CROW MOON

CROW MOON

ANNA MCKERROW

Quercus

First Published in Great Britain in 2015 by

Quercus Editions Ltd
55 Baker Street
7th Floor, South Block
London
W1U 8EW

Copyright © Anna McKerrow 2015

A CIP catalogue reference for this book is available
from the British Library

Paperback ISBN 978 1 8486 6957 4
Ebook ISBN 978 1 84866 956 7

10 9 8 7 6 5 4 3 2

Printed and bound in Great Britain by Clays Ltd, St Ives plc.

For Ally

Chapter One

And then he said, 'No one should distract an ordained knight from his thoughts in a discourteous way, for perhaps he has either suffered a loss or he is thinking about the woman he loves best.'

From *The Mabinogion*

The fire in the middle of the circle casts flickering shadows over our faces: we stand obediently in its fierce warmth, following the words of the monthly full-moon ritual.

I raise my hands up to the star-riddled Cornwall evening just like everyone else, just like every month, and feel nothing. I chant along with the whole village, as they follow the woman at the centre of the circle with their eyes; her head is thrown back, black hair blowing in the evening air, arms outstretched, long wool cloak rippling against her thin shoulders, conviction written across her brow. My mum, the head witch. El supremo.

Sorceress. Disciplinarian single parent. Poster girl for our eco-pagan Greenworld.

'She who is the beauty of the green earth, and the white moon among the stars, and the mystery of the waters. For She is the soul of nature, who gives life to the universe. From Her all things proceed, and unto Her all things must return,' we intone as a group.

I puff out my cheeks and exhale loudly at the end of the litany.

Boring.

My gaze zigzags across the circle to Sadie, who catches my eye and gives me her slanty little grin. She's a sorceress too, in her own way. All she has to do is smile at me.

Back in the circle, Mum's bringing things to a close. She walks round the perimeter of the circle, blessing everyone, and returns to her altar at the centre. The altar is a tree stump; we're in the middle of the village, on the green. An old maypole stands off to the right, its red and white paint peeling away. We still dance round it like idiots in the spring. We have to.

She brings her arms down by her sides and bows her head for the end of the ritual, and people start filtering out of the circle. I walk over to Sadie. Usually we'd slink off together at this point, but this time she goes up to Mum, who is packing her tools away. Wooden wand made out of a branch from our apple tree and engraved with sacred Celtic spirals; witch's knife; candles; a cup of water; a pack of tarot cards; crystal ball; five-pointed star made from branches; figurine of Brighid, the Greenworld's patron goddess.

As I approach, I can barely hear what they're saying, but Sadie reaches out to touch the cards, and Mum's eyes widen in panic as she pulls them away.

'. . . special energy. You can't touch them, dear,' Mum's saying icily as I get to them.

Sades looks affronted. 'Sorry, I just . . . Oh, hi, Danny.' She turns back to Mum. 'Sorry, Zia. I was just curious. I've never seen them up close. I was just wondering if . . .'

Mum stuffs the cards into her bag and smiles a thin-lipped smile at Sadie: her definitely-not-happy expression.

'That's all right, dear. But they are special. Witches' tools are powerful. No touchy-touchy.' She wags her finger at Sades, only semi-playfully, and Sades smiles and opens her mouth to say something else, but she's cut off by someone elbowing her way through the crowd.

'Sadie! Sadie! What are you doing?' yells a voice like a saw, and Sades' mum Linda comes waddling over. Without stopping, she pulls Sadie's still-outstretched hand away from my mum and drags her away from us, like we're lepers.

'What have I told you? Don't go near those things! They're evil!' she shouts at Sadie.

Mum's shoulders square up and her chin juts out. Here we go, I think.

'What did you just say?' she demands, and the

3

villagers who were heading home start turning round when they hear raised voices. A fight's one of the only decent bits of entertainment we get down here in the middle of nowhere.

'You heard. I don't want my daughter anywhere near those things,' Linda says, jabbing her fat finger in the general area of Mum's witch tools on the stump.

Mum raises her eyebrows. 'She's no more than three metres from them every month when we do this, and I don't usually hear you complain about it. Well—' she smiles coldly – 'I do hear you, actually. It's just usually easier to ignore—'

'Don't be so holier-than-thou, Zia,' Linda spits. 'We're allowed to have our opinions, aren't we? If we're not, we may as well be in the Redworld.'

'You're free to go anytime you like, Linda,' Mum counters, and points towards the village boundary, which we can just see over the rooftops: a barbed-wire fence that surrounds our village and protects us from the lawless people outside. 'Don't let me stop you. Give my regards to the gangs.'

Linda laughs nastily. 'Oh, you'd like that, wouldn't you? You'd like us to leave. Then you could get on with brainwashing everyone with your magical hippy rubbish. I'm the only one they've got if they want any real history or facts about what life was like before the Greenworld. I'm not going anywhere. I've got a duty to these people.'

Mum sighs and turns away from Linda, gathering her stuff into her bag.

'So have I, Linda. So have I. And it's not rubbish, as well you know. It's our sacred Celtic spirituality. Why do you come to the ritual if you think it's so pointless? And don't blame me if your daughter's interested in the craft. Maybe she's got a bit more talent than you, eh?' I can see her smile to herself, still turned away from Linda.

'Over my dead body. Teach my girl any of your mumbo jumbo and you'll regret it,' Linda threatens, and pulls Sadie away. 'Come on. Home,' she says, but Sadie wriggles free.

'Goddess, calm down, Mum. I'm going for a walk with Danny for a bit. I'll see you later,' she says, and she takes my hand, challenging Linda with her eyes.

'No you're not, my girl. I don't want you seeing him any more. He's a bad influence.'

I choke back a laugh at that, cos if she knew what her darling daughter wanted to do on our 'walks', she wouldn't think it was me who was the debauched one.

Sadie tugs at my hand. 'Come on, Dan. Mum, you're making a scene. Everyone's looking at you. Go home.' And we walk off, not giving Linda a chance to argue. Winning the battle of wills, just like she always does.

'Danny – don't be late for dinner now,' Mum calls from behind me, and I can hear the grin in her voice. She's not exactly in love with Sades, but she just wants to make Linda even madder, I can tell.

'See you later,' I call, and we drift through the crowd.

Sadie blows her red hair off her forehead and grins up at me as we walk.

'What was all that about?' I ask. 'I didn't know you were interested in the cards.'

She shrugs. 'Yeah, well. Just fancy learning something new, y'know? Something other than school.'

'Reflective Greenworld Journaling not enough for you?' We're supposed to each keep a creative journal at school in which we can express our thoughts about living in our eco-pagan Greenworld, like anyone really cares.

She makes a face. 'Surprisingly, no. Or t'ai chi.' She screws up her face in imitation of our teacher doing her spiritual-concentration face. 'Find the chi within you, Danny! Find it!'

'I haven't found it yet,' I say, scuffing my feet along the dirt path. We're heading out to the boundary, a scrubland where nobody goes except kids. It's somewhere to go when you want to be alone.

'You're not going to get anywhere with that attitude, young man,' she mock-lectures me, wagging her finger in my face. I grab it, then her hand, and pull her towards me.

'Educate me, then. If we kiss long enough some of your smartness might rub off on me.'

She pulls her hand away. 'I don't want anything of yours rubbing off on me, thanks.'

'Stop pretending. I know you want me.'

'I know. I'm just hiding it really well,' she banters back, sarcastic as ever.

I hold my hand out. 'Come on, Sades. School isn't my thing. You know that.'

She grins, but doesn't take my hand again. 'I wonder what school's like in the Redworld?' she muses.

'Dunno. Got to be better than ours, though. Thankfully it's almost over.' We're both sixteen. Just a few more months and it'll be done.

'You can't fool me. I know you like reading.' Sades' mum Linda is one of our teachers, and her house is a kind of village library. I do visit quite a lot to read, but also as an excuse to see Sadie.

'Mind, the more I think about it, there are probably other things we should be learning apart from water desalination and forest craft,' Sadie says thoughtfully. 'Like, Mum speaks other languages. I'd like to speak another language.'

I shrug. 'What's the point? You're never going to need it.'

Where we live, at the far end of England, the old place of fairies and smugglers, cut off at Devon from the edge of the Redworld – we don't meet anyone that doesn't speak English. We don't meet anyone new at all. We'd still be living in the Redworld now if Mum and all her mates hadn't decided to branch off on their own and make us this weird little witchy closed community. It's still out there, the Redworld, after all, going strong

7

beyond the Devon border. Burning what's left of the small amounts of fuel that can still be ripped out of Mother Earth; fighting; looting; exploiting the weak; buying and selling.

We walk on in comfortable silence for a while. She plaits her red hair as we're walking along and tucks it into her blue woollen jacket. Wool is big in the Greenworld.

'What are you going to do, then? After school finishes?' I ask her, ticking off the options on my fingers. 'Farming, spinning, dyeing, folk traditions, community work . . .'

She scoffs. 'What, looking after little kids? No thanks.'

'It's probably what I'm heading for. Working on the water systems, house maintenance maybe.'

'Not farming?'

I mime a retch. 'No thanks. Can't stand the smell.' In a community that has to grow everything it eats, compost is revered as some kind of holy shit – pardon the pun. Mum might think there's something magic about it, but the truth is that it stinks.

Shit is the signature scent of the Greenworld.

'Mum's got me in with folk traditions,' she says, rolling her eyes.

'Cool.'

She shoots me a withering look. 'Hardly. She's the one that likes telling old stories, not me. But it's the best of a bad lot anyway.' She groans, stops walking,

8

throws her arms up dramatically to the sky. 'Bloody folk stories and the oral tradition. There's only one oral tradition I'm interested in. Everything's bloody cold, and damp, and BORING! I'm sick of it!'

'Well, what're you going to do about it?'

She sighs, and slumps, bending at the waist and trailing her fingers on the ground. 'Nothing, I s'pose. Join the gangs, maybe,' she mutters into her knees.

I smile. 'Yeah. We all say that.'

'I might, though. I like the idea of it – soldiers of fortune, living on our wits. Outside the law. It's romantic. Can't you see me as a gang assassin?' she asks, head between her thighs, grinning at me, and jerks upright, fingers in the shape of a gun. 'Kapow! Gotcha. Gangs, one; son-of-bossy-village-witch-and-general-waster Danny, zero.'

I push her hand away. 'So much for your assassin skills. You'd make a crap gang member.'

'I wouldn't. I'd be great. I don't believe in anything. I have a natural aversion to authority. I'm ideal.'

'I'd like to see you last five minutes out there. They'd put you in a pie and eat you, Little Red Riding Up-to-No-Good.'

She laughs. 'Well, I s'pose I'll think about it a bit longer.'

'Wise of you.'

We're almost at our usual spot, but she's still ranting. I hope she'll shut up in a minute so I can kiss her.

'It's their choice, though, you know? They opted out. They don't know what it's like to be a first-generation Greenworlder. One hundred per cent restricted to Devon and Cornwall. Forever.'

I shrug. I know this, but I can't do anything about it, so why bother?

'I mean, look at my mum. She doesn't know how lucky she was, growing up in the Redworld. All that clean shit. I mean, CLEAN! Squeaky! Not like the mud-covered, cold shitholes we live in—' she gestures to the houses we can see from the boundary – brick-built but getting tatty, or thatched cottages that haven't been re-thatched that expertly. 'Do you know how you make things really clean? CHEMICALS. Not vegetable soap.'

I smile. 'I don't mind things a bit dirty.'

'I bet you don't. Just imagine, though, Dan. Real booze. Cars. Disposable, delicious, greasy, wonderful, additive-rich food. Stuff that wouldn't rot in a day.'

I hold up my hands. 'I know, I know! You don't have to convince me.'

She picks at her fingers. 'Don't you wonder what the Redworld must be like, though? Really, truly like?' She looks at me over her chewed cuticles.

I shrug. 'Course. I want to visit, you know, cross the border somehow, but Mum would go mad,' I say, which is what we always say, regardless of whether we mean it or not. Most Greenworld kids are either genuinely fascinated with the Redworld, or know that it's cool to appear to be fascinated by it.

10

She looks at me critically. 'You'd be all right. They like that unkempt look in the Redworld, or so I hear.'

I run my hand through my longish mess of black hair, trying to tidy it a bit. Mum says I look like a Romantic poet. I'm tall and skinny. Brown-skinned, though lighter than Beebs, who got more of Dad's colouring. Dad's family were originally from India, which is unimaginably far away. I got Mum's eyes, green like a cat, her longer face. Despite my supposed Romantic poet-ness, I can never work out why Sades likes me. I mean, I think she likes me. Who knows with girls?

'Maybe I should come over and work out a plan. A detailed plan to get through the border. I might need to sleep over if we really want to get the detail right,' I say, sighing theatrically.

'Shut up,' she shoots back, and we walk on in companionable quiet.

'So what're you doing for Samhain, then?' Sadie asks, all perky again.

'Dunno. Probably same as last year. Light a fire, remember the dear deceased, drink cider, get wrecked, piss in the bonfire. Get yelled at for not keeping the candles burning.'

Samhain (the pagan word for 'Halloween', which the Redworlders probably still call it) is in a week's time, and it's Mum's busiest night for fortune telling. Most of the villagers come to our house and get their predictions for the year ahead.

'You didn't always own up to being a witch in the red days, apparently,' Sades ponders. 'People thought it was weird, then,' she says, shrugging, cos, for us, a witch is the person in charge. It's weird to us that it was weird then. 'Knowing about medicinal herbs, reading the cards. Energy healing. You know.'

I do know. Some anyway. But Mum's not just a fortune teller. She's in charge of the village here – she's the protector, the figurehead, the witch. Every village has a witch in charge, to protect it and do witchy things for the villagers, even blessing marriages and burying the dead. It's a full-time kind of deal. The witch is supposed to hold the safety of the village in her hand; at every village boundary there's a picture of a woman's hand holding a cluster of buildings in it. We all celebrate the Celtic pagan festivals, cos that's the history of this neck of the woods – the old Celts. The Greenworld honours Brighid, Mother Goddess of the land, and we take part in the moon ritual once a month, but the witches are the ones with the real magical skills and knowledge.

'Your mum's so cool. Would she read my cards, d'you reckon?' Sadie asks as we walk past the burnt-out van.

Cars are not needed here in the Greenworld, we're told. Pity. All us kids want one, but unless we can figure out how to build one that runs on grass cuttings, none of us are driving anywhere. And anyway, where would we go?

'Don't see why not.'

'Wouldn't she think I was too young?'

'Dunno. Maybe.'

'You're a lot of help.'

'I don't really know much about it.'

'How can you not know? You're there every year.'

'I know, but it's not like I go in and listen to what she's telling them.'

'Hmmm. Maybe I shouldn't. She might see us doing it in a vision.'

'I can provide you with a first-hand experience of that if you're interested.'

'Shut up. You're so forward.'

'Yeah, and you're so impressionable.'

She waves her hand at me. 'No, but seriously, I wish I could read them. The cards. Or even have some of my own, but where would I get them? No one has any apart from Zia, and she's made it clear she's not going to show me.'

'Other witches have them too,' I say unhelpfully, thinking of the times Mum goes to covenstead meetings – where all the witches from all the villages in Devon and Cornwall get together. 'You could make your own,' I suggest.

She looks thoughtful. 'Maybe. But I wouldn't know what they're all called and what pictures they're supposed to have and stuff.'

'I could show you the pack, maybe, without Mum knowing, and you could copy them,' I offer before I've thought it through. 'Write down the names anyway, make a start.'

She jumps on the idea. 'Oh, really? That would be great!' she says and claps her hands together.

Too late to take it back now; already this doesn't feel like such a good idea.

'I'll get the cards after Samhain. Mum probably won't use them for a while after then: she'll have done all her readings for a whole season that night.' It'll be fine, I rationalize.

Sades smiles her snake smile. 'Sounds like a plan, Dan.'

We've stopped at our usual spot – the wind blows aggressively through the barbed wire and makes her shiver. I pull her to me.

'S'cold,' she murmurs. 'Warm me up.'

When I get back home later, Gowdie thumps down the hall, barking excitedly. We've had her since she was a pup and now she's a big floppy-eared lolling-tongued drool machine, but we love her. Mum named her. I think it was after some historical witch or other. Typical. We couldn't have a normal dog name.

I walk into the kitchen and my sister Biba is cutting up the veg for dinner, probably without being asked, the supergreen. Mum is nowhere to be seen, but calls hi from upstairs.

'How's the tin drive, Bibalicious? How's the

efficiency manifesto coming along?' I ask, looking in the cupboard for something to eat. There isn't anything.

She looks at me haughtily from her chopping. 'Don't make fun of me.'

I do make fun of her, all the time in fact, but that's my job as an older brother. Biba gets teased at school sometimes too, though. She's darker-skinned – and small, and less charming than me – and for some of the kids here that's a reason to push her around. Despite this being the super-wonderful-liberal-Greenworld. Some parents haven't quite forgotten their Redworld roots, I guess. And on those occasions – not too many of them, considering who our mum is, but still sometimes – I have to remind those kids what we believe in the Greenworld. That there's no colour here. Not even the red blood that they wipe away under their noses after I've finished with them.

'That's my job, Beeball. Don't sweat it.'

'You're the sweaty one.' She sniffs the air around me in an exaggerated way. 'Eurgh! You reek!'

'Oh – you think I smell?' I look at her with fake concern and sniff my armpit.

'Like a compost heap.'

'Oh. See, I can't smell anything. I wonder if I can just get you to . . .' And I grab her and stick her under my arm.

'Ugh! Get off! Ugh, Danny, let me out!'

'Suck it in, Beebs. You won't get this off you for days.'

She's making trapped-bird noises under my arm and spluttering about her constitutional rights when Mum comes in.

'Daniel Prentice! Let your sister go!'

Reluctantly I release Beebs from under my arm. She shakes her shiny black hair in disgust. She got Dad's straight hair – I got Mum's. Curly. Both as black as ravens.

Beebs shoots daggers at me. 'Ugh. You're so disgusting.'

I shrug. 'I'm your big bro. That's what I'm supposed to do.'

'Mum – Danny was making fun of me.'

'Stop making fun of your sister, Danny,' Mum says automatically.

'How's your good self, Ma?' I say, and give her my most winning grin.

'Danny, remember you were going to find me some stuff for the bonfire. Can you do it tomorrow? It's a bit late now,' she asks, mussing Biba's hair affectionately, and eating a piece of raw carrot from the bowl.

I eye our yard, which has been stripped ready to burn. 'No problem,' I say, keeping her sweet. 'Have I got time for a wash before dinner?' She nods distractedly and so I head upstairs. I hear Beebs start to tell Mum about her Young Greenworlder Association meeting as I walk away.

'It's exciting, Mum, cos we've got a new plan. We

16

need to get all the kids together, strike hard at the Redworld.'

I smile at Biba's tough revolutionary talk. Before Samhain, you could tell Mum you were going to the moon and all she'd say would be 'Get me some cheese while you're there'.

Whistling, I head to the bathroom and pass Mum's room, happening to see her tarot cards in their little sequinned bag on top of her dressing table. They catch my eye as they're hardly ever left out. It's usually 'Don't touch'; it's 'Those are our living, kids'; it's 'This is what makes us special, this is what keeps us protected'.

But, nevertheless, there they are, winking at me, saying, "Danny, Danny, pick us up! We're your one-way ticket to Sadesville; one-way to L.O.V.E.! We want to be liberated. Liberate us, Danny! Liberate the hell out of us!" And so without thinking I nip in, take them, put them under my shirt and get in the bathroom double quick. I run the taps in the sink and slyly open the window. I've got out of here before on many occasions. I turn the taps off and bolt the door.

I turn on the radio in the bathroom, an old wind-up gig. It's been set so that it only picks up a Cornwall Greenworld station. I've heard they have music on the radio in the Redworld, and, man, I just wanna dance. But instead I hear the ultra-boring *Bull's Greenworld Gardener's Guide* – 'Save it, hive it, share it' – transmitted from somewhere near Zennor. However, in this instance, the radio serves a purpose: if Mum knocks she'll think I'm in here abusing myself quietly to new-world eco-pagan propaganda. Not often, but sometimes, being a teenage boy works for you.

I edge out of the window and down the pipes to the side of the house by the water butt, then slink on to the side lane and round the back. I get on my toes and I'm tapping at Sades' window with a long stick in five minutes. Her red head pokes out and she gives me that little slanty smile. I wave the sequinned bag at her.

'Got the cards for you,' I hiss.

Her face lights up. 'Ooooh. Already? Yay,' she says, and holds out her cupped hands.

She wants me to throw them up to her, so I give it my best pitch. As they leave my hands I feel a tingle of betrayal. I haven't really thought about this and now it's a bit late. It looks like she's not even going to let me in.

'So, like, no hassle, but I'm going to need those back before Samhain,' I say, hoping I don't sound like a massive hard-on. She pulls a mean little face. 'You can have them again after that, it's just cos she needs them for the big fortune-telling night,' I add hastily. Sades's probably wondering why I didn't just wait till after Samhain anyway, and I'm already regretting bringing them, but with the hinted-at promise of Sadie, what boy wouldn't lose his mind a bit?

'Course. I'll bring them over Samhain morning,' she says, like she has to be nice, but already she's got what she wanted and wants me gone.

'Cool,' I say, and give her my least dorky smile, the

18

one I hope makes her think, Oh, that intriguing boy, I must sleep with him soon.

She's shutting the window so I whisper up to her, 'So maybe tomorrow we'll hang out?'

She remains elusive and kind of nods and shuts the window.

I slink off. Too late, I think, this might be a situation.

Chapter Two

Save it, hive it, share it.

From *Tenets and Sayings of the Greenworld*

When I get back to the house I climb back into the bathroom, have a strip wash and get dressed again speedily. I turn off the radio, which has now started spouting the memoirs of various luminary envirowarriors. Enviros are anyone – mostly the men, though – that have left the Greenworld to patrol the border, or be an anti-war activist on the front line – sabotaging Redworld tanks, or trying to stop mining or fracking. But most enviros aren't heroes, they're like my dad: wanted to have a purpose; wanted to feel functional again. They'd prefer to fight for the last traces of fuel left in the world than live here, not using it at all. If you're strapping homemade bombs to the underside of supply trains or organizing picket lines you don't have to take turns doing the laundry by hand, shelling peas, digging manure into the plots or taking part in the community storytelling sessions, and he hated all that. My dad said before he left, 'This is survival, it isn't life.' Mum had said, 'This is what life is now.' She says he wanted to be a hero. The reality is that living even a month in this shithole makes everyone a hero.

I go downstairs and to the kitchen where Mum and Biba are dishing up dinner. Bean stew. It's OK, I guess. We eat a lot of veg. Mostly the meat we get is chicken – we all have a few in the garden, as long as the foxes don't get them. We haven't got round to eating fox yet but it's a distinct possibility – they're bloody everywhere. Fruit in the summer from the apple tree in the garden, a bit of rhubarb, some plums for like two weeks in the summer. We trade apples with our neighbours cos we get so many, and we make cider every year. The village grows its own grain and we all make our own bread; we even grow tea and coffee. We also farm some animals for meat, but not many – meat gets kept for the seasonal festivals. For a while when we were kids there was still a bit of hoarded canned food around, left over from the Redworld days, but that's gone now. And there's strictly no trade with the Redworld, so we live off what we have.

We sit down to eat. For once I'm glad to listen to Beebs go on about her supergreen friends and what they've been up to this week, as it will take Mum's mind off anything to do with her cards or Samhain. She babbles over the watery bean stew until Mum breaks into my thoughts.

'I heard you listening to the radio earlier, Danny, was there anything good on?'

I shake my head, remembering just in time that I left it on when I slipped out. 'Oh, right – no, just the usual.'

Mum sighs. 'I'd give anything to hear some real music again. Greenworld folk singing only goes so far,' she says, pushing her stew around her plate.

'All ready for Samhain, Mum?' Biba asks brightly. She's always been tactless; insensitive to the undercurrents. Neither Dad or Biba could ever read the mood in a room.

Shit, I think. Shut up, Beebs. She doesn't want to talk about it.

'Oh yes, all ready, thank you, darling,' Mum says and plays with her fork. The whole thing takes so much energy out of her she wants to save up as much as possible in the week before. Now we've had the community full-moon ritual, it can be a quiet week for her until Samhain. I asked her once, wasn't it good to know everyone's secrets? But she'd said, 'Danny, there are some dark things curled up in the hearts of others.'

'So how many people do you think will come for readings?' Beebs ploughs on, unheeding. I cough but she doesn't take the hint.

Mum is picking at the rough wood round the edge of the table, something she usually shouts at us for doing. She is smiling in a not-smiling kind of way.

'Oh, well, it's hard to know in advance,' she says. 'You know how it is. I just leave the front door open and they form a line. Danny organizes things.'

Supernatural receptionist wouldn't be my top choice of job for the night, but it's what Mum needs so that's that.

Beebs blunders on. 'Don't you think it's weird for Danny to do it, though, Mum? I mean, he's only a kid.'

I expect Mum to get on her high horse and tell Beebs off, like what she says is holy writ, but instead she just shrugs. 'Maybe you're right, darling,' she says. 'He is still very young.'

Now, don't get me wrong, I don't particularly love providing off-the-cuff anteroom consolation and embarrassing chat to community members of a Samhain night. As soon as they get through that door on that one night of the year they seem to think that the gloves are off, and they don't even want to wait for Mum. They'll get hold of me in the hall as I'm bringing through glasses of water or taking coats and pull me into a doorway to 'talk'. They don't mean talk, though, cos that implies a two-way conversation. What they really mean is they want to know, can I do it too? Am I a seer, a prophet? Do I read the cards? So I have to say, 'No, I have no insights for you. No, sorry. Can I take your coat? Mum will be right with you.'

So it's a weird night. And made weirder by the fact, which I have never told anyone, that sometimes I do have flashes of knowing about people. I can't say when it's going to happen or for who, but now and again it's like a bit of a movie that plays in front of my eyes.

'Er . . . yeah. Anyway. I've finished. Need to do some, errr . . . homework,' I mumble, scraping my spoon against the home-made clay bowl, and leave Beebs to regale Mum with her tin-drive update. Keep a low profile, Dan, I think, so she can't find you to ask you about the cards. Even if she can't find them, she might think she's mislaid them somewhere. As long as they're back where they should be by Samhain.

The next day I get up late and head downstairs for something to eat. It's not a school day. Mum isn't even up, which is a result. I whistle as I make my tea and bread, thinking about Sades, thinking about spending some alone time with her, and what might happen.

I leave it a few minutes to check the coast is clear and head out. Gowdie raises her head sleepily from her basket as I pass, and I ruffle her ears. 'Not today, girl,' I whisper to her. As I close the front door behind me I see Mum coming down the hall looking like she wants to talk to me, so I shut it and jog down the path. I start walking up the hill to Sades' place. It's a pretty nice morning all in all so I whistle my way along. My dad used to whistle sometimes, when he was working in the garden. It's one of my favourite memories of him.

I get to Sades' house and she hardly lets me in the door, just opens it a crack, and all, like, reluctantly, lets me in. I slide in like a snake with an agenda. We go upstairs. I get the impression I'm being smuggled in. Sades pushes her bedroom shut behind me. So far, so good. But she's looking all weird, pulling the hair of an old doll she's holding. Her room is full of old toys.

'Ummm, Danny,' she says, and all of a sudden I can feel the blood draining away from my underwear region. 'Danny, ummm, the thing is, I don't have your mum's cards any more,' she says, looking at her feet.

'What? What does that mean?' I ask unimaginatively, but I know what she's going to say. Oh Holy non-existent Goddess, not the cards.

'Well – don't be angry at me, Dan, I didn't know she'd—'

'She'd what? Who? What's happened, Sades?'

'I was looking at them just now, you know, making a list of all the titles, when Mum came in. She said, "Where did you get those? Only one person has those. They're evil; get your hands off them,"' she blunders on.

'What happened then?' I say, but the answer seems horribly clear when I look at Sades' tear-stained face.

'She took them off me,' she says despairingly, dropping the doll, her hands open as if to demonstrate this fact. Sades is always so composed, so cool, and it's a bad thing to see her panicking like this. I walk out of the room and go down the stairs cos I've got no choice; I have to get them back.

Sades wails down after me, 'She said she's going to

burn them!' and so I start running down the stairs to the kitchen and burst in to find Linda sitting at the kitchen table, watching the fire, which is burning merrily. I can see the curling edges of the cards as they get sucked in and charred, burned – The Tower, The Ten of Swords, The Eight of Cups, chaos and disaster – turning to dust before I can do anything.

Linda sits there, greying yellow hair falling out of a ponytail. She looks at me full on, flat eyes like a shark smelling blood in the water.

'Oh, Danny, won't you have a cup of tea? Come and sit by the fire; it's nice and warm.' She doesn't break eye contact. Bitch.

Instinctively I grab the first thing that comes to hand and smash it on the floor. I don't know what it is, but it makes a glassy crash and Linda jumps up from her seat. I lunge towards the fire, and try to pull the cards out, but it's too late – the fire has eaten them and cackles wildly at my misfortune.

I whirl round to Linda, and Sadie, who is standing in the kitchen door looking aghast. But Linda's face is set in a determined grimace as she picks up the shards of glass from the floor.

'You shouldn't have done that. How could you do it? Why?' I shout, and she looks up at me, smiling.

'I warned her. I warned her what would happen if she tried to involve my girl in all that rubbish. I keep my word, Danny. You tell your mum that. I keep my word.'

My stomach aches at the unfairness, and the guilt of knowing that Mum had no hand in this at all. She's going to be furious when I tell her what I've done, and for what? I look at Sadie, clutching her doll again and staring at us with round eyes. For her. I brought them here to be destroyed, for her.

'Why didn't you stop her?' I ask, thinking of how Sades usually refuses to be told what to do, but her shoulders slump and she won't look me in the eye. She doesn't reply.

I look at her helplessly for a moment, but I can see she's not going to help me. I walk out. Then I run and run and eventually find myself at the edge of the village where there's a big pile of burnt-out cars. There's nothing I can do and I'm furious at Linda, that smug old whore, for doing what she did. But I'm more furious at myself.

'Give me a break!' I scream at the wind; it blows ash back on me.

I trip up as I'm walking and see I've fallen over a big branch. I pick it up and whirl it around my head. It feels good, so I batter the boots and hoods of three cars, one after the other: crack, crack, break your mother's back. I hammer the blows down, thinking, You bitch, Linda, you've ruined everything. I just stand there over the pile of dented car bonnets and start to cry, cos I know that really *I've* ruined everything and it's all my fault.

I sit there for about an hour in one of those shitty

rusted-up cars, and think about my options. I know I only really have one, which is to go home and confess to Mum and take whatever comes. But the thing is, I can't do that. Maybe I'm not strong enough, but when Dad left, he said, 'Danny, you're the man now. Look after your mum and sister.' I'm not supposed to be the one crying in the burnt-out car pile-up. I'm supposed to be strong.

Without the cards Mum's far less special; they were part of her witchy armour to protect us from the gangs outside. Part of her power as head witch. Tools of the trade.

I feel sad to do it, my heart really aches at the thought, but I know what I have to do.

Getting out of the boundary is easier than you think, cos no one really wants to leave. The village is protected by wooden posts covered in barbed wire – not very inventive, but with power in short supply or non-existent it can't be an electrified perimeter. I mean, we do have some solar panels that work, and a few basic handmade wind turbines, but the energy they generate is generally about enough to boil an egg. The boundary marks us out as a community, like a line drawn round us in pee, and it's reinforced psychically by Mum, like a magic protective bubble. Apparently. That is, I don't know if I really believe that. But if everyone believes it then there's power in that belief.

Back in the days before the regime change to the

Greenworld, nobody would've cared if some middle-aged woman had her fortune-telling cards burned in a fireplace. We'd all say, 'Who gives a crap?' and move on with consuming the planet and covering everything in plastic. But now, it really matters. As soon as the gangs know a witch's tool has been destroyed, they'll start circling, like dogs sniffing meat left in the sun. What's happened is a sign of weakness. The witch's power is supposed to hold the village, after all, to protect it from invaders with a magic circle. Her word is truth and all her tools are sacred: knife, cup, candle, cards, crystal. Her image as all-powerful witch has to be without doubt or scrutiny.

For Linda to burn the cards is a really big deal, cos it shows that Mum's power isn't total. The gangs will think if she couldn't protect those, maybe she can't protect the village.

That's why I'm going straight to Lowenna, Mum's friend in Tintagel, the witch at the next major village from us. She's the only person that I can think of who can help. We've got to make sure this doesn't get further than the village walls. I creep between the barbed wire and through to the scrubland beyond, and without looking back start running into the unknown.

Chapter Three

We are called the Greenworld as green is the colour
of life, regeneration and purity.

From *Tenets and Sayings of the Greenworld*

Between deciding that this was what I was going to do
and finding myself nudging through the barbed-wire
fence, I set some things in place. I scribble a note to
Sadie and on my way out of the village push it under her
front door – really hoping she gets to it first and not her
mum. It doesn't say much, just what it needs to:

> Sades, I'm going away for a few days. Keep
> your mum away from mine till I get back. Don't
> let her tell anyone about what she's done.
> Danny.

I think I'm going to be three days max. Get to Lowenna's,
get another set of cards, get home again. It should give

me plenty of time to get them back for Samhain. I leave a note for Mum too, and even though it's short it's murder to write; with every letter I feel guiltier and it feels like I've swallowed a ball of knives. I write:

> Mum, Linda burned your tarot cards. It's my fault. Gone to Lowenna's to get new set. See you in three days.
> Sorry.
> Danny.

I leave it on the kitchen table so she won't miss it, take some snacks and a sandwich to eat on the way and leave. There's nothing else to say. I'll miss a day of school but I don't think anyone's that bothered whether I'm there or not.

Gowdie looks up at me from her basket as I make my way stealthily down the hall. She looks like she's going to bark so I shush her, kneeling down by her basket and ruffling her ears. She whines and paws at my bended knee. She knows something's up. I try to stand up and pull her paw off my leg, but she whines louder.

'Shut up, Gowdie!' I hiss at her, but she's not having any of it. She follows me down the hall, claws clicking on the wood floor. I get to the door and she looks at me expectantly, as if to say 'What adventure are we going on today?'

'Too much adventure for you, girl,' I whisper, and open the front door quietly, trying to hold her back with my foot, but she hops over it and stands on the front step, wagging her tail. 'Get back!' I try again. Maybe she's not that daft. Persistent, definitely. I sigh.

'All right, then, come on,' I say to her and she yips happily. Damn dog.

I've only been to Tintagel once before, a long time ago when I was a kid, and so I hope I can remember where I'm going. Once past the boundary walls, and the peeling-off picture of the hand holding the village, I just run and run for ages with my guilt spurring me on – out into the wide open moor, green and purple, thick and mossy.

Tintagel is on the dramatic, often-stormy north Cornish coast, north-west from here. We're inland people here in Dartmoor, as much as any part of Devon and Cornwall can be imagined to be inland anyway, cos you're never far from the sea down this way. We know the heathers and the miles and miles of open moor. Stone circles, strange outcroppings of rock covered in moss that turn almost neon when the sun hits them. Boulders in the middle of nowhere that look like they've been left behind from giants playing catch. Little streams winding through the grassland, full of icy clear water, even in the summer. Eerie quiet, blanketing thousands of years of magic. Tintagel and those other places, like Boscastle, Treligga, Port Isaac – they're all about the grandeur of the sea, the roar and break of the cold waves against black rock, into shadowed caves, with only the gulls and witches to watch.

One of the first things I run past is our local stone circle. Scorhill. A few tall jagged standing stones in a circle with a lot of smaller ones in between. It's wide, one of the biggest circles in the south-west, so they say. No one knows why it's not named after the village, as it's right next to it, but instead it has its own name. Scorhill, an old Norse word for 'steep'. Sades and me snuck out here a few times at night to look at the stars. Nothing happened – well, I mean, nothing magical happened. But there is a funny vibe to it, that place. Not bad, not good – just charged, somehow.

I don't stop, even though Gowdie stops and sniffs around the stones a bit. I've got to run, get some distance between me and Gidleigh – and I've got to keep on the move out here in the in-between space. No man's land. Purgatory.

However, an hour or so later, I'm out of breath and flagging, so I stop; I want to conserve my energy, so I eat an apple. It's sour but it goes down well enough. There's a little stream near to where I've stopped, so I drink a few cupped handfuls of cold, clean water. It's so quiet out here, and it's kind of nice, and I know not to get too comfortable and all like attuned with nature – but it's hard to ignore the wide bright blue sky, the crisp cold October-morning air and the orange-and-gold leaves falling from the trees. But it's not nature that matters out here, and you shouldn't get distracted by whatever blue skies or purple sunsets or mossy boulders you see. There are gang eyes everywhere. This is their place, the wild in between. No laws. They can take you and nobody can do anything about it, not even witches: it's out of their territory. I walk on carefully, whistling quietly for Gowdie who comes and trots happily at my heels.

Our relationship with the gangs has changed over time. When I was a kid there was much more crossover – Mum had several gang boyfriends soon after Dad left, one after the other with their gangland tattoos. I think they made her feel protected. They were mostly cool; they strutted around the place and were loud and swore a lot but they knew good music or they told me dirty jokes, how long their tattoos took and how much they hurt or the best ways to beat someone up. Weirdly, at the time Mum looked on and smiled. She didn't seem to mind.

Omar was the guy she stayed with the longest. He was tall, black, muscled all over; he had a shaved head and bizarrely massive eyebrows (as if to compensate), and he always smelt sweaty, but somehow not in a bad way. Like all of the gang boyfriends he seemed to almost worship Mum, and if he was telling a sexist joke or talking about breaking someone's ribs and she walked in he'd shut up, make her sit down and ask her what she wanted for breakfast, or that he'd noticed the water wasn't draining properly and would she like him to look at the drains? Omar was the one I liked best too. I always got the impression there was real love there, the way they were with each other – I remember cos you find it disgusting when you're a kid – grown-ups hugging and kissing. They were always mucking around. I remember Mum's happy-but-outraged face when Omar would pick her up, hoist her over his shoulder and tickle her feet. She'd kick and demand to be let down, but you could see in her flashing eyes that she loved every second.

He'd do his Champions of the Wild routine to entertain me and Beebs, who was just a baby then – two or three. This included stretching both huge arms behind his head, locking his fingers and bringing the arms down into an arc, with a 'hurgh!' sound. He'd pretend to come at me and strangle me with his big hands, and muss my hair at the last moment or tuck Beebs under his arm and run up and down the garden with her.

Those guys were struggling to survive, just like us. Not everyone liked the gang members, but Mum welcomed them. She said a repentant sinner is the most loyal soldier. And Omar was useful to her. He went back and forth to the Redworld all the time, through the border. He must have had contacts cos that border's a mile wide, all feral dogs and barbed-wire fences. He'd get us Redworld toys sometimes, but Mum mostly wanted witchy things. Stuff she couldn't get here – crystals, exotic smelly resins, other mysterious things. And so Omar used to tell us stories about the Redworld – how dangerous it was. How people lived – locked away, never going out, having everything delivered if they could afford it, or running the risk of being mugged or worse if they couldn't. The streets were run by criminal gangs and security organizations equally, working together – creaming the money from the rich who needed protection or the poor who didn't have any. I remember Omar describing those streets of shanty houses right next to the big gated mansions, with grey armoured vans patrolling the roads and guys with machine guns at the end of every street, and I'd feel scared and excited at the same time, thinking that all that was just a matter of miles away from us.

I stop walking and running after another couple of hours and eat half the sandwich. You have to be fit, living in the Greenworld. The good thing about being used to not having much to eat is that you don't get that hungry. Plus I'm living off adrenalin right now. I can feel it pumping through me like liquid steel. I am full of purpose. 'I will prevail!' I say to myself. I decide it's going to be my new mantra when I start running again. I say it out loud to Gowdie, who gruffs at me. She's probably hungry too, so I give her the other half of my sandwich, which she gulps down in two seconds flat.

The place we've stopped at has these three huge, gnarly trees in one spot. They look like they're on their own little hill, but really it's their massive roots that are making that blip on the landscape. In this part of the moor there aren't any other trees nearby; there's the start of a forest off a way to my right, but these big old guys are just here by themselves, standing really close together like they're talking. For the first time I wonder where I'm going to sleep tonight if I don't get to Lowenna before dark, and it reminds me to move on.

I jog on, thinking, I will prevail, I will prevail, all medieval-sounding and shit, chanting it in my head to the beat of my footsteps. I know I'm going west, where the sun sets. Follow the sun to Lowenna, I think. I just hope I don't lose the trail before dark. It gets dark early this time of year.

I look back at the trees one last time – I kind of liked them, those old guys – and blink, cos for a moment I think I see someone standing under the tilting tree. I stop, but the shape moves really quickly and I can't tell whether it's someone hiding behind one of the trunks or just a trick of my over-anxious, adventuring, man-on-a-mission eyes.

Gowdie's seen something too, cos she barks at the trees. I hold her collar. If there is someone there I don't know who they are or what they'd want – and maybe they're hiding from me cos they're afraid of what I might do too.

'Come on, girl,' I say, and tug the dog's collar. I don't really have any choice but to run on and hope it was my own brain messing with me. It's spooked me, though, and it spurs me on.

I run, on and off, for the rest of the afternoon without seeing anyone else. I'm pretty pleased with myself, I won't lie: I'm fitter than I thought I was. *Like a whippet, you are*, Mum says to me sometimes. Give me a few years, some more time to build myself up, and I'll have arms like Omar. I'll be able to crack nuts in the crook of my elbow. I'll carry a pig under each arm. I'll walk the earth setting things right. I'll disappear like in those old stories and when I come back many years will have passed and no one'll recognize me.

As I run I think about Linda. How could she have done that to me, to Mum, burned the cards, such an act of war? I mean, I know they hate each other, though I don't know why, but she must know the shit Mum's going to get into if anyone finds out her cards have been destroyed – and, ipso facto, the trouble the village will get into too. And there's something else – something about burning tarot cards. It's like burning books. How can you destroy such a source of wisdom? It's an evil thing that she's done. I have to stop thinking about her cos it makes me too angry, so I focus my thoughts on Lowenna.

A weird thing happens when I think of Lowenna – I'm still running, still panting and sweating, but it's like suddenly I see her in front of me. She's sitting on a bench shelling peas. She looks a bit surprised to see me, but she says, 'Hello, Danny. Long time no see.' She looks older, more grey in her hair, more sags round her oversized green eyes, but it's Lowenna all right. She always wore these faded tops with old band slogans on them. She's wearing one as I see her but I can't make out the name of the band. I start to say, 'Lowenna, I need your help,' but just as sudden as the vision comes, it goes.

I stop running. As I stand there and stare off at the horizon I know it was just like the occasional visions I've had before, but this time I seemed to make contact with Lowenna. I saw her, and she saw me too.

All in all, after I think about it for a minute, it feels OK, so I start to walk on. Nothing horrible happened: I was thinking of Lowenna, that's all, and the visions are coming more frequently nowadays. In a sense this one was useful. Maybe it will tell her I'm on my way, if in fact it was actual contact and not just an odd waking dream or something.

But as time gets on it gets dark, and the darker it gets, the more noises start up. Hooting, clicking, crackling, howling; it's not reassuring, and my mood of adventure starts to evaporate. By five o'clock it's almost completely dark and I know in half an hour or so I won't be able to see my hand in front of my face, never mind where I'm stepping next. So I have to find a sleeping place and fast, cos I don't want to be out here on the moor: easy prey for too many predators, gangs included. I look around at my options. The problem is that the land is mostly grassy, with patches of long grass and weeds, and sometimes marshy land where you definitely don't want to step, but other than that, the only option is the forest to my right. I don't like the look of it: the trees are really densely packed, all jostling with each other, like they're prisoners and they can't get out. But I know it's my only option, so I make my way over. Gowdie runs ahead of me into the low branches. I walk in and look for something I can use as a shelter till it gets light.

Not too far in I find a tree that's fallen at an angle to another, making a cosy little crawl space. I look inside and actually it looks OK. It's dry and the forest floor is covered with crisp leaves. I look around, remembering forest craft from school, and find a big fern nearby. I take loads of its big furly leaves cos they're soft and lay them on the floor of my hideout. There's nothing to cover myself with but I decide to risk a little fire outside the entrance. It's a pretty big risk as everything is fairly dry, but otherwise I might freeze. I rationalize that if I start a forest fire a) this forest could stand to be thinned out anyway, and b) hopefully I'd wake up and escape. I make the fire and light it, tapping a piece of flint I keep in my pocket against a stone. The dry moss I've heaped over some twigs and branches catches, and I guide the flames to the bigger kindling. The fire makes me feel safer, and as soon as it's at an OK level and I've surrounded it with rocks, I sit back for a while, thinking about my journey and staring into it like a prophet. After a while my eyes get heavy, but I manage to stamp out the fire and cover the remains with leaves before I fall dead asleep in my fallen-tree cave, even though it's still early.

Before it's fully light, I wake up suddenly. I've heard the snap of a twig or something very close by. Now very awake, I listen as close as I can for another noise, heart beating like a Redworld train, ba-BUM, ba-BUM. I try to tune out the forest noises and listen for the thing that is out of place. There's nothing, nothing, and then, close by, the noise of a tread breaking a fallen branch. I hold my breath. Then I hear a man's voice, very low, saying something I can't catch.

I peer out of a little crevice and see a pair of legs and heavy boots just to my left through the trees. If he turns round and walks through the next row of trees he'll see the shelter. I swear to myself. I know the only option I've got is to keep quiet. I put my hand over Gowdie's nose, and thank Goddess she sits quiet.

He looks like he's just turning my way, and I'm trying to decide what my story's going to be when he catches me, when he flicks his head round the other way and makes a 'hmph!' noise. I can see now he's holding a rifle and he's a big man, dressed in camouflage clothes, all greens and mud colours, those heavy boots caked in mud, a knitted hat. As he turns his head away I see the shadow of a tattoo on the back of his neck, something big: it stands out even in the half-light of early morning here in the forest. It looks like – I can't be sure, maybe a cockroach. Anyway, I hear what he's heard, something sounding like it's breaking through the forest, running. It's probably a deer. To my extreme amazement, he walks away from me and towards it.

Knowing a reprieve when I get one, I slip quietly out of my hideaway and scatter the fern leaves around and rough up the whole area a bit, so hopefully it doesn't look as if I've been there. Cautiously I tiptoe to the edge of the forest, leading Gowdie by the collar and shushing her, and look around. To my right, at the edge of the trees a long way down, I can see some movement. A man breaks on to the flat moorland dragging something behind him. I can't be totally sure but I'm pretty convinced it's the same guy. I frown and can't quite see what he's dragging, but whatever it is, it's not dead; it's making these crying sounds, which I can hear – the wind must be blowing my way, and anyway, there's nothing else happening out here in the middle of nowhere. It's a horrible sound, that crying, and I try not to listen. It stops all of a sudden and I realize that the man has killed the deer. I see something glint in the distance and think it must be a knife. I watch, and the man drags the carcass away. After about ten minutes, he disappears over a hill in the opposite direction to where I'm going.

I take that as my cue to get out of here. That guy may only have been hunting, but there's no guarantee he wasn't hunting me, and so me and Gowdie hightail it out of there, heading in the other direction. The sun is behind us now, rising in the east, so it's harder to get my line to Lowenna straight in my head. Still, I think I have it, so I push on. My morning adventure has reminded my adrenalin levels to stay high, so I run as fast as I can out of there. I've lost the enjoyment of yesterday's journey and now all I can think of is getting to Tintagel, and for Lowenna to give me a cup of her disgusting leafy tea. And since I 'saw' her yesterday I've had a feeling in the pit of my stomach like a rope pulling me to her. Gowdie races along with me too. I think she feels the same urgency to get the hell out of Dodge.

An hour later I'm taking a rest and walking for a while past a rocky ledge in the moor. Dartmoor's got tons of these weird things, ice-age rocks that appear out of the grass – and then I reflect that I've probably left Dartmoor by now. So where am I? Bodmin, maybe. Still the moors, but that much closer to the coast. Maybe five hours walking – less if running too. I run my hand along the ledge of rock that runs waist-high out of the heather and grass. It's crumbling at the edges, and I work a piece free with my fingers. I'm rolling it over in my hand, looking at the grain of the cold granite when someone jumps out at me from behind the ridge and pulls me to the ground.

'Don't say anything; I'm here to help,' says a voice in my ear.

I don't believe it for a second – I push them off roughly and get up, but a moment later I hear a heavy tramping of feet approaching and I'm pulled down again.

'By Brighid! Stay still! Do you want them to see you?' a girl's voice hisses at me. I try to look at her but she holds my head down with some force. I'm expecting Gowdie to bark and tear her face off, or at least nip her leg, but the girl whistles a low note and Gowdie trots over and curls up next to her, easy as you like. Traitorous dog. She might be daft but usually you can rely on her to protect you, but this girl – this woman, whatever – seems to have some kind of magic hold over her.

'Who?' I hiss back, mouth full of grass, face squashed into the dirt.

'Gang hunters. Three of them. I've been following them for about an hour. Knew they were looking for you,' she says in a low voice. I wonder how she knew that, but she puts her hand over my mouth. A huge centipede crawls over my hand. I don't brush it off, but it takes a lot of willpower not to. I decide to stay put for the moment – better the devil you know, or, in this case, better the devil that doesn't have a neck tattoo and a hunting knife.

The sound of footsteps is much nearer now and it's more than one person; it's as she said, three or four. I keep my eyes closed and start praying to a goddess I don't really believe in. They're right by us now and we can hear three men's voices. They haven't seen us but it sounds like they're looking for me, especially when one of them says, 'I thought I had him in the forest.' This must be the tattoo guy, and I shiver. So he *was* looking for me.

His friends don't reply. There's a lot of puffing and blowing going on; they must have just stopped after a long run to find me. I manage to turn my head, loosing her hand from my mouth, and sneak a look at who this woman is, and almost give us away, cos there's no mistaking that this is a girl, and this girl is a knockout.

She looks like she might be tall and she's got almond-shaped hazel eyes and some of her dark blonde wavy hair has come loose from her hood. She puts her finger to her lips for quiet. But she smiles. It's a killer smile.

The gang men look expectantly at the tattooed man; he's in charge.

He doesn't say anything; he's staring at the horizon, looking west, in the direction of Tintagel. 'He's heading that way,' he says, and nods to where the sun will set later in the day. 'Doesn't matter if we wait to pick him up there. Let's move,' he grunts. They start to march on past the ridge. They don't look around them; they're focused only on what's ahead. I shudder, and the girl puts her arm round me. We wait until they're out of sight before either of us say anything.

She rolls over, as her legs have been kind of draped over mine all the time we were lying there. As she does so I can't help noticing her jacket is a little open. She catches my eye checking out her boobs and shakes her head disapprovingly, hauling me to my feet. She lets go of my hands. 'I'm Bersaba. I've come to rescue you.'

We get up and dust ourselves down. She is tall, like I thought: great posture, lazily poised like a lioness. She pulls her hood off and her tawny mane of hair spills out – streaks of blonde and gold glow in the harsh Cornish sun.

'How come you came to meet me?' I ask, ignoring the idea of this being a rescue. I was taking care of myself, wasn't I? Shaking her hand, I notice her palm is rough and she has mud under her fingernails.

'Mum saw you and knew you were on your way to us, so she sent me to make sure you got here OK,' she says.

'Mum? What, so you're Lowenna's daughter?' I didn't know she had a kid.

'Yeah. I've got a twin, Melz. Well, Demelza really.' She rolls her eyes. 'Mum wanted us to have traditional Cornish names. Bersaba's the Cornish version of Bathsheba, but everyone calls me Saba. Demelza means 'hill fort'. Talk about random.' She gestures to the horizon. 'We need to walk.'

We start moving away from the ridge, Gowdie following.

'What does yours mean?' I ask.

'My what?'

'Your name. What does it mean? In Cornish?'

She looks embarrassed, all pink and glowy, and there's just something about her that makes me think, Hell yeah. This one's special.

'It's corny.'

'Tell me.'

She sighs. 'Daughter of an Oath. It's like the title of a bad romance novel with loads of heaving breasts on the cover.'

I do a mock-ogle at her boobs. 'Suits you, actually.'

She punches me in the arm. 'Shut up!'

'Ha – urgh! No . . . it's nice. Unusual. Pretty and mysterious, like you,' I say, trying to put some of the Danny charm on her, but she just grins.

'You've got to try harder than that,' she says, and I grin back.

Happy to, I think.

We go a bit further without saying much. I follow Saba's lead — she walks quietly and quickly, keeping to a line of trees here or a crumbling wall there. It kind of puts my open-land ranging to shame, but, hey, I'm new at this. And after last night I am thankful for some extra vigilance.

The landscape is gradually changing as we journey along, and I look around me with a fresh eye at my surroundings now that I've left the moor's thorny wildness. It's softer, this landscape — misty green fields, icy dew on broken stone walls. This is more hilly too, not like the open, windy stretch of Dartmoor, which is miles and miles of heather, the horizon draped in shifting mists. And the hardness of it too — rocky outcrops, strange ancient standing stones like weathered secrets. There's an old, old vibe on Dartmoor, and not always a friendly one; it's harsh, but it's beautiful, like the hard granite line of a tor as it stands against the cold whiteness of a winter dawn.

Saba motions for me to stop as we walk into a wooded glade; the sun's shining now and it's beautiful there as we stand in the long tree shadows. She offers me a drink of water and I take it gratefully.

'How far is it?' I ask. I don't want to sound like a baby, but I am pretty tired.

'Not far,' she says. 'I would have come out last night

but it's too dangerous. I had to wait for first light to set off.' She looks at me. 'I'm surprised you got under their radar. The gangs, that is,' she says.

Is that admiration in her eyes? Yeah, girl, I think, I'm a hero. Don't forget it.

'The one with the tattoo on his neck almost found me in the forest, but I gave him the slip,' I say, waiting for her to be impressed, but she frowns.

'Yeah, that's Roach. That's what the tattoo is on his neck. He's the leader – overall leader, as far as we can tell. They used to have lots of little groups, maybe just ten men here, fifteen there,' she says, taking the bottle back from me and drinking from it. 'And then there got to be more and more of them, and they became one group. With Roach as the leader. Still stretched out regionally, between the Redworld and the Greenworld, but they report to him. Have done for probably ten years,' she explains. 'They used to be just small groups of people, or individuals that wanted to do their own thing, didn't want to settle down with us. But then when Roach took over, they got organized, and they got a lot more dangerous. Raiding, raping, killing sometimes. Taking what they want.'

I nod. It's the same at home. I wonder why he's interested in me.

'So why are you coming to us?' she asks. She's beautiful with the dappled sun on her face, all healthy flushed cheeks and tousled hair. Just in that moment I forget we're in danger, I forget how I've betrayed

Mum and Beebs and the whole village, endangered them: all I can think about is how beautiful this girl is. Guiltily, a second later I remember Sadie, feel that my loyalty should be with her. It's too complicated. I look away.

'I need to get something from Lowenna for my mum,' I say. That's not exactly a lie and not exactly the truth, just the bare bones.

'Your mum's Zia, right? I remember her. She was here a few years ago for a meet.' She smiles. 'We raised the roof that night, all right. Haven't seen her at the last few, though.'

I look at her. Surely she's way too young to be a witch, but only witches are allowed to the meets. To be fair, my frame of reference is Mum and Lowenna – both ancient.

'You were there?' I ask.

She doesn't answer. She's been looking around since we stopped and suddenly snaps her fingers. 'Yes!' she says and runs over to a little clump of plants. She takes out a bag from her jacket and picks the leaves from a particular plant, folding them into the bag and closing it carefully when she's finished. There's a wild rosebush nearby and she looks at it appraisingly.

'Do you think we could pull that bush up?' she calls over to me.

I shrug. Course. I can do anything as far as this girl knows. I go over.

She nods and unfolds a big sack from her other pocket. She winks. 'Always be prepared,' she says.

'Why do you want it, and what was that other stuff?' I ask. She's wrapping her jacket round her hands. She doesn't tell me what she found first. That's two questions she hasn't answered now — she's mysterious enough to be a witch at least.

'Protect your hands; this has thorns,' is all she says.

I take off my jumper and wrap it over my hand like a mitten. We dig round the roots of the bush with our hands and with this silvery little trowel Saba produces; it doesn't look big enough to do anything but actually it gets to the roots pretty well. We stand up and grab the main trunk of the thing and pull. Gowdie frisks around, yipping, thinking it's a game. 'Stay!' I call to her, and point to the ground near me, but she ignores me and races around.

Nothing happens for ages, and we pull and pull, and then suddenly the bush comes free of the earth and we fall backwards.

Laughing, Saba stands up. 'Let's put it in the sack,' she says, and we manhandle it in.

'Thanks,' she says, looking into my eyes. She's standing really close and there's a second when I think, Is she making a move on me? I'm ready to; been ready ever since I took that first look at her. But the moment passes — she turns round and hefts the sack on to her back.

'Come on, we better head off,' she says.

Chapter Four

Knowledge comes from the earth more than any book. Listen to the songs of the trees, the beat of the soil, the caress of the wind on wheat if you would be wise.

From *Tenets and Sayings of the Greenworld*

After a while I see the outer wall of Tintagel village in the distance and breathe a sigh of relief. We've been taking turns carrying the rose bush and I gesture to Saba that she should give it to me for the home stretch.

'You didn't tell me why we dug this up or what that other thing you picked was,' I say, hefting it on to my shoulder.

'Mum wanted a rose bush for her garden so I thought we'd try to get it as we saw it there, and the plant was belladonna, which we need,' she says.

'Another weird Cornish name?'

'Belladonna is a sedative. We use it for medicinal purposes.' She's stretching out her shoulders as she walks. Her tawny hair catches the sun like (I imagine) a mountain lion's coat catches the moon. 'It's also a poison.'

I know all about that, I think. Last year one of the guys in the village was pestering Mum and wouldn't take no for an answer, so in the end she slipped something in his tea. I don't know what it was, but he went home with a stomach ache and never came back. No proof, of course, that she did anything. Mum said the sad thing was that she wouldn't have had to do it if Omar was around, but since the village had decided that even a reformed gang member was still a gang member, a dangerous threat, they had run them all out. Even Mum couldn't stop that. 'Mob rules,' was all she'd said, but she didn't speak for two weeks after he left. 'Even if I'm a protector of the people, Danny,' she'd said, 'if the people decide they don't want Omar here, my opinion doesn't mean crap.'

I don't say anything to Saba, just nod. We're getting closer to the main entrance, and as we get nearer I can see a picture like ours, of a hand holding a village. The weird thing is, though, that this mural features five hands linked round a picture of houses, not houses sitting in one cupped hand. Plus, it looks much fresher and better maintained than ours. I look at the barricades around the village. They don't look as though they've got any gaps.

As we approach the perimeter, Saba stops me by placing her hand lightly on my chest. 'Wait,' she says. 'I have to break the circle for us to get back in.'

'There's actually something here?' I ask incredulously. I thought that was a kind of metaphor. Like, if we all believe we can see an elephant, we can see it, never mind if it's not there.

She looks at me confused, brow furrowed. 'Of course. Psychic circle. Magical protection. You of all people should know about that,' she says.

'Well, I don't. I mean, I know the theory – I just didn't know it was an actual thing. I've been outside the village at home more times than I can count without opening and closing some kind of invisible door.' I don't mean to sound sneering, but it kind of creeps into my voice anyway. These people are way more paranoid than they need to be. Nonetheless, I put my hand on Gowdie's collar.

Saba just looks at me, clear hazel eyes taking me in as we stand there together in the bright day, with the sound of the waves crashing against the rocks – Tintagel's famous ragged, rocky coastline, full of caves and mysteries.

'Perhaps your mother feels her protections are adequate as they are,' she says finally, after a long silence where it feels like she's mulling something over. 'But I would say that an untended boundary is a weak boundary. If you walk out through it any time you like without respecting its power, who's going to stop people from the outside trespassing? Forcing their way in?' She turns away from me and bends, trailing her fingers across a patch of grass. As she does it, she continues talking to me.

'Has it occurred to you that your mother's lack of attention to the upkeep of the psychic protection of the village might have something to do with why you're here?'

I ask her what she means, but she waves her other hand at me. 'Don't interrupt,' she orders.

Saba traces the shape of a door in front of us with her hand four times over. She's murmuring something under her breath as she does it, and then bows her head, bringing her hands out to her sides, palms upward. She brings them together over her head and then down in a prayer position over her heart. It doesn't take long, and then she turns to me and beckons me through. We both step forward, and the dog, and she repeats the process again behind us. I don't continue the conversation and neither does she.

When we enter the village, everyone we pass says 'Good morning' and 'Blessings' to Saba. They nod at me, curious but not asking anything, and the question stays in their eyes. It's much friendlier than my village. People are out and about even though it's still pretty early, chatting away to each other, walking about with baskets of veg and all kinds of organic-looking crap. There are brightly painted shopfronts on a main high street where you can barter goods, by the look of it.

They look much better supplied here than us, and the whole place is a lot tidier and nicer. No burnt-out cars that I can see. The paths are cobbled, not muddy tracks. There are hand-painted signs above the doors of some places — APOTHECARY, THERAPY, MUSICAL INSTRUMENTS.

We come to what feels like the middle of the village; we've been walking briskly in more or less a straight line for about twenty minutes. I remember Lowenna's house as soon as I see it, though there are some symbols painted on her blue front door I don't remember being there before. All Greenworld kids know the five-pointed star — symbol of perfection and balance — and the triskele — a triple-spiral symbol, proper old Celtic, representing Brighid and fertility and the cycle of life. Birth, adulthood, death, and back again.

'Ah. The tricycle,' I say, which is what the kids call it at home. Fun religious slang.

'What?'

I point to the white spirals on the door.

'You know. The tricycle. Holy spokes.'

'Are you serious?' She looks furious. Talk about a sense-of-humour failure. I give in.

'Oh, come on. Can't you take a joke? I know what it is. The triskele. Symbol of Brighid. I did learn something in school, you know.'

'Clearly not the proper reverence you should have for that symbol. It's the symbol of the Greenworld as well as the Goddess, you know. Of everything we've accomplished. Of the sustainable and organic beauty of our community, of its strength,' she replies haughtily and scrapes her key in the lock.

She looks back at me. 'We really care about the Greenworld here, Danny. You'd better watch your mouth,' she says, and all of her previous twinkle is gone.

Lowenna pulls the door open before Saba finishes opening it. She looks just like in my vision the day before: older, greyer with more lines on her face than when I last saw her – laughter lines, I remember she calls them. The only difference is that today she's wearing a long blue dress with a loud pattern on it – swirly flowers, psychedelic – and not one of her band T-shirts. She laughs and holds out her arms to me, and though it's not cool at all, I have this big red rush in my chest and give her a huge hug. To my own amazement, I start to blub. I manage to stop myself after a minute, but for a while I really need that hug. It's been a rough couple of days.

I pull away and Lowenna looks at me for a couple of seconds, taking me in. Then she's all smiles and she turns down the hallway, showing us in, chatting away to Saba mostly. Gowdie runs ahead of Lowenna, snuffling at anything and everything.

Lowenna takes the sack from Saba's hands and hefts it on to the kitchen table.

'My dear Bersaba, have you been shopping again?' She laughs and peers into it, and claps her hands together. 'Oh, how exciting! A wild rose! I've got just the place for it. And did you find the, er, other item?'

'Don't worry, he saw me get it,' says Saba, and gives Lowenna the little pouch with the belladonna in it.

Lowenna smiles at me. She motions to me to take a seat. 'Needs must, dear, when the devil drives. You must be starving, both of you,' she says, and puts a loaf of bread and some cheese on the table in front of me, and a glass of water. 'Start with those, and I'll make you some eggs.' She looks down at Gowdie, who is slinking round her legs, whining for food. 'And I suppose you'd better have some too,' she says, and puts down a bowl of water and a plate with some vegetable mush in it. Gowdie's pretty much a vegetarian dog anyway and she must be starving cos she wolfs it down.

I don't need telling twice either, and as Lowenna turns away and gets busy with the frying pan, I cut thick slices of this still-warm bread and give one to Saba, and slip a slice to Gowdie under the table too. We cover our slices with the soft, sweet cheese and dig in, gulping down glass after glass of the cold spring water. I start to feel a bit less shaky and start to notice where I am a bit more, to remember the place.

Lowenna's kitchen is a room that seems to stretch out up to the sky and into the wild. To say it's a kitchen is wrong; it's too big, for one thing, it's almost all made of glass and too much other stuff happens in it, not just cooking and eating. When you're at Lowenna's you spend pretty much all your time there except when you're sleeping, or out in the garden. In the day you feel like you're in the garden anyway as only the glass separates you from the huge plants and bushes and whatever the hell it all is; plus there's these massive plants indoor too, so you're always brushing up against something or other. There's shelves upon shelves containing blue or brown glass jars with mostly unreadable labels on them. Probably the most noticeable thing though is the round table. It seats thirteen and it looks like it was made out of a tree trunk and root system. It has a star carved on the top with thirteen spikes, each pointing at a place to sit, and the triskele symbol in the centre of the star. I remember suddenly that this is where the witch meetings take place; a witch from each of the boroughs that make up the south-west Greenworld attends one meeting a year. I'd forgotten until I saw it again. And the witches call those boroughs covensteads, even though everyone else still calls them villages. That I do know.

At night in the kitchen, when the sun sets and the stars come out, you're in a different world. With all the candles lit the glass dissolves and you feel like you are at one with the earth. As a kid I remember lying on my back in this room with Mum and counting the stars. My heart pulls a little when I think of Mum. My eyes wander to the walls, and see pictures I don't remember from before. Pencil or charcoal portraits mostly. They're good. I see Lowenna and Saba, and lots of others I don't know.

'How come we never met when we were kids?' I ask Saba.

'We used to live with our dad, but he went off to the war when we were four, so we came here,' Saba says matter-of-factly. Another dad lost to the war for fuel.

'So how is your mum, Danny?' asks Lowenna, still with her back to me. I guess she knows already why I'm here.

'She's OK,' I hedge. Now that I'm here, I don't really know where to start with my story, and I'm starting to feel stupid.

'Has she lost something?' Lowenna asks, turning round from the fireplace. She slides fried eggs and some cooked mushrooms on to two plates and puts them in front of each of us, then sits down.

I don't know how to answer. Lowenna looks me in the eye. Saba is quiet, already chewing her breakfast and looking out of the window. I sigh.

I tell them both everything; from Sades borrowing the cards and Linda burning them to me making the journey here to find another set, and being chased by the gangs on the way. I tell her about seeing someone by the three gnarly trees, then Roach almost finding me in the forest, and Saba saving me, though obviously I don't use the word 'saved'. Saba just smiles at that part, but doesn't correct me. She seems to have forgiven me for my former light-heartedness at the expense of the Greenworld.

Lowenna looks admiringly at Saba. 'Well done! So you did it!' she cries, clapping her hands in delight and Saba's eyes twinkle.

I look back and forth between them.

'I threw a protective sphere around us, when we were lying there by that rock, so they couldn't detect us,' she explains, biting her lip, but looking proud of herself. 'It's like a psychic bubble; nothing can get in or out, or nothing you don't want to anyway. It's what we do to protect the village, but that's a lot bigger so it needs more of us,' she says, and Lowenna smiles.

'One of the jobs for my little school,' she says.

'School?' I ask. I swallow a bite of wild mushroom on the fresh-baked bread and frown. There's no witch school at Gidleigh, or anywhere in Dartmoor.

'Five of us in all. I've been training Bersaba and Demelza since they were young, and then later, Beryan and Merryn came to me from the village, wanting to become witches. Other people have wanted to, but they weren't suitable. You have to have some natural power to start it off, the training.'

'Oh. So do they live here too?'

She shakes her head. 'No – Beryan and Merryn live in another house in the village. There's not enough room here.'

I lean down and stroke Gowdie's ears – she's curled up under my chair, snoozing. It was a long journey.

'So have you got a tarot pack I can take for Mum?' I

ask. We've got sidetracked and now that I've eaten, the direness of the situation returns to me.

Lowenna bends down and feeds the dog with bits of mushroom. She sighs and straightens up. 'I've already sent a tarot pack to your mother; it'll be with her by now. As soon as she found out hers was gone, she told me. All's well. Don't worry, Danny, about what happened. You've come here for another reason.'

'Told you? Told you how?'

'Bush telegraph.'

'Eh? What bush?'

She laughs. 'No, dear. I mean, we communicate psychically. Talk to each other in vision when we need to. "Bush telegraph" is just an old expression. A way of communicating across the wilderness.'

'But . . .' I say and trail off. I don't know what to say, except couldn't she have told me that when I walked in, and how come I didn't know about this system her and Mum have cooked up? I feel like I've wasted my time and taken all those risks for nothing.

'How do you send stuff like that?' I say instead.

She just winks. 'Witches have their ways, dear. Don't give it another thought. But you've come here for other reasons, Danny. That's what we should talk about now.'

'Eh?' What other reasons could there be?

'You manufactured the problem of the cards for yourself as a reason to come here, dear. Your subconscious is much more powerful than you realize –

61

there was something deep in you that awoke and pulled you here without you really knowing why.'

I look at her askance. What?

'Tell me: how long have you been having the visions?'

Even though I've come to the conclusion that seeing Lowenna when I was running yesterday was probably some kind of vision and not my brain playing tricks, I'm still a bit shocked when she asks cos I'm so used to keeping it a secret at home.

'Not long, I s'pose,' I mumble, thrown off guard a bit.

'How long, exactly? And don't mumble,' she snaps. Something tells me I'm not getting out of this easily.

'About a year.' As soon as I say it, though, it feels as if I can move my shoulders a bit more freely.

She nods. 'And have you told anyone? Have you told Zia?'

I shake my head – no.

'Why not?' Lowenna asks, and I think, Well, that's the question. Why not? I don't really know, except that I've seen the life of a witch in our village, and I don't want it: too many secrets, too much fear, that rancid undercurrent of awe and aversion. People need her and fear her, but they don't like her. I don't want it to be my hand painted on the village boundary. I'm not ready for that kind of responsibility.

'I think if I told anyone they wouldn't leave me alone; they'd always want something,' I say, looking at my hands. 'And Mum hasn't got many friends. They, like, they seem to hate her sometimes, the people in the village.'

'Is that really the reason?' she asks quietly.

I look at my hands. 'No.'

'Why, then?'

'I s'pose cos she'd want me to help her,' I say, feeling crappy. You're not supposed to say you don't want to help your mum, not in this day and age. See, I do help her, but only with the practical stuff, cos that's safe. It makes me feel safe. It makes me feel like a man. The visions and all the rest of the witch crap, that doesn't make me feel like a man. It makes me feel sneaky and underhand and weird. I don't want to help her with that.

She looks at me steadily. 'I do understand, Danny. Really I do. But sometimes life hands you a grenade when you were looking for a butter knife.' She sighs and gets up from her chair and pats me on the arm.

'I don't know what you mean.'

'I mean, you may not want power, but you've got it, like it or not, and you've got to learn to handle it safely. But that's for later. For now, eat and drink. You're safe.'

I look around me, at Saba, at the witchy kitchen, at Gowdie snoring under the table. I am safe, and Mum has what she needs. So why do I feel like there is something weird going on?

Chapter Five

Lament for the life cut short,
Lament for vitality waned;
Keen for the spirit taken away,
Cry for the loss of the world.

Suggested lament for the dead (short version),
from *Greenworld Prayers and Songs*

After the last couple of days I'm pretty whacked out, and after breakfast I'm starting to feel a bit sleepy. I sit down in a comfy-looking chair. Saba brings me a cup of tea and I lap it up – anything from her sweet hands, and I'm so, so tired. As soon as I've drunk half a cup I can feel my eyelids drooping, even though it's still only the afternoon. I feel the cup being taken gently from my hands and, as I pass out, Saba's voice is saying, 'I gave him just enough.'

Suddenly I'm walking down a cobbled path behind

two figures wearing long, hooded robes. They don't look back at me but they are walking very purposefully, and murmuring to each other. I can't quite pick up what they're saying, but I follow them. It's as the two figures ahead of me turn a corner that I catch one of them in profile and realize it's Saba. The other bulkier figure, I realize, is Lowenna. Where are they going, and how am I following them? I am weirdly aware that I am definitely asleep on Lowenna's easy chair right now, and yet here I am, feeling the cobblestones under my feet, smelling the cool air, with my mind like a knife: alert, aware. I don't feel at all muggy and hazy like I did after drinking the tea. I don't know how I got here; I definitely didn't wake up and leave the house. I realize this must be another vision, but it's already a longer one than I've ever had before.

There's something about the look of Saba and Lowenna in their grey wool robes and the way they're walking — briskly but with heads down, as if they definitely have somewhere to be — that makes me think they're on witch business. And then, like a clear shot out of nowhere, it comes to me: Roach is close by. And I know that they're going to stop him. A massive chill goes down my back. This is dangerous. And I feel guilty cos I've brought Roach and his gang here; they wouldn't be troubling this quiet, nice little village if it wasn't for me and my stupid ideas. But why does Roach want me?

I follow them to the outskirts of the village, and there are fewer and fewer and then, finally, no people around. We pass the outer wall of the village. I shiver: it feels exposed out here already. I find myself in this band of scrubby grass outside the wall but inside a further fence. Part of this fence is a huge gate, part of the outer perimeter. We definitely didn't come this way earlier cos I would have remembered it. The gate is a piece of artwork really. It's made of iron bars like any gate, but it has ornate mouldings that stretch between the bars. At the top of every bar is a spike, and on top of each spike is a kind of ball of something. I can't make it out, but then Saba walks right up to it and reaches into her pocket. She has to climb on to a step that is built into the linking fence to get up there; it's pretty high. What happens next makes me heave. She brings out a bird's head and shoves it on top of one of the spikes, pushing it down. A crow, it looks like. The blood runs down her hand. I realize that the ball-type shapes on top of the spikes are all crow heads. I close my eyes. I am so shocked I want to cry, and crying's not something I do that often. I hold it back, but I'm disgusted. All that preaching about the goodness of witches, and here they are, having fun with dead birds.

In the Greenworld all animal life is sacred. If you kill an animal, and it's not absolutely essential for food, you have to commemorate the animal in a community ceremony: write a poem, sing a lament for it, whatever. Which means that no one kills animals, either cos the idea repulses them or cos the idea of having to write poetry does. I'm the second – not worth looking like a

66

saddo in front of a future girlfriend. Girls like widdle fluffy animals. Ergo, if you harm one you're one lonely guy.

Nonetheless, I watch them. I'm compelled. I've never seen Mum do anything like this. Lowenna has started sweeping the area behind the gate. There's a twig broom in a little outhouse near to them, which I guess is where they keep all their magic stuff. Saba goes in there for a little while, then comes out with a handful of shapes that she hangs on the gate, like it's a Yule tree or something.

Still in the vision, somehow aware that I am asleep in the soft chair in Lowenna's kitchen, three other robed figures appear. They all confer for a minute and then form a ring, holding hands. They start chanting, and then one of them – I can't tell if it's Lowenna or Saba or one of the others – breaks their grasp of the others and walks round the outside of the circle, intoning something. She gets back to where she was and traces a symbol in the air. It happens again another three times with three different figures – they all trace the outside of the circle, return and make a symbol in the air. Then they start skipping round the circle, hands joined again. They are chanting as they do it, and I notice that the air inside the circle is getting hazy. It's like the space inside the circle is becoming a yellow-gold kind of cone of light, like water down a plughole but the other way up. I squint and see individual little vortexes of the same yellowy-white light coming from the foreheads of all five witches, feeding into the middle.

All of a sudden, they stop dead. Their hands stay linked, but one of them, and I'm pretty sure it's Lowenna cos I recognize her voice, starts to speak, and what she says chills me.

'Brighid, Lady of Vision, bless my voice with your authority and power. I command those unwelcome in this place of peace to appear. I command those who attempt to enter our community with avarice and violence in their hearts to step forward. I command those who keep their faces and intentions veiled from me, appear! For nobody who enters the sacred space with malice shall be allowed.'

Lowenna's voice is deep and loud. The space in the middle of the circle shimmers and roils like the sea. As I look, shapes seem to be forming within it. Shadows. They flicker and get stronger: grey shapes in yellow soup.

'Appear! Appear!' Lowenna intones loudly, and all of a sudden there are three men inside the circle. I couldn't say how or when they got there, but one second there are these wavering shadows and the next Roach and his two buddies are standing in the middle of the five witches.

'What is this?' Roach shouts, wheeling round. He's looking for a way out, I can tell, but none of them seem to be able to move within a pace of where they are. Caught like rats, I think.

'Capture,' says Lowenna. She seems taller. I can't see the gate any more, or the rest of the witches – just Lowenna towering over these guys. I actually feel sorry for them.

'What have you come for?' she asks, and her voice is like a bell under the ocean.

'None of your business, bitch,' says Roach.

'Do not dare to insult a priestess of Brighid; do not walk on Her land with evil intention,' she booms back. There isn't really any emotion in her voice; she sounds almost detached, but incredibly scary at the same time.

'Where are we?' he asks. The other two say nothing. I think they're in shock.

'At the boundary; within my grasp,' she replies. 'Did you really think you could evade my gaze? Did you think you could trick your way into this place? Did you doubt my power, our power? Did you doubt the Five Hands?'

The women throw back their hoods and I see their faces, stern and resolute. But one of them is no longer herself; instead, she is red-haired, dressed in a long green gown covered in Celtic patterns with fire – fire! – streaming out of her hands, and crowned with deer antlers. I realize in disbelief that Lowenna – only her face is missing from the circle, so it must be her – has somehow become the Greenworld's patron goddess, Brighid.

Either that, or she's got the world's best fancy-dress costume.

The two goons are rendered speechless, but Roach seems undeterred.

'What do you want?' repeats the Goddess/Lowenna, and she holds up her hand as if beckoning him to speak. The flames curl around her fingers and up her arm. I recall vaguely from school that Brighid is associated with fire.

'The boy,' he mutters. Lowenna's fingers curl inwards a little more, pulling more words out of him. He coughs.

'Who?' she asks again.

'Daniel Prentice,' he spits, and I shiver.

'Why do you want him?' she demands.

There's silence. He's fighting her.

'None of your business,' he manages to pant.

'Tell me!' Her fingers start to dig into her palm, and he groans and bends over, clutching his chest. Still with her hand in a fist, she flicks her wrist and the flames in her hands stream towards him warningly.

He flinches away from the heat. 'Pow . . . pow . . . power,' he grunts, with some effort.

'You want his power. What for?'

He gasps. 'No . . . none . . . of . . . your . . . business!' he cries out, and stands straight, pushing his hands out in front of him as if to repel Lowenna, but if he can match her then he can't beat the five of them together.

The five witches raise their arms towards the sky. Both Lowenna's hands are now fists.

'You can't have him. You have no power here.'

They speak as one voice.

'Be gone.'

And that's it: Roach and his buddies are gone from the centre of the circle, and all of a sudden everything is back to where it was. I see the witches in their plain grey wool robes. They are no longer holding hands. Their hoods are down and Lowenna has her normal face again.

I open my eyes and I am back in the soft chair in Lowenna's kitchen.

Chapter Six

The moment is all we have and the one thing we cannot keep.

From *Tenets and Sayings of the Greenworld*

When I look up after rubbing my eyes like Wee Willie bloody Winkie, the witches are looking down at me.

'He's all tuckered out,' one says.

'He's had quite a time of it,' says another one that I don't know. They're towering over me like nurses over a newborn; just for a minute, they are impossibly huge. Then I sit up and perspective goes back to normal; I am a boy again and they're just a group of chicks. They have taken off their wool robes and are back to normal, apart from Saba, who is glowing like some kind of primeval marble-sculpted goddess. I attempt to stand up but as soon as I try to get my knees and elbows to work it feels like they're made out of yoghurt, and I sink back into the soft turquoise-flowered chair.

'Whoa, boy; just give it a minute. You've got a face like a whitewashed wall,' says Lowenna's voice, and there she is, rubbing herbs between her fingers over a pot of boiling water. 'Just getting a brew on and we'll all have a bit of refreshment,' she twinkles. She's just like she always is again, merry and bossy; the woman-goddess with the voice that could split mountains is gone. I sit there, like I have a choice, and Saba introduces me to the other witches.

'Danny, this is Merryn. She's our chief healer. And this is Beryan. She's our trance and vision specialist.'

Merryn has a soft smile and rosy cheeks, all rounded apples and cotton undies. Wholesome. Beryan is a bit more serious, thinner-faced, blonde hair pulled into a tight knot. She's wearing overalls. She hasn't made up her mind about me, I can see from her frown. Both of them are a bit older than us, but not much – they're twenty, maybe twenty-two.

'And this must be Melz,' I say, smiling at the frowning girl picking her cuticles. Saba's sister, who disturbs me in a minor way. She's got something of the vampire about her, chipped black nail varnish, intense eyes, dressed all in black. She stares at me without smiling for a moment, then goes back to her nails.

Lowenna comes over and offers me a cup of her herb concoction. 'Drink it. It'll bring you back to earth,' she says, and I sip it. It's disgusting, but it does clear my head, and after a few sips I feel a lot better. The witches draw up a chair each and form a circle with me in it; six of us sipping tea, lounging in Lowenna's overstuffed chairs with their crazy patterns and cushions with the filling spewing out. No one says anything for a minute, and then Saba says quietly, 'We know you saw what just happened.'

'What?' I ask. I haven't entirely worked it out in my head yet, what actually happened.

'Lowenna thought you might,' says Merryn and smiles over at me.

'Before we left I, er . . . I put something in your drink,' Saba confesses. 'We had to deal with Roach and we couldn't take you with us, but we didn't have time to fully explain what we were doing to you.' Her foot is curled underneath her, dirty sole turned up.

'If you had a vision, you'd witness for yourself what we did; if you didn't, you'd get the rest you needed. The tea would make it easier, either way,' Lowenna adds. She passes me a chipped blue tin. There's a piece of paper stuck on the outside with green italic writing: Turnera diffusa, Hypericum perforatum, Asperula odorata, Verbena officinalis. Written alongside these ingredients: Visioning Tea.

I turn it over in my hands thoughtfully. 'I don't understand how I do it, though. The visions.'

'Some people just have a psychic ability. They can see into the future – you have that. And sometimes, people who can do that can have real-time visions too.

Especially if you're helped – herbally, in this case. You can link to people. See what they're doing. A kind of telepathy.'

'But I followed you, in the vision. It took ages. I watched you do it all, even the . . . that weird thing where you looked different . . . like Brighid. I mean, was that real . . .?'

'Yes. Strange, but real. I took on the face of the Goddess. Brighid is the patroness of the Greenworld, after all; I'm dedicated to her, and I've worked with her long enough to be able to . . . channel her sometimes.'

'Oh.' I'd assumed I was hallucinating. It was real?

'The tea helped you stay with us for as long as you did. But being able to do that at all is rare, very rare without training. I was curious to see if you'd be able to.'

'So it was a test?'

She smiles. 'In a way, dear, yes. A safe way to assess some of your capabilities.'

'Why do you want to assess them?'

'Well, that's the question,' she says quietly.

'I can't get beyond you changing into the Goddess, though. Just like that. Sorry. How could it be real? And . . . and why did you do it?' I demand, confused.

Melz butts in scornfully. 'Why can't it be real? Why doubt the evidence of your own eyes? You saw her transform. Roach saw it too. And why do you think he disappeared? We moved him. We can do that. We are the Five Hands!' She's in my face, all worked up, and

75

Merryn puts a calm hand on her arm. Melz shuts up, but she still looks mightily pissed off.

Lowenna raises her hand for peace. 'All right – that's enough. Melz is very passionate about the work we do, and she's right to be so. She has been working as a witch since she was eight,' she says, and smiles affectionately over at Vampire Girl, who only looks slightly mollified. 'The Goddess persona is very effective, but takes a lot of energy. It's not something I do very often. But it is real, Danny. She is real. Have no doubt. But that's not for now. What is important is that you know who we are. We are the Five Hands; it's our hands that are painted on the walls on the village boundary. We hold this village together, the five of us,' she says proudly.

'OK. So why does he want me so badly? Roach? Why has he followed me here?'

'He said he wanted to use your power,' Merryn says, hands folded.

'Well, given that I didn't know I had any until very recently, that's kind of weird,' I say.

'Maybe not all that strange,' Lowenna says mysteriously. 'But it's more about what he wants to use your power for. That's what's unclear.'

'Am I really all that powerful though? Like you? I mean, I don't know anything about what you do.'

'Some people are naturals. Some people discover their gift with training. Everyone needs training, either way. But you can still have power and not know. Not understand it,' Beryan says.

76

I look at them all, thinking about Mum.

'So why does our village only have one witch? Why hasn't she ever taken on any apprentices?' I ask.

Lowenna sighs. 'I often talked about it with her, but she was never convinced that she could trust anyone with her secrets – not even you,' she says sadly. 'Even when you were young we both knew you were psychically gifted.' First I've heard that anyone ever thought that. 'Those talents are why I want to train you as a witch. I've already told you that.' She really is serious. But I'm not prepared for what she says next. 'You are the Sixth Hand, Danny. I think this is why you've come to us. We've been waiting for you.'

There's an expectant silence, and as the seconds tick past and no one says anything, it gets uncomfortable. Finally I break it.

'Oh. OK . . .' I don't know what else to say really. I mean, what did she think I'd do? Bite her hand off for a chance to join in with a load of women chanting and drinking tea? But I don't want to be rude. And there is a small part of me that's a bit intrigued to see what would happen. I feel like I should have more to say. I don't.

Saba saves me.

'Mum, I think Danny needs some time to think. It's a lot to take in, all this. And he's knackered. Why don't we all just hang out for a while, and Danny can see what we do? Make up his mind that way?' she smiles at me. 'He probably thinks we're all mad.'

They might be mad, but you're an angel, I think, and grin back at her.

'That'd be great . . . I mean, Lowenna, it's an honour that you think, er, you know, I'm the Sixth Hand and everything, but I don't really know if I'm up to it and . . .'

Lowenna waves my words away. 'Of course, Danny. You're both right. Stay with us for a while and learn what we do. Decide for yourself. Explore the village. Make new friends. Enjoy!' She hugs Saba to her.

Saba catches my grateful gaze. You're welcome, she mouths at me.

I spend the next two days being shown around the village by Saba and introduced to what feels like everyone – the butcher, the baker, the naturally-fallen-wood-carved-with-Celtic-iconography-candlestick-maker. I'm polite and shake hands and endure the questions – and the stares. Visitors to any Greenworld village are mini-celebrities cos they're so infrequent, even if they're only from another Greenworld village two days' walk away – and never mind if they're brown – but, really, all I want to do is chill out and get pissed in the woods.

It's the second day of getting-to-know-you; it's mid-morning and everyone looks purposeful, and cheerful greetings and exchanges fly from one person to another across the street like starlings.

Saba turns to me, smiling that incredible smile. 'Where now? I've got everything I needed to get, so it's up to you. We could visit some more people, hang out at Merryn and Beryan's, do some gardening?'

Wow. That all sounds ultra boring.

I cough. 'Errr, yeah. Sounds good. But actually I think I might just have a walk on my own, if that's OK with you? Just take it all in? The village?' It's great being with her but if I have to look at her hands caressing another candlestick I might explode. I need some time out.

Disappointment passes over her features for a second, and she touches my arm briefly. It sets my whole torso tingling.

'Of course. You know your way around now, and if you get lost, just ask anyone. They'll bring you home.'

Home. I smile back at her, thinking about Mum and Biba, and feel a sad little tug at my heart. I've never been away from home before. Not that I'd ever admit to being homesick. I'm a man now, after all.

She pauses and leans in suddenly and pecks me on the cheek, a kind of unnecessary goodbye-for-now kiss. I only realize what she's doing when she's pulling away, and lean in to return it, only I miss her cheek and get the tip of her ear instead. It's totally awkward.

'OK, see you later,' she says, and hurries away. I wonder if she was just being polite, but I rub her kiss into my cheek like a salve anyway. A salve for horniness. Rub in twice a day to the afflicted area for the best effect.

My cheek isn't the afflicted area.

I wander off in the opposite direction, towards the outskirts of the village. At home that's where kids go for some alone time; I'm curious to see the boundary again, walk round it a bit. See if it's as well protected all around as it looked when I came in. See if there are any holes. And yeah, see if I can get some privacy . . .

I find myself in the same kind of scrubland outside the main part of the village that we have at home – the idea is to keep it purposefully unkempt so the village won't look too appealing to the gangs. Although I'm sure they know what it's like really. The fences stretch around the village, and I don't see any gaps here either – long, strong wooden fences curled round with barbed wire. I walk round slowly, following the grain of the wood with my fingers, listening to the quiet.

I'm walking west, with the Witch's Gate behind me to the north of the village, I think, when I see someone outside the fence – a kid, a boy, maybe eight or ten, talking to a man. I can't see the man's features; they're face to face, cross-legged on the grass, the boy's back to me, outside where the energy circle is supposed to be. I look at the fence panel and see, a few metres along, a pile of kicked-up earth a bit further on. I go and look and see that the kid – or maybe another kid before him – has dug under the fence just enough for a small body to wriggle through. Underneath and out into the open.

I call out to the boy, kicking at the mud by the hole to clear it away.

80

'Hey! Hey! Kid! You're not supposed to be out there. Hey!'

The boy looks round at me, startled, and gets up.

As he moves, I see the man's face.

It's Roach.

My heart starts thumping and I kneel down, scrabbling at the damp red earth with my fingers. I'm shovelling it as fast as I can, but it's not fast enough; I'm skinny but the hole's still way too small for me to get through.

I look up again and shout helplessly at the boy. 'Kid! Come back! You need to come back, this way, come on!' but Roach has his hand on the boy's shoulder. The kid doesn't look frightened, just mildly surprised – he looks down at the heavy hand on his shoulder and then at me, like, *What's all this noise about?*

'Bloody FENCE!' I mutter, and pull at the rusted wire. I scrape my hands, but I see a rip at the bottom and pull it apart a little before the wire tears too deeply into my palm, and I pull it away, grimacing in pain.

Roach walks the boy towards the fence, his big arm now across the boy's chest, elbow down, his fist by the boy's ear. He's smiling, but the boy isn't.

'Hey, mister. You're hurting me. Let go,' he says, squirming, but he can't get free.

'Shut up,' Roach says.

I scrabble more earth away from under the fence and pull the wire apart as hard as I can. It comes apart a bit more, but not much.

Roach stops, still some metres away from the fence.

I stand up and look him in the eye.

'Daniel Prentice,' he says, smiling. 'Aren't you coming out to say hello properly?'

'Let him go, Roach,' I call back, as authoritatively as I can.

He hugs the boy to him in the same aggressive grip. 'No need,' he calls back. 'We were having a nice chat till you turned up. Never hurts to recruit early.'

'What're you doing here?'

'Watching. Prowling. They may have banished us but I thought I'd hang around. See if you sensed me out here. Seems like it was a good idea. Here you are, right on cue.'

'I didn't sense you. It's just coincidence.'

'Nothing's a coincidence, Danny.' He ruffles the boy's hair, looking at me. 'So. You going to come and free the rabbit from the trap, or do I take him home and make rabbit pie?'

'Leave him alone.'

'I will, if you come out here instead. Come on. Burrow under that fence like a good little bunny. I know you can do it.'

I look at the boy's frightened eyes. See, this is what happens when you break the rules, kid, I think.

I kneel down in the mud. 'S'OK, kid. I'm coming. Don't worry,' I call out, and put my head under the fence. Slowly I pull my shoulders through, and press my body as hard as I can into the earth.

My coat is too bulky; I pull it off and slither under the fence in just my T-shirt, the wire tearing at my arms like hungry crows. There's only just enough room.

I walk cautiously towards them, hugging my bloody hands under my armpits, my breath coming quickly and making clouds of panic in the air between us.

I hold out my hand. 'Let him go, Roach. He can go now,' I say, trying to sound commanding like when Lowenna faced him and his goons at the Witch's Gate, but failing.

Roach looks at the kid thoughtfully. 'Nah. I might hang on to him for a minute. Insurance. You understand. Come on now. Let's observe the niceties, shall we? We haven't been properly introduced. My name is Radley North, or Roach. I don't mind either. I've been looking forward to meeting you.'

'Charmed,' I say, sounding more offhand than I mean to. I don't take my eyes off the boy.

'What's your name, kid?' I ask him direct. I read once, Goddess knows where, that if you know the name of your captive, you're less likely to kill them. I mean, I don't know if it's that serious, but he's definitely in danger.

'Kevin,' the kid snuffles, and starts to cry. 'My mum told me not to come out here, but I wanted to see what it was like. Outside. I've never been outside,' he sobs, and Roach looks distastefully at him.

I try to smile and look like everything's OK, like

I used to for Biba when some kid had made fun of her at school and she'd come home crying. She might be a pain in the ass, but she was my little sister.

'It's a bit shit really, isn't it?' I make my tone calm and friendly like we're all having a laugh. 'Don't worry. We'll go home in a minute.'

'No, I don't think so,' Roach says. 'I've been waiting for you, Danny. Waiting a really long time out here in the middle of nowhere. And now you're here, we need to talk.'

I reach out for Kevin's hand; Roach tightens his grip and pulls him back slightly, away from me, but I inch forward and clasp Kevin's palm. I squeeze it. 'Talk, then. Why do you want me? I'm just another Greenworld kid.'

I don't take my eyes off the boy.

'No, you're not. You've got power, Danny, but I don't think you know how much.'

I frown. The Hands knew about my weird stuff, my abilities. Mum knew, apparently, but didn't let on. But they're all witches.

'How did you know? About me?'

'I saw you in a vision one day. This young, skinny kid. And I saw the power in you. I knew I had to get you working with me. That I needed you to achieve my plan. Though "plan" is such a meagre word.'

'You saw me in a vision?'

He looks at my expression, reading it. 'Yes. In a vision.'

'How do you know about visions? I mean . . . how did you . . .'

'They haven't told you about me,' he states, like he's confirming something to himself. 'No, why would they?'

'Told me what?'

He looks at Kevin, smiles at both of us and takes a large hunting knife out of his pocket with his free hand. Maybe the same knife he had when he tracked me on my way here.

Kevin's brown eyes widen and he gets even paler. Roach polishes the serrated knife against his thigh.

I've got to get this kid away from Roach. Like, now. I try to pull Kevin to me, but Roach tightens his grip, challenging me with his eyes. Standing this close to him I see the lines in his face, the few days' stubble hardening his features. He's got an angular face. Snaky. There's no softness in that face, no room for manoeuvre. Every line and shadow has been drawn from long nights, fights, loneliness. It's a face that has been out in the cold a long time.

'About my place in the history of your precious Greenworld,' he says. 'Want to hear a story?'

'Not really,' I say, but at the same time I think maybe if I listen to him it'll get him a bit more on side. He'll relax and I'll be able to get Kevin away. So I shrug, trying to look careless. 'But I guess you're going to lecture me anyway.'

'Think of it as an education, Danny. See, once

upon a time there weren't any witches. It was something that kids read about in books, old women in black hats, turning people into frogs—' I think of Melz immediately when he mentions black hats – she's by far the most stereotypical witch of all of us – 'but at the same time the world was coming to a crisis. There were so many earthquakes and floods and the oil reserves, coal reserves, were almost gone. And there was panic. When people panic, Danny, they start making funny decisions. And there was a group of people, me included, who decided maybe all the industry and technology and medicine and physics and space travel, maybe all that stuff had caused all this disaster, and maybe it would be better to go back to a kind of pagan existence, living on the land, in the way that we thought our ancestors did.

'And so we made the Greenworld, Danny. Groups of people who didn't want to live in the cities any more, or who lived in the country already – we came out here, to the south-west, to live a more spiritual life, to live a life closer to nature. And we brought back the role of the witch, the wise woman, in the community. I say brought it back, of course, Dan, cos we believed that it really had existed before.'

There's a lot of people who make out that the Greenworld is all part of our spiritual heritage, a tradition of witchcraft, especially down here in Cornwall. But I've never been sure whether I really believe that.

I look around us for any help at all, but there's

no sign of anyone else either out here or behind the fence.

'Yeah,' I say. 'I know all that. So?'

'So, I'm a founding member of the Greenworld. Did you know that? Did you know I was one of them once? It was a different Five then. Me, Lowenna, your mum. A couple of others. So that's how I saw you in a vision. So that's how I know you've got power. Because I have it too.'

'You're a witch?' I ask incredulously, looking at the knife and at Kevin. He must be joking, because, holy crap, what witch holds an eight-year-old kid to ransom with a knife?

'I'm a witch, Danny. Just like you.'

I look in his eyes and I know he's telling the truth.

Why didn't I know? Why didn't anyone tell me?

'Well, even if you are a witch, I'm never going to be on your side, so you may as well give up,' I spit back at him, trying to brave it out, but the truth is I'm scared. A lot scared. But also a little intrigued. I want to hear more about this amazing power I have, and what part he thinks I'm going to play in his wacko stab at glory. Whatever that is.

He laughs. 'Giving up isn't in my vocabulary.' He peers into my face, his craggy features centimetres from mine; Kevin shrinks between us. Roach seems unaware he's there still, but I am.

'Yeah. I can see it in you. You're the same as I was. Young, stupid. You don't know what you've got.

87

But with a bit of training . . . You're meant for great things.'

'What things?' I ask in spite of myself.

He laughs again. 'Aha! Yes, there it is. Curiosity. I knew it.'

He opens his mouth again to continue, and there's a loud crack to my left. I look at the grass by my feet, which seems to have exploded.

Roach jumps and lets go of Kevin, and I pull him to stand behind me. I whip my head round and see Saba and Melz standing at the boundary fence. Melz is holding something that looks very like my dad's old shotgun. She fires it again a metre or so to our right, cocks it and reloads.

'Got your attention,' she calls, and aims the long barrel at Roach. 'We told you to get out of here,' she shouts, her scrawny face frowning, black hair coiled up on her head like snakes.

He looks at the kicked-up ground on either side of him.

'You're not much of a shot,' he calls out, but he looks rattled.

She fires a shot just past his ear in response, so close that his hand instinctively goes to his head.

'Correction. I'm an incredible shot. The first two were warnings. The next one can be five centimetres to the left or five centimetres to the right. Your choice, Roach. Leave them alone.'

I take the opportunity to get the hell out of there

while Roach is distracted. I guide Kevin back to the fence and Saba kneels in the mud, holding out her hands to pull him back under the wire. I crawl back through after him carefully and painfully. As soon as I'm back on the right side of the fence my hands start throbbing. Saba opens them carefully and sucks in her breath at the cuts, which are muddy and bleeding.

I look back, and Roach bows theatrically, smiling, but he's angry, anyone can see that.

'You won this one, but they won't always be there to protect you, Daniel Prentice,' he shouts.

Melz fires just past his other ear. 'Leave. Now,' she orders.

He makes his fingers into a gun shape and mock-fires at us. 'Till next time, my friends,' he calls, and walks away.

I see Kevin's scared face and wonder what mine must look like, whether I'm still doing such a good job of seeming OK.

'You all right?' I ask, and he smiles bravely, but he's terrified.

Saba catches my eye. 'OK. Let's get you home,' she says brightly to Kevin, and puts her arm round his narrow shoulders. She steers him away, back towards the village, talking animatedly. She's distracting him so he'll keep walking, so he won't think about what happened. Yet.

Melz shakes the dead shells out of the gun barrels, clicks the gun shut and balances it against her shoulder.

'Thanks,' I say.

'Don't go out there again. It's too dangerous.' She avoids eye contact, refusing to let me be human, to let me be sorry.

'I know that now.'

'You should've known anyway,' she snaps. 'It's lucky for you that Saba had an inkling something was wrong. If we weren't witches you might be dead by now.'

'If you weren't witches I wouldn't be here,' I snap back.

'Well, we are witches, and you'd better realize you are too.'

'I'm not. You choose to be a witch. You can't just be one, like it or not. I haven't chosen.'

She looks at me critically, and I wonder what she'd look like without the black eyeliner. Softer, maybe. Nicer.

'No. Well. That's your problem, isn't it? You're afraid what'll happen if you do make a choice. If you commit yourself to anything other than being a waster.'

'I'm not afraid,' I lie.

She gets up in my face. 'You damn well should be. That just shows what an idiot you really are. You're not even smart enough to be scared.' She strides away and joins Saba and Kevin.

But I am scared. Scared enough for all of us; scared enough to keep looking over my shoulder as I follow them home at a distance, trailing behind them like a curse.

Chapter Seven

So they took the blossoms of the oak, and the
blossoms of the broom, and the blossoms of the
meadow-sweet, and produced from them a maiden,
the fairest and most graceful that man ever saw.

From *The Mabinogion*

A few days later I'm sitting with Saba and Melz,
meditating in the garden. There's been no more word
from Roach; he seems to have, at least for the moment,
gone to ground. It's a cold but clear start to the day,
and the late autumn sun is filtering through the tops
of the trees, warming our shoulders. I have a hot cup
of tea steaming on the grass next to me, and I can
hear Lowenna talking to Gowdie in the kitchen. But
even among all this goodness and positivity, I am on
edge: brittle and filled with broken glass, my senses
jangling. Every time I close my eyes I see Roach, so I

don't close them. Meditation isn't going all that well today.

I sneak a look at Melz, with her streaked morning eyeliner leftovers, her whiteness to the point of invisibility, her raggy black clothes, all of which seem to involve lacing of some kind. As sisters her and Saba couldn't be less alike – like the sun and the moon. It must be hard being Saba's twin; she's so perfect. It's like Melz has deliberately taken the other path – the henna-dyed, kohl-lined black way of the witch – to be seen at all. I smile ruefully when I think of her with the gun, though. *Correction. I'm an incredible shot.* We all definitely saw her then: avenging angel-come-sharpshooter. Where did she learn to shoot like that?

I look down at my hands, bandaged and sterilized. After we took poor Kevin home to his mum, Lowenna cleaned the cuts with alcohol and iodine – not that gently either. I could tell she was annoyed with me, I guess for not making up my mind about being a witch. But it's not exactly a casual decision, is it? She muttered, 'Watch your back, Danny. Roach can sense the power in you as well as I can. So until you decide – whenever that might be, whenever you decide to bestow us with the gift of your commitment, and until you learn how to look after yourself – be careful. Keep the girls around you.'

I didn't reply. I was too shocked and too tired to come up with one of my usual smart remarks, and the cuts in my hands really hurt.

I think about how Kevin's mum was so relieved to see him that she forgot to be angry. 'Thank you for protecting my boy,' she said to all of us, and the girls said, 'Think nothing of it, but keep him safe.' She clutched the boy to her, hard, and I saw her fear of us in her eyes, as well as the fear of what could have happened to Kevin. And I realized that was my fault. I brought Roach here. And that puts all these people in danger.

But Kevin's mum was afraid of witches in general too. I saw it in her eyes and the way she hurried us out of the door. So maybe when you live in a barricaded village run by witches, you're counting the days until your son gets sacrificed or abducted or mixed up in something weird. Because as much as your rational mind knows that the oddest thing that's going to happen in a usual year is you dancing round a maypole feeling like a bit of a dork, maybe after a few years, your irrational self starts waiting for the poisoned apples. I always knew that life in our frontier villages meant being scared of what was outside, but for the first time I realize that some of the villagers might be afraid of what's inside too.

I dutifully try to clear my mind, breathe, relax behind my eyes, breathe, but it's hard. Melz can tell I'm not concentrating. Saba seems blissfully unaware. I peek at her from below my eyelids and she's sitting perfectly still, legs crossed, breathing deeply. She's beautiful. A lioness. A witch princess. Melz's voice cuts into my jangling senses: thinking about Roach – bad; watching Saba – good.

'I think that's enough for today, Danny,' she says, and she's up and brushing at her skirt.

Saba is unfurling herself like a cat on a warm day. She smiles over at me. 'It's so good to start the day like this. Makes it magical from the beginning,' she says and yawns. 'Follow me. I've got a job you can help with.'

I get up to follow, but Melz grabs my arm. I wince at the sudden pull – my back and my hands are really sore.

'He'll be with you in a minute,' she says, and Saba shrugs and goes into the house. Melz turns her smudgy gaze on me and her look is stern. 'She's off limits,' she says. No preamble.

'What d'you mean?' I give her the wide-eyed look but she's wise to me.

'Don't give me that. I know you like her, Danny, and it's not allowed. Anyway, Saba's got a boyfriend.'

First I've heard of it. I raise my eyebrows coolly. 'Oh yeah? Who?' I say like I'm not bothered either way.

'Tom. He's one of the gardeners. He's a really nice guy. Kind, thoughtful, funny, great-looking, tall, strong . . .' The inference is that I am none of these things. I notice an oddly zealous gleam in her eyes as she talks about him.

'Sure he's not your boyfriend, Melz?' I grin at her, trying to get a smile.

'No. But he's a really good friend of mine. I wouldn't want you to upset him.'

'Goddess, all right.'

There's a silence.

'And how long have they—' I start to ask.

She cuts me off. 'A long time. Forever, really.'

'Oh. OK. Well, good for them.'

'Yes, it is. So don't try it on with my sister. She's not interested.'

Could have fooled me, I think, but smile. Melz seems annoyed by it.

I shrug. I just wanna kiss the girl, man! I think.

'Just keep your hands to yourself,' she says, and releases her hand on my arm.

'I'll consider myself warned,' I mutter and head after Saba into the house. Talk about pissing on my bonfire. Thanks, Melz.

Saba and I leave the house and start to walk through the village, leaving Gowdie peacefully snoozing in a box with a blanket in it. I'm desperately racking my addled brain for something cool to say to this teen witch goddess. Really and truly she is probably out of my league, my dark side taunts. I shouldn't fancy her. She's powerful: if I piss her off she'll turn me into a frog. Or whatever the fashionable creature is now – an otter or something.

When we've been walking awhile she asks me if I recognize this street. And I look around and it does seem a bit familiar.

'You followed us along this road in your vision. When we banished Roach from the village,' she says.

I look again and see that I did come this way. Not the same way as when I ended up at the boundary with Roach and Kevin.

'Didn't work, though, did it? He still came for me. And I still don't know why.'

'It worked insomuch as he stayed outside the boundary, Danny. You shouldn't have gone out to him.'

'What was I supposed to do? He had Kevin.'

'I know. But still.'

I look at her questioningly. 'But what? You're not suggesting I left him out there?'

'No. But you're . . . important. You need to be more careful.'

We walk on a few more steps.

'Did you see his mum's face? When we took him home? She was terrified of us.'

Saba dismisses the idea calmly. 'She was just worried about Kevin.'

But I want to make her understand. 'No, Saba. She was afraid of us. You, me and Melz.'

She frowns. 'Why would she be afraid?'

'Because we've got power and she doesn't. Because she lives in this village, cut off from everything and only protected from the gangs and Goddess knows what else with a bit of barbed wire and your magic. Because strange men are turning up and threatening her kid with knives. Isn't that enough?'

She shrugs. 'I think you're making more of it than it is. You're scared; it's understandable, given what's happened, but don't blow it up out of proportion. Roach wants you for something, but every time he tried to get you, we stopped him. I rescued you. The Hands banished him. Then me and Melz saved you. We're powerful and we can protect you. Kevin's mum knows it and you know it. Just remember that.'

We approach a crossroads. 'Do you remember where we go next? To get to the Witch's Gate?' she asks, changing the subject.

I can't think, can't remember, and I shake my head, but it's not just that I can't remember. I don't want to go anywhere near the boundary again, but I don't want to look gutless in front of her.

'Come on. The only way to get over it is to go back out there. You don't need to be afraid; I'll be with you. OK?' she says.

I shrug, casual. 'I'm fine. I don't care.'

'OK, then. Close your eyes and focus. Left or right, or straight ahead?' she asks, and so, to please her, I close my eyes and concentrate.

First of all I just feel like a tool standing in the middle of a street with my eyes closed, but then I take a deep breath and concentrate. I visualize the streets leading east, west and north. 'Ask for guidance,' Saba's voice suggests, and so in my mind, out of nowhere, I think, Spirit of the crossways and protector of travellers, guide my feet and take me in the right direction.

Mum told us when we were young about the faeries – the nature spirits that live in the woods, in rivers, in gardens – and how there's always a spirit that lives at a crossroads. In my mind's eye, the path to the left, the west, lights up as if clouds had parted and the sun shone through. I open my eyes and point uncertainly to the left.

She nods and smiles. 'You're a natural, see?'

We follow the quiet street for a while – we've turned off the main drag where the shops and services are – recycling points, market stalls selling fruit and vegetables, a laundry, a couple of cafes – and this street just has houses on it. Not many people are around yet; it's still early.

My insides are coiling. I really don't want to go back there.

'What is it, exactly, the Witch's Gate?' I ask, mainly to distract myself. 'I mean, I know I saw you all meet there and work magic in the vision. But I saw that you, err . . .' I cough. I don't want to make Saba hate me by suggesting that she is some sort of animal sadist, but the truth of it is that she did ram animal heads on the spikes of the gates, and as far as I'm concerned, that's not cool.

'That I what?'

'Ummm . . . that you put those animal heads on the top of the spikes. I didn't think witches did anything to harm the natural world. I mean, that's one thing that I did learn from my mum.'

'Oh, that. Well – you're right, of course. We work in harmony with nature. We honour the power of animals and plants and everything in our environment. But, sometimes, and only very rarely, we ask the Goddess for special permission to use the powers of her creatures. In this case, the dark goddess. The Morrigan. Her animals are crows, ravens.' She sighs. 'I know – it's not a fitting end for a free life, to be displayed in that way, but we need to do it on occasions like the other day with Roach.'

'Well – it's not so much the displaying as the killing, I'd have thought,' I blurt out. I'd hate Gowdie to come to some kind of sticky end for the sake of witchcraft.

Saba stops her brisk stride and looks at me, aghast. 'But we didn't kill them!' she exclaims. 'We occasionally use the bodies of already dead animals that we find in the wild to help us with our magic.' She shakes her head vehemently. 'Invasion is something we have to guard against, and sometimes, like it or not, our methods have to be hard. Brighid is our goddess. But sometimes we have to call on the dark mother. The Morrigan.'

'I don't really remember her from school,' I say. Mostly what you learn is Brighid: patron of fire, spring, heavenly inspiration, poetry, agriculture, motherhood. All the nice things.

'Well, we don't tend to make much of her in our overall culture, but witches work with her now and again. She's Melz's patron goddess, actually. We say

99

she's dark, but that's not right really. She's the necessary death; transition; growth; rebirth. She's a war goddess, too. She helps people in strife, in bad times. She helps those that protect the land. You call on her in times of trouble.'

'She doesn't sound very friendly,' I say, thinking of Melz and how appropriate it is that this warmongering bitch-goddess is hers.

Saba flicks her fringe out of her eyes, smiling. 'No, well, it's not her job to be friendly. Sometimes life calls for crows.' She reaches for my hand. 'It's OK – you were perfectly right to ask about it,' she says. 'It's good to know that you care about our animal friends. That makes you a good witch.'

'I'm not a witch,' I argue.

We walk the rest of the way to the gate hand in hand, and neither of us mentions it.

When we get to the Witch's Gate it looks different to before – less threatening. The bird heads have been removed. Now it stands and gleams in the morning light. My heart beats a little slower – even though this is a different part of the boundary to where I crawled out under the wire, I still didn't want to come out here. It feels too exposed. I look around, expecting to see Roach out there, but there's only the sun on the grass and the wind in the far-off trees.

We walk right up to the gate, and I see that close up it has a lot more detail than when I saw it before. The bars are thick and strong, and there's writing engraved on the curlicues that connect them. The triskele and the pentagram sit in the centre of the gate, the spirals within the star. I read what's engraved around them.

Saba traces the writing with her finger. She recites it like a spell.

'Strong is the fortress, early and late; iron are the
    bars on the Witch's Gate.
Keep out the evil and keep in the good; honour
    the power of the wild and the wood.
Protect the people and maintain the sight; keep
    the circle in sun and moonlight.
Ever the village together will stand; kept by the
    wisdom and love of the Hands.'

'Wow,' I say. 'Who wrote that? And who made the gate? How long has it been here? How come you've got one but our village doesn't?' I bombard her with questions.

She has brought a bunch of flowers with her and she gives half of them to me. 'Thread them through the bars,' she says, not answering my questions. She starts making a kind of weave through the bars with the long-stemmed flowers – roses and carnations, I think they are. I'm not good at flowers. I ask her what we're doing.

'A nicer way to decorate the gate,' she says, smiling. 'We are honouring a sacred site, a magic place.'

We continue threading the flowers. Then concentrating, with a frown on her forehead, she tells me about the gate.

'It was built years ago by a man that lived here once, Omar. I think that was when your mum lived here too. It was the end of the Redworld for us and the start of the covensteads. A woman, Linda, wrote the words. Omar engraved them. At first, the gate was just a nice entrance into the village, but as the gangs got stronger and we needed to protect ourselves more, it became more and more important. Mum decided it would be permanently closed. It's become iconic, I suppose. Powerful.'

I stop threading the flowers and take all this in. Was the Linda who wrote the words on the Witch's Gate the Linda who burned Mum's tarot cards? Sades' mum, Linda? And Omar built it! Omar with his biceps and triceps, his 'guns'? Omar, who used to swear when Mum wasn't around, who taught me about fighting and engines and life on the road? So Linda was a part of all this once. Why did she hate Mum now, and everything connected with witches? What happened?

'You've met her, my mum, haven't you?' I ask. I'm curious to see what Saba thinks.

'Oh yes.' she replies. 'She's so magnetic. Glamorous, even, I'd say. A natural. Some of us are born and some of us are made – but Zia, she was born an enchantress. She's the type men die for,' she says a little wistfully. I can't understand why she seems wistful, as if she'll never attain that level of desirability – Saba is the most compelling girl I've ever met. I wonder if she knows it. She looks up and catches me staring at her. We are standing very close together and for a long moment we just stay in that moment, that perfect second. Then, all thoughts of possible chaos forgotten, I lean in and kiss her.

It's a long kiss, a good kiss. We stop and she looks up at me and strokes her hand over my hair, my cheek.

'I've never kissed anyone like you before,' she says. 'You're so . . . different. Beautiful.'

'Sorry – I didn't mean to, I . . .' Half of me doesn't really love the idea that she might've only let me kiss her out of novelty value or something – the only brown boy in the village, but the other half is just thinking whatever made that kiss happen is fine. Better than fine.

'Shut up,' she says, and kisses me again, longer and deeper. I have the impression of us being inside a comet, all reds and yellows, the heat of our lips together. The world has been replaced with Saba; I'm burning in her.

This time she pulls away. She looks guilty. 'I shouldn't have done that.'

'You should.'

She smiles. 'I wanted to. But I'm . . . I've . . . I've got a boyfriend.'

'Your sister may have mentioned it to me earlier.'

'Did she? And you still kissed me?'

'You still kissed me.'

We both smile.

'So what now?' I ask.

She sighs. 'Look, Danny, I really like you, but . . .'

I take her hand. 'Saba, don't worry about it. If you don't want me, let's just be friends,' I say. There's all the time in the world to win her round. I'm not in a hurry.

She smiles, that cat smile, her hazel eyes glowing.

I touch her cheek. 'He's a lucky guy, that's all I can say.'

She holds her fingertips to my hand, still on her face, and her eyes meet mine for a long moment.

'Friends,' she says. 'Well, I guess that'll work.'

We've finished with the flowers, and Saba stands back to admire our work. 'Lovely. See how nice it looks now.'

Better than the crow heads, I think.

'Yeah . . . it's good.'

'You have to keep sacred spaces special. Tend them,' she says, drawing a triskele and a pentagram in the air in front of us. 'There. Done. We can go.'

She takes my hand and we walk quietly for a minute.

I change the subject. 'Did you always want to be a witch, to follow in your mum's footsteps?'

'Yeah. But to be honest there wasn't much discussion about it – Mum assumed Melz and me would want to be witches. We'll take over control of the village one day, I guess.'

'Are you cool with that?'

'Yes, I am, but at the same time there are other things it would be nice to do. Melz wants it more than

104

me, I think. The magic. Always did. She works much harder than me at it. But I seem to have more natural talent.'

I consider that for a minute. 'Do you think she feels like you're the favourite?'

She shrugs. 'Maybe. Sometimes. Melz feels things pretty intensely. She loves hard, she hates hard.'

I snort. I get that.

'I guess I'm more laid-back than her. She worries all the time – about us, about the village, about the war, everything.'

'Do you think the war will ever be over?'

'It has to end one day. But not any time soon, no. My dad's out there fighting,' she says, flinging her arm out, presumably to indicate Russia, where the battle for fuel is raging as we speak.

'Mine too,' I say. I don't usually talk about Dad, but I could talk to Saba about anything.

'Do you miss him?'

'Dunno. Yeah. But he's been gone a long time now, you know? Sometimes I think I've forgotten what he looks like.'

'I miss my dad. I was four when he left. I can't remember him that well either, but I still miss him,' she says unhappily. 'Sucks, doesn't it?'

'Yeah, yeah it does.'

'What do you miss the most?'

I think for a minute. 'Lots of things, you know, the small stuff. His laugh. Reading books together, ones about dragons and wizards and stuff. But I s'pose what I really miss is . . . I don't know . . . his solidness. He was just together, solid, you know? Someone I could trust, who wouldn't bullshit me. I don't know.' I kick a stone in the dirt.

Saba smiles a little sadly. 'I know. Dads leave a big hole in your life when they leave. If I ever have a kid, I'm never splitting up with its dad. I couldn't break anyone's heart like that.'

'Yeah. But who'd ever leave you, Saba? No one would be that stupid.'

She smiles. 'I'm sure it's possible,' she says.

'I don't believe it.' I smile at her; she smiles back wickedly.

I kick a stone along the path for a while, thinking about my choice of male role models since Dad left. There are slim pickings in the Greenworld, with easily two-thirds of the population being women.

She digs me in the ribs. 'Redworld penny for them.'

'What? Oh. No, I was just thinking, I don't know who to be like, you know? Sometimes I think I should be like Omar. Or a free man in the gangs. Be my own man, not our mums' vision of how a man should be – like some sort of eunuch.'

She frowns, but doesn't comment.

'Look at Roach. I mean, he's got power,' I say.

'You want Roach to be your role model?' she says disbelievingly.

'No. Not really. But who else is there?'

'I don't know, Danny. Maybe you need to become a role model for others.'

We walk on, and I think about that. Laughable. Who'd want to be like me?

Saba breaks into my thoughts. 'Hey, you should come out with us later. Melz and I are meeting the gang. Kind of a pre-Samhain thing.'

I'd almost forgotten it's Samhain tomorrow. My stomach lurches out of recent habit, but I calm myself – it's OK, the cards aren't a problem now. Relax. Still, I don't feel good about being away from home on the most important night of the year. And I'm scared of Roach finding me again.

'A gang? What do you mean, Roach and his cronies?'

She punches me in the arm. 'No, silly. Our gang. Some kids we know. Come along!'

I wonder if Tom the Boyfriend will be there.

'OK. I mean, is it safe? What're you doing?'

'Just hanging out. There's a few of us. I've got some of Mum's elderflower wine stashed,' she says with a winning smile. She takes my hand. 'You'll be OK. Honestly. It's a really out-of-the-way place and anyway, me and Melz will be there to look after you.'

I look at her hand holding mine and feel her blood pulsing in time with mine, through the bandages.

'I'm there,' I say, and think, Watch out, Tom.

Chapter Eight

Love the land; share its bounty; grow with love; harvest well.

From *Tenets and Sayings of the Greenworld*

That night, after dinner, Saba, Melz and I head out of the house under Lowenna's watchful gaze. 'Take care, all of you,' she calls out as we leave. The night is a different time around the villages – we all know that. At home around now the wind blows in off the moor, carrying the smell of damp dark earth, which I've come to associate with the threat of what lies beyond – the gangs. But here it's the cold salt sting of the sea that hits your nose as you walk out, the faint roar of the waves battering Tintagel Head. I miss the moor, but at the same time there's a tinge of excitement in the sea being so close; it's primal, I guess. Who doesn't feel the pull of the tide in their blood when they hear the rush of the water? It makes you feel alive.

Melz has linked her arm through Saba's and is pulling her along the village high street. Gowdie runs ahead of us, exploring the paths and running back to me every so often, as if to check on me. I walk fast to keep up with the girls.

'So where are we going?' I ask as we pass the bakery and grocery in quick succession.

The grocer is still putting away the last of his unbartered vegetables. He nods to us as we pass by.

'Evening, Bert!' Saba calls, and the old guy straightens up a little at the velvet touch of her young voice.

'Evenin', darlin',' he calls back, and, quick as you like, flicks an apple over to her.

She catches it deftly and takes a juicy bite. 'Gorgeous!' she calls back to him, winking playfully.

We're still walking, and she turns to walk backwards and waves to Bert.

Melz frowns, little lines crinkling above her nose. She doesn't say anything to Bert, just pulls at Saba's arm. 'We're going to be late,' she says, chivvying us as if we were ducklings.

I look at Saba's smile and the apple juice dribbling down her chin and can't help grinning at her.

'We meet the others at our secret spot,' Saba mumbles around a chunk of apple. 'Means we can have a few drinks without anyone sticking their nose in. S'fun. We have a fire, dance, that kind of thing.'

I know what kind of thing. I often had the same kind of nights with Sadie at home, at the boundary or in the stone circle.

'So who's in your gang?'

'Umm, well, there's us, Tom, Jennie, Bryony and Ennor. Oh, and sometimes Bali and Skye.'

'All witches?'

'Oh no. Just me and Melz, and you, maybe. Well, you're a half-witch. Tom's a gardener. We went to school with Jennie and Bryony – they're a year younger than us. Ennor's a mechanic's apprentice. Fixes stuff. Skye and Bali live . . . outside the village.' She delivers the last part somewhat vaguely.

'What do you mean "outside the village"? In another covenst—'

Melz breaks in impatiently. 'No, stupid. She means they live with the gangs.'

I look at Melz to see if she's joking, but her gaze doesn't waver. 'But . . . we're not supposed to . . . I mean, the gangs are . . .'

She shrugs. 'I know. But they're all right. They saw us having a bonfire one night a couple of months ago and came over, made friends. They're not bad people. They get us stuff. Steal it off their dad.'

'What stuff?' I ask to clarify.

She rolls her eyes, like I should know. 'You know. Stuff. Booze. Redworld stuff. You'll see.'

I think about Omar's trips and how he used to get us stuff.

Saba takes my arm and squeezes it, so I'm linked in with her and Melz. 'Don't worry, Danny. It's all right. You don't have to have a drink if you don't want to. If it's your first time or something.' She's being genuine, and it makes me laugh cos if she knew what a party animal I was, she'd know how off the mark she is.

'No . . . I'm all right, ta. I can look after myself.' I smile back at her. 'I'm just surprised Lowenna doesn't mind about you consorting with the enemy.'

Melz sniggers. 'Goddess, Mum doesn't know, what do you think? She'd go mad. None of the parents know, or Merryn and Beryan, so don't mention it to them. They'd think Bali and Skye were up to something, but they're OK.'

'They're even less dangerous than Melz,' Saba teases, and Melz punches her in the arm.

'Hey!'

'Shut up, Melz. You know you study too hard.' Melz gives her a look that Saba ignores. 'Poor innocent Danny. We'll save you from the evil gangs,' laughs Saba. She glances at her sister. 'Speaking of. Are we picking Ennor up on the way?'

'Yep.'

'Why "speaking of"?' I ask.

'He goes out with Skye, but don't tell his mum,' she whispers as we walk up to a white cottage with a black trim. Even though winter is coming, the garden is filled with flowers and herbs, and the door has a tree painted on it.

'Wow,' I say, taking it in.

Melz knocks on the door, using a knocker in the shape of an apple. 'I know. It's amazing, isn't it? Ennor's mum Maya's such a wonderful artist. Wait till you see inside,' she says, flashing a rare smile.

The door is opened by a short, plump woman with grey-streaked black hair in a red wool dress and a necklace that looks like it's made of coins.

'Ah, the young witches!' she exclaims, smiling, and ushers us in. 'He's just finishing the washing up for me. Ennor!'

Ennor comes out of the kitchen as Maya pushes the door shut behind us. He looks like his mum – same dark hair, dark eyes – average height, but bigger than me – I'm skinny, and Ennor has some fighting weight. He's got one of those naturally frowny expressions, but there's a twinkle in his eye when he talks.

'What do you think of it, then?' he asks, nodding to the mural that runs the length of the hall. Trees, cliffs, the ocean – it's the Tintagel coastline, the stormy sky with the wind in the waves.

'It's amazing,' I say honestly, cos it is.

'I've seen better,' he says, and ducks as Maya mock-slaps him.

'Rude young man,' she says, smiling, and he just gives a half-grin back to her.

'Be back late,' he says, buttoning his wool coat and pulling on a dark knitted hat.

'Not too late, Ennor. You've got work to do tomorrow,' she says, and he waves his hand absently.

'Yeah, OK. See you later!'

He ushers us out of the door before Maya can ask any more questions – or that's the impression I get anyway.

Once we're out on the street again he holds out his hand. 'Ennor,' he says. A man of few words. The strong silent type, I guess.

'Danny,' I say, and shake his hand, which is rough, from manual labour, no doubt. Not many of us get to keep soft hands in the Greenworld.

He nods.

'Ennor doesn't say much,' Saba teases. 'We like him, though. We can tell him all our secrets and he won't blab.'

He just gives that half-smile again and holds his hands up. 'You got me,' he mutters.

'So how did you get to be part of the gang?' I ask. How does a strong silent type get to be friends with two witches?

'We used to play together, back in the day,' Melz butts in. 'Maya used to look after us when Mum was doing head-witch stuff. We'd stay at Ennor's house. Make up stories about what was happening in the murals.' She smiles at the memory.

Saba leans in confidentially. 'Maya trained Melz as an artist,' she says.

I didn't know that about Melz. Guess I don't know that much about her at all.

'Yeah. Well, we spent enough time there. I picked it up,' Melz says, making it sound like it's not a big deal to her.

'I didn't. Haven't got an artistic bone in my body. Melz is the arty one. She did all the portraits at home. Always sketching. I'm just the dumb blonde,' Saba sighs mock-theatrically at me.

'Don't you believe it,' Ennor says to me. 'You've got to watch this one. She'll enchant what she wants out of you and leave you wondering what happened.'

'Oh, En! That's not very nice. Say sorry!'

'I'm just warning him.' He smiles at me.

'Ennor's like our little brother,' Saba says to me. 'Though he's all grown up now, and thinks he's funny.'

'Pack it in, Sab,' he says gruffly, but there's affection between them all – I can see that.

'So, what sort of stuff do you repair? Not cars any more.'

'No. Though we do have one in the garage. We tinker with it when we get the time, but it needs loads of parts, and we can't get them.' He opens up as soon as he's got machines to talk about. 'No, we maintain people's lawnmowers, repair windows, fix door hinges, build a bit of furniture here and there. There's a lot of machinery that isn't electrical,' he says.

I know the lawnmowers he means – heavy rollers with blades that curve round a metal cylinder. We've got one at home and it takes bloody forever to mow the grass with it.

Saba pulls us forward, running. 'Come on, boring boys! Stop talking about mending things. Let's race! Last one there gets the warm beer!' she cries, and she and Melz speed away. Saba's face is wickedness and excitement; Melz's set in competitive concentration. I start to run after them, and Gowdie runs along after me, barking excitedly. She can feel something in the air tonight too.

After about five minutes of running I see Saba's back disappearing into a shadowy door in a long, faded red-brick wall. We've been heading out of the village for a while and I can tell we're near to the boundary now – my sense of direction has always been good. I shiver a bit more than just from the cold; knowing I'm near the boundary makes my stomach twist, but I follow her.

It's got pretty dark, but we're outside what looks like a run-down farm. I slip through the same door and see it's been wedged ajar by overgrown grass and a thorny rosebush. The red paint is faded and peeling and the wall is half falling down. I feel I can safely conclude that nobody lives here.

Inside the wall, I can see more cos of the flickering light coming from a campfire in the middle of what must have been the farm's garden, and I follow Saba through what looks like a mini orchard – all apple trees, though most of the fruit has rotted on the ground. The oversweet smell of the apples mixes with the smoke in the cold autumn evening.

A girl wearing an oversized jumper and her red hair tied up in a scarf walks round the fire to meet me; without breaking stride, she leans forward and kisses me on both cheeks.

'Welcome! I'm Jennie. Saw you round the village. Hoped the girls would bring you along tonight.' Her eyes sparkle with the firelight.

Ennor, Melz and Saba cluster round the fire, warming their hands. Jennie waves to a petite blonde girl in a long green coat walking through the apple trees towards us. The coat gathers in at her small waist and with her long, carelessly braided hair she looks like a faery princess in one of Biba's old storybooks.

'Hey, Bryony!'

Bryony comes over and smiles up at me. 'Hi!'

'Nice to meet you, Bryony,' I say, with equal parts sincerity and flirtatious eye contact.

She flushes. 'Oh! Yes, hi! So you're the new witch?'

'Well, I'm thinking about it,' I purr, projecting my own supercoolness. 'Like, I could be a witch whenever I want; I'm just playing the game for now.'

I feel a hand on my arm. 'We've got to persuade him to stay and train with us, Bryony,' says Saba, reappearing at my side and looking at me with her laughing eyes, 'So anything you can do to help would be appreciated . . .'

Bryony blushes. 'I'll do my best.'

She smiles a shy little smile, and Saba laughs. 'Tom! Come and meet Danny!' she says, and holds out her hand to a tall, blondish, shaggy-haired boy, who is bundled up in a thick jumper on top of overalls and talking to Melz. She's got her sketchbook out on her lap and he's peering at it, making her laugh about something. Tom comes over, and I'm briefly reminded of a Labrador trotting up to his mistress. I suppress a smile at the thought.

'Danny, this is Tom. He's one of our village gardeners. Tom, this is Danny. He's going to train with us,' she says.

'You sound pretty sure about that, toots,' I say, and playfully punch her in the arm. It's on purpose; I want to see how he takes it. A foray into his territory. But he doesn't seem to notice. And he also doesn't seem to notice that Saba hasn't introduced him as her boyfriend, just as Tom, the gardener. But I notice.

He nods his head over to Melz. 'She's got a good likeness of you in that sketch, Saba. Boobs not quite big enough, though.'

She punches him in the arm. 'Sexist pig. Go to the Redworld if you want massive mahoomas. All plastic, all uniform, no waiting.'

He feigns thoughtfulness. 'Might do, might do. Anyway, good to meet you, man!' he beams, and shakes my hand warmly. He's strong, I can tell from the handshake, and he's bigger than me. All that digging and hands in the earth. Instinctively I like him, which annoys me. He's the competition, I remind myself.

'Yeah, you too.'

Gowdie noses his boots and yips at him, which means, 'Hello, I like you, pet me.'

He bends over and strokes her head. 'Nice dog. What's her name?'

'Gowdie. She likes you,' I say grudgingly.

More evidence that he's a good guy. Gowdie's radar for good people is never wrong.

'Oh, like the witch.' He smiles and squats in front of her, tickling her under her ears, which she loves. 'You're from a witchy family, then?'

'Just my mum.'

'Well, you must have something if Lowenna's recruiting you. She wouldn't waste her time.'

I shrug. 'We'll see.' I don't want to give anything away, and I also don't want to bond with Tom. I need not to like him cos I want to steal his girlfriend. But he keeps talking to me.

'So you're from Dartmoor, are you? I've never been. What's your village like?'

'S'OK. Same as anywhere really. Total Greenworld.'

'Yeah. Sucks, doesn't it?' He smiles, and hands me a bottle. 'There you go, man. Cheer you up, being away from home.' He clinks his bottle against mine. 'Down the hatch!'

I look at the bottle. It's not one I've seen before. It's a Redworld brand, totally forbidden. I laugh and take a big gulp. It tastes of betrayal and pollution and sex and corruption and I love it.

We're all sitting round the campfire and a few beers into a stash of bottles when the last of the group turns up – Bali and Skye, the gang kids. I'm curious to see them – will they be covered in tattoos, be packing guns, look murderous? But when they push their way through the orchard, kicking aside the leaves and rotting fruit, they look normal. The girl, Skye, slides round the campfire to Ennor, and they get into a pretty full-on clinch, like, right away. I'm a bit embarrassed (I mean, there's a lot of tongue going on there) and look away and catch Saba's eye. She's smirking, and as I look at her we both burst out laughing. I know what she's thinking, cos it's the same as me: Get a room! I've got to hand it to Ennor – he's got a way with the ladies if Skye is anything to go by.

Eventually they unclinch and come over to say hello, with a shambling Bali close behind, who just nods. Skye's sweet, long-lashed, wide-eyed, dreamy, holding Ennor's hand, but when Saba says I might be training to be a witch she gives me a surprisingly sparkling smile, like the lights were just turned on.

'A new witch? And a boy too. That's different.' She grins up at me. 'Shame I'm taken. Wouldn't mind seeing how a witch kisses,' she teases, and rubs Ennor's arm when he looks aghast at the very idea. 'Oh, En. As if I'd want anyone else,' she coos exaggeratedly.

She rustles around in the hand-stitched cloth bag she's carrying and pulls out a little book – probably not more than eight pages in a black cardboard cover.

119

'This might interest you, then,' she says, holding it out to me. I take it and look at the cover – *Cornish Charms and Witchcraft*, with an illustration of a warty witch on a broomstick against a white moon.

'What's this?'

'Read some of it. It's hilarious,' Skye giggles, looking under her lashes at me and then Ennor.

'Where'd you get that?' he asks.

She curls her hair round her finger. 'Found it at home.'

I'm surprised. Gangs aren't supposed to be interested in this stuff.

'Read it! Read it out loud!' she says.

I turn to the first page and start reading. 'It is probable that Cornish children enjoyed more than their fair share of stories about wicked witches on broomsticks, because a deep-rooted belief in witchcraft – that is, the power of magic – persisted in this remote corner of Britain much longer than elsewhere. The persistence of such superstitions and beliefs, which are largely a survival of pre-Christian practices, is more understandable when it is realized that, about a century ago, Cornwall had few connections with the more sophisticated England across the Tamar.'

Saba snorts. 'More sophisticated! What is this crap?' She reaches for the book and reads on from where I stopped.

'Moreover, in those days, neither the Church nor the standard of education offered much of a

120

corrective to such age-old beliefs; if anything, they were strengthened by that natural desire all Cornish people show to cling to the past. It is a past made more immediate too, by the presence throughout the countryside of numerous prehistoric remains in the shape of giant burial chambers, mystic stone circles and standing stones, which in the country people's simple minds often assumed supernatural and horrific significance.' She shrugs, looking up from the page. 'It's just an old book for tourists about witches. Pre-Greenworld.'

She holds it out to Skye, who takes it and flicks forward a couple of pages. 'No, it wasn't that I was laughing at. Where is it? There's a list of traditional charms. I was going to ask if you and Melz ever did any of them.'

Melz has drifted over now too, and everyone's standing around Skye, listening.

Skye flicks one more page and her dirty fingernail jabs the page. 'Ha! Here it is. Listen to this. To cure the whooping cough: make a bread-and-butter sandwich with a hair from the head of an ailing child. Feed this to a dog, hoping that he coughs, because from then on the malady will have left the child and entered the dog.'

We all laugh and I tickle Gowdie under the chin. 'Did you hear that? Beware bread-and-butter sandwiches, Gow.'

Skye is flicking through the book still. 'Ah! Listen to this, then. How to destroy a witch or her spells:

One. Make an effigy of the witch in clay and pierce it with a long pin or skewer. Two. Write the witch's name across her portrait or photograph and throw it into the fire. Three—'

Before she can finish, Melz has torn the book from Skye's hands and put it in her pocket.

'What're you doing? I was just reading that.' Skye reaches for the book, still smiling, but Melz looks furious.

'Well, you shouldn't be reading it. It's not funny.'

'Melz, don't be a pain. We were just having a laugh. Give it back.'

'No way.'

'What? It's mine. Give it back.'

Melz shakes her head. 'You shouldn't have something like this.'

Saba frowns. 'Come on, Melz, she didn't mean any harm. We're just having some fun. Give it back.' She goes to take the book from Melz's pocket but her sister pulls away.

'No! Why was she reading out the bit about destroying witches? Does she want to destroy us? Is that why she's here?' Her eyes are spitting hot embers. Poor Skye, I think. No one likes being on the receiving end of Melz's sudden tempers.

Saba sighs and looks up at Tom. 'Tom, tell her.'

Tom unwraps himself from Saba and steps towards Melz as if he was approaching a hungry lion. 'Melz, it's not your book to keep,' he says gently, and tilts her chin

122

up with his finger so that he can look her in the eye. 'Come on. It's all right. It's all superstition. We're just having a laugh.'

'You don't understand, Tom,' Melz says, but her tone softens when she talks to him.

'Well, no – but I know you're not afraid of a stupid little book like this, are you?' Carefully he holds out his hand for it. 'Come on. Give it back. You're upsetting everyone, and I know you don't want to do that.' He smiles gently at her, and unbelievably the threads of a smile pull Melz's face into something less raging harpy, more average girl once more. She sighs and pulls the little book out of her pocket and hands it to Tom, who places it back in Skye's hands.

He smiles. 'Well, thank Brighid for that! Now, let's get this party started, witches and non-witches. And no trying to destroy each other!'

Ennor pours something from the bottle he's holding on to the fire, and the flames surge up in the night-time air. Melz is standing by the flames, screwing up a page from her sketchbook, and tosses it into the flames. She catches my eye. 'I didn't do it right this time,' she says, looking a little shifty.

'Don't be so hard on yourself. You're good.' I've seen the portraits she's done at Lowenna's.

I'm offering the olive branch, but she gives me a half-smile and turns away. 'Not good enough,' she mutters.

I watch the fire lick the paper, the edges curling

and blackening. And just for a few seconds I see the image she's thrown away: Saba's face, with Tom's, but she's drawn them looking away from each other. As if they don't know the other one is there; as if they were two unconnected sketches on the same page. The charcoal lines forming the faces are deep and black, as if Melz scrawled them in a rage, with all the pressure she could muster. They aren't like the finer, more detailed drawings of hers I've seen. I look up, but she's turned away, and stands with the fire at her back, staring silently into the night. Her flickering shadow falls across Saba's as her twin leans in to kiss Tom.

About an hour later I'm lying flat on my back on the cold, hard red earth, listening to the fire pop and staring up at the stars. Thousands of them. Beautiful. Everything's quiet and beautiful.

'So you've joined the Hands.' A voice interrupts my reverie. Bali's lying close by, over by the fire, his head resting on his arm.

'Maybe. Haven't decided yet.'

He takes a minute to consider this. 'Why not? What would you do instead?'

'Dunno. Haven't really thought.'

'You may as well, man.' He upends a beer bottle, draining the dregs. 'Sod all else to do round here.'

'Yeah. But I don't know if it's for me.' I take a long glug of my beer.

He sits up. 'At least you've got a chance at something.

A talent. Me, what have I got? Being a waster just like my dad?'

I roll over to look at him.

'What's it like, being in the gangs?'

'It's all right. I mean, people think we're all killers, rapists, thieves. But a lot of us don't do anything like that. We're just living, you know? Outside the bloody covensteads. I mean, how do you cope with all that Greenworld stuff, man? Doesn't it get boring?'

'No . . . well, yeah, obviously, it is boring. But it's all right.' I want out find out more about life in the gangs. 'So where do you live?'

He waves his arm loosely to the right of the farmhouse.

'Yonder. Me and Dad and Skye got a caravan in the woods.'

'Have you ever met Roach?'

He shrugs. 'Yeah. He's all right. A bit mad; you don't want to get on the wrong side of him. As long as you do what he asks you then you're all right.'

'Are you going to tell him about me, and this?' I wave my hand at the bonfire and the garden, where the rest of them are dancing under the trees. I reflect that I might feel vaguely alarmed at the thought if I wasn't so wasted.

'Nah. What's the point? Just make things worse between us and the village. Anyway, Skye's seeing Ennor, isn't she? If our dad found out about that he'd skin her alive, and me for bringing her here.' He wipes his mouth with his sleeve. 'Don't trouble trouble unless trouble troubles you, that's what I say,' he slurs, and I grin back at him.

'Fair enough.'

He reaches into his coat, frowning, and pulls a box-like metal thing out. I squint unsteadily at it.

'What's that?'

He holds it up to his eye, closing the other, and presses a button. There's a click, and a blaze of white light. I hold my hand over my eyes.

'Smile,' he says, and the light flashes again.

'Ow! What the hell's that?' I peer over the top of my arm.

He laughs. 'Old camera of my dad's. Takes pictures. You know, photos. You must have seen them in books an' that. Bit of a hobby.'

'Oh.' I look at the metal box and at the glass circle on its front. 'Where is it, then? Where does it come out?'

He shakes his head and puts the camera back in his coat. 'Nah. You have to develop the film.' He shakes his head at my confused expression. 'Bloody hell, you Greenworld kids. Develop the film. In chemicals. In the dark.'

I look at him blankly. I have literally no idea what he's on about, and my head is starting to reel. Slowly, Bali and the bonfire start circling me, and the stars whoosh past in between.

He nods over at the trees. 'Think someone wants

you.' I look around to where he's looking, with some difficulty. He nods again over to a shadow standing under a tree. I can see it's a girl, and in my blasted state I can only think it's Saba.

I get shakily to my feet and weave my way over, but when I get there Bryony looks up at me with her cornflower-blue eyes.

'Hi,' she says shyly. 'I was, I was, errr . . . wondering if anyone's given you the tour of the farmhouse?'

'Oh, uh . . . no, no, they haven't,' I slur. I hold onto the tree for support, but she takes my hand instead. 'Well, then, follow me,' she says and leads me through the trees towards the house.

I look back as I stumble after her, spiderwebs from the branches catching in my hair and fruit squishing under my feet, and am surprised to catch Saba looking after us. She's sitting on her own next to the fire – everyone else, even Bali, is suddenly dancing drunkenly beyond, their figures like jerky shadow puppets in the firelight, but in that moment a message passes between us. And I'm sure that message is 'Don't go with her'. But I'm too far away, too wrecked and Bryony's pulling me towards the house; the promise of passion is in the air. I look away from Saba and smile down at Bryony, pulling her towards me and kissing her deeply. At this moment I can't be doing with these does-she-doesn't-she-like-me mind games. Bryony is here, and she likes me. If Saba's got someone here then so will I. The kiss grounds me for a moment, and the world stops circling as dangerously, slowing the stars' erratic movement to the rhythm of my blood.

The next morning, Samhain, I wake up in my bed at Lowenna's house feeling like a wardrobe has fallen on my head. My mouth tastes as though I've been eating roll-ups doused in badger's wee. I sit up. Too much. I lie down again until the dizziness fades. I think back to last night and realize I have some gaps in my memory. But I remember two things very well: making out with Bryony, and catching Saba's look.

And it may be the beer, or the wine, but I realize that I want to stay and do the training. I need to do it for Mum, to help her, but I also need to have a reason to stay here. Cos although I was with Bryony last night, I've fallen in love with Saba. Hook, line and sinker. And I don't care what I have to do to get her. Now that I'm sober (or almost) I know that look meant something. I know it.

Resolved, I get up as quickly as I can and make my way down the stairs – I'd run if I could, but though the spirit is willing, the flesh is weak – and crash into the kitchen, where Lowenna is sitting at the big table, talking to one of her many cats. Gowdie's in her basket looking on warily. She's afraid of cats, the big wuss.

'I want to do the training,' I blurt out, and she looks at me with a surprised expression as I stride up to where she's sitting.

'And good morning to you, Danny!' she replies, laughing at my solemn face.

'I'm serious. I want to become a witch,' I say. I try to rearrange my face into a look of focus and poise. 'I'm serious. I want to do it,' I repeat.

She stops laughing.

'I'm very glad to hear that, Danny. What changed your mind?'

I pause. 'I think it's my destiny,' I say, and it's true. Just not in the way she thinks.

Chapter Nine

And it was not in our name that the Redworld burned.

From Tenets and Sayings of the Greenworld

'Then there's no time to waste,' Lowenna says and pushes her cup of Greenworld tea into my hand.

'Drink that and follow me,' she says. It's like *Alice in Wonderland* here. Eat this, drink that. All designed to alter your perceptions in some way. But I sniff it and it smells safe. Just manky old leaves soaked in water. I slurp it gratefully and follow her.

She leads me upstairs and into what must be her bedroom, cos there's a messy pile of stretched-out old band T-shirts in a corner by the door and a rumpled bed. The room smells of incense and there's five mouldy teacups lying around that I can see. I stand in the door, thinking, Is there any time it's not weird to be in your mum's best friend's bedroom? But she's over at a cupboard and impatiently waves me in.

'Come in, come in, take a seat,' she says, indicating the bed. 'Don't worry, I won't romance you.' She scrabbles around some more in the drawer she's looking in and mutters, 'Aha!' When she turns round she's holding a green silk-covered box. 'Here you are,' she says and brings it over to me. I wonder if I can look inside. She waves her hand impatiently. 'Yes, yes, look inside. It won't bite.'

I open the lid of the box and see a package. I look at Lowenna. I reach in and take it out. It's wrapped in yellow silk.

She closes my fingers round the tarot pack. 'I give this pack to you, Danny; go well; see clearly.'

I almost drop it. 'F-for me?' I stutter. Uncool.

She's drawn up a chair and is sitting opposite where I am on the bed.

'You of all people should know that the tarot is a witch's tool. If you're going to start training, you need a set. So this is yours.'

I turn the package over in my hand. Weird. These were always Mum's thing.

'Open them up.'

I slowly unwrap the yellow silk. The cards have a kind of star-and-sea design on the back, and the fronts are full of kings and queens, swords, stars, moons.

'There are so many of them,' I say like a dork. But

there are. How am I ever going to remember what they all mean?

'Don't worry. You'll get the hang of it,' she says. I guess I will.

'Let me tell you about what I do here, Danny,' Lowenna says. She smiles. 'Get comfortable, dear. It's not every day you begin as a witch. There's a lot to learn, and you won't take it in all at once.' She looks at me speculatively. 'But perhaps you should tell me about what you understand a witch does. And how we came to run the covensteads.'

Oh hell – just like school.

'Oh, well, er . . . well, there was the war,' I begin hopefully.

'Yes . . . and?' she says, waving her hand encouragingly.

'Er . . . Well, the war's about fuel,' I say.

'Yes it is.'

'It's still going on.'

'Sadly.'

I start warming up a bit. 'Nobody was prepared. The Redworld realized it had almost run out of fuel. Burnable stuff. Coal and oil.'

'So what happened?'

'They realized there was still some of that stuff left over in Russia. Eastern Europe. So they went to get it.'

'Well, it's not as simple as that, Danny. You can't just wander into someone else's country and take their fuel. Especially when there are shortages everywhere.'

'But they needed it.'

'We aren't concerned with what the Redworld needs,' she snaps.

Touchy. I better get back to the history lesson.

'So some people decided to opt out of the Redworld. The people that didn't agree with the war. Not In My Name. All that.'

'We thought that we'd do the planet a favour and stop using it altogether. Live cleanly.' She's nodding, with that zeal in her eyes they all get, our parents, when they talk about this stuff. Apart from my dad. He just used to blow out his cheeks and make faces at me and Beebs when Mum was talking about how great everything was, now that we didn't have any electricity or heat. He'd come to the Greenworld after it was set up, out of curiosity – at the beginning you could do that. There was more coming and going, not like now – and he stayed because of Mum, then us – and then, one day, that wasn't enough any more. Mum was furious when he left. 'None of our business,' she'd said. 'We've opted out. Don't care about the war. Care about the Greenworld.'

He left when I was old enough to notice it – quite old enough, thank you. Beebs was younger, but she still knew. Still woke up in the night crying most nights for months, wanting a hug from him to make it OK. I remember the way he was in the days before he left – sad, sort of sucked-in and defeated. Not like how he usually was, alert and watchful, and a bit spiky, but with

133

a twinkle in his brown eyes and the creases round them in his weathered brown skin that could either frown dangerously at you or crack into giggles all of a sudden.

It has often struck me that I don't know if he's alive or dead. If Mum knows, she's never told us. She's so secretive, like a closed-up suitcase.

So I like to think of him alive, fighting the war for fuel in Russia. I hear they still have electricity there. And so I sometimes imagine Dad sitting at a clean scrubbed table somewhere, bundled up in a rough jumper, lit by the harsh cold of an electric light, writing a letter to me. And what's in that letter has changed over time. First of all it said:

Dear Danny, I miss you so much and wish I was there with you, but I am forbidden from coming home. Every day I work on my escape plan to get away from here, but they are too strong for me. I am being held against my will and forced to fight, and you must know that I would do anything to come home and be your dad again. I will find a way soon. Love always, Dad

But then, after a while, it said something like:

Dear Danny, Just writing this in between fighting. The battle is going well. I miss you and Biba but I know most of the time that I made the right choice — the noble choice. I am doing this for the greater good. I hope you are doing well in school. Love, Dad

And eventually the letter, when I even thought about it, said something like:

Danny, Just a short note to let you know I am OK. I'm sorry I forgot your birthday but I hope you are doing well and growing into the man I wanted you to be. All is well here. I have met a good woman and have moved in with her and her two children, Laszlo and Lili. They are great kids. You would like them. Love, Dad

Truth be told, I haven't thought about him for a while now. I focus back on Lowenna, who's still rattling away.

'OK – so you know that witches became the heads of villages here in Devon and Cornwall when we rejected the Redworld?' she asks. I nod. Everyone knows that. 'We wanted to go back to the idea of having a local wise woman or man who could be the local healer, seer, herbalist, agony aunt, whatever. We split Devon and Cornwall into covensteads. But as time went on and the gangs started and got more powerful, people wanted protection. We put up boundaries and fences and walls, but they didn't keep the gangs out. They still robbed people, attacked those who went out walking between the towns. And the towns worked out that they needed something more than wood and bricks. They needed fear to keep the gangs out.' Lowenna picks up a teacup and turns it over and over in her hands as she talks. 'See, we didn't make this decision; the people did. The mob, if you like. They wanted the gangs to be frightened of something, and they decided we were it.'

'And there used to be cities in Devon and Cornwall too, didn't there, before the Greenworld? But no one lives there now?' I ask.

I've always found it weird that in Plymouth and Exeter, a way away, there are a couple of pretty much deserted cities – office blocks, houses, train stations – cos cities don't fit into the Greenworld. They cost too much to run; they're hard to live in without electricity; they don't have enough green spaces for growing food; there's too much dead steel around. Stuff that can't be used – cars, trains, aeroplanes, computerized stuff. The Greenworld works best in the countryside. The people who used to live there either moved into the covensteads or the Redworld, so that they could continue living in cities – or joined the gangs, I guess.

Lowenna smiles sadly. 'It's a terrible shame, but there have to be some casualties in a regime change.'

The Greenworld is Devon and Cornwall, but there are rumours about other rebel communities across the world. I don't know if they even really exist, or if it's just us cut off, down here with the waves and the moors.

Thinking about the gangs makes me remember what Omar said about them.

'Omar used to say that the people in the gangs are just the people in between – they're not into Greenworld ideas but they want to live outside the Redworld too. They're not necessarily all evil.' I'm watching her face as I say this to see what she'll say, especially after last night with Bali and Skye – gang kids. Lowenna would surely go nuts if she knew her witch daughters were hanging out with them.

She raises an eyebrow. 'Well, Omar has his own experience . . . his own opinions. I wouldn't argue with him. I think the gangs might have started off in that way, but they've become criminal. Thieves, drug dealers, thugs, murderers, even. All of them,' she finishes darkly.

That's not what your daughters think, I whisper in my mind.

'So how do we manage to make them so afraid of us, then? If they're such badasses?'

It's something no non-witch really understands. I mean, we get that the witch protects the village. We just don't really know how. Real ways, or smoke and mirrors?

She smiles ruefully. 'They are afraid of what we can do.' She stops for a minute and looks out of the window.

'What, exactly? I mean, what can you do?' I'm curious.

'You saw. If they try to invade us in small groups we can repel them with magic.'

'What else?' I ask. If she wants me to train she has to spill her guts. I want the good stuff.

She sighs. 'Oh, well . . . you know. Plants and herbs have their uses.'

'What, you mean, like, poisons?'

137

She just nods, pulling her lips tight into a line.

'What else?'

'Sorcery. Enchantment.'

'What does that mean?'

She looks at me for a moment, deciding, then goes over to a wicker casket, pulls out a large leather-covered book and brings it back to me.

'This is a book of spells. A grimoire. Ways to make people do things. It's old, but very effective.' I reach out to open it, but she pulls it away. 'Not for the uninitiated,' she says, smiling.

She taps her finger on the tarot pack sitting in my lap. 'A witch's tools are very important; a witch has powers, but she also needs her tools to maintain the covenstead's belief in her. The more they believe and trust in her, the stronger her power becomes, and therefore the more she can protect and help them. So when Linda burned your mother's cards it was a problem. You knew that. These are yours now, and they'll help you more than you know. But there's something else that's even more important. It's the great secret of the witches.'

Dah-dah-DAAAAH, I think. Here it is. The big moment.

'All right.' She takes a deep breath. 'I'm going to trust you, Danny. Do you know what an energy portal is?'

'No – I mean, I can imagine, maybe, but, no . . .' I stammer. Great, Dan, way to look dumb.

She sweeps her hand dismissively. 'There's no reason why you should. Let's see. Now, do you know what energy really is?'

I shake my head. Not really. I mean, I know Mum sees auras, colours around people, but that's where the knowledge stops. That's when I usually tuned out anyway.

'Energy is hard for most people to detect. But it's just natural life force. It can be shaped, commanded. That's what magic is.'

'So what's a portal?'

She leans forward towards me, her too-big eyes popping slightly, silver-grey hair shining in the candlelight. She looks mildly deranged.

'I'm getting to it. Our world has its own natural energy system, and that is completely dependent on a natural flow of life, death and rebirth. In the spring, a flower grows from a bulb. That's life. It dies in the winter. The leaves and petals decay and become a part of the earth. The earth provides the nourishment for the bulb to flower again the next spring. That's rebirth. And all the while the energy isn't lost or gained, just goes from one state to another. Death is just a change in energy, after all.'

I raise my eyebrows. That kind of comment always sounds so flip when people say it. Usually when people like Lowenna and Mum say it.

She ignores my expression and plunges on. 'So that's what a portal is – an energetic passageway between life and death and back again. Human energy flows through it, from life to death and from death to rebirth. When we die, the portal is our way through to the other side – whichever portal is the closest. Same when we're born.'

'OK.'

'I cannot express to you how important these portals are. We have to ensure their secrecy as well as their health. How they operate.'

'What do you mean, health?'

'These things aren't to be messed with, Danny. If non-witches – people without the proper training, the proper reverence – if they started using them, trying to enter them, go over to the other side for a laugh, for a dare, just to see what was there – the portal would become polluted. It would stop working. And souls wouldn't be able to cross over.'

'Are there any polluted ones? Ones that don't work?'

Her expression goes dark. 'Yes. Sadly. Quite a few, in fact. And it isn't always necessarily because of individuals, even. The other problem is pollution. Fracking. Drilling. Disruption. Chemicals. The Redworld, essentially. The Redworld doesn't know portals are there, and even if they did know, they wouldn't understand what a portal does. They wouldn't believe it. They'd think it was silly, like faery stories. So they drill and poison the earth wherever they like, and sometimes they destroy especially powerful natural places. That's part of Tressa's work. My sister, over in

Boscastle. She keeps track of what's happening with portals all over the world.'

'How many are there, then?'

'A few hundred, maybe.'

'So everywhere there's a witch, there's a portal?' I ask, thinking of all the covensteads in Devon and Cornwall. That's a lot of portals just in our thin little sliver of land.

'No. There's two here – Tintagel and Scorhill circle. Your mum's. Some in the rest of Britain. The rest are all over the world, but sadly most of them aren't protected by witches, as far as we know. You find that portals are often round stone circles, burial mounds, that kind of thing. Earlier civilizations than us knew about them.' She sighs. 'I have to tell you that the situation is getting worse and worse. The war, in particular, is killing the portals in Russia and Eastern Europe.'

'So where's yours? Tintagel's, I mean?'

She looks at me. 'Guess. There's only really one logical place.'

I think about it for a bit, and then it hits me. Of course.

'Tintagel Head?'

She smiles. 'You'll make a good witch, Danny. Yes. It's a very special place. The medieval kings knew it; King Arthur knew it. We know it.'

'I didn't think King Arthur was a real person.'

She glares at me. 'Don't be stupid. Of course he was. But I'm not getting into that with you now.'

Heaven forbid you should have to defend your opinions, I think. Nevertheless, I'm curious. 'Can I see it, then, this portal?'

She grins at me. 'If you're going to become one of us, it's essential that you do.'

Chapter Ten

This is the night when the dark is thin.
Welcome, ancestors! Enter in.
The fire is lit, the table set.
You have passed and we, not yet.
Brighid bless the Samhain fire;
Flame of creation in the funeral pyre,
Crows dance in the dark, shadows in flight:
Goddess bless us all on Samhain night.

Song for Samhain,
from *Greenworld Prayers and Songs*

Later, I'm standing on Tintagel Head with the Five Hands, almost being knocked over by the wind. It's the evening of Samhain – Greenworld New Year. The end of everything and the beginning of everything. I didn't intend it, but I've ended up becoming a witch on a pretty auspicious day.

We are on an island that's really just a big cliff, linked to the mainland by a thin path – a neck of rock with a wooden walkway over it – that stretches from one side to the other, linking land, knowledge and normality to rock, magic, wind and water. The crash of the waves against the sides of the island are like bass drums; the air is as sharp as sapphires.

Lowenna and I made our way down together. It was scary leaving the village, crossing the boundary, but somehow I knew it would be OK. I trust her; if I'm not safe in the company of the head witch of the Greenworld, I'm not safe anywhere.

The other four witches are here waiting when we arrive.

'How did they know to come?' I ask, panting, as Lowenna and I reach the top of the rock.

'Bush telegraph, remember?' she says.

I look around me. They've been busy, the other four: a circle is laid out among the famous remains of Tintagel Castle. There's an altar at one side, with a sword pointing into the circle, storm lamps, a cup, a five-pointed star, a triskele painted on a stone, a long stick, figures of Brighid and two others – the crow goddess, Morrigan, and a crude male figure with a spear. The four witches stand solemnly outside the circle. Lowenna leads me to them.

I've come to see the portal, though, and push the wind-whipped hair out of my eyes. 'I don't see it.' I feel disappointed. Somehow, with my newly recognized power, I thought I'd see whatever it is straight away, but there's nothing here, just the wind and the castle.

Lowenna tuts. 'Well, you won't do, will you? It's closed. There's no point it being visible for any old Tom, Dick or Harry to see. Then where would we be? No, we have to open it. And anyway, even when it is open, it takes a witch to see it.'

'Why does it have to be a secret?' I ask. Just to clarify.

'Don't you listen?' Lowenna tuts again. 'I told you. It's a gateway between life and death, this world and the next. Do you think the average person would be able to deal with that?'

I shrug. 'Dunno.'

'Well, let me tell you, they wouldn't. And they'd be wanting to mess around with it, and if you don't know what you're doing with the portal, it's dangerous.'

'Why? What happens?'

'I told you earlier about it being the way between life and death. The dead can get lost here, on earth, if they can't access the portal to move on. And a living person going in, if they worked out how to – they could get lost there. Disintegrate. Or get lost in the River of Death. Even beyond that. There's a point you can't come back from. You'd die.'

I shiver at the thought and look around at the witches. 'Have any of you ever been inside it? What's it actually like?'

'We all have,' Beryan says. 'It's strange. You can

go in with your real body if you've got the right focus. It's debilitating being in there for any period of time, though. Especially if you go as far as the river, but there's no need for any of us to do that.'

'So, the River of Death is . . .?'

'Where the souls go when they die. They enter the portal, follow the tunnel to the end, to the river. They have to cross over it to get to the next life. Once across, there's no way back, as far as I know. It's like a kind of assessment place. Looking back at your life before you go on to the next stage.'

Lowenna takes my hands in hers. 'I think it's important to teach others the right way of protecting it; share the guardianship with those I trust.'

'You trust me?'

Lowenna looks me square in the eye. 'Yes, I do. Look, Danny. You've been given some very special gifts. You shouldn't waste them.' She's deadly serious. 'You are a witch. You're here to be trained. I've foreseen it. I've told Zia and she approves,' she says, weighing up my commitment in her oversized green eyes.

'Are you sure you want to be one of us? Now's the time to say no if you don't,' Melz interjects, her heavy black hood covering her face. 'It's hard work, being a witch. So if you're in it cos you think it looks cool or to impress a girl——' she looks at Saba, then back at me — 'forget about it. There's other ways to get laid.'

She's a good enough witch to have noticed, at least. The rest of them look on impassively. No one pulls up

Melz on being mean, so maybe that's what they all think of me. Just cos I'm a boy I've only got one thing on my mind. Well – technically that's true, but I'm damned if I'm going to back down now and prove them right.

I square up to Melz, to all of them. 'I'm sure. I want to be . . .' I search for the right word. 'Initiated.'

Lowenna steps forward. 'All right. Let's begin,' she says, and signals to Saba, who opens the circle just like she did that first day we met, coming into the Tintagel boundary. We all file in behind her.

We do the usual calling of the Goddess Brighid to be with us – that's the same as at home, in the community ritual.

Saba leads the invocation: 'Be with us, Great Goddess Brighid: She who is the beauty of the green earth, and the white moon among the stars, and the mystery of the waters. For She is the soul of nature, who gives life to the universe. From Her all things proceed, and unto Her all things must return. O Brighid, burn this witch in your sacred fire; cleanse his soul and purify him, for he is your servant. Lend him your powers of healing, creativity and your fiery resolve. Be ever with him, O Blessed One.'

Lowenna picks up the male figure from the altar, and intones: 'Be with us, Great Spirit, Lugh; shed upon this witch your powerful light of courage and strength. Take him for your own, in your army of warriors of the light. Give him the power to believe in himself, the courage of his true instincts and the strength to lift himself and others from fear. Give him the discipline to hone his skills to perfection, and the joy of laughter and friendship. Be ever with him, O Shining One.'

Melz picks up the figure of the Morrigan – a thin female figure with a crow head, carved in wood and painted black. 'Be with us, Great Goddess Morrigan; take this witch under your feathered wing and give him your strength in times of conflict; help him be reborn as a protector of the Greenworld. Fill his enemies with fear and his allies with courage; protect him, O Dark and Beautiful Goddess; fill him with wisdom. Be ever with him, Queen of the Shadows.'

Lowenna leads me in front of the altar, picks up the sword and points it at my heart. 'So now, Danny, I have to ask you: will you submit to my teaching? Will you honour the will of Brighid, of Morrigan, of Lugh? Will you protect the portal and your fellow villagers? Will you keep the Greenworld safe? And will you let the force of your power flow through you, increase with each moon, and be true to yourself at all times? Better you should run at this sword than take these words in vain.'

I have a moment. Do I really want to go down this road? Do I want to be a witch? Is Saba worth it? Surely there's still time to back out. And then a strange calm comes over me. 'I submit,' I say quietly.

'Then receive the Fivefold Kiss.'

She touches me lightly with her finger – forehead, left foot, right hand, left hand, right foot.

Saba traces the triple-moon symbol on my forehead with blue paint. 'Receive the sign of Brighid as a reminder that She rules this Greenworld, and we are all Her servants.'

Lowenna opens my shirt and paints the shape of an arrow on my chest. 'Receive the sign of the God Lugh: the arrow. Be blessed.'

Melz takes the paint pot from Lowenna and draws a triskele over my heart. 'Receive the sign of the Morrigan, of life in death and death in life,' she intones.

Here we go then, I think, and even my jaunty devil-may-care inner voice doesn't sound as confident as usual; as much as I might think I'm doing this to get close to Saba, there's another, deeper voice inside that says, This is serious, Dan. As I hear that voice, the magic of Tintagel Head starts to spread through my feet and up through my legs into my body; the heartbeat of the rock resonates in my blood. I look up into the wide grey sky with its fast-scudding clouds, feeling the wind blow through me. It feels good. Serious, but good.

Melz bends down and takes something out of a blue velvet bag. 'Hold out your hands,' she says, and places a knife across my palms.

I turn it over in the twilight. It's a beautiful thing – white bone handle, shining steel blade engraved with Celtic symbols.

'This is your athame – your witch knife. You will use it to channel magic and to make magic tools and charms. You must never use it for non-witch purposes, or to harm anyone or anything.'

I nod. 'Thank you.' I trace my fingertip over the blade.

Next, Lowenna places both her hands on my shoulders, and unrolls something from her fist. I look down and see a line of red wool snaking towards the ground. She holds one end by my head and Beryan comes forward and holds it by my foot, and gives that end to Lowenna. She stands up and wraps the wool once round my head, then once round my chest. I look at her questioningly.

'Your measure. As high priestess I keep everyone's. This is a part of you. Keeping everyone's measure symbolizes keeping everyone's loyalty. And secrecy.'

I don't know if I like the idea of that, but it's too late to argue now, as she places the wool in her pocket.

She stands back and smiles at me. 'Welcome, Daniel Prentice; witch and man. You are blessed by the elements in this holy place. The Gods guide your hands and heart,' she says, looking into my eyes.

Merryn follows her and kisses me on both cheeks. 'Welcome,' she says. The rest follow.

'Welcome, Danny.' Saba is last, and holds my hand as she kisses my cheek.

She breathes in my ear. 'I knew you would.'

'Now for the portal,' Lowenna says, and starts to trace symbols into the air and hums slowly. I feel the temperature around us rise. I start to see something ripple in the middle of the rock. It's like the heat haze coming off the pavement on a hot day, and when my eyes focus directly on it it's less visible, but I find if I relax my eyes, I can see it better.

It's a dim orange. And it's big, like twice as tall as me, and several metres wide. The centre widens like a ripple in a pool, and I start to feel energy pulse from it and through my body like an intense heartbeat. I notice Lowenna is sweating. She's still making symbols with both hands, until suddenly her last symbol seems to push definitively into the energetic mass, and the swirling slows. It doesn't make any noise you can hear with your ears, but being next to it kind of makes you feel a bit breathless somehow, like the pulsing heartbeat of it takes charge of your lungs and makes you want to pant.

'Jeez,' is all I find to say, freaked out but also not wanting to disturb it in case it eats me or something; I limit my smart remarks out of respect.

Lowenna looks shagged out and is dabbing her top lip with her sleeve. She catches my Whoa-this-is-weird expression. She reassures me. 'It's all very new to you, I know, but believe me, there's nothing to be frightened of.' I stare into the orange swirling mistrustfully.

She nudges me in the back. 'Go in.'

I step backwards. 'No, I'm all right thanks . . . maybe next time?'

I don't fancy it at all now that I've seen it, but she gives me a look.

'No. This time. I've just initiated you. You are, now, a witch. One of your jobs is to understand this portal. Attune yourself to it. Be able to open and close it correctly; be able to enter it if needs be. Know how it should feel, so if its energy is ever disrupted, you'll be able to sense it.' She is as breathless as I feel.

'So it really is a matter of life and death,' I joke, but no one laughs. Tough crowd.

I clear my throat, take a deep breath to even out the push and pull in my lungs. 'OK, OK. What do I do?'

'Just walk forward into it, and visualize yourself becoming transparent. Imagine yourself taking on the colour of the portal. Imagine that your body becomes fuzzy round the edges. Lose your definition. Merge into it.' She sits down on the cold ground and breathes deeply.

I look around at the other Hands. 'You make it sound easy,' I say.

'It is easy, once you know how. Might take a few attempts, but you should be all right,' Beryan pants.

Just standing by it makes you feel like you've been running: how will it be inside?

'And what will happen once I'm in it? How do I get out?'

'Just walk out, imagining the reverse. Your body getting more solid, less fuzzy. Walk out imagining walking on the island again. That's all.'

'That's all,' I repeat. 'That's all. OK, let's try it.'

I take a deep breath, close my eyes for a minute

and imagine my body becoming less solid. I imagine having a less well-defined outline, and open my eyes, walking forward, focusing on the portal. Orange, I think. Orangeorangeorange. Fuzzyfuzzyfuzzy. And I try to keep my breath even. But it doesn't work; I walk straight through the thing as if it were a cloud hovering on the rock and find myself looking out over the sea.

'Try again,' Saba calls, a smile in her voice.

I walk back round and try again. This time, it works.

It's hard to say how, but one minute I'm standing on Tintagel Head, cold and wind-whipped, and the next I am in this circular corridor, leading off into the far distance. Colours pulse around me – orange, like on the outside, but pink, purple, white too. If I had to say what it was made of, it would be like a dense gas: like being inside a cloud maybe. Inside, the pressure on my lungs is worse; the thud-thud-thud of the energy beating through the portal is stronger, more of a sound now I'm inside, and it resonates through me steadily, even though I am thinned-out here – a kind of diluted me.

I walk along a bit. It's just a long, long corridor – a tunnel, perhaps. Nothing happens. I'm definitely still in my body, but my feet don't make a sound.

Then, a kind of wormhole opens in the side of the tunnel a few metres in front of me, and a person falls into the tunnel. The hole closes immediately, and the person – an old woman – stands there looking around her, a bit puzzled, like I'm doing. But unlike me, she starts losing definition almost straight away, becoming more translucent with every moment. A spirit, I suppose. And she seems to know where to go because she drifts away from me, down the tunnel, and after a while I can't see her any more. She merges with the colours and the heartbeat-like rhythm, melting into the portal.

OK, I think. Time to come out now. It's fine in here, but maintaining this fuzzy state is getting kind of hard, and my breathing is definitely laboured. Or maybe it's not the keeping fuzzy, but the being-able-to-become-unfuzzy when I get back that's the problem, because there's part of me that wants to stay here and just drift along like that old woman. I feel the desire to surrender to the thudding heartbeat of the place, to be dissolved into its rhythm. And that wouldn't be good. Not for someone alive anyway.

Instead, I pant, 'I am leaving now,' which sounds kind of dorky, but I don't know what else to say, and feel that saying it out loud is a good idea. I turn round and walk slowly back the way I came, away from disintegration. I get more solid, darker, less opaque. I feel the rocks and the grass under my feet, and find myself back on Tintagel Head. I walk clear of it and crumple down on to the ground, trying to catch my breath.

'Good!' Lowenna looks pleased as I walk out, and Melz takes time out from looking pissed off to look surprised instead. I guess I was quick or something. 'How was it?'

I look up from the cold grass, wheezing. 'All right,' I manage to get out.

'A bit more detail?' Lowenna chides, tapping her fingers on her thigh. No sympathy for my breathless state.

'Oh . . . right . . .' I heave a lungful of air in and start to feel a bit better. 'Well, it was a colourful tunnel, and this . . . this old lady appeared through this kind of hole, and she drifted on. I guess . . .' I cough. 'Excuse me. I guess to the other side. She died, I s'pose. And I came back.'

Merryn coughs and steadies her breath. They're all suffering from it, the thudding energy making them gasp. 'Good to hear you're so unfazed with seeing dead spirits,' she says.

I think about it. 'Well – if she was dead then she was in the right place, wasn't she? That's what's supposed to happen? So – yeah. It was all right.'

'All right, then. You need to learn to open and close the portal,' Lowenna says.

'Show me,' I wheeze.

She turns to the portal and waves her hands around again for a while, and the swirling colours vanish. We are back on the plain rock. No orange vortex. Immediately the pressure in my lungs disappears.

'Thank Goddess for that,' I mutter, breathing in the cold air from the sea and relishing the sudden calm.

'Your turn now,' she says.

She takes my hands and manipulates them, showing me the opening sequence. It's a bit like t'ai chi. Power rushes through my hands and the portal reappears, the colours getting brighter and brighter. Then suddenly it levels off, with a low noise like static.

'That's how you open it,' she says.

I look at my hands, hoping they remember what they just did. The pressure comes back in my lungs, but slightly less than last time.

'You'll get used to the shortness of breath, to some degree,' she adds. 'It gets better.'

She rubs my hands in hers, her many rings glinting. 'I fancy a nice cup of tea. What about you? Just show me now that you can close it and we'll go back home and make one. It's the same as I showed you, but backwards.'

I concentrate. Remembering the process is hard enough, but remembering it backwards is harder still. As I repeat the symbols, the circling starts to decrease. A few seconds later the whole huge orange vortex has vanished, and Tintagel Head is back to normal: rocky, mossy, the open sound of the sea.

Lowenna takes my arm. 'Well done,' she says quietly.

I smile. 'I think I'm ready for that tea now.'

Chapter Eleven

Dreaming should form a large part of your journal's observations. Observe your dreams daily; record them regularly. Notice recurring patterns and symbols; look for puns and metaphors. Sometimes meanings only become clear when you write them down.

From *A Guide to Reflective Greenworld Journaling* (schools edition)

Later that night, the Hands do Samhain for the village, which is like a souped-up version of what Mum does at home: fortune telling for all, village bonfire, cider. They put me on bonfire duty cos there's no way I'm ready to do the cards.

Saba waves me off. 'Have a good time! Don't get too close to the fire! Don't eat too many apples!' she calls after me as I trudge up the street. It's not much of a job really – just be present at the fire, wish everyone well from the Hands – that is, the ones that won't be going to Lowenna's house tonight to cross the witches' palms with silver. The gardeners make the fire and set it alight. When I get there and see it blazing I feel doubly useless.

I'm standing next to the crackling flames, trying to keep warm and cracking the sugar coating off my Samhain apple with my teeth, when Bryony appears at my elbow.

'Oh, hey, Bryony,' I say. Should I kiss her? I've got no idea – honestly, I haven't thought about her at all since leaving the orchard.

'Hey,' she says shyly.

'Happy Samhain.' I offer her a bite of my toffee apple.

'I've just had one, thanks.'

'Cool.'

There's an uncomfortable silence. I can't think of anything to say to her.

I fill the gap in the conversation. 'You not getting your cards read tonight then?'

'Oh, err . . . no. I don't really believe in it,' she says, smiling timidly.

I'm surprised. Most people do. 'Really? Why not?'

'Dunno. Just don't. Can't see how it would work, I guess.'

'Your choice.' I'm surprised that I, as someone who has never had any interest at all in Mum's witchy activities in the past, and someone who thought it was all basically a load of crap, now feel protective of this tradition of ours. Who would have thought? I smile to myself. The initiation has had an effect already.

There's another silence as we both stare at the bonfire.

'So . . . Danny, I, err . . . I was wondering whether you wanted to go out sometime, maybe? I . . .' She's looking at her feet and talking quietly, shyly, and it's painful. I'm just not interested in her – I would have been, back home – definitely, but I hear myself saying no. Something's changed.

'I think you're great, Bryony, but I've just become one of the Hands. Just started my training. I don't know – it just feels as though it would be wrong right now. I'm sorry.'

'Oh. Of course. I . . . I understand . . .' she says, immediately apologetic as if the very idea was completely ridiculous.

'I'm sorry about the other night. I was drunk, and I wasn't thinking.'

'Oh – well, I . . .'

'I don't mean I'd have to be drunk to kiss you. You're really pretty. I just . . .' I can't finish the sentence. The rest of it goes something like: I can't go out with you, Bryony, because I like someone else. A lot. And she's the only one I'm interested in. And it's complicated, cos she's got a boyfriend, and we're both witches and we're not supposed to be together that way. But I still don't want to be with anyone else. Sorry. I mean, bloody hell. This isn't me. But it's how I feel. Stupid and pointless and hopeless. I sigh and look at my boots.

'It's OK,' she says, and we both stare at the bonfire again. Now there really is nothing to say. I cringe with the uncomfortableness of it all.

'I'm going to get some cider. D'you want any?' she asks, blue eyes staring up into mine. Sweet girl. Why can't I be interested in her?

I shake my head. 'Better not. Supposed to be representing the Hands tonight. On duty, kind of. Stay sober.'

Goddess, what a tool you are, I think to myself, but it doesn't make any difference. She's defeated.

'Oh. OK, then. Well, I guess I'll see you around,' she says, and slides away into the crowd.

'See you,' I reply weakly.

I'm broken. Saba has stolen my ability to flirt.

That night I dream of Roach.

It takes me ages to fall asleep at all. I feel weird. Too awake, too tuned in. I feel like I can hear the wind buffeting every leaf on every tree in the garden, that I can feel the whispering thoughts of everyone in the house. Finally, I sleep, but go immediately into a vivid dream.

I am back on Tintagel Head, but the sea is bright turquoise and the grass a deep emerald rather than the grey, muddy colours of October in Cornwall. The colours are too strong, too loud, like they're shouting. Despite the brightness, there is no sun: when I look above me it's the night sky I see, with a full moon. The constellations I've been studying with Lowenna are marked out in the sky with lines, just like in the textbooks – Pegasus, Andromeda, Cassiopeia, but much brighter than usual.

I have the sense, in the dream, that there's someone else with me, and I feel a hand on my shoulder. For a second it reminds me of Dad, and I turn round, but it's Roach. I remember his hard stare; I see the cockroach tattoo at the base of his neck, the tail curling round his throat. I pull away from his hand and try to run but realize I am standing at the edge of the island, the waves crashing on the rocks far below. I turn round, reeling, and he's right in front of me. He takes a long knife out of his belt, and, holding my arm tightly so I can't pull it away, he cuts the flesh of my forearm. I can't see what he's cutting but I can feel him dragging the point of the knife through my skin in different motions. I pull away from the pain and stumble at the edge of the rock; stones crumble away and fall into the sea below. I clutch at my bloodied arm, which throbs under my fingers.

'The Sixth Hand,' he says, holding his knife under my chin.

'Why do you want me?' I cry out.

'We can do great things together,' he smiles, wiping my blood from his knife with his sleeve.

'But why me? Why not the others?'

161

'You're special,' he says, and holds a long red thread up for me to see. 'Be careful, Danny. They've got your measure now. They control you. Be careful you don't become too like me. They might not like it.'

He wraps the red wool, the wool Lowenna measured against me in my initiation, round his wrist and round mine. The blood from my arm drips on to it, soaking it an even darker red.

'Now we're both witches, we're really connected,' he says. 'Dream of me, Danny. Let me in.'

I wake up, gasping, my arm throbbing.

Some weeks later we have a group visualization exercise. That's when one of the witches tells a kind of story and we all have to imagine being wherever she says and doing whatever she says. They are weird exercises and I never know if I'm really doing them right, but they all seem happy enough with my progress. We do them, apparently, because they strengthen the imagination, and imagination is what makes magic. I don't mind the visualizations, but a lot of the other training's pretty dull. Learning the magical properties of plants. Basic physiology. Latin, even. It's worse than school.

I didn't tell anyone about my dream of Roach. I put it down to post-initiation paranoia and general weirdness: it was Samhain; I was initiated as a witch on Tintagel Island; I was given a knife. All of that just mixed up in my head. Probably.

Sometimes dreams are just dreams. You have

to keep one foot on the ground with this kind of shit.

The fire in the grate is crackling and the early December rain is pelting down on the glass roof in a persistent rhythm. I close my eyes and listen to it: hypnotic. Beryan's voice leads me into my imagination like a ball of silky string. 'You are in a hallway,' she begins, 'and this hallway has many doors. You walk along it slowly. You are in no hurry. You come to a door and open it. It opens, and you walk down some steps into a garden. It is a beautiful place.'

Beryan's voice has wrapped me in its spell – I feel as though I am right there. I see myself in a huge garden, like the kind I saw once in a book about rich people's houses in the Redworld: marble pillars, bushes cut into the shapes of animals. I see a crow, a lion about to pounce, a cow. The moon is huge, like a murky silver wheel hanging heavily in a black-blue sky. It is dead quiet, with the occasional sound of an owl.

'You walk through the garden and notice the life it holds,' continues her voice, 'and you see that there is a place to sit. You breathe in the night air and feel entirely at peace. Now, you see there is someone else in the garden, and they are coming towards you. The person sits down beside you. You are pleased to see them. They speak to you now and tell you something important. What is it?'

Beryan goes quiet for a while, I guess to allow the

experience to happen. In the garden of my mind I am sitting on a white marble bench, carved with a kind of curly design at the ends. I do feel very together sitting there, listening to the owl. It's nice. I could stay there a long time.

I turn my head to the left and see a figure coming towards me. I can see it's a guy from his build – tall and muscular, but he walks gracefully. As he gets closer I see his long reddish-blond hair and a long sword hanging on his belt; he's wearing sort of normal-ish Greenworld clothes – rough-spun cotton shirt, leathery trousers, but I see the triple-spiral design tattooed on his forehead. And the strange thing is that he seems to kind of glow, like he is lit up from inside. He sits down next to me and nods politely.

I nod back, thinking, Err, well, what next? What am I supposed to say to this person?

He laughs, quite gently really, and claps me on the shoulder. 'Well met, young Daniel: man of the witches!' he booms.

I nod again. I can't really think of anything else to do.

He smiles a huge smile and starts whistling under his breath (like Dad, it occurs to me). He doesn't seem in much of a hurry to say or do anything, so I start to relax. I look at him in some more detail. His sword has a pretty special-looking holder. Sheath, is it called? Holster? I don't know. But it's all tooled, like leather embroidery, in Celtic symbols. The skin on his hands is rough, but he looks like a young man. He's still whistling, a faint smile on his face. He turns to me. When he speaks, it's less speech than a kind of sonic boom in my head.

'The moon watches over us and gives us wisdom,' he says.

I nod. A weird conversation starter, but there's no way I'm going to argue with him.

'The sun gives us life, but the sun sets and the moon rises; always night into day, day into night,' he continues. 'I am the sun, child. I am the force of light, the force of war, the trunk of the tree, the iron in the fire.'

As he speaks, a weird thing starts to happen. I feel a kind of humming on the skin of my arm and look down at my forearm. As the man speaks, words are writing themselves on my skin. It doesn't hurt: it's just like a tickle, but the words lick over my skin like a brushy lightning. They are written in a kind of flowing script, and each line arranges itself so that it becomes part of a verse. He's still speaking and I look up, amazed.

He smiles down at me. 'Call on me, boy, when you have need of strength, of fire, of fight; I will be with you. I am the Smith, the Mage, the Warrior. I will be with you when you call; I will pulse in your blood and walk in your dreams.'

I watch, astounded, as words continue to write themselves on my arm.

He stands and lays his hand on my shoulder again

and I feel a rush of something like adrenalin pass through me and whizz out of my toes. 'We'll meet again, Daniel, when the time is right,' he says, and walks away.

Before I can do anything, Beryan's voice continues as if no time has passed and nothing out of the ordinary has happened. I'm almost too stunned to follow what she says but I concentrate and pull myself together – a good witch has a strong mind and an invincible memory is what they keep telling me, after all. 'You get up from where you have been sitting and walk slowly towards the steps,' she says softly but clearly. 'Bid goodbye to this garden; you will return to it soon. Ascend the steps in your own time and open the door at the top. You walk down the corridor until you find the right door. Now, open your eyes. You are back with us.'

I open my eyes and find myself back in the glass kitchen again with Lowenna and Beryan. They are both looking at me expectantly.

I look down at my arm. Slowly I unbutton the cuff of my shirt and roll the sleeve up to my elbow. The writing is there on my skin, unmistakable.

Chapter Twelve

Gather the holly, crown the king!
Seed of a new sun; let the bells ring!
Feast and be well; keep the hearth burning.
The cycle of eight; the new year a-turning.
Turn, turn, turn, turn.
The cycle of eight; the new year a-turning.

Song for Yule,
from *Greenworld Prayers and Songs*

When I come round from the meditation they're looking at me like lionesses round a carcass.

'Who did you meet in the garden?' fires off Beryan, aiming straight for the bullseye. She's about as subtle as an axe in the nuts.

I describe the figure to her as Lowenna hands me a glass of water and I slurp it down, hot under their combined stares.

'Lugh,' says Lowenna. 'The masculine force. The world is a place of polarity – creation and destruction, light and dark, mystery and clarity, masculine and feminine. There is a god for the Goddess. We invoked him at your initiation, remember? That's who you saw. He has taken you for his own.'

The writing is still on my arm. Unbelievable. It's written in a scrolling text that follows the contours of my arm. I hold it out for them to see. I touch it gently, then lick my finger and rub it hard over the surface of my skin. It doesn't blur or rub off.

'What does it say?' Beryan asks, leaning in.

I read it aloud:

'I am the spear, the slingshot, the smith,
The poet, the warrior, the magician, the gift;
The trunk of the tree, the arrow of war,
The movement of time, the lover at dawn.
I am the sun, the heat of the day;
The might of the land; the great bird of prey.'

'Is this normal? I mean, what the hell is this?' I turn my arm under the light.

Lowenna runs her fingertips over my forearm, and as she does so, my recent dream flashes through my mind. Roach cutting my arm after I was initiated. I didn't know what it was all about then, but I do now. Only there was no pain; no blood with the way it actually happened.

'Sometimes this happens; a magical mark that appears after a vision, or an initiation. Not to everyone, though. We call it a witch-brand,' she says, unbuttoning her blouse and showing me the dark blue outline of a circle flanked by two crescent moons on her brown, lined skin. 'I have the triple moon. It appeared on my chest during my initiation, all those years ago.'

I look away, embarrassed by looking down my mum's best friend's shirt. 'Do you all have something different? The people that have it?'

'I've only ever seen three types. Triskele, the triple-moon sign, and . . . this.' She peers at it again and looks meaningfully at Beryan. 'Danny, I don't want you to worry about . . . About who else has this,' she says.

'Just spit it out,' I say. 'I want to know.'

She pulls her lips in a line. 'I had a student, some years ago. A young man, like you. As gifted as you, but with a strong desire for power. It became clear over time that he wanted to misuse the power he already had and the skills he was learning here. He left before I finished his training, and now . . .'

I know who she's talking about.

'It's Roach, isn't it?' I ask, and she nods quickly, as if it pains her to admit it.

'Yes. It didn't happen as soon for him as it has for you, but it was on a similar guided-path working that he made contact with Lugh. We were delighted, of course. We'd never seen the text before. Only Zia and myself had witch-brands then — the triskele and the triple moon.' She sighs. 'But soon after, he left us.'

'But what does it mean? That I have this . . . poem,

and so does Roach?' I ask, looking down at my arm. Inked in a vision. Amazing.

'I don't know,' says Beryan. 'We've never known why some people have them. Most of us don't. Zia, Lowenna, Roach; Demelza; now you. You're the only ones. For some reason, the Gods have chosen you for something.' She looks a little downcast. It must be pretty annoying for some upstart like me, and a villain like Roach, to have something she clearly wants. Maybe that she deserves. I mean, Beryan, Saba, Merryn – they're great witches. Powerful. So why no brand?

Melz pushes the door to the kitchen open, as if on cue, shaking the rain from her hair. Saba follows her. They've been out getting some food from the barter shops, but they pick up on the mood in the room immediately.

'What's up?' asks Melz.

I hold out my arm, sleeve rolled up to my elbow.

'Whoa,' says Saba. 'Sorry, I mean – that's some witch-brand. What does it say? I've never seen actual writing before. That's weird.'

I read out the text written on my arm.

'Roach has it too. The same brand. Word for word, I think,' Lowenna adds.

Melz looks at me with what I like to think is a new respect and whistles through her teeth. 'This must be why Roach wants you. Why he followed you here. He knows, somehow, that you have something in common with him. Do you think he knew you'd get the same witch-brand?'

I shrug. 'Maybe. He didn't mention it, but he didn't get the chance, I guess.'

My apparent coolness masks a sudden panic. Roach did know. He knew because he cut this same witch-brand into my arm in my dream. I know it, even though in the dream I didn't know what he was doing, just that he was cutting me. Did he brand me? No. That's crazy. It was Lugh, I know that. It was a good thing, a special experience.

But Roach knew. Lowenna might have known I was going to be the fabled Sixth Hand, the light-bringing saviour or whatever, but Roach knew I'd be branded the same as him.

He knew before anyone. And that worries me.

Lowenna gets up and starts pacing the room. 'This puts things in a different light. Until now I thought Roach had just sensed the same kind of power in you that I had. I thought he wanted you for general troublemaking; you being a boy, a male witch, like him – to make himself seem more powerful in the gangs, to set you against us – that would appeal to his warped sense of humour. I thought he might try to tempt you away from us, as revenge for us disowning him. In his eyes anyway. But now—'

Melz breaks into her mum's train of thought. 'If he knows you have the same witch-brand as him, and if he knew you were going to have it before it appeared, then it's more than troublemaking. He feels a kinship with you. Perhaps he thinks it's a sign.'

'Of what?' I ask, but she shakes her head.

'Don't know. We've never known why the people that get the witch-brand get it at all, or why they get the one they do – only that when you do get it, you become dedicated to that one particular god or goddess. I mean, you getting the same as Roach – Lugh's brand – is only the second time it's ever happened that two people have the same one. I have the same as your mum, the triskele. We're both priestesses of the Morrigan.'

I didn't know that – Melz and Mum having anything in common. But in a way I see it – both kind of harsh, mysterious, strong.

'What about your triple moon, Lowenna? Hasn't anyone else got that?'

'No,' Lowenna says. 'No, just me.'

There's a silence. Lowenna continues to pace the wood floor. 'The covensteads are due to convene here for Yule. It's not far off. We'll have to discuss it with them. Find an answer. He's obviously not giving up on you,' she says.

'Until then, you need to stay protected, Danny,' Merryn says. 'I'll teach you some advanced psychic self-defence.'

I make a face, but Beryan puts her hand on mine. 'You need this. Believe me. If he's got the same witch-brand as you, that means you've got a connection of some kind. We don't know what that might mean. It might mean a psychic connection. You've had at least one vision of him already, and he seemed to know that you'd go out to the boundary when and where you did, so that he could talk to you.'

Saba sits down next to me and looks into my eyes seriously. 'Beryan's right, Danny. A psychic connection is dangerous, especially with someone like Roach. You can't risk that. You can't let him in your dreams. You can't let him in anywhere. He's got power, Danny, and until we know what he wants with you, you have to learn to keep him out. Even when we do find out what he wants, you'll need to. You can't let him get inside your head.'

You can't let him in your dreams. Does she know, somehow? It's too late to tell them now. They'd want to know why I didn't say something before. Does Saba know about him tying us together with the red wool of my measure, the witch's symbolic tradition of keeping witches loyal? Without meaning to, I'm keeping his secret. He's made a bond between us whether I like it or not, and I don't like it.

'Don't worry, I'll help you.' Saba's eyes are earnest.

Melz, my fellow branded witch, says nothing. No kinship between the chosen, then.

'OK,' I say, and avoid all their eyes.

When the solstice comes – Yule, 21 December, the darkest time of the year – I don't know what to expect. I've been hoping that I'll see Mum again at the covenstead meeting.

We meet after dinner in the kitchen; it's lit up with loads of candles that throw a creamy glow on the faces of the people sitting there. There are a lot of them. Gowdie's been banished to my room while the meeting's happening, but Lowenna's three cats line the backs of the easy chairs.

I see the other Hands first, and I'm looking for Mum, but I don't see her cos someone else is there that I recognize, among the middle-aged women and the young girls. He's standing up, massive arms crossed over his chest with a grin as big as a pirate ship. Until I see him I don't realize how much I've missed him: Omar, with the tattoos that navigate his deep brown skin like a faded treasure map. I forget all about being cool and sophisticated and run over to him. He hugs me hard, lifting me off the ground.

'Good to see you, Danny boy!' he drawls. We slap each other on the back. He puts me down and looks me over. 'You look good, man!' he exclaims. 'These witches been taking care of you all right?'

'Yeah, OK, OK.' I wouldn't say it but it's good to see a familiar face.

'Playing it cool as ever I see,' he booms.

'Where've you been?' I ask.

'Danny, my man, we can crack a beer later and catch up on where our lives have taken us, but for now I think there's someone you want to see even more than me,' he says seriously, and nods to a person on the other side of the room. She's been standing in the shadows and now she steps forward. The candlelight glows on her cheeks and in the dark circles under her eyes. She looks tired, I think, and she walks over and gives me a huge hug.

'Mum, I've missed you,' I whisper into her neck.

'Me too, Danny; me too,' she says. 'Your sister's here as well. She's really missed you.'

'Biba? She's with you?' My heart jumps, and I realize how much I've missed my little supergreen sis. I can tell Mum's smiling, even though my head's still on her shoulder.

'Well, I couldn't very well leave her behind, could I? She'd be running the village by the time I got back.'

'Where is she?'

'At Beryan's house, keeping their cats company. We'll see her after the meeting.'

I smile, and hug Mum more fiercely than a teenage boy should in front of anyone. She smells like home – of sweat and rosemary and vegetable soap, and I breathe her in gratefully.

Lowenna claps her hands together and the rabble that is thirty-odd witches in the same room – at least two from every covenstead – shuts up and looks at her expectantly. She's left off her traditional band T-shirt tonight and is wearing some kind of busy-print kaftan-type garment; she looks like a ship moored on a bed of coral. Thing is, she might not have any fashion sense, her eyes might stick out slightly too much and she might have mad hair that she obviously cuts herself, but she is one formidable chick. I've seen her be scarily strong, picking up her huge compost bin and carrying it across the garden; I've seen her become the Morrigan and make gang members crap their pants with fear; I've seen her cook a breakfast for six and lecture us on psychic ethics without breaking a sweat. And I've been at the mercy of her patience for weeks of trying to remember chants, herb names and properties, and the histories of various deities. I realized a long time ago why Lowenna is in charge of this whole shebang.

'Welcome, one and all, welcome to my home and to this communion and sharing with your fellow witches and with the spirits of our witch ancestors. We've come together to celebrate the winter solstice, discuss ways forward with the gangs and to share news of an important event. However, let's start with our customary toast.'

Lowenna raises a glass of her herb wine. I've had a few glasses before: it's pretty strong stuff.

'Merry be our meeting and wise be our ways; inspired be our nights and bright be our days,' they all chant, and toast each other solemnly.

There's a few pinched lips and puckered cheeks after drinking the wine. I take a sip of mine: pure rocket fuel. Try not to cough, I remind myself. I catch Omar's eye – he's suppressing a laugh. I focus back on the group.

The floor goes to a plump woman in her fifties with a blonde-grey buzzcut wearing overalls and boots caked with mud. She looks like she could take Omar on in a brawl and come out on top, but when she speaks it's giggly and breathy like she's telling secrets in the girls' changing room.

'Hi – for anyone who doesn't know me, I'm Tressa; I'm Lowenna's sister. My covenstead's Boscastle and thereabouts; I'm keeper of the Archive—'

'I wonder whether you could just explain to our new members, Tressa, what the Archive is? I think it would be useful to bring everyone up to speed?' queries Lowenna, butting in.

Tressa looks a bit annoyed. 'Of course, dear.' She drawls a long Cornwall 'rrrr' in 'course'. 'Well, as I was about to say, at Boscastle we have the Archive – that's the largest collection of witches' tools and paraphernalia in the country. There was the museum for a long time, but now there's not the coming and going of tourists that there was, so we protect the artefacts. Cornwall was always a witchy place and we can be grateful to have had so many wise folk in the area before us; what we have is some of their possessions, hundreds of years old, found in their houses when they died or passed down to their families. For example, we have Granny Greenhorne's spell book, her coral claw for spellcasting, her recipes, her scrying mirror. We have the skulls of the whole family of the Trevarren witches. Among other things, we have the only record of all the known portals in the world. That's one of our main jobs at Boscastle – to keep the *Book of Portals* correct.'

I hold my hand up. 'So there's, like, a directory of where all the portals are?'

'Yes, dear,' she trills. 'It's important that we try to keep a handle on what's going on with the portals around the world.' But then her expression changes and I see the resemblance to Lowenna in the way that she can be jolly and mumsy one minute and suddenly formidable the next. 'So, I have a concern about one of the portals. Zia – what's been happening at the Scorhill circle portal? You don't seem to have been available much to confer on the energy,' she says, and all eyes in the room swivel sharply to Mum.

I notice Omar lay a protective hand on Mum's arm. She looks composed, but anyone who knows her can tell she's been caught out a bit cos she blinks a few too many times.

'Ummm, well . . . It's been fine really, no real problems,' she says, and Tressa's eyes narrow.

You have to do better than that, Mum, I think, they're not going to buy it.

It's a revelation to see Mum in this position, though. I've never seen her have to report to anyone, not having been to one of these meetings before. I've never seen her sweat it before, been asked to account for herself. She's a strong woman, an in-control mum – get your feet off the seats, Danny; go and get firewood, Danny.

Don't get me wrong, it's all good, not least cos growing up with her has definitely helped me be around so many opinionated and powerful women, in this gnarly, strangely developed mandrake root that is my new teen-witch life. But I start to will her to do better. I imagine her standing tall, shoulders back. I imagine her calmly and powerfully telling them all what's what in no uncertain terms, them all watching her, taking in her every word.

The off-the-wall thing about this is that as I start to imagine it, it starts to happen. That is, I start to lose the ability to decide which is reality and which is my vision. The more I imagine Mum as a fiery powerhouse capturing the attention of the whole room, the straighter her back becomes, the brighter the glint in her eye and the stronger her words. Instead of umming and mumbling, her voice is steady.

'You ask what is happening in my covenstead, the place I protect with an open hand and an open heart. Desire and dissolution is rife. I will be honest. There is division in my community. I cannot see the outcome: something is blocking the energy flow. I would appreciate the group's help, the magic of their combined hands.' She bows her head regally before the group.

I step towards her, taking her outstretched hand and feel the power pulsing within it. I knew something wasn't right at home.

The group join hands until we are all standing in a big circle, and quite naturally the circle starts to sway, and sing. I follow the words as if in a dream.

All of a sudden I'm somewhere else. I squint and realize I'm standing in the lane behind my house, my real house in Gidleigh, in the lane that leads into the woods. I can see two figures leaning over a bonfire, and their voices are a warm hum as they chant. With a start I see in the flickering light coming from the fire that it's Linda and Sadie. What are they doing? I can't make out what they're saying, but it's unsettling. However, not as unsettling as the smoke above the fire, which is shifting unnaturally. I watch it for a few seconds and realize that the smoke is making the shape of a face. A face I recognize. Roach. It hangs there in the smoke, then opens its eyes and looks past Linda and right at me. I jump, and lose focus. I open my eyes and realize I am gripping Mum's hand.

I know I'm safe in the circle but I'm still shaken. It was scary as hell to see Roach like that, and sense that he saw me looking, weird as that is. I have to say I'm pretty happy to be back in the safety of the kitchen with the hearth and the comforting plants.

The rest of the group open their eyes and come back to earth. We sit cross-legged and exchange visions. Many of the group seem to have also sensed that there is some issue with Roach, but they can't tell what it is. I share my vision of Roach's face in the smoke. There are some raised eyebrows.

Beryan shakes her head. 'I told you. Psychic connection,' she says, looking at Lowenna.

'I think this would be a good time for you to show the group what happened in our visualization yesterday, Danny.' Lowenna nods at my sleeve.

I turn the shirt cuff backwards and roll it up, holding it for them to see.

Mum grabs my arm and scans the lines, then stares at me. 'Where did you get this?' she demands, like I stole it or something.

'Where'd you think, Mum? It's a witch-brand,' I say a little bit proudly.

'Would you read it for us, Zia?' Tressa pipes.

Mum takes a deep breath and reads the words on my arm out loud. The witches start looking at each other as she reads and an excited chatter reverberates around the room.

Beryan turns to the group. 'Danny received Lugh's blessing in a guided visualization yesterday. And, you may not know this, but Roach has the same brand. Text. Writing. Poetry, even. I know that none of us have that. What do we think it means? I mean, it feels logical to say that there must be some kind of psychic connection between Danny and Roach, if they both have the same brand – but what's the link, and is it why Roach followed Danny to the village?'

Tressa looks quizzically at me. 'And you've had this vision today about Roach. His face floating in the smoke.

Do you think Roach is blocking the Gidleigh portal? Why would he do that? And what's his connection to Linda?'

'Does he want control of the village?' Melz asks. She's picking her nails, appearing typically disinterested, but I know she is, even if she is too cool for school.

Mum sighs and shakes her head. 'I can't imagine why he would – why he'd want control of any of the villages. He chose to join the gangs precisely because he didn't want to be involved in a community with rules and cooperation. He wanted his freedom; that's why he left Tintagel. But I can answer the question of the link to Linda, I think. You see, they were an item once. They must have stayed in touch. And I've always wondered about the girl, Sadie. She looks like him. She's got his smile. I've thought about Roach every time I've seen that child smile for the past sixteen years. I don't know what they're up to, but I can believe that they're working together in some way – to cause trouble for me in the village.'

Lowenna shakes her head. 'I always wondered what happened between them. So, we can assume that they're trying to block the energy from the Gidleigh portal in some way. Probably Roach is instructing Linda how to do it. I doubt she has that kind of expertise. Zia, you're going to have to put a stop to it. They don't know what they're doing. It's dangerous.'

Mum sighs. 'You're right, I know. But there's already so much discord in the village, I—'

'There's discord because you're letting it happen, Zia. There's discord because your energy portal is being polluted by whatever Roach and Linda are doing. There's discord because you need to be stronger. Restore your defences. Repaint your mural. Lay down the law, Zia. Otherwise this problem is only going to get worse. For all of us.'

Mum smiles neutrally. 'I'll do my best,' she says quietly.

'No, Zia. You need to do what's necessary. We have to always do our best, otherwise we lose what we've fought for. You have to be in control. Always.'

Mum nods, looking away from Lowenna, biting her cheek. Lowenna looks like she wants to say more, but she just nods and lets it go. They're friends, and it can't be easy for either of them to have a barney in front of the other witches.

Mum smiles at me brightly – perhaps a little too brightly. 'So my son can see things I can't now. Things have really changed!' There's a few chuckles that go around the room, but it's a diversion. She doesn't want to be told off any more.

'So where do we go from here?' Tressa asks.

'What's been happening with the Redworld recently, Omar? Anything that might have relevance to this?' Lowenna asks.

There are a few surprised faces. I don't think everyone's aware that Omar still goes to the Redworld now and then. It's supposed to be forbidden, but he's our go-between. Obtains items that can't be found here. Sometimes information.

He blows out his cheeks, mulling. 'Well, now, I don't know. Things are pretty much the same most places. The war's not going very well – fuel's running out fast and they can't find any more over in Russia, so there's still the rich few that are paying through the roof for what they can get. The vast majority are living like us, without power, except they don't have any food-growing organized, any community – they're living off crime and what that can get them. People are getting pretty desperate.'

Tressa grimaces. 'What a state to live in.' She tsks. There's a touch of smugness in her voice, though. Like she wasn't stupid enough to stay there, but those people were.

'It is. And don't think it's not going to affect you either,' he warns. 'That many people, if they can't feed their kids but they've heard about you and your fields and livestock – you've got to expect them to start coming through the border soon. You're going to have a refugee problem on your hands in the next year, I reckon, unless the war doesn't find more fuel.'

Tressa looks horrified. We all do. Things are tight enough without a wave of new mouths to feed. I mean, we're used to the odd new person joining villages, very occasionally, having come through the border from the Redworld. But more than that?

'But they can't!' she exclaims.

Omar smiles at her. 'Why can't they, Tress? What's going to stop them? If they get through the border and past the gangs they're heading straight for you.'

She looks aghast. 'Well – magic! They won't be able to get past the village borders. We don't have to let them in!'

He shrugs. 'Guess you don't. But what are you going to do, sit in the village square and listen to their children crying when they haven't eaten for days? Let them starve? Let them die of exposure, cos they don't know anything about living off the land, finding shelter?'

'Well, they should think about that before they get here,' she spits back. 'We've worked too damn hard for what we've got to have some freeloaders come along and take it all.'

'I'm sure your mother goddess would be very happy to hear that,' he says drily. 'Look – it doesn't bother me what you do. All I'm saying is, it's going to happen unless something changes pretty soon.'

She looks like she's going to argue a point, but snaps her mouth shut and turns away instead.

Mum looks up from tracing the lines on her hands with a long fingernail. 'He's right. We have to remember how closeted we are, down here. We forget there's a whole other world out there, and there's more who are suffering than living in luxury. And anyway, I don't know that magic circles would keep those people out. They're set up to propel away danger, threat and malice. They're not there to keep out hungry children and desperate mothers. Or, even if they would, I don't know whether they should.'

There's a silence. Who can argue with that? We worship a mother goddess; we live in tune with the earth. How can we refuse to help families that need food and shelter?

Lowenna sighs. 'I think that's something we have to think hard about. Thank you, Omar, for letting us know. For the moment, though, Roach is our most immediate threat. Have you heard anything about what he might want?'

Omar shakes his bear-like head. 'Nah. Roach is less known in the Redworld than you might think. They've got their own criminal kings there – although some of those guys are getting interested in the Greenworld. They hear a lot of rumours about us, same as we do about them, and most of it's about as true. But it's possible he might have been to talk to them. I don't know; he knows how to get through the border. Tell you one thing, though. They're interested in witches, the Redworld criminals. There'd probably be jobs for all of you if you wanted to defect.' He looks around the room. 'Any of you. Especially the pretty ones. Lot of money to be had in the Redworld if you've got skills to trade.'

I suppress a grin. That's Omar all over – he likes to mess with the witches.

Tressa smiles thinly. She doesn't have a sense of humour about the Greenworld, you can tell.

'I think we're quite happy here, Omar, but thanks for your concern,' she says icily. She turns to her sister. 'Wenna. Wenna! Are you still with us?'

Lowenna looks introspective. She starts, and looks apologetic. 'Sorry. Miles away. Thanks, Omar. Will you keep me up to date with any developments?'

'Sure.'

He's our link to anything beyond the border, and Lowenna, at least, knows she should keep him on side. She turns to Saba. 'Saba, dear – you're leading the Procession of the Maidens tomorrow, I believe?'

'Yes, I am.' Saba blinks, like she's not sure what's coming next.

'I'm wondering whether you might take Danny with you, dear? To experience the event, and perhaps be inspired with some helpful wisdom?' She's almost wheedling.

For once Saba doesn't just say 'Yes, of course' and get on with it. She's got a problem with it, I can tell.

'Well, it is supposed to be a women-only event, you know; it is of quite a sensitive nature, and—'

Lowenna interrupts her. 'I understand your feelings, love, but I think, given that Danny is rather prone to visions, that he might be inspired with something useful tomorrow.'

Saba knows better than to argue, especially in front of everyone. And so she bows to it. 'Of course,' she says. 'Of course he can come along.'

When the meeting breaks up a hubbub of witches

forms quickly around Omar, all firing off questions about the Redworld. Is it true that anyone can have a car? Are there really so many different types of chocolate? What does their music sound like? Do people really have metal legs and arms? Are there really drugs that can make you fly? It's all the younger witches asking the questions – all the kids that grew up with those tantalizing rumours about the dangerous, illicit Redworld, but have never seen it. Tressa's incensed, you can tell by looking at her. She doesn't say anything, just stands in the corner, fuming. Omar catches my eye and grins.

I stifle a laugh, and Mum gives him a look. 'Such a wind-up merchant,' she mutters, smiling, and puts her arm through mine. 'Come on, young man. Let's leave him to it. Your sister's waiting to see you.'

Chapter Thirteen

Community, family, covenstead. All one and none
separate.

From *Tenets and Sayings of the Greenworld*

We head over to Beryan's house and as soon as I walk
in, Beebs runs at me and gives me a massive hug, almost
knocking me over.

'Hold on. Goddess, go careful,' I chide her, trying
to steady my balance, but I hug her back just as hard and
muss her hair like I always do — and then, after we've
said I missed you in our own way, we go straight back
to being Danny and Biba: that is to say, tormentor and
tormented. I grab a handful of her hair after making it
all messy, something she hates. She's not a particularly
appearance-obsessed girl, but she does like to be neat.

'Needs a cut, this, Beebs. Hang on, I think there are
kitchen scissors here somewhere . . .' I start crashing

around the kitchen, dragging her with me, by the hair. Not too hard, mind.

She's squealing like she always does. 'Let GO! Let go, Danny! Mum, tell him!'

Mum grins. 'Let go of your sister's hair, Danny,' she says obligingly.

Beebs knows I'll always do what Mum says, at least if she's in earshot. I sigh theatrically and sit down at the table; Biba follows, slightly warily, as if I might pounce on her at any moment. When we're sitting close to each other like this I like to make sudden, twitchy movements now and then, just to make her think I'm about to attack. Keeps her on her toes.

'So what's been going on in Gidleigh with the supergreens, Beebs?' I ask.

She starts rambling on about all the usual stuff — committee meetings, preserving resources, blah blah blah, and then suddenly Sadie's name crops up.

I catch Mum's eye and give her a quizzical look. 'What?' I ask. 'Sorry, what was that about Sadie?'

'I was just saying that she's got quite interested in the Young Greenworlders since you left. She's come to a few meetings. She's helping us formulate our next step.'

'And what might that be?' I'm suspicious, especially after my vision earlier about her being in contact with Roach. It can't be good.

Biba assumes her officious, you-wouldn't-possibly-understand expression. 'I can't tell you. It's secret.'

I look at Mum, who raises her eyebrows at me as if to say 'Tell me about it, I've tried'.

'I don't know if that's such a great idea, Beebs. You don't know what she's like, what she's involved in. Her dad's a gang leader. He wants to kill me, according to my vision,' I explain, expecting a bit of concern, but she looks at me scornfully.

'Don't tell me what to do. I'm not the one who got Mum's cards burned and then ran away. Don't try to pretend you're all grown up and responsible all of a sudden, just because you've decided you want to be a witch—' out of the corner of my eye I see Mum trying to suppress a laugh, and frown at her – 'and anyway, Sadie told me she hates her dad. Her and Linda do. The only reason they've stayed in Gidleigh all this time is because they can't think of anywhere safer to go.'

'Well, that's interesting,' Mum chips in. 'What else did she say about Roach?'

Beebs sticks her tongue in her cheek, thinking. 'Not much. Just that hopefully they'd be free of him soon.'

Mum looks at me. 'Funny, then, what you saw about them. Why would they be helping him disrupt the portal if they hate him so much?'

It doesn't make sense. I trace the carvings on the table with my finger. 'Dunno. That's weird. But seriously, Beebs, I don't think you should be hanging out with her. Sadie's trouble.'

'Shut up, Danny. I—' she starts, but Mum gets her

laying-down-the-law face on and she shuts up pretty quick.

'No, Biba. Danny's right. I don't want you spending any more time with Sadie. She's up to something and I don't trust her. There are other things happening that she's a part of too, I think, that you don't understand.'

Beebs just gets that square-jawed look and doesn't say anything.

'Why does Linda hate you so much, though, Mum? I've never understood it,' I say.

Mum looks sad. 'We were good friends once. We had a bit of a falling out about witchcraft when I took over at Gidleigh, but then she came to live there too and I could never really work out why. It's always been weird – you remember that day at the full-moon ritual, when we had that argument. That's nothing new – she'll come to rituals and then complain about them. But it makes sense now. I'm thinking maybe if she thought that we – me and Lowenna and the rest – if we were responsible for how Roach turned out, developing his power, and if he used it against her, against her and Sadie, I can see why she'd be angry with me. But I've never known that I was protecting her and Sadie against him so specifically. That's the only reason I can think of – why they've stayed.' She shakes her head. 'Life is full of little ironies,' she mutters.

She takes Biba's hand and squeezes her fingers affectionately. 'Please, Biba. Don't get involved with

Sadie. It's all too complicated. Let me deal with it when we get back, OK?' she says.

Biba huffs. 'Goddess, all right, if it's that important. The Young Greenworlders aren't going to be happy about it, though.'

Mum smiles tiredly. 'If anyone can make it OK with them, darling, I've no doubt that you can,' she says, sighing.

The next morning we set off very early for the Procession of the Maidens ritual that I'm so very not bothered to be a part of, and definitely wouldn't be here at all if it wasn't for Lowenna making me. There's still a massive moon in the greyish sky, pendulous and heavy, like an omen.

I trudge along, two skats behind – that's Cornish for bringing up the rear. The phrase reminds me again how much I've missed Mum, and how nice it is to see her. She loves the old Cornish dialect, uses loads of weird old words like 'teazy' for irritable or 'heller'. Like you'd say, 'That kid is a real little heller', meaning bad or naughty. She used to say it about me, but not Beebs. I don't think Beebs gave her as many sleepless nights. But even Mum isn't as old Cornwall in the way she talks as some people. Some of the people in our village, you have to get an ear for the way they talk; the words all run together in rrrs and eees, like 'Oweenawthaa?' means 'How do you know that?' or 'Perdee, inna?' means 'Pretty, isn't it?' Mum's got that old Cornish blood, and so I have too I guess. 'Magic in this blood,' she'll say sometimes, touching my hair.

We've gone somewhere we never usually go, to the beach. It's not far from the village but cos of the gangs the people don't go there much. Today there's a special deputation with me included. Saba's leading the way and there's a line of nine girls following her – not witches, but girls from the village, all between about fifteen and twenty I'd say. No one older. It's freezing; the girls are wrapped up in wool cloaks and heavy shoes and are trudging along behind Saba like cream being pulled through a cauldron of soup by a spoon. She strides along through the grassy, brackish land, head up, not seeming to feel the cold. Ignoring me, or doing her best to.

As I understand it I'm here in an observation capacity only; this is women's work. Saba's stiff back shouts 'You shouldn't be here' as she marches along in the cold December morning. It's the first time that gender has come into it, and I'm surprised. I thought they were all cool about men's work and women's work; that is, in this spiritually advanced Greenworld hippy community we live in, no such thing exists. Everyone does everything. But apparently there are still divisions of responsibility, and Saba feels like I'm muscling in on her territory. I don't want to piss her off; I haven't actually done anything apart from what I've been told to, and I tried to talk to her when the meeting broke up last night, but I got caught up with Mum, and then when we got back to Lowenna's house, Saba was gone.

Merryn told me last night that the Procession of the Maidens is an annual appeal for protection from Brighid – kind of renewing her protection of the village, and when I asked what kind of protection, she said, 'You'll see.'

As we left the village the Hands set a protective energy bubble around us; it will deflect the eyes of anyone seeing us when we're out, like a cloak of mirrors.

We're nearing the sandy beach and Saba whips her head back, tawny hair twisting in the salty early-morning wind as we make our way down steep steps cut into the cliff. Her gaze catches mine. She half smiles and my tender heart leaps.

We gather on the cold beach with the salt stinging our eyes. The girls cluster around, chatting and laughing nervously and not really knowing how to be with each other – they know what they're here to do, but they've never done anything like this before. New girls are chosen each time. We've brought along a couple of the older women of the village too, and they start building up a campfire and setting out their preparations for some food and drink – I guess for after the ritual.

Merryn explained that the village leaves most of its witchery to the Hands, but a couple of times a year the townspeople are required to take part. This is one of those times, apparently. At Yule, the winter equinox, nine maidens (by this I think they mean virgins) go to the beach and wade into the ocean waist deep and ask for Brighid's blessing for the coming year. It's not something I've come across before, but I'm learning that Tintagel has its own way of doing things. The sea, the waves that crash against the cliffs all day and all night in the winter – it's a big part of their lives. It's the sound against which they live their lives. They're a water people, and for them, Yule doesn't just mean stuffing yourself full of roast potatoes and cake; it also means a kind of sacrifice, a sacrifice to ensure another year's protection for the village.

'What kind of sacrifice?' I'd asked.

'Blood,' Merryn had replied.

So these nine maidens offer something of themselves to the ocean. What do they offer? How can I put this? The Hands choose the nine girls who say they're likely to be on the rag at the time of the ritual. It's not anything I want to see or be involved with, but here I am – knight and protector of nine wringing-wet bleeding virgins. And Saba. Whose sexual status is as yet unknown to me.

Saba is leading this ritual. She doesn't need me to do anything, just observe, she says to me as she passes me on the beach. I ask whether I should do anything, and she shakes her head and says just to keep out of the way. She calls to the group to form a line facing the sea. Only Saba knows how cold that water's going to be cos apparently she's done this ceremony for the last two years.

Saba waits for the nervous chatter to hush down and then starts singing, a low flat-toned song that I can't quite pick up, and slowly walks towards the water. When she gets a few steps away she throws off her wool cloak and kicks off her shoes. Underneath she's wearing a floaty white gowny dress and I see the glint of a silver necklace round her neck. I know that there's a crescent moon on it as a pendant, made of silver and a glistening type of white shell; she always wears it.

The maidens pick up the song – they must have rehearsed it before – and follow Saba into the water, casting off their heavy robes and wading slowly into the water in matching white dresses. I have to say that none of them stops with what must be the incredible coldness of the water; a few flinch, but they press on. Nobody shouts 'Bloody hell, that's cold!' Not so much as a 'brrrr'. They spread out so they're in a line, just about waist deep in the incoming tide, singing this weird song. It's among the stranger things I've ever seen.

They stand and sing, and sing some more, and raise their arms up towards the horizon and nothing happens. And then more nothing. Then just when I'm giving up, there's a kind of ripple over the water and the waves still themselves – the tide stops coming in. All of a sudden I notice that the sea has become like a lake: flat, still. Completely flat and completely still, dead quiet and black.

At this sign, the hush of the water, Saba motions

to the maidens and they continue singing, but they've changed it. Now it's 'Brighid, Mother Goddess, give us your blessing', over and over again. And then it's like I've been taken into a vision, but it's not a vision or a pathworking or a visualization or any of that happy crap that I've been doing with the Hands for the past two months now, but this is really happening and I can't believe my eyes cos a huge goddess figure – Brighid, in all her glory – is walking over the ocean towards us.

Now, when I say huge, I do mean monstrous. Like, her hands look like they're the size of the cliffs. She totally fills the sky and horizon and we're all just gazing up at her like lovesick prawns. I find myself digging my toes into the sand for security; she looks like she could crush us with an eyelash. It's hard to say really what she looks like; I just get this sense of vastness and power. Her robes are the water: grey and blue and green, flexing and flowing like a massive waterfall. All the girls are looking up at her, mouths open.

As I stare up at her I start to feel dizzy, and at first I think it's just because my head's at an angle and it's the effect of her sea-as-robes, of the swirling on my eyes, but then I feel like a hand touches me on the forehead. A sudden electrifying power surges through the centre of my head, down through my heart, my stomach, legs and out through my feet. There's a buzzing in my ears, like bees, and a voice – inside, outside my head, I can't tell – says 'Be blessed with vision, young witch'. I close my eyes and let the vision come.

First, I see a shadow moving over the full moon until it is totally hidden. An eclipse, when the earth, sun and moon are in a line. Not like a solar eclipse you aren't allowed to look directly at, a darker, more spectral event. Lunar eclipses are the kind of thing people get nervous about in Gidleigh, despite Mum telling then not to worry. When you live by the power of the moon – the monthly community ritual, sowing your seeds and harvesting your crops by moon phase – it's a big deal when it disappears so dramatically.

I look down from the eclipsed moon to my feet and I see I'm not standing on normal ground but inside the portal, on the pulsing colours and the strange dream-like cloudiness. But I can't walk; my ankles are bound together. I'm confused and there's a panicky tightness in my throat; I'm thinking, What the hell? What the hell's happening now? But when I look up Roach has appeared from nowhere, right next to me, and he's holding a knife to my throat. 'I can cut you here,' he breathes in my ear. His breath is hot and I try to pull away from him but I can't. Then he whispers, 'This is the way.' He throws me over his shoulder and carries me down the tunnel. I scream and try to kick but he is too strong.

Next, the moon becomes full again and I am back outside, but I'm a crow flying above a crowd, and I realize it's a battle. Blood spatters my wings and I plunge down into the chaos.

I see the faces of Tintagel villagers contorted with

pain as I fly over; I try to reach out to them, to help, but I am constricted inside my bird body. Screams ratchet through the air like knives. I watch as a woman about Mum's age stabs ineffectually at a middle-aged man with her small knife, but he rips it out of her hands, grips her hair and smashes her face down on his knee. I hear her nose break as loud as a gun retort. I watch as a grizzly grey-bearded man in camouflage gear clumsily fires a pistol into the crowd; the bullet tears a hole in a boy's neck, a kid maybe even younger than me. He falls down, clutching at his throat, eyes darting madly from side to side, and the blood pumps crazily out of his artery, pooling under him like a second shadow. My crow's sense of smell picks up the blood: ripe, coppery, hot.

And then I see Roach standing on top of Tintagel Head, laughing over at us. Because this is like a dream I can see his face even from so far away. He stands semi-silhouetted against the orange portal, which is open and swirling behind him; he turns and walks into it. Yet, instead of disappearing slowly and merging with its energy, he gets brighter, darker. His outline gets more definite; he seems to grow taller, as if being stretched.

And then, he bursts into flames.

I snort awake from my semi-trance, shaking, and Brighid is still there. I stare up at her vastness blankly, the image of Roach's flaming body still glowing in front of my eyes. What the hell was that? I slump down on the sand heavily, as if soaked in seawater.

Brighid, Mother Goddess of the Greenworld, draws a five-pointed star and the triskele in the air over us, and instinctively I know she is drawing them in protection over all the villages. There is a sound – and if sounds were colours, this sound would be cerise, a kind of intense pink – a choir singing an unnameable harmonic for one long second, and then she's gone.

Everyone stays dead still for a few minutes; there's a real quiet over the whole beach; the waves remain flat, as if the weight of peace is upon them. I don't know what everybody else saw, but if it was anything like my vision, they'll need to pick their guts off the floor.

The girls wade slowly and thoughtfully out of the water, not seeming to mind that they're wet through and freezing. They all come out with the same expression: thoughtful and elated, each with a glow. Maybe no burning men for them. No war. No blood. They wrap themselves in blankets as they come out and help themselves to tea that's been brewing on the campfire, though the mumsy types make them take tea towels to wrap around the hot mugs.

I go and get a tea and a sandwich and eat it staring out to the horizon. I come back to earth slowly, my heart gradually returning to its usual rhythm. What does it mean? Will a real battle come to the village here? Why? I mean, what could possibly bring that kind of carnage to the Greenworld? I think again of the blood pumping out from the boy's throat. Of the noise of the woman's nose breaking, that hot snap of agony. My mind can't stop turning the impressions over with a kind of fascinated dread, and all the time with the remembered smell of blood. If it is a prediction of something to come . . . I don't know. How would we even prepare for something like that?

After about half an hour a figure appears beside me: Saba, dried off and changed into a jumper and warm trousers. She knots her scarf round her neck and ties her long hair into a damp plait.

'Let's have a sip of your tea,' she says, and she warms her fingers on the mug. She gulps it down and wipes her mouth with the sleeve of her jumper – an ordinary gesture she makes look sexy as hell. I look at her warily. I think she's still angry with me for being here, but I catch a glimpse of her face and it's beatific: still, peaceful, radiant. I've never seen her look so beautiful. I really, really want to kiss her, despite the craziness in my head. Despite the horror.

'How was it?' she asks, hazel eyes searching mine.

I shake my head. I don't know what to say: either to tell her how beautiful she looks or just how freaked I am by what I saw. The two sensations make a kind of jagged sense together, like a jigsaw that you force to join, despite one piece being blue sky and one being a shipwreck.

She mistakes me shaking my head to mean I didn't see anything and her brow furrows.

I start to babble. 'No, no – I mean, it was . . . weird. She was . . . I don't know. Powerful. Power itself.

Did she bless the village, was that what that last part was?'

'Yeah. That's the main point of the ritual, to ask for blessing and to worship Brighid, to submit ourselves to Her. But usually anyone involved gets a vision or a message, something personal. Did that happen?' she asks.

I try to gather my thoughts. 'Yeah. It was horrible, though. There was an eclipse, and Roach kidnapped me. Inside the portal. Then I was a crow flying over this battle.' I shudder, seeing the pooling blood, the boy clutching at his throat and the woman having her nose broken. 'And then . . .'

'What?'

'I saw Roach again. But he sort of exploded. Burst into flames.'

'Exploded?'

'Well, no. More just . . . suddenly he was on fire. Standing by the portal. What did you see? I mean, just now. In the vision She gave you. A battle? Something?'

She frowns. 'No. No battles. Just . . . something personal. Something nice.' She smiles non-committally and looks out on to the horizon for a moment, avoiding my eyes.

I follow her gaze to the hazy blue-grey line where sky meets sea. 'Well, maybe that's a good thing. If you didn't see anything disturbing, maybe that means a battle's just in my messed-up head.'

'Maybe. But you really do have a psychic

connection with him. You need to be careful, Danny. That connection goes both ways. If you can see him in vision, he can see you. See what's in your heart, in your future.'

'I guess so.'

'Hmmm. And the crow — that's a symbol of the Morrigan, remember? We don't really worship her so much. Death and destruction. She's Melz's goddess, not mine. The Morrigan's always freaked me out really.' She shivers and wraps her arms round herself. 'Give me Brighid any day of the week.'

'Hmmm,' I say, staring out at the horizon, thinking. 'It didn't feel bad, being a crow. It was more what I saw. What does it mean?'

'Dunno. Usually people get nice messages. Not people burning to death.'

'Well, I don't know if Roach actually died, he was just kind of . . . consumed,' I say.

'Consumed by fire. Died. It's the same thing,' she says a little haughtily.

It makes me a little annoyed, like, Don't tell me what I saw. Don't tell me what I felt, Saba. But obviously I don't say that.

She turns round and calls to the girls to get their stuff together. She looks back at me, concern in her eyes. 'We're heading back now. You know that you need to tell Mum what you saw, right? I mean, even if it's nothing, or not what it seemed. People suffering . . . dying . . .' She shudders. 'I've never known anyone have that type of vision at the procession before. Or any time, in fact. She'll want to know if there's any chance that the village might be in danger. There's an eclipse coming up. You have to tell her, OK?' Her almond eyes are afraid – of what I saw, but maybe – maybe of me too, I can't tell.

'Yeah. OK, I guess.'

'Good,' she says, and squeezes my hand briefly. The electricity flashes between us again, and I know she feels it because she pulls her hand away too quickly. She looks away. Is she a little flustered?

I watch as she goes to help one of the older women pack the mugs away in a wicker carry basket, her back to me. Busying herself to ignore that moment. Maybe to ignore what she knows she felt.

I wander off slowly, following some of the girls that have started their cautious and cloaked way back to the village, but when I reach the path through the cliffs at the edge of the beach she catches up with me.

'Come on,' she says, smiling again, and her eyes have something more than friendliness in them.

We've shared this morning, this special moment together, and it means something. I know it does. She holds out her hand to me again and I take it. This time she doesn't pull it away.

Chapter Fourteen

War is not for the Greenworld. We leave war to
those that have not found peace.

From *Tenets and Sayings of the Greenworld*

When we walk back into the village Tom's waiting for
Saba at the Witch's Gate. It's a jolt back into reality,
and it hurts. I'd forgotten there was a Tom, a good-
natured tall blond boyfriend, a guy I reluctantly like.
Saba snatches her hand away from mine and I know she
has the same jolting feeling: like we were in our own
little world down at the beach, and now here we are
back home where the old rules apply.

Saba smiles and waves, dropping the 'Tom's
girlfriend' persona over herself like a robe.

I arrange my face into a pleasant expression.

'Hey, baby,' he says, and kisses Saba as she gets to
the gate.

'Hi, Tom,' she says a little guardedly, or am I imagining it? 'I didn't know you'd be waiting for us. It's so early still!'

He smiles. 'Well, got to support my girl, haven't I? And I thought I'd bring some veg over for tonight's dinner,' he says. There's a big box of muddy Greenworld organic veg by his feet. All grown by his fair hands, no doubt.

'Dinner?' she asks blankly. But I remember. Tonight we're hosting a Yule dinner for some of the villagers. It's a regular thing – various townsfolk come to have some quality time with the witches. To see we're normal people, I guess, not a bunch of cackling, wart-munching weirdos.

'Yeah, you know, the gardeners are coming tonight,' he says.

I nudge Saba. 'Come on, Sabs, the big dinner. How can you forget? Lowenna's got us on spud-peeling detail.'

'Oh, right. Yeah. Sorry. Still a bit spaced out, I s'pose.' She smiles up at me. At me, not him.

'It was a pretty heavy ritual,' I say, by way of explanation to Tom.

'I guess it was,' he says slowly, looking at me, looking at her smile. And I know in that look that he gets it. That I like Saba. So I give him that look back – Yeah, brother. I do. So let the best man win.

The rest of the village girls tramp past and there's a slightly uncomfortable silence until Saba breaks it. 'So d'you want to come back to the house?' she asks Tom, but he shakes his head.

'Ummm, no, actually. I've just remembered I've got a lot to do today – finishing early to come to yours later – so I better get going.' He shoves the box of vegetables at me. 'Dan can take these,' he says.

'Oh . . . OK,' Saba says, a little bit flustered. 'See you later then.'

He turns away and gives a backwards wave to us, not looking back.

Saba looks put out. 'Well, that was odd,' she says. 'What's up with him?'

I know exactly what's up with Tom, but I'm not telling the tawny-maned temptress Saba, the one that men would slay dragons for.

'Maybe he didn't want to peel potatoes,' I say, and she smiles.

The dinner comes after a day of food prep. There are twenty gardeners and ten apprentices to feed – kids in their early teens learning the trade – as well as six hungry witches, Mum and Biba. Omar's here too. The rest have gone back to their villages. Tonight I'm interested to see what Tom does or doesn't do. I feel kind of sorry for him. I mean, he is a good guy. In a normal situation we'd be friends, but my aim here is getting Saba, and all the bets are off.

Lowenna's in charge of roasting the meat for the meal – a rare luxury. She's turning two lamb legs on a spit in the garden when Saba nudges me out of a vegetable-peeling trance. 'Tell Mum what you saw this morning. Go on.'

As if I could forget. I've been trying to – concentrating on the food prep like it was a masterclass in mindfulness. Staying in that moment of perfection, trying to peel every potato in one precise curl. Hasn't helped, though. And I know I've got to tell Lowenna, but I don't want to speak the words and make those visions even a tiny bit more real.

Reluctantly I put down the almost-blunt knife and poke my head out of the glass door. The rich aroma of charring meat hits me immediately; the blood smell is almost too rich for my usually vegetarian nose.

Blood. I remember what Merryn said. The maidens offer a blood sacrifice to the sea for our protection. But what if today's blood wasn't enough? Will Brighid demand more? Was that what I saw? A battle for our freedom, our safety?

Lowenna looks up from turning the handle of a heavy iron contraption. Kind of like a medieval torture device. 'Ah, Danny. I could do with a break. Here . . .' She peels off her gloves and hands them to me, straightening up slowly. 'By Brighid, an electric oven would be a boon on days like this. Still, reap what you sow.'

I put the gloves on and start turning the spit slowly. The fat drops from the meat on to the coals below and hisses, sending up smoke. 'How long do you have to do this for?' I ask, already starting to feel my muscles burn.

'A few more hours,' she says, eyebrow cocked. 'Don't tell me you're tired already. I thought having a young man about the place would mean I didn't have to do all the heavy lifting.'

I look at her thick, muscular arms, then at my skinny ones. 'Don't be sexist,' I say.

She laughs. 'Ha. No, quite right. Quite right. Did you want something, or did you really come out to help?'

I look back at the glowing coals in the fire pit she's built on the patio. They'll leave a scorched mark when it gets swept up tomorrow. 'I saw something. At the beach this morning,' I say to the stone ground.

She reaches into her pocket and brings out some tobacco and a handmade wooden pipe. 'Aha,' she says, stuffing the brown leaves into the pipe bowl and lighting it from the coals under the spit.

'Yeah. Errr . . . well, it was a bit disturbing.'

'Hmmm. All right then, let's have it.'

'I was a crow, flying above this battle.'

'The Morrigan. The crow, it's her animal.'

'That's what Saba said.'

'Hmmm. A battle, though? What d'you mean, exactly? A few people fighting?'

'No. hundreds of people. Dying. Fighting. Hand-to-hand combat. Guns, knives.' I shiver. 'Blood everywhere.'

'Who were these people?'

'I'm not sure. I didn't recognize a... but I knew it was Tintagel. The villag*in particular,*

'Fighting between themselves?' She*...* intensely, her pipe momentarily forgotten*...*

'No. I didn't get a sense of who they we*at me* but Roach was there, so I guess it must have*...* gangs. Anyway, I was flying above this battle.*...* were getting hurt. Blood everywhere . . . kille*...* and before that there was an eclipse. And then . . .*...*

I stare into the flames, thinking about Roach, a*...* the sweet smell of his burning flesh in my vision turns*...* my stomach.

She looks up sharply. 'An eclipse?'

'Yeah. Sorry, it's all jumbled up in my head . . . I was in the portal with Roach. There was an eclipse. And he kind of kidnapped me.'

'What do you mean, kidnapped?'

'My ankles were tied. I couldn't walk. He said something.' I try to remember. 'He said, "I can cut you here." He had a knife. And then he said something like "This is the way" and carried me off to the end of the tunnel.'

'What then?'

'Then I was the crow, and there was the battle, like I said.'

She frowns and pokes the coals with a long branch, blackened at one end. 'Was that the end? Was there something else?'

urning the spit. It makes me sick
'No, I . . .' I st saw Roach. He was burning. He
when I think of was horrible.'
burst into flame says under her breath. 'What was
'By Bri s happened? When he was burned?'
he doing nding by the portal. Laughing.'
'H l again.' she says, more to herself than
ttle.'

a pulls in a long drag from her pipe and
e smoke over her shoulder, away from the
looks pensive, an unusual expression for her.
know that there's an eclipse soon? In a month

shake my head. 'No. Well, Saba mentioned it earlier today. Why, do you think something's going to happen?'

She takes the blackened branch and draws a circle on the stone slabs of the patio, then draws lines across it to shade it in. Make it black.

'I keep seeing this in my dreams. The dark moon of the eclipse. And I see you, shadowed by the moon. I can't see your face. And I think it's just the moon's shadow over you, and then I see Roach behind you. With a knife. And I realize it's his shadow, his darkness, over you. And then I wake up.'

She looks at me and I'm shocked to see fear in her eyes.

'Goddess,' is all I can say.

'That's not all of it, though. Just last night I had

another dream. I was in the middle of a battle, fighting these men; there were men coming at me from all angles. Coming at all of us, pouring out of the forest in droves. Guns and knives. One of them pushed me over and was about to stab me through the heart. And just before I woke up I realized I wasn't me in the dream. I had a different body. I was a boy.'

'You've seen a battle too?'

'I see a lot of things. Being in charge of the Greenworld's no walk in the park, you know. People come to me with their problems, their fears. And even when they don't, it's my job to know what those fears are and try to assuage them.' She sucks deeply on her clay pipe and the tobacco glows like feral eyes in the bowl. 'I feel all the negative emotions and thoughts of the whole village, Danny. All the time. And I work to transmute it into positivity, or banish it into neutrality, at least. Well, all the Hands do. So if I have a dream about a battle, that doesn't necessarily mean there will be one. More likely it represents a tension somewhere in the Greenworld, a fear of some kind. If you hadn't told me about your vision I'd have put mine down to a more or less constant fear of the gangs from the people in Tintagel. But now . . .'

'Now? You think there's an actual battle coming? Not something symbolic?'

She puffs the smoke out into the air thoughtfully. 'I don't know. Maybe. Here's what I know. I know you were sent here for a reason, for me to train you. I know Roach wants you. I know I have to protect you, and I have to protect the portal. But I don't know what Roach wants you for. And . . . if there was a battle . . . I don't know how we would even do that. I mean – we're not fighters here. We don't have weapons. I just can't imagine it happening.'

She looks suddenly frightened, as if the prospect of a battle is actually hitting home for the first time. The idea that magic might not be enough to keep conflict away forever is not one Lowenna wants to entertain. *War is not for the Greenworld. We leave war to those that have not found peace.* Another stupid tenet.

Except that it's not that simple. You can practise peace as much as you want, but what do you do if someone makes war on you? What do you do then? Betray your peace and fight for what you believe in or surrender it in the spirit of non-violence?

When I was a kid and I came home from school one day crying cos some kids had made fun of my dark skin and black curls, my dad hugged me until the tears stopped, and then he said, 'Never start a fight, Danny. Never be cruel. But if someone hits you, you hit back harder.' Mum had intervened and told him off, told me I should just ignore bullies and feel sorry for them. That picking on others means you're unhappy. That you don't get enough love. And they got into a big fight about it and me and Biba got told to go and play outside, which was what always happened when they had a difference of opinion and wanted to yell it out.

And I remember hearing Dad say, 'It's all very well

for you, nobody dares say anything to you, you're the witch. But I know what it's like down here. I'm not having the kids go through what I did, bloody small-town mentality,' and Mum said, 'Don't exaggerate. There's no colour in the Greenworld.' And Dad laughed and said, 'If you believe that, you're not as wise as you think you are.' He left soon after that, but he taught both me and Biba not to stand for any shit. If someone hits you, you hit back.

I touch Lowenna's arm gingerly. She smiles wanly and grips my hand, lacing her fingers through mine.

'We have to be sure, one way or the other,' I say. 'If there really is going to be a battle, we need to be prepared. As much as we can be anyway.'

'Yes . . . I suppose . . . I'm just not convinced. I mean, I just can't believe it would ever happen. Would Roach really attack us? Over what? You? The portal? It seems ridiculous.'

Not that ridiculous, I think, but I can see the resistance in her just like with Mum rejecting the idea that anyone in her precious, liberated Greenworld could ever make fun of her kids for the colour of their skin. We made a beautiful new world. How could anything go wrong?

'OK. We know more than we did yesterday anyway, thanks to your vision. We know he'll try to get you – and the portal, maybe – at the eclipse. So we've got some time to prepare. It's all right.' She's talking as if she's calming herself down, rationalizing.

She looks inside to the kitchen where Saba and Melz are laughing about something. 'Don't say anything tonight,' she says. 'I'll talk to the girls tomorrow. And Merryn and Beryan. We'll work out a plan. But tonight, let's not worry. Well – I'll worry. But they won't know.'

I look at her doubtfully. I expected more than this, but she's deliberately ignoring this because she can't believe it. Won't believe it.

'All right . . . I won't say anything. Saba knows what I saw, though,' I say doubtfully.

'Saba is very good at not mulling things over,' Lowenna says dismissively. 'I wouldn't be too concerned about her if I were you. Saba isn't – how can I put this? – she's not one to waste her time worrying about other people.'

I look inside at the sisters. Light and dark, sun and moon. 'That's not a nice thing to say about your daughter.'

Lowenna laughs. 'Oh, she'd agree with me. It's not a bad thing, don't get me wrong. It's a gift to be able to avoid worrying. Why worry anyway? All that exists is the moment we are in. Nothing else has happened yet, and everything in the past is past. Other people spend their whole lives trying to be as unworried as Saba.'

'I suppose . . . when you put it like that.'

She gives me a sudden hug. 'Don't worry. All will be well. Everything, eventually, happens as it should.'

'I guess,' I say, but I'm kind of angry. This whole live-in-the-moment, everything-happens-as-it-should thing is OK, but it doesn't mean Lowenna should just sit back and refuse to take responsibility. There's a very real possibility that people will die, if our visions are correct. And mine have been pretty spot on so far.

Saba knocks on the window, waving the blunt knife at me.

'Go on,' Lowenna says and takes her gloves back. 'There are few more important things in life than food. Today I need you in the kitchen. Tomorrow, who knows?' She pushes hard on the spit and the old iron creaks back into life again. Conversation over.

I expected more than this. I go back inside with a weight in my stomach. Before, the vision scared me. Now, it's worse. Now, I'm scared that it might come true and nobody's going to do anything to stop it.

At about seven p.m. the door goes and Melz answers it. There's laughter and she comes back in with Tom and two other guys I've seen around.

'Danny, this is Denzil and Aaron, and you know Tom.' She smiles up at him with far more adoration than her sister does. Melz is a hard nut to crack, usually caustic and snappy, but all of a sudden here she is, Miss Warmth and Hospitality.

I shake hands with the guys who seem as laid-back and friendly as Tom.

'Hey, man, how are you?' asks Denzil, a tall, rangy boy of about seventeen. Aaron looks older, maybe mid-twenties and has a gingery beard. Beards are big in the Greenworld.

'Good, thanks. Good to meet you,' I say. 'Hey, Tom,' I add, and hold out my hand.

Clearly he's composed himself since his hissy fit earlier in the day cos he takes it and we shake hands in the proper manly way.

'All right, Dan?' he asks, and hands me two bottles of home-made wine. 'Put these somewhere, will you?'

I take them, and point at Biba, who's gazing up at him with a funny expression on her face.

'This is my sister, Biba. Beebs, this is Tom.' I don't honour him by adding on 'Saba's boyfriend'.

Tom smiles his warm nice-guy smile and shakes Biba's hand. 'Didn't know you had a sister, Dan. Pretty one too. She doesn't look much like you. Hi, Biba. It's really good to meet you,' he says.

I look at Beebs, who is uncharacteristically silent. I nudge her, and she wakes up. 'Oh . . . err, yes, hello. Nice to meet you too,' she mumbles, and I look at her in disgust. Not you too, Beebs, I think.

He leaves her and goes over to Saba, who is working on dessert. 'Evening, gorgeous,' he says and kisses her. She definitely kisses back, I note, putting her hand on the back of his neck in a familiar way, and my anxiety over the battle morphs easily into the more familiar jealousy. 'So what's for dinner?' he asks, looking around.

'Hungry men, is it? Come to eat me out of house

and home?' Lowenna walks in from the back garden with some herbs in her hand, and to my surprise gives Tom a big hug. 'How are you, Tom? Haven't seen you in a few weeks.' She is all jollity and warmth, and there's no sign that she's worried about what will happen at the eclipse. Or worried about an impending battle.

Deception is part of a witch's skill set, after all.

She catches my eye. 'I've known this one since he was knee-high to a grasshopper, Danny. He and the girls used to play in the paddling pool naked. Grew up together, they did. Now look at him! Big lug!' she says, laughingly reaching up to muss his hair – which is quite a task, as she's average height but Tom's well over six feet.

He laughs. 'Lowenna's my second mum,' he says. 'We were always in the garden out there as kids – me, Saba, Melz, playing. We had so many good times!'

The picture's becoming clearer, I have to say, now that I know this. So Saba and Tom are an item from way back – almost like brother and sister. Does it feel like that to her? I wonder. Did she resign herself to ending up with Tom, whom she loves, but more as a brother than a boyfriend? And then found herself having feelings for someone else? That's how I want it to be.

I also wonder at what point Tom and Saba became an item, and not Melz and Tom? Cos looking in Melz's eyes I can see that's what she wanted, and still wants. Her gaze could melt walls – anyone with eyes can see she adores him. Are they both just used to Saba coming first in everything? Melz always the second sister? Who knows. But it makes me think that if that was me, I'd get pretty tired of not being noticed.

Gowdie, the traitor, comes running in at the sound of Tom's voice and jumps up at him excitedly. Goddess, everyone's so pleased to see him. It's like bloody Father Christmas has walked in or something.

'Gowdie, get down,' I say, and pull her off Tom.

'Nah, man, she's all right, aren't you, girl?' he says, and fishes around in his gardener's bag. 'Now, what's this I've got in here for you?' He brings out a meaty bone and gives it to her. She goes ape. It's the first meat she's seen for months.

'Oh . . . thanks, Tom.' Why does he have to make it so hard to dislike him?

We stand around the kitchen drinking the home-made wine and wait for the others to arrive – we're using the big covenstead table with a couple of other tables joined on, so there's less room than usual and we're all herded into one end of the kitchen, knocking into pots and pans and trying not to spill jars of dried herbs and witchy stuff everywhere. As more and more of the gardeners arrive we get more and more squashed up there. It's hot with so many people there and the fire crackling away merrily. As I back further in to let more people in I bump into someone. Turning round to say sorry, I see it's Tom. Saba is across the room talking to Melz and Denzil.

'Hey, man,' I say.

'I know what you're doing,' he says.

OK. Right to the point.

'What am I doing?'

'Don't make me spell it out. Saba. I know you want her.' He's serious – frowning, as if he doesn't want to have this conversation.

'Why do you think that?' I don't deny it, but I'm waiting to see what he's got before I show my hand.

'I can tell by the way you look at her. Don't think just because you spend so much time with her something's going to happen. She's my girl. So just leave her alone.'

'OK, man, whatever you say. But shouldn't we let her decide who she wants?'

We're standing close to each other cos of the crowding, but Tom leans in closer so his face is centimetres from mine.

'I'm serious, Danny. Don't think I can't fight you for her, cos I can. I'm not that much of a Mr Nice Guy. Leave her alone.'

He means it – he's mad as hell. I just nod.

'All right, then,' he says, and turns away from me, pushing his way through the crowd. I look up and catch Saba's eye – she looks concerned, and I wonder if she saw us talking. But right then Lowenna's voice rings out above the hubbub.

'Dinner, everyone! Take your seats! Sit anywhere! Let's eat!' And there's a big scraping of chairs on the slate floor as we all find somewhere to sit. I'm nowhere near Saba and find myself next to Aaron, Mum, Biba and Omar and a bunch of the apprentice gardeners, who proceed to get pissed on the wine. We have a good time and Aaron's good company, for a gardener. He talks passionately about gardening and the Greenworld and how it's all great, and Beebs joins in, and they hammer out a plan for world domination as we eat our potatoes and turnips. But amid the laughter and shouting, my gaze happens to range up the table to Saba, who looks up at the same time and smiles at me. And I think about how I've never really cared about anything before, but I care about her. And I'm not going to be warned off, not by anyone. As long as she wants me, then I'm going to do everything I can to get her.

It's our turn for clean-up after the big Yule dinner and we are the last ones up. I'm doing the washing up and Saba's doing the drying, cosy as you like. It's late and the moon is shining in through the glass-panelled kitchen roof like a peeping Tom. Saba's singing a tune under her breath – we're not talking, just companionably passing plates, stacking them. The dinner and a few glasses of wine have made me relax a bit about the whole Lowenna-not-believing-a battle-could-happen thing; as I pass a bowl to Saba I reflect that maybe Lowenna's right, and the visions were probably a result of picking up on the village's general anxiety about the gangs. If I truly looked deep into myself I know I'd find that I don't really believe that, but I don't want to look deep right now. Right now I just want to be here with Saba, alone, feeling good and slightly hazy.

Saba's wearing some kind of long-sleeved top that keeps slipping off her shoulder, and she pulls it up every now and again. It stays for a minute and then slips again. A few minutes later she notices it and pulls it up. I'm enjoying watching her out of the corner of my eye.

I hand the last washed plate to her and our fingers touch. There's a crack of electricity that has nothing to do with the weather – it's a connection between the two of us, right then and there, and we both jump. I meet her eyes and she's staring at me. I stare back at her and neither of us drops the gaze. I lean in and kiss her, and my lips meet that soft, warm, peachy mouth.

We stand in that position for a couple of long minutes. She draws back, finally, and I realize I'm still holding the plate.

I laugh, embarrassed, and put it back on the sink. 'So,' I say. Unoriginal.

She smiles. 'So,' she says back. She hikes up her top again and looks at the floor.

I reach over and push the sleeve off her shoulder again. 'Looks better that way,' I say, and lean over and kiss the soft skin on her shoulder. She smells like peaches too, with an undercurrent of incense.

She puts her arms round my neck. 'Do you want to go for a walk?' she breathes.

'Happy to go,' I tell her. I'm not fond of walks in

the night in winter for no reason, but you don't say no to girls like Saba.

We tiptoe out of the house, pulling on our heavy boots and wool cloaks. They have good leather workers here in Tintagel, and it's the first time in years I've had good shoes that didn't let in the water. The cloak is grey and hooded, and the wool helps keep the hard night air out of our bones. Tonight, I'm too excited to be cold. Adrenalin is keeping my blood pumping and my hands sweaty. I have to keep wiping them surreptitiously on my wool trousers. For once, Gowdie doesn't demand to come with me – maybe she's getting smarter, or some of these witch skills are rubbing off on her. She knows we want to be alone, and just wags her tail as I pass her.

'Where shall we go?' I say, looking one way and then the other down the street. There's no one around: in one of the Redworld cities at this time of night there'd be action everywhere you could see, no doubt – looters, whores, packs of feral kids, dogs, weirdos. But here everyone's in bed, or if not, cleaning up after their Yule celebrations. I hear singing in the distance: some committed Greenworlders singing Yule songs to welcome in the new sun. Beebs would love it here, if she was allowed to stay. She loves a good singalong, and we don't do as much of that kind of stuff at home. I miss my little sister being around, and seeing her has only made it worse, in a weird way.

Saba pulls me down the street, away from the route

we usually take to the village centre or the Witch's Gate.

'Where're we going?'

'You'll see,' she says, smiling.

I don't care really where we go, as long as I have a shot at those lips again, and maybe more. I take her hand and she squeezes my fingers.

'What're you thinking about?' she asks.

'My little sister,' I say. 'I was thinking how she'd make more of being here than I do. If she spent longer than a couple of days here.'

'Your sister's Biba, right? I don't really know her that well. What's she like?' Saba's clear hazel eyes look up into mine.

'She's cool, really. Not that I'd tell her.' I think of Biba's earnest brown eyes, her straight black shiny hair, always tied back neatly. 'She's a supergreen. Massive nerd. But, I guess she cares about things, you know? A lot of kids in Dartmoor don't really give a shit. But Beebs believes in the Greenworld. Believes in the future. Her friends are all the supergreen kids, y'know, the nerds.'

'Weren't you a nerd?' She looks at me playfully.

I snort. 'No! Tried to stay out of school as much as I could. Party when I can. You know,' I say, trying to be cool.

'Am I a nerd?' Saba asks, smiling – she knows she's not.

'No way – you're hot. You're way too hot to be a nerd. Girls like you can't be nerds,' I say.

'But I do my homework on time.'

'You're not a nerd.'

'I do extra reading.'

'Not a nerd.'

'I stay in most nights reading *The Common Herbal*.'

'No way. That is pretty supergreen. Still not a nerd, though.'

'I don't really like drinking. It disagrees with me.'

'You're sexy enough that it doesn't count.'

She stops in the street. We're almost at the boundary of the town, where she first brought me into the village that day after rescuing me from Roach. She looks up at me, all serious again. 'I like you.'

My heart starts pounding, but I try to look cool. 'You know I like you too. But you're with Tom. You made a point of telling me.'

'I know. Tom and I . . . well, we grew up together. Everyone just assumed we'd couple up, so it seemed like the obvious thing to do. He's a really, really good person, but . . .'

'There's a but?'

She looks up at me, wickedness and nervousness fighting for dominance in her cat eyes. 'Yes,' she breathes, and her hand finds the back of my neck. She leans in slowly and her lips meet mine. Joy pierces me like lightning. My hands find her waist and I pull her to me, our bodies aligning perfectly. She pulls back from me. 'But what about Bryony?'

'Bryony? Oh, right, yeah. No. I mean, no. She's

all right and everything, but she's not you. I only went with her cause you were unavailable. You practically set us up. What was I supposed to do?'

She looks rueful. 'I know. I thought if you got stuck on someone else I'd stop wanting you.'

'Did you?'

'No.'

I take her hands in mine, which are shaking. I hope she thinks it's just the cold. I take a long breath in. 'Saba, I think you're amazing. You're the most beautiful, talented, sweet, intelligent girl I've ever met. I just want to be around you. Cos you make me laugh. Cos I can be myself around you. I don't have to worry about being cool or saying the wrong thing. You're just . . . you're just perfect.'

'Thank you, Danny,' she says softly. We kiss again.

Saba is the one that eventually breaks away from the kiss.

'Come on. I want to show you this place, and it's late already.'

'OK, lead the way.' I'd follow her to damnation. The Redworld. The Russian front line. Anywhere.

I'm surprised when we reach the boundary of the village and Saba opens the energetic circle for us to get out. I don't say anything, but it's rule-breaking. We walk on in silence for a while and I know that Saba is concentrating on protecting us in an energy shield while we're out here in gangland territory. We both know we shouldn't be out here, but we're here anyway;

if Saba wants us to walk this way then we will. I trust her, though maybe if everything wasn't so hazy from the wine and the kiss then I might be more worried, considering the visions of bloodshed and all. I hold her hand as we walk – the moon is so bright that it almost seems like daylight. Good for not tripping over anything – bad for being noticed. We make occasional small talk but really we're keeping it low – we know we're taking a risk being out here, witches or not.

I start to hear a noise, which is kind of like a banging, kind of like a rolling *shhhhh*, and I realize we've come to the top of a cliff and stopped just centimetres from the edge; almost under our feet the grass and stone drops away to nothing and I see the stark cliffs of Tintagel, opposite Tintagel Head, plummeting straight down to choppy waves beneath. The cold salt of the spray off the waves catches in my lungs as I gasp in surprise.

'Amazing, isn't it?' Saba murmurs, hugging her coat round her. It's colder by the water but it's also a chill of awe that runs up my spine as well as cold. This is a different cove to the one we enacted the ritual at. The cliff curves round a small deserted pebbly bay, and you can tell that this was never somewhere for picnics or ball games. It has a magic about it, a wild beauty. The waves that buffet the shore are greenish-grey in the moonlight like dull jewels: wintry, cloudy, dramatic. The sound of them is like a salty heartbeat or a low song with no words. Saba's face has the reflection of the water's broken sheen and her hair has come loose from its ponytail – it whips behind her and across her face like a flag. She belongs to this place, I realize as I see her. It's as if she has come home.

Before I realize what's happening she's pulling my hand and stepping out as if on nothing, towards the waves. I try to pull her back, but she turns her head back and smiles a kind of wild sea-nymph smile. 'It's OK. There's a way down. Follow me.' Already her voice is starting to get carried away by the sea wind that blows through this place. I follow, gingerly placing my feet where hers have been.

It's a steep climb down and the steps that have been chipped out of the cliff are narrow and slippery. They're made for smaller feet than mine and I slip more than once, almost falling into Saba, who seems to be dancing down the face of the cliff with no more trouble than a mountain goat. Finally, my pride almost intact, we get to the bottom. This is a different path than the one to Tintagel Head, though that's also narrow and dangerous.

The sea's really wild the closer up to it you are, and I wonder what we can get up to down here – I mean, it's freezing and wet. The pebbles that aren't being lashed with the tide are streaked with seaweed, slippery and lethal.

Saba still has me by the hand. She laughs and pulls me to the right of the bay. 'This way! It's much drier!' she says, and leads me past some rocks that contain little basins filled with limpets and seawater to what looks like the shadowy cliff wall. At the last minute, though, I realize it's not a shadow but an opening to something. She pulls me in.

'Stand there for a minute,' she says, and I can hear a kind of rustling sound. Suddenly, a flare of light flickers, spits and settles into an amber glow. 'There, that's better,' she says.

The fire throws strange patterns on the walls and I look around me in wonder.

We are dry and comfortable and warm in a cave. It's high enough inside to stand in and about the size of my bedroom – perfect for two people. In the centre is a large flat rock, a little like a bed, which is where we're standing. The fire starts to warm the space up.

'Here – hang your cloak over this rock to dry,' she says and takes off her own. She goes over to one corner and I notice with amazement there's a kind of chest there, from which she takes a rug and a couple of candles. She lays the rug over the flat stone and lights the candles with an expert flick of flint on rock. It's totally dry inside and I can see no water's got in here for a long time – I guess if it did she'd never be able to store anything in the chest cos it'd get ruined.

'What is this place?' I ask – I can hear the child-like awe in my voice but I don't care. I can't believe I'm sitting in a secret cave with Saba in the middle of the night, lit by candlelight as the sea rages outside, with a campfire that smells like apples and cedarwood. The fragrant smoke lingers in the cave and then blows out to sea.

'I come here sometimes to think, to meditate — sometimes just to be on my own,' she says. 'I found it when I was out walking one day. Exploring.'

'But you're not supposed to go past the boundary on your own,' I say, sounding like a nerd.

'I can look after myself.' She shakes her wet dark-gold hair out of her eyes with a touch of defiance.

I know she's got the power, the self-assurance, to protect herself as much as anyone. I mean, she came and rescued me that first day after all, when Roach's gang was after me.

'Does Lowenna know?'

She shakes her head. 'No. No, I don't think so. But it's OK. Really. We'll be safe here,' she says, and suddenly I wonder what I'm doing wasting time with wondering whether we should be here when I could be kissing her, tangling my fingers in her mane of silky hair. I cautiously reach up to her face and stroke her cheek. She leans her face into my hand and kisses my palm.

'What now?' I ask softly.

'This,' she murmurs, and leans across to me. Her lips brush mine, tenderly, and brush again. The kiss deepens. We go under, into the world of oceans. I can hear the crash of waves on the cliffs outside, smell the salt of the beach. It mingles with the honey smell of Saba's skin, the warm closeness of her. Gently she pulls me down so we're lying on the blanket kissing. It seems to go on for hours, being lost in each other's shadows. Her lips are all the clichés my defective brain can conjure — rose petals, peaches. I've got a hard-on the size of a monolith, the weight and girth of a hot boulder. I'm trying to control myself, and stop my doubts from multiplying in my paranoid brain — Does she really like me? Does she want me to do anything else? Is Tom better than me? Does she want him more? Is she thinking of him?

I hope I don't seem distracted, but she seems happy to lie here and stroke each other and kiss forever, and hey, I'm more than happy with that. My hands stray to her T-shirt and run over her breasts, her tight little belly. Cautiously I run my hand up on to her warm skin under the shirt. She doesn't seem to mind, just sighs, in a good way I think. My hand, intrepid explorer that it is, takes more initiative and reaches up to one breast, unfettered by a bra. The Greenworld has a few major benefits, and bralessness is one of the sweetest.

The sea crashes outside and the dark takes us. At a point I don't remember, I fall asleep in her arms, like a sailor caught by a mermaid.

A few hours later, I wake up stiff, sore and sober. Lying on a rock, even with a few blankets, isn't that comfortable I guess. Saba is standing up, re-plaiting her hair by the cave opening and looking out. She's a siren — she's got the sea in her somehow, in her blood. That wildness, that elemental force. Tempting a boy like me on to the rocks, into danger. I like it, the illicitness of our being out all night together beyond the boundary.

'Morning,' I say a little shyly. What do we say to each other in the light? The dark, lit by candles, listening to the sea, was a different us – a different magic world, full of the thick strings of sensual energy. The morning is rationality, light, communication on normal terms.

She turns and smiles at me. 'Morning,' she says, and comes back to kneel and kiss me. She runs her hand through my long black curly hair, which is a bit bed-heady. 'We better be on our way before anyone works out we're gone,' she says.

'What time is it?' I yawn. It's lighter in the cave but there's that harsh early-morning feel to the sea air.

'Early. About five,' she says.

Hell. Five a.m.

I get up. 'OK, we better head off,' I agree, and shiver.

It's cold out of the blankets and without Saba's warm body next to me. I wonder when the next time I hold her all night will be.

Chapter Fifteen

And someone called me by my name:
It had become a glimmering girl
With apple blossoms in her hair
Who called me by my name and ran
And faded through the brightening air.

From 'The Song of Wandering Aengus'
by W. B. Yeats

We make it back fine, up the rock steps from the cave to the cliff, across the open country, through the energetic boundary outside the village and back into our beds by six. It's bloody freezing, even indoors, as none of the hearth fires are lit yet, and as I get into my own room I wonder how the hell I actually managed to sleep in a cave in Cornwall in the middle of winter. Fortunately none of the witches are up. I blow a kiss to Saba as we separate and enter our own rooms. I plunge into bed, grateful for the chance to warm up and replay the night's events in my head without interruption.

I nod off, evidently, as the next thing I hear is Omar's deep voice laughing somewhere in the house. I look at the clock – it's past ten and I can hear activity downstairs – crockery and cutlery, the domestic clatter of breakfast. I'm glad he's still here – I decide to zone in on him for a manly one-to-one, cos if anyone knows anything about loving a witch, it's him.

After cruising by the kitchen for a cup of tea and a slice of toast I find Omar on the roof of Lowenna's house, adjusting the solar panels. Lowenna's house has some of the few panels in Tintagel; likewise, Mum's house in Gidleigh, but it's funny how the witches have them and no one else. Still, they don't work any better here than Mum's. Maybe half a warm bath a week.

He looks down to where I'm standing in the garden below and beckons me to come up. 'I could do with a strong pair of hands up here,' he calls down. 'I suppose I'll have to settle for your puny little paws, though.'

I climb up the ladder against the side of the house and find myself on the sloping tiles. Trying not to look down, I inch myself across. Not easy balancing a mug in one hand and toast in your teeth.

'Good to see you, Dan,' he says. He's not lost his old habit of chewing tobacco – a nod to the Wild West. He's strutting his way across this roof, his footsteps a warning to the women below, as if to make his mark. Will he piss off the roof when he needs a leak? I wonder.

He points to the bottom left corner of the solar panel that's slipped out of place. 'Push that towards me,' he says, and I push.

It's pretty heavy but I don't let on. I think I see a glimmer of a smile around his mouth, but he just clears his throat. 'So, my man. How you finding it here?' he asks.

'S'OK, yeah.' I don't really know how to broach the subject of Saba. I want to lead up to it, not blurt it out like some kind of virgin.

'How you getting on with the ladies?' he asks – a bland enough question. 'Hand me that hammer.' He starts banging nails into the tiles round the panel.

'Err, yeah, it's fine. Like, it's weird being the only man. But I guess it's OK.'

'There aren't many male witches,' he says. Is it a fact, or just an observation?

'Why's that?' I ask, chewing my toast.

He shrugs. 'Don't know. Just not enough interested in it, maybe. See it as work for the women. Don't want to be some warty crone chanting spells over a cauldron. Other tougher work out there if you want it. Stigma attached to it, I s'pose.' He says all this with nails between his teeth. 'Mind you, you're used to being the odd one out, I suppose. You and Biba.' He's talking about us being non-Greenworld-standard-issue-white.

'I guess. It's different here. At least at home everyone was used to us. Here it's like you can hear they're thinking, Ooooh, look at that boy. He's not the right colour.'

'Tell me about it,' he grunts.

'Yeah, but you don't live here. You come and go. It's different for you,' I say.

'You'd think so. The Greenworld forgets what a closed community it actually is. Very different in the Redworld – that's one good thing about it, at least. You and me – we're nothing remarkable there. But you're a witch's kids. That gives you some protection, doesn't it?'

'Most of the time.' I watch his practised hands placing the tiles expertly, one after the other, and think how we're veering off the subject. 'But what about you?' I blurt out. 'You built the gate. Are you a witch? Were you one of the Hands?'

Omar doesn't miss a beat and keeps pounding those nails into the roof. 'I was here when it started, the Greenworld. Your mum was here, and Lowenna, Tressa, Linda – your friend Sadie's mum? Yeah, and Roach. We were all here. We were the Six then. Times were hard, man. We had to protect the town. We were interested in the old times, old religions. Your mum and me were together, had been since we were kids. School sweethearts, that's what it was. Always loved her. Always her, no one else. She lit up every room she went into. Still does.'

He stops hammering and sits back on his heels, hunkered down on the roof. He takes my tea from me and drains what's left without asking.

237

'So why did you join the gangs?' I ask. Why wouldn't it be enough to be one of the Hands? And when I first remember Omar he was in the gangs already, had been for a long time. He was full of their bravado and swearing; he was an outsider.

'Partly tactical, partly personal. When Radley became Roach and left the Hands we got worried he'd take our secrets and give them to the wrong people, so I went to stay close to him, try to talk him back. But he was my friend too, you know. We were tight for a long time.' He smiles wistfully. 'We used to double-date – me and Radley, and Zee and Linda. Go walking on the cliffs, bonfires on the beach . . .'

I still find it weird that Roach and Linda used to go out.

'Once I entered the gang, though, it was hard to be in two headspaces. I couldn't spy for one side, either side. And after a while I was away too long. Your dad came along and Zia gave up on me. I hadn't managed to stop the gangs. I hadn't managed to bring Roach back. She was disappointed in me, I guess. She moved on, and I stayed as an outsider.' He looks off into the distance.

There are a few minutes of silence, but I don't want to stop talking to Omar. There's so much more I want to know.

'Do you and Mum . . . I mean, are you still . . .?' I don't know how to say it.

He smiles at me. 'Course I do, Dan. I love her more than anything, you know?'

'Does that mean you're together?'

I wouldn't mind if they were. I mean, he's not my dad, but he's the only one of Mum's boyfriends that I ever cared about, and who cared about me and Beebs.

He shrugs. 'Kinda. It's complicated. But I'm always there if she needs me,' he says. They're both staying in the same room at Lowenna's, though. The same saggy double bed. Work it out for yourself, Dan, I think. But I know he's not welcome back home, in the village. So this is some kind of temporary arrangement, maybe. Adults. They're such hypocrites – telling us not to sleep around, be peaceful, cooperate in the community – and all the time they're banging each other like the last days of Rome and waging wars on each other.

War. I wonder if I should mention the conversation with Lowenna yesterday to Omar, about her basically refusing to believe that a battle could take place here, although I don't know why that battle might occur, but he interrupts my thoughts.

'Enough of all that, Dan. How's your love life, then? Got your eye on someone, have you?'

He nudges me and I almost fall off the roof, so I gingerly move away from the edge.

'Yeah,' I sigh. I push war and battle and vision aside in my head and concentrate on Saba. The nicer alternative. I may as well spill my guts – that's what I came up here for anyway.

'Thought so,' he grunts. 'Who is it? Saba?'

Oh Goddess, is it that obvious?

'Er . . . yeah,' I manage to get out. 'Does everyone know?'

'Don't know. You are living with some very psychic people, you know, Dan. Plus they're women. Nothing's a secret, man.' He chuckles. 'Well, she's nice. Very pretty. You're about the same age, so what's the problem?'

'She's got a boyfriend.'

He shrugs. 'Not for much longer, though, if she likes you? Has something happened?'

I nod. 'Yeah. Yesterday, in fact. The boyfriend's not going to be too happy about it.' I pick at the edge of a roof tile gloomily. Not looking forward to that confrontation.

He laughs. 'I doubt he will be. Do you love her?'

I shrug. 'I think so, maybe. Yeah. I mean, I haven't been in love before, so I don't know what it's like, but I want to see her all the time. I don't get bored of her. And . . . like, it's weird, but yeah, she's gorgeous and beautiful, and I do want to sleep with her, but it's not just that. Like, I've learned loads from her already. Like, she's my friend too, you know? I just like being with her.'

Omar claps me on the back and almost pushes me off the ledge I'm clinging on to. He's smiling and looking wistful, if that's possible for a man of his bulk.

'Ah, well, Danny. That sounds like true love to me. No man's a match for that. You better love her, boy;

you better really want her, cos loving a witch's a roller-coaster ride.' He shakes his head. This is the end of the conversation suddenly. 'Come on – let's go down now. I could eat a horse.' He takes himself down the ladder with surprising speed and I try to follow at the same pace.

At the bottom, I put my hand on his massive bicep. 'Don't tell anyone about me and Saba, though, will you? Not yet,' I ask.

He smiles. 'I am the keeper of many secrets, Dan. Don't you worry.'

Later, I'm up in my room taking some alone time with Gowdie – I've done my chores for the day and feel like I need some time to piece things together. Life's been pretty fast recently. I'm curled up in bed with Gowdie sitting on top of the blankets thumping her tail happily on me.

I raise my forearm to the light and look at the script curling round it. What does it mean? What if it means I'm evil? The mark of a kind of brotherhood with Roach?

'What do you think, Gowdie?' I ask the dog, but she just nuzzles my arm. If she knows, she's not telling.

While I'm mulling it all over I look out into the garden below. Saba is sitting cross-legged on the grass in the fading evening, reading. As I watch, Mum appears in the garden. I have to remember that they know each other; they've met before at the covenstead meetings. Saba looks up and smiles, and beckons to Mum. Shows her what she's reading. They sit down and start chatting away like old friends.

I go back to reading my arm. It's cool having a tattoo – oh, excuse me, a witch-brand – not least cos it a) didn't hurt and b) was supernaturally achieved. When I've been wearing short sleeves or just roll up my sleeves when I'm walking around it gets people's attention. I like that.

About half an hour later I'm deep into *The Common Herbal* when there's a knock on my door and Mum peeks in. 'Hi, Dan. Can I come in?'

I sit up. 'Course.'

'I'm heading home soon. Just wanted to say goodbye.'

I get up and give her a hug. 'You're doing so well, my lover,' she says into my hair.

'Thanks, Mum.'

She tickles Gowdie's head. 'How's the witch dog?' she asks and strokes her brown fur.

'OK. Seems to like it all right here.'

'Even with the cats?' she smiles.

Gowdie ruffs. She doesn't even like the word 'cat'.

'Yeah, I think so.'

Mum looks me over. 'Look at you. You've changed already. The power is increasing. I can see it.'

I shrug and she sits down on my bed and looks at me meaningfully. 'You know, I'm glad that you've chosen to be a witch. I'm glad that you're learning new skills. But don't think that just because you've learned a few magic tricks that you've suddenly grown up overnight. Being a witch isn't all magic spells and potions and energy spheres – it's about being able to function in the normal world too – to work, have relationships, make your place in the world. To understand yourself. Believe me, that takes a long time.' She sighs, and traces her fingers on the blankets. 'Mind you, I'm surprised that you didn't pick up on what Sadie's been up to, seeing as you saw her and Linda in your vision.'

'What has she been up to?' I realize I haven't thought much about Sadie since I've been here. Saba has eclipsed her.

'Sadie's been bothering me for witch secrets. To tell her things, train her. She won't leave me alone. Every time I look up she's there, it seems, knocking at the door. I don't know if Linda knows about it. I thought you'd want to know, as she was your girlfriend.'

'She wasn't my girlfriend.'

'Oh. It started after you gave her the cards, I think. After Linda burned them. The witch blood is in that girl; you can see it. She might have her father's abilities.'

'She might do. I don't really care.'

She looks surprised. 'I'm sorry, love. I thought you were a bit of an item.'

'Well, we're not. Especially not now,' I say, almost saying too much. And then I think, Saba. They were talking just now.

'Did you just tell Saba about this?'

'I mentioned it.'

'Why?'

'We were talking about the meeting last night, and your vision of Linda. And I was saying that it's strange that Sadie has been pestering me to train her. I was wondering, now that I know that Roach is involved with them somehow, whether Linda had sent her, or whether she was genuine.'

'Did you tell her Sadie was my girlfriend?'

She looks confused. 'Was there any reason I shouldn't?'

I get up and punch the door frame in frustration. I can't tell her the reason. 'Whatever, Mum, OK?' I mutter.

I can tell Saba will have taken this the wrong way, cos I've never mentioned Sadie to her. No need to – nothing to do with me and her, and Sadie and me were never official. We just hooked up sometimes. But Saba might not see it like that.

Mum gets up and catches me by the shoulder. 'Hey. Hey!' She reaches out to hug me, but I push past her as she stands in the doorway, not stopping to explain.

I look around downstairs but Saba is long gone. My guts feel like a molten ball of worms. I'm nervous about how she's going to see this. I don't want to go back into the house. I decide to walk out to the Witch's Gate; I have a sudden strong feeling that Saba is there.

I follow the familiar path through the village. The houses thin out close to the boundary, and I turn the last corner and there it is ahead of me, glinting in the early evening. Saba is sitting at the base of one side of the gate, looking out into the scrubland and at the horizon. I put my musings to one side as I approach her, and I am unbelievably glad to see her smile as she sees me – not a grin, not a huge where-have-you-been-all-my-life beam – a sad little half-smile, but a smile nonetheless. I sit down beside her and follow her gaze to the horizon.

'I wish we could leave whenever we wanted, no magic needed,' she says wistfully after a while.

'Yeah, me too.'

'I get so tired of having to be so careful all the time. Not being able to go anywhere. Staying clear of the gangs. Do you ever wonder if they're really that bad? I mean, Bali and Skye are all right,' she says, looking at me.

'I dunno. Remember Kevin?' I look down at my hands – no more bandages, but the scars are still there.

'Yeah. I s'pose they are that bad.'

'Sorry about Mum,' I say, by way of starting an apology.

She looks at me sharply. 'I can't see that anything was your mum's fault,' she cuts back quickly. 'Did she forget to tell the girl she was romancing that she already had a girlfriend? No.'

'She's not my girlfriend. We just went to school together.'

'So you never slept together?'

'No, I mean, yeah, we did a few times.'

She looks nonplussed. 'If you've slept together, isn't she your girlfriend?'

'Well . . . no, not really. We were friends, kind of, but we fooled around. You know, for something to do.'

'No, I don't know! I'm never short of anything to do!' she says sarcastically.

This isn't going well, and I'm starting to get angry with her, mostly cos I feel like she's making me out to be a criminal and I don't think I've actually done anything that wrong.

'I'm allowed to have had girlfriends, or whatever, before I met you. Stop making me out to be some kind of villain. You haven't broken up with Tom yet anyway. When's that going to happen?'

She doesn't say anything.

'Saba?'

'It's complicated,' she mutters, looking off at the horizon.

'How is it complicated? You were with him, now you're with me. Simple.'

'I'm not necessarily with you just because we had one night together.'

My heart sinks. 'Oh. Well, are we or aren't we?'

'Tom and I have been together a long time, Danny. I can't break his heart.'

I look at her but she refuses to make eye contact. 'Saba. Saba, look at me.'

Reluctantly she turns her head to me. 'You don't understand. There's a lot of pressure on me to be with

Tom. Everyone loves him. We've known each other forever. Mum, Melz . . . they'd be so upset if—'

I cut her off. 'I don't care what your mum and Melz think. It's you and Tom or you and me. It's that simple.'

'It's not that simple at all.'

'Why? Why isn't it?' I stand up and start pacing around. Need to get rid of the mounting tension somehow. I thought this would all be plain sailing – we like each other, we become a couple. Maybe I was being naive. Suddenly it's 'not that simple' and I don't get it.

'I might not be in love with him, but I love Tom. I care about him. It's not his fault I don't want to be with him in that way any more.'

'That's fine, Sab. I understand that. Let him down gently. But it's not fair to keep seeing him and me. It's not fair on either of us.'

She draws with her fingertip in the earth – a star, traces it over and over.

She looks up at me. 'I know. But he's supposed to be sent to another village soon to train the gardeners there, some new method of growing or something. He'll be gone for ages. It would be so much easier if we just waited for him to go, and then told him when he got back.' She smiles that killer smile, a twinkle in those almond eyes.

I sigh and sit down beside her. 'Can't you just tell him now? Be upfront about it?'

247

'I don't want to do it that way, Danny. Please don't make me.'

'I'd rather you told him outright. It doesn't seem as honest your way.'

She takes my hand in hers and traces the same star on the back of my hand. As ever, her touch increases my brain static. She must know what effect she has on me.

'I know. But this way seems the kindest. This way, we'll be apart anyway, and when he gets back, things will just have moved on naturally. I don't want to break his heart. It will be easier for him this way.'

And for you, I think, but not for me.

I gaze at my feet. I want her so much; what if I push her on this, what will she do, will she leave me? I suppose this way avoids a confrontation.

I find myself squeezing her hand. 'OK, Saba. Do what you think's best,' I say, and am rewarded with a kiss that blots out the moon and the stars. Everything goes black for a while.

Chapter Sixteen

Respect Nature, for She has no respect for you.

From *Tenets and Sayings of the Greenworld*

Because of my vision and Lowenna's dream, we are preparing for the eclipse. Preparing for Roach to make his move. On the portal, on me, on the whole village – any of these are possible, even if it's only me that really believes that.

An eclipse is an important time in magic, cos it's the time when portals are vulnerable. In the time of an eclipse, lunar and solar, portals are open, and it's possible for less trained or skilful people to be able to enter them – either on purpose or, more likely, by accident. Hence an eclipse is a time when the portal has to be protected more than usual. Roach knows this. In the month that's passed since Yule, that's most of what we've been doing. Preparing.

Lowenna's acknowledged that Roach might threaten the portal at the eclipse, but as I feared, she's basically ignored the shared visions we had about a battle, as real and bloody as they were, and that's making me feel anxious. The day after the Yule dinner, after Saba and I had our magical trip to the cave, I expected her to do something. Convene a meeting, talk to the Hands, talk to Omar. Anything. But she didn't. When I asked her about it, she said she'd thought about it some more and our visions were probably the result of general worry about Roach following me here, about him grabbing Kevin that time at the boundary. That my vision was a result of that and me witnessing the sea ritual, of thinking about the village's need for protection.

Basically, a big denial. She can't believe the battle will happen, but I'm becoming more and more convinced it will. But what do I know, right? I'm the trainee. She's the head witch.

Psychic preparation for the eclipse and worrying about the battle-visions isn't all I've been doing. Saba and I have been doing a fair bit of sneaking around, seeing each other when we can, but I'm feeling less and less comfortable with it as time goes on, and, worse, Tom is showing no signs of leaving.

I'm in the kitchen making tea with Saba and having a muttered conversation so no one hears. We're having this conversation a lot lately.

'Want to go to the cave later?' She smiles at me under her lashes, and don't get me wrong, that smile still does things to me, things I can't control, but I'm starting to resent being kept on the hook, or so it feels. Not even starting to resent it, really. Just straight out resenting it.

I avoid her look and pour the hot water from the cast-iron kettle into some mugs. 'Yeah, maybe,' I say.

'Don't you want to?'

I do want to. There have been a few cave visits now and things haven't progressed further than stroking and sighing, and I'd be cool with that apart from it's because she doesn't want to go all the way while Tom's still around. But I shrug, and duck outside the back door to get the milk – makes sense to keep it outside when it's this cold.

'What does that mean?' she asks, mimicking my shrug.

I slosh some milk into the mugs. 'Any more news on Tom leaving?' I ask pointedly.

She drops her eyes and looks shifty, which is what she always does when I bring up the subject. More and more, I'm seeing that Saba has Lowenna's gift for self-deception. Neither of them wants to face difficult things.

'I told you. It's been put back a few weeks, he said.'

Yeah. And he told her that last night when they hung out. At his house, just the two of them.

'Sab. I can't do this much longer. I can't spend one night with you and know he's seeing you the next. It's too hard.'

Her eyes flash at me. 'I've told you. I don't want to break his heart. It's just a few weeks longer, Danny, then we can be together. Properly.' Her hand reaches out for mine on the stone kitchen worktop. 'Danny. Please.'

Oh for being together properly. But there's also a part of me that wonders is it more than not wanting to hurt Tom? Is it also that I'm too different to be with openly? Not normal enough? Not white enough to walk around the village with, hand in hand, without attracting the wrong kind of attention?

I pull my hand away and am about to say, 'No, Sab, this isn't OK any more,' when Melz comes in. She looks less scary first thing in the morning when she hasn't put her make-up on yet. Softer, more smudgy round the edges.

'Mmmph,' she grunts, and her sister turns on a smile.

'Hey, Melz. Get out of bed on the wrong side?' Saba twinkles. It's as if our conversation never happened – she's all brightness, no anguish.

I look back at Saba, who smiles innocently at me. She's off the hook and doesn't have to answer any more difficult questions for now.

I turn away and walk out. I don't want to forgive or let it go. But I still want her, what little of her I do have. I head out to get Merryn and Beryan to start the long day's work of eclipse preparation with us. Their house is a few streets away, and I see the early-morning business of the village as I often do when sneaking back with Saba from a night in the cave. Today, though, I feel like I'm allowed to linger – I've got nothing to hide.

There's a bakery stall at the end of Lowenna's street – the far end of a food market that does a brisk trade every morning. Bread, fish, fruit and veg. Cakes, honey, cheese. Good things. I stop and breathe in the fresh-baked bread smell, warm in the sharp morning air.

'One of my favourite smells,' says a girl's voice, and I look across the brown crusty loaves cooling in the Cornish winter air and see Bryony's blue eyes and generous mouth.

I smile. 'Mine too. Haven't had breakfast yet.'

She comes round from the back of the stall and hands me a warm brown bread roll. 'Here. Have one on me. Can't have you starving, can we?'

'Thanks. Do you work here, or do we need to get ready to make a break for it?' I bite into the roll – it's delicious.

'It's my dad's stall. I help on weekends. In the bakery or here.'

'It's great, thank you.'

She smiles her sweet smile. 'S'OK. Where were you off to? Or were you just cruising the stalls? Waiting for someone to take pity on you?'

I laugh. It's the first actual conversation we've had that isn't awkward or drunk.

'No. I'm going to Merryn and Beryan. Witch business.' I make a face and she laughs too.

'Nothing serious, I hope?'

'Oh well. You know, the balance of life and death. Omens. Times and tides. Forces beyond our control. The usual.'

She nods, grinning. 'Oh, that. I haven't got time for such trifles. I've got bread to sell, you know!'

'You do trifles as well?'

She bats me on the arm. 'Cheeky. Go and save the world, witch. No sweets for you here.'

Before I know what I'm doing, I catch her hand. 'You sure about that?' I ask quietly and look down into her big blue eyes.

They widen in surprise. 'I . . . I thought . . .' she stutters.

You thought I wasn't interested, I think, and I wasn't. But I'm sick of being kept on the hook, and I know you like me.

'Listen. I'm busy right now, but do you want to hang out later? Meet at the old farmhouse?' I ask, just like that.

She looks at me as if she can't quite believe what I'm saying, but she nods quickly. 'Yes, sure. OK. OK, I'll be there.'

I give her hand a squeeze. 'Cool. Say eight?'

She nods again, and I walk off, biting a chunk out of the still-warm bread roll. It tastes good. Satisfying and straightforward. Wholesome. Whistling, I head on to Merryn and Beryan's house.

*

Later, when we're all together in the glass kitchen, Lowenna clears her throat. 'As you know, everyone, today there is a lunar eclipse and that means that the portal will be vulnerable. I believe that Roach is going to try to enter it. So we all need to keep vigil. Are you all ready?'

We exchange glances. 'Ready as we'll ever be,' Merryn says.

I can tell she's a bit scared. I think we all are.

First, we raise the psychic defences around Tintagel Head, something we can do from home. We chant and burn special protective herbs and resins. This is the kind of work that all those visualization exercises were edging towards, because as soon as we close our eyes I can see a golden bubble forming around the whole massive rock island as clear as day. I imagine that it's an impenetrable glass bubble, keeping good energy in and keeping negative energy out. We imagine the rock as a fortress; I imagine a medieval castle, complete with turrets, archers with their bows ready at the slit windows and buckets of boiling oil at the ready to pour on invaders. I've seen a picture of it in a book.

I open my eyes to see Lowenna nodding at me approvingly. 'Very good, Danny,' she says, and I feel a flare of pride in my belly.

The chanting goes on for a few hours. I'm glad I'm doing a lot of yoga because you have to be strong to do this kind of work, and keep focus.

For the portal itself, we have to actually go to

Tintagel Head, and I suddenly remember my date with Bryony. Hell. I'd forgotten all about it. Can I get away and meet her quickly and get back without anyone noticing? It'll be tough. I consider just not going, standing her up, but I don't want to do that. It's too late to catch her at the stall. I look at the clock; an hour until we leave for Tintagel Head. The farmhouse is a good twenty-minute walk. I can do it, as long as no one guesses. And, for once, especially not Saba.

I think on my feet and let out a theatrical yawn. 'Wow. Tough day. Think I might go and centre myself before we head off. You know, prime the energy.'

Lowenna looks up from the table where she's preparing incense with a heavy stone mortar and pestle. She clicks her fingers at me. 'Good idea. Get some downtime. Go and focus. All of you, in fact. I'll call you when it's time to go.' And so we all head off to our rooms. Brilliant. This actually makes it easier.

Saba smiles and brushes my fingers as we head up the stairs. 'Want me to come and help you focus?' she whispers.

I smile – no point in letting her know there's anything going on, not yet – and yawn again for her benefit. 'I'm actually pretty tired. See you in a bit,' I say, feigning sleepy eyes, and go into my room.

She looks a bit surprised. I've never said no before.

Inside my room, I wait for all the doors to close, pull on a couple of jumpers to keep the Cornish evening out of my bones, crack the window open as quietly as I can and climb out and down the trellis that runs conveniently under my window to the ground. On the street, I check no one's seen me and then head off, running down the country lanes to the border of the village. There's already a freezing mist coming in off the sea and my lungs start to ache as I run and gulp it into my chest. The farmhouse appears in front of me and I edge my way through the door in the wall and into the garden. She's there already, hugging her arms round her, her breath making clouds in the creepy shadows cast by the bare trees.

I walk up behind her and wrap my arms round hers. 'Hey,' I murmur into her ear.

She jumps and turns to me. Her wide blue eyes are lovely, but I find myself comparing them to Saba's amber gaze. With an effort, I push Saba out of my mind. She's not here, and Bryony is.

'Oh, hi . . . Cold tonight,' she says, making conversation. 'Why don't we go inside? Make a fire or something? The old kitchen still has a fireplace. We could—'

'Sure,' I break in, 'but I can't stay long. I'm really sorry. After I saw you this morning something's happened and I have to get back. We're going to Tintagel Head tonight. It's a whole big witch thing.'

'Oh.' She looks at the frozen muddy ground. I put my finger under her chin and tilt her head up.

'It really is something important. Out of the blue. I didn't want to stand you up, I wanted to come and tell you, but I have to get back. Honestly.'

Her eyes search my face for a lie, but she doesn't see one. 'OK. Well, it can't be helped, I guess.'

'No. But do you want to get together tomorrow night?' I stroke her cheek. 'I'd really like to make it up to you.'

Her smile widens. 'Sure. OK. Yes, yeah, that would be nice.'

Shyly she takes my hands and puts them round her waist and reaches up to kiss me. She's shorter than Saba, but her mouth is luscious and hot, and she might seem like a shy girl but bloody hell she doesn't kiss like one. We're both encased in layers of wool, but as the kiss deepens I pull off my gloves and reach under her cloak and dress and make contact with her warm, soft skin. I'm horny as hell – weeks and weeks of kissing and touching but nothing more with Saba, with the ever-present spectre of Tom hanging over proceedings have taken their toll. I pull Bryony towards the farmhouse.

'What are you doing? I didn't think you had time?' she murmurs, but follows readily enough.

'I'll make time. I'm a witch,' I say over my shoulder.

The world can bloody stand still for a moment. I want her and she wants me. We fall, giggling and breathless with cold and desire on to the stone-flagged floor of the dim room, and every second lasts longer than it should.

*

258

Later, we Hands make our way stealthily to Tintagel Head. It's dark, and our grey cloaks meld into the winter heathers; our heads are down, battling the icy winds rolling in off the sea. I'm chilled to the bone, cos unlike the rest of them I haven't been tucked up in bed, meditating like a good boy, but I keep that to myself along with the very recent memory of Bryony's moans and her hot, sweet mouth.

When we get to the cliffs my breath is ripped out of me by its salty gusts. The sea is grey-green, tipped in white foam and it pounds on to the spiky, wet Cornish rock as if in a rage; the noise pounds in my ears. It's not for the faint-hearted, this place in winter. We stand in our wool cloaks at the jagged tops of the cliffs and feel like we're at the edge of the world; that we are the only ones alive.

We cross the thin rock walkway to heart-shaped Tintagel Head holding hands in a shaky line; it's treacherous underfoot, wet and slippery. One step wrong and you'd fall to your death. Melz is ahead of me and Saba behind. I grip Saba's hand firmly, and feel her warm hand beneath her woollen mittens grasp my fingers. She squeezes my fingers and I squeeze hers back, feeling guilt mixed with an illicit excitement.

I look at my fellow adventurers. Lowenna's in her no-nonsense don't-mess-with-me mode. Her hair's as mad as ever and looks like a ring of yellow fire around her head. Melz seems to have dressed up for the occasion and maxed out on black; as well as looking like the Bride

259

of Dracula she's wearing a huge cat's-eye stone on a long heavy chain. Egyptian-style eyes, cowboy boots. She sees me looking at her and scowls. We're all in black under our cloaks – it's a psychically protective colour. Plus it looks cool. Saba's hair is pinned away from her face in a tight bun – she's also got the Egyptian-style make-up on – maybe Melz did it for her. They have few things in common – and usually look so different – but tonight I see the resemblance between them. The power in them both. Saba, the sea siren; Melz, the dark priestess.

On top of the rock we form a circle of protection around the portal. We can't use candles up here as they'd blow out in the wind, so we've brought storm lamps – heavy glass cylinders with candles inside that we weigh down with rocks. We place five of them round the circle. Beryan has brought some purple beetroot dye and she marks out the circle with it, and Saba paints symbols round the circle – air, fire, earth and water. And most important, she draws all the protection symbols we know.

We draw the power of the moon into us with the words of our ritual, to make us powerful enough to hold the space all night. I can feel myself fill up as if with water; I can feel the power of the moon sloshing through me, and then flowing in and out of me as if I were a battery. The energy is buzzing – I'm sweating with it, even though it's so cold here on the rock.

And cos of the eclipse, the portal is already open.

It's just what it does, as responsive to the natural rhythms of the world as a daisy opening its face to the sun, and just as unstoppable. We watch its orangey-gold light swirl faster and faster. I steady my breath like I've been practising – a whole night next to an open portal will be hard on the lungs. I feel its deep thumping beat through my whole body and concentrate on aligning my breathing with it, not fighting against it. The other Hands say it makes you a bit light-headed but it's better than passing out if you resist it.

I put my thoughts of Bryony and Saba aside. That's for later: this is our work for now.

Chapter Seventeen

A quilt is a web of time, a document of the Greenworld, stitching life to life, season to season, memory to eternity.

From *Tenets and Sayings of the Greenworld*

It's a long, boring night – minute upon minute piling themselves in layers of dead time like old leaves, as I meditate and breathe, synced with the portal. Each minute starts as a minute in which something could happen and ends with the life sucked out of it: limp and consigned to history. My mind starts to stray to Bryony, but I get rid of that thought pretty quick. There's something in a communal meditation, different to doing it yourself: more charged, more powerful, and if someone else thinks about something you can pick it up – you can get a flash of whatever thought has entered their minds. It's not anything I want anyone here to know.

I'm getting tired, and what I really, really want to do is to relax the backs of my eyes and sleep with my eyes open. Perhaps I could just have a five-minute power nap. No one would have to know.

After a while I realize that I can see a light criss-crossing around me in the night air – very regular, like snowflakes. The more I look at it the more I see – liquid sugar made into hard candy, all perfect angles, squares, triangles, merging into each other. I start to see that the patterns, meshes really, are moving and merging together; I am hypnotized by the movement and the perfection, the extreme perfection, of these patterns.

I've been staring at the patterns for a while, I don't know how long, when I realize that there are elements of colour bleeding through them. Shadowy shapes like mist, just a couple of shades darker than white, so that they're almost not noticeable, but slowly that changes and the shapes draw in. I start to see green shapes and the scene around me starts to recede, melting like ice on a spring day. And after some more time it feels as though I'm not sitting on the hard ground of Tintagel Head at all, but somewhere with more knots and irregularities, and I touch the surface with my fingers. It's a log. There's something else – a smell. Rain on pine trees and a fresh breeze. I look up and realize I can see the moon in a sky edged with waving leaves and branches. The picture slots into place as my eyes come back down to head height and I meet Roach's eyes across from mine.

Somehow he's drawn me here, into some kind of communal hallucination or vision. I remember Lowenna saying I had a talent for making telepathic links to people. But I didn't initiate this one.

I immediately try to focus back on Tintagel Head to take myself back there into that safe, sacred space, but somehow the picture doesn't form in my head.

'No use trying, Danny: you won't be able to go back there for a while,' Roach says, eyes twinkling.

'What have you done? What do you want?' I demand.

I try to stand up and rush him but as soon as I do ropes bite into my wrists and ankles.

'Not so fast, witch boy,' he says. 'Do you think I would let you go so easily? Having worked so hard to get you here? You're the guest of honour, Danny. Relax!'

He stands up, stretching, and groans, snapping his neck. 'Really takes it out of you, all that bloody meditating, doesn't it, boy? Hours of it. Knackering.'

He walks over to me and behind my back. I jump as he lays a hand on my shoulder. I try to move my wrists but they're tied tight, no movement at all.

'You may as well stop trying, Dan. You're tied up nice and tight. Just accept it.'

'What do you want with me?' I repeat.

He reappears in front of me and now he's holding something down by his leg – concealed in cloth, and I don't like the look of it.

He doesn't reply, but raises the arm he's been keeping by his side.

In his hand there's a long glittering knife with a black ornate handle, like it's been carved. The same knife he held against Kevin's throat, the same knife I saw in my dream, cutting into my arm. He brings it closer to me, in front of my face. I see when it gets closer that the carving on the handle is a cockroach. The blade has some kind of text on it too, but I can't read it; it has symbols on it as well, but none I've ever seen before, which worries me.

'Oh, you're admiring my athame,' he says, smiling at what must be shock on my face. A witch's knife, like mine.

'What about it? I've got one. We've all got one,' I say. I don't add, 'But I don't usually threaten people with mine.' He's got a duplicitous-looking smile, slanty, and I can see Sadie's smile within it.

The athame is right under my nose. Swiftly and without warning he slashes it on my arm. I jump and try to pull my arm away but the rope is holding me fast. I can't actually feel anything, and Roach chuckles and reaches down. I fully expect to see a gash running down my arm, to see blood dripping down on to the rope that binds my hands, like the nightmare that keeps lurking at the back of my mind, but he's only cut the material of my sleeve away, not touched my skin, which says something about the sharpness of the knife.

He rolls my sleeve up and bends down to look at the

writing tattooed on my arm. 'So you really have it,' he says, looking at my witch-brand.

'Yeah.'

He rolls up the sleeve of his khaki shirt and holds his forearm in front of my face. 'The same as mine. But you know that already, don't you?'

'I'm not going to do what you want, whatever it is. You know that,' I say, braving it out.

He looks at me keenly. 'I know that those bitches are lying to you. I know that they haven't told you the truth about me. That's what I know.'

'Why do I need to know the truth about you? I know enough. You were one of them. You chose to leave. You chose evil.'

He bursts out laughing. The sound of it makes me realize that the forest seems unnaturally quiet. Like, there haven't been any animal or bird noises since I've been here, or any sounds like leaves falling from trees: just the wind in the leaves.

'Evil! Bloody hell, that's a bit overdramatic, isn't it? Is that what they're calling me?' He snorts. 'Evil. Goddess, nothing that exciting, Dan. I'll tell you what I chose. I chose to disagree.'

'Disagree with what?'

'A lot of things, but most of all, the ownership of the portals. The new covensteads, they rediscovered the portals, those pathways between life and death, and decided that wherever possible, portals should be owned by the witches – decided they always had been, in fact. In practice, that's just two in Devon and Cornwall. You know about those.'

He runs the tip of his athame down my arm and I try not to wince in anticipation.

'And, of course, most of your average townspeople don't know what a portal is or what it does. They've accepted witchcraft down here because it seems to work. They don't care about the details, and the ones that care enough become witches. So I thought, why do Lowenna and Zia and the sisterhood have to be in charge of those portals? Were they elected? Cos I didn't vote for them, man. Did you? No. You didn't. And that's the thing that really gets to me.'

He's pacing around where I'm sitting now like a dog in search of a hidden bone. He wants something from me, and I guess he's going to take his own sweet time letting me know.

As he mentions the Hands my entire self jumps, and there's a kind of shimmer at the corner of my eye. For a moment I think I see Melz's Egyptian kohl-blacked eyes looking at me, and then they're gone.

As Roach paces, I notice that I can't hear his feet on the ground. He's walking silently on what looks like an earth covered in pine needles and twigs – definitely something that should make a sound when you walk on it – but it's soundless, as if he's wearing slippers on a smooth wood floor. This is an incredibly complex vision-place he's created, and he's brought me into it. This is not good; it must mean he's way more powerful than me, and if that's the case, how the hell am I going to get out of this? Am I here really? Where is my body? Is it back at Tintagel Head? Is it here? Where is here? Are we inside the portal?

I try mentally connecting with Melz, with any of them. Nothing happens for a minute, and then very faintly, I see a hazy figure dressed in black appear and then fade out again over by the trees. While I'm doing this, Roach is still rattling on.

'So let me enlighten you about what happened when I left the covenstead, or was pushed out, which is more like the truth. I was the chosen one, Dan, just like you. I had this . . .' He runs his fingers over the brand – the same as mine but older, a little faded. I look away. 'And they didn't know then what it was for – why it was words, not symbols. And they still don't know. It marks us out as different, Dan. It means we've got a separate destiny.'

'What, then? What's so different about it? It's still a witch-brand. Lowenna, Mum – they've got them too.'

'Yeah. But this means something else. I think it marks us out as leaders. Gods, even. Do those bitches have this kind of instruction written on them? This call to war?'

He reads the first three lines of the brand aloud.

'I am the spear, the slingshot, the smith,
The poet, the warrior, the magician, the gift;
The trunk of the tree, the arrow of war.'

'That isn't necessarily a call to war,' I say. That's

never occurred to me. 'I mean, there's poetry and magic in there too.'

'Well, I think it is. I think it's a war. God against Goddess. Us men against them. Don't you think it's too one-sided? The goddess sorority, the sisterhood? No time for the God, my god. Yours. Lugh, God of light and magic and war. I've found brotherhood in the gangs, out here with the survivors, Danny. You could too.'

He's standing a few metres away from me now, looking away from me and into the forest. I think I can hear him muttering something, but I can't make it out. Maybe he's reciting some mantra, some spell, to keep me there. So I call over to him, hoping to distract him from what he's doing. But as he turns round, a wall builds itself out of nowhere around us, brick by brick, higher and higher, so that in a matter of seconds it seems to reach to the tops of the trees.

'As you can see, I've hidden us just a little further from prying eyes. Just until we're finished, you understand. They're nosy. They're going to be trying to crash our little party, and I want it to stay just you and me for a while longer, Danny. Just a while longer.'

He smiles and raises his hands, palms open and facing the wall on either side of us. In a flash, the bricks turn into what looks like a black-crystal wall. In terms of a psychic defence it looks like it's going to be hard to crack.

'And now, Danny, I'll cut to the chase. We are

269

destined to go to war with the Goddess, that's true. We have a sign from Lugh. I think it means he's supposed to be in control, not Brighid. Not the Goddess. Us. But that's only half of it. Because when we win the battle for control of the villages, when the God wins and overturns their stupid basket-weaving, herb-loving goddess community, I'll take the portals. I want control of both of them – Tintagel and Gidleigh.'

'But what do you want with the portals? No one can really own them. They're just there.'

'But the witches think they own them. They think they're protecting them, keeping them pure, blah blah blah. But really, they're not maximizing the potential of these things. Typical Greenworld, they're living in the past. Want everything to be simple and organic and mud poultices and charms to cure the pox.'

It's the kind of thing I've said myself about the Greenworld, but it's one thing for me to think it. I live here. He's an outsider.

'You know what I'm talking about. Look, I know you know that a portal is the way to the next world – where we go when we die, but I don't know if you realize its potential as a practical, usable energy source. And I've got a way to realize that potential, Danny, but I need you to help me. I need your power as well as mine to make it possible. And when we've done that, we can change the world. No more starving, corrupt Redworld because everyone will have all the fuel and power they need. We won't need a separate Greenworld. There won't be a war. But if you say no, I can't have you using your power to try to stop me. So either you join me or I kill you right here and now. It's your choice.'

He's standing in front of me again and brings his athame blade to my throat again, digging it in hard, but not quite hard enough to break the skin.

I gulp and try to steady my breath. 'I don't believe you. If it was possible to stop the war it would have been done already.' I can't believe for a second that deep down, Roach might have a point – or, worse – care about humanity's survival. 'You can't hurt me if we're in a vision. You can do what you like,' I say, braving it out.

He just laughs. 'Oh, Danny! Haven't they told you? Don't you know what will happen if I cut your throat here? In this little scene, this collection of dream matter I've shaped to my own will? Do you think it won't hurt? It will, you know.' He leans in and peers into my eyes. 'I know you know. You dreamed it, didn't you?'

My eyes dart to my arm involuntarily, remembering the shock of seeing the blood dripping from the cuts in my dream. 'I don't believe you. You can't do that.'

He shrugs. 'If that's what you think, Danny, try it. See what happens. This is a magic knife, after all. Do you think it's possible that your old witch mother and all of them – don't you think perhaps there's things they still haven't told you? Do you think you know everything there is to know?'

My mind recalls Mum at Lowenna's telling me

about being a witch – that it takes years, a lifetime really. That it's not all spells and potions.

'We've been chosen, Danny, by the God. By Lugh. We're powerful. We've been chosen to take control. Of the portals, of everything! That's what the brand means!'

Roach grabs my arm and twists it hard. I gasp as real pain floods through my arm up to my shoulder. The pain makes me think twice about what he's saying about being able to hurt me.

'Do you really believe that?' I gasp, and he lets go.

'I know it. For years now I've known. It came to me in dreams, a little here and a little there, over the years. That there was a secret to unlocking the portals, and I was the key because of my brand. That they could be something more than the pathway between life and death. They had some other power. But I couldn't do it on my own. I had to wait for the other key.'

I wince, because what he's saying about the lack of balance in the Greenworld is something I've always felt. That all the power is with the female, not the male – but that's how it's always been for me, and I can't change that. Just like there's not many non-white people down here, and me and Biba – and Dad, when he was around – we stood out. But all this about us being able to magically unlock the portals for some kind of other purpose is surely the result of Roach's paranoia and obsession. Of too many nights alone with his bitterness at being excluded from the witch community.

'I've seen it, Danny. There will be a battle for the portals, and you can either be with me or against me. But we both know that we're the ones with real power. We can unlock the portals. Make them give us the one thing the world desperately needs.'

I remember my vision at the beach – seeing myself as a crow, flying over a battle, and I gulp as I see those images again. The boy gulping desperately for air as he swallows his own blood. I knew. I knew it was real. Not a symbol, Lowenna. Real blood. Tintagel's people.

'You think a portal can give us fuel?'

'Yes. Usable, burnable energy. And it will make us incredibly rich, Danny.'

'I don't see how that's possible.'

He turns round, and at this moment, I know I have to do something and do it quick. I have to get out of here: I'm not taking any chances about whether he can hurt me or not.

I focus all of my power and energy on the wall around us. Just smoke, I think, it's just smoke that can be blown away. I take a deep breath and exhale, pushing air at it. Nothing happens. I close my eyes and think as hard as I can about Melz and Lowenna and the rest of them. I imagine them reaching out to me and us all forming a circle, holding hands. And this makes me feel stronger. I imagine that the black-crystal walls are still made of smoke, and that a great storm is coming. I screw up my eyes and imagine gusts of wind and sleet driving at the walls. Imperceptibly, the air around me moves. I keep concentrating, and suddenly there is a rush of wind from behind me, then another. I open my eyes and see that the black wall is now blowing like a dense fog or the smoke from a bonfire. I look up, and I feel a drop of rain on my cheek. Melz's voice, suddenly in my ear, says, 'Don't give up, Danny,' and I focus my mind again. This time a huge gust of wind ploughs through the wall. A gap appears in the curling black smoke. A sheet of rain flies across us like an eagle's wing. Roach looks up, surprised, and I know it's now or never. I push all of my power out of me and into the shape of a lightning bolt. It hammers down from the sky and into the ground at my feet, slicing through the ropes on my wrists and ankles. I stand and jump through the hole it has made in the mist. The last thing I see is Roach's face, his expression a mixture of surprise and frustration. Then blackness.

They tell me later that I've been in and out of consciousness for days, but it all seems like a long dream to me. At one point I come to for a while – I'm in my bed and Saba is sitting by me, holding my hand, and there's an acrid herbal smell in the room. Dimly I'm aware of Gowdie as a warm fuzzy lump on my feet. But for the most part I feel like I'm drifting, floating; not unpleasant, really, but I'm just atoms, occasionally grouping, and then disintegrating and becoming something else.

Finally, I wake up properly.

Saba is in the room, looking out of the window. She looks round when she hears me stir. 'Hello, stranger.'

'How long have I been out?' I croak.

She comes over and holds a glass of water to my lips. I try to sip it without spilling it on myself, but I still do.

She wipes the water off my chin. 'On and off, two days,' she replies. 'It really took it out of you.'

I just stare at her for a while. Her outline seems to be sharper than it's ever been before, and the colours of her are even more vivid. I'm still not a hundred per cent back in the room. I can feel there's a part of my brain on a leash somewhere, being pulled back in from miles and worlds away.

'Your psychic reintegration has almost finished, but it's taken ages,' she says.

I look at my chest. It's covered with symbols, numbers, formulae. They must have really crapped themselves if bringing me back has taken two days. I must have been pretty far gone.

'How far away was I?' I ask her.

She raises her eyebrows. 'Lazarus,' she says.

I look at her, puzzled.

'Raised from the dead,' she says with an impatient look.

I catch her hands as she brushes my forehead with a cool wet cloth. 'How did you even get me back here? From the island?'

She shushes me. 'We carried you.'

'I didn't know where I was. One minute I was on Tintagel Head, the next, I was in this weird place. Like a forest, but no forest sounds.'

'Your body stayed with us. I think he took advantage of the fact that you were meditating and in a trance and he entered your mind somehow. His body was elsewhere – somewhere safe – and he merged with you. Your mind.'

'What about the portal, then? He didn't try to get it?'

'No. He wanted you this time, I guess. Maybe you being close to the portal made it easier, I don't know. For him to enter your mind like that. He knew it was a time you'd be there. He's a witch; he knows how we protect the portal at an eclipse.'

'Saba, I was really scared. I thought he was going to kill me. He had me tied up and I couldn't move. If it was only in my mind, why couldn't I just get up and walk away? I imagined the wall being blown down.'

She traces a fingertip across my forehead. 'Belief is the strongest thing, Danny. You didn't know what was happening, so you believed what he made you see. You saw and felt the ropes. When you'd worked out it wasn't a material space, you escaped.'

'So it wasn't real?'

She traces her finger to my lips. 'What is real? Am I real? Are you? How do you know I'm really here?'

I reach up and hold her hand. 'You're real,' I say,

and pull Saba down towards me and kiss her deeply. She kisses me back hard. It's all quiet in the house.

My heart wells up in my mouth cos she says I almost died, and I love her. I love this girl so much. I was almost gone, never to come back. I don't think of Bryony. I need to show Saba with all my body and spirit and heart how much I love her, and I feel that same love radiating back to me from her heart, her stomach, the whole red-hot trunk of her body pulsing with energy: passion, bonding, wanting to connect. There is no more delaying, no thoughts of Tom, no more waiting.

I hold her as close as I possibly can, in some way hoping that if I hold her close enough it will stop her from pulling away. Our hearts slam into each other like hammer on anvil. It's a world away from Sadie or Bryony; this takes my breath away. If I have any thought at all it's a kind of disbelief that it's me making love to this goddess – unworthy, lowly Danny. I am hardly aware of our bodies moving together; I am turning with her in space. There is nothing else but her. Finally, the energy peaks and blows us towards and apart from each other at the same time with the force of a bomb. We lay panting on the single bed and come gradually back to our bodies. There is nothing to say. Our hands are interlinked, and as our energy slowly sinks back to normal, only our palms retain the intense heat.

She sits up suddenly after a few minutes of lying there, and looks at me mischievously. 'Want to go to the cave?' she asks, eyes twinkling.

'What?' I'm disoriented, and just want to lie there in the wonderful glowing moment, holding her hand.

She pulls my arm. 'Come on. Let's go. I want to be by the sea.'

I sit up shakily – I really don't feel that great.

'Ummm . . . I feel a bit tired, actually, Sab – can we just lie here awhile? My head's spinning.'

She pouts. 'Come on. You're fine. I want to show you something.'

I don't want to break the mood, so I sit up and put my feet on the floor. My heart flutters like a sick bird. 'Ah – Saba, I . . .'

'Oh, stop malingering. The worst is over. You should have amazing powers of recuperation, what with all your power. You're in the prime of your life. Get up!' She pulls the covers off me.

I don't want her to think I'm weak, so I stand up and start getting dressed slowly.

She throws me my wool cloak. 'Put that on. It's cold out.'

I pull it on, pain lacerating my body.

We steal out to the cave and curl up together under a couple of thick blankets. I'm still pretty shaky. It's another freezing Cornwall day, and we're squinting in the half-light of the cave, lit by candles. We left before anyone knew I was back, and hopefully no one will notice. Saba's shuffling her cards thoughtfully and staring at the wall of the cave. I lean in to kiss her but she pushes me away playfully.

'Want to see something new?' she asks.

I shrug. 'Course,' I say. 'Always up for a new magic lesson. A kiss'd probably come first on the list, though.' I'm still reeling with the reality that we have made love to each other; she seems far more composed and ignores me.

'Shut up. I found this spell in an old grimoire in the Archive when I went there to work once, a few years back.' She pulls a card from the pack. The Empress. A picture of a beautiful crowned woman reclining in woodland with fruit and animals all around her. The Earth Mother, like Brighid. Desirable and beautiful, just like Saba.

I watch Saba. She's staring at the card intently and muttering something under her breath. Nothing happens for ages. I shift my weight from one elbow to the other. My back's getting stiff, and though the pain has levelled off, it's still pretty uncomfortable.

I'm just starting to consider eating some of the pasties we hastily brought with us to stop an imminent stomach growl when I happen to look at the card again and notice a kind of 3D effect, like a hologram. I blink. There's definitely something wrong with that picture. And the thing that's wrong, or different, is that the picture is coming out of the card. It's rising up, getting bigger. And, faster and faster, it grows until the Empress, trailing grapes and apples and with a bloody deer frisking around her (I mean – a deer? Really? It's like Snow White has appeared and is going to start singing 'Whistle While You Work' while giving the cave a really thorough clean), stands in front of us.

I stare dumbly. I had no idea this was possible, and briefly consider it might be an elaborate hoax, with Beryan and Merryn giggling outside the cave with an old video projector flickering away next to them. But obviously that isn't possible. But then, neither is this.

Saba nudges me. 'Ask her something,' she whispers.

'Eh?'

'Ask her a question. She might have something interesting to say, you never know.'

'Oh. Right. Yeah. Ummmm. I don't know what to say.'

I look helplessly at Saba who addresses the woman in front of us directly. 'Thank you, Empress, for attending our rite. Blessings upon you,' she purrs smoothly. Confident. Ever the professional witch.

The Empress smiles warmly. 'Blessings to you, priestess. Blessed be the stars and the moon. Blessed be the harvest and the warm earth. What is your request?' Her voice is thick and warm like a spiced cake fresh from the oven. As she talks, I see that her dress is made of butterflies and bees, clustered lovingly against her skin. I try to focus on her face, but her features keep shifting.

Saba nudges me again. 'What is your request?' she hisses.

'Oh. Right. Umm . . .' I flail around looking

for a question, and then it comes to me. 'Who is my soulmate?'

'The one that is most like you,' the Empress says.

I smile and squeeze Saba's hand. 'Will we always be together?' I ask, feeling sure of the answer.

'Together, and apart.'

'When will we be apart?'

'Your hearts will come to twine together.'

'So when will we be apart?'

'Life gives us quests and challenges.'

'Who? Saba or me?'

'We all have our own lessons to learn,' the Empress replies enigmatically.

It's like talking to a sphinx. I'm getting worried. It was all sounding great to start with; not so much now. And a voice, out of nowhere, in my mind, wonders suddenly if she is even talking about Saba.

'What else is it important for me to know?' I ask. I might never get this chance again. She's beginning to waver, to be less solid than before, and I sense that Saba's concentration might not last that much longer.

The Empress reaches out to touch my hand, and her touch is no more than a sparrow's breath.

'Share the energy, young priest. It is your path to bring them together,' she sings like a low bell, and is gone.

Chapter Eighteen

'We thread the needles' eyes, and all we do
All must together do.' That done, the man
Took up the nearest and began to sew.

From 'Cuchulain Comforted' by W. B. Yeats

A few days later, Lowenna calls another witches' meeting. All the head witches are invited, even from far-away covensteads. And this one is different, cos for the first time, the normal village folk are invited too.

Melz is making coffee in the kitchen as I teeter down the stairs; the chocolatey deep smell of it makes my mouth water. I'm still in need of a hit of that sweet black stuff after all the shitty herbal teas the Hands have been making me drink. Being in psychic recovery is no joke, and Saba's and my secret jaunt to the cave has done me no favours. I'm as stiff as a board and weak as water. The goth cowgirl looks up with a raised eyebrow as I stumble in.

'Give us one of those,' I say imploringly. 'I need a pick-me-up, Melz.'

'Junkie,' she says disapprovingly. 'What do you think you've been given for the past week? Pick-me-up, he says! It took a lot of powerful herbs to pick you up from death's door.' However, she sloshes some of the Greenworld's best greenhouse-grown into a mug for me and brings it over.

I take an apple from the fruit bowl and practically tear it apart with my teeth. 'Goddess, I'm starving,' I moan. 'What is there to eat?'

Melz shrugs. 'I don't know. We've all had our breakfast. Look in the cupboard, magic boy,' she says and disappears into the garden where she sits down and starts sketching, shooing Gowdie away from her.

Friendly as ever, Melz, I think, but Gowdie doesn't care. She just runs around barking.

Weak as a day-old kitten, I slump over to the window, tapping on it for the dog to see me. The result is instant: her brown furry ears prick up and she ruffs, yomping down the garden to fling herself at the door. Bless her leathery paws. I open the door and she jumps up at me, yipping happily.

'Take it easy, Gow!'

I'm so weak she can almost knock me over. I bend down and give her a hug.

Dog practically hanging on my leg, she's so happy to

see me, I root through the cupboard. There's some cake in a tin and I push handfuls into my mouth hungrily. I've got my back to the kitchen so I don't see Lowenna come in, and am so absorbed in eating that until she puts her hand on my shoulder I don't know she's there. I jump, inhale at the wrong moment and start coughing.

She bangs me on the back until I wave at her to stop. 'We thought we might have lost you once, Danny – don't conk out now on Beryan's cake.'

I smile between the coughs.

'So how are you feeling?' She rinses a cup under the tap.

'OK,' I say. 'Getting back to normal.'

'I'm sorry we didn't get you out sooner, but Roach is stronger than I thought.'

She indicates two of the easy chairs and we sit down. 'It seems he was able to create a communal vision and hold you there quite effectively,' she explains. 'You know,' she says, taking my hand, 'it's very difficult to admit to yourself that you've made a mistake when you train someone. I thought that Roach was the great new hope for the Hands once. Even before the Greenworld I'd had premonitions about a powerful male witch, a male witch I would train. I really thought it was him. My premonitions never actually included a vision of his face, you see. But I knew this male witch would come to me through Zia, and Roach was a friend of hers in the beginning. But I can see now that I was wrong, love. I had to wait a lot longer for you to arrive.' She squeezes my hand.

I give her a half-grin. It's weird being referred to as some kind of spiritual saviour when you're a sixteen-year-old kid. I don't know how to take it.

I pull Gowdie up into the chair with me and rub her ears so she calms down a bit as we talk. 'He wants control of the portals – Tintagel and Scorhill,' I say. 'He says we'll go to battle over them. Real battle. Like my vision,' I emphasize, and she frowns, like she resents being reminded.

'He was just beginning to tell me about some way that we're meant to unlock the portals to make fuel, and that we could get really rich by doing it. Bring order to the world. He says with the fuel it would provide, there'd be an end to the war and no need for the Greenworld any more. And he thinks the reason we both have the same brand is that it a sign from Lugh, that we're supposed to be in control, not Brighid. Not the Goddess.'

She snorts. 'Well, that's ridiculous. If there's anything that history has taught us, it's that masculine gods are destructive. We've had quite enough of that, thank you. What a load of nonsense. I mean, the earth itself is female!'

I choose not to argue the theoretical masculine/feminine balance that's supposed to exist in the natural world.

'But what about the fuel thing? Do you have any idea of what he's talking about?'

'Make fuel? Out of what? No. That doesn't make sense,' she says slowly, frowning. 'And the end of the Greenworld? Who wants that? We've taken so long to make it what it is. The Greenworld's about more than living without electricity. It's a holy place. The land of the Goddess.'

I wouldn't be so sure, I think, remembering Kevin's mum. How wary she was of me and Saba and Melz, and she was probably right to be. For some people being here is more about survival than visions and blessings. The Greenworld knows how to survive without power. A lot of people here know that the Redworld's days of even very limited power are numbered, and what then? At least here we have food and water, no crime inside the villages, law and order.

A lot of the people in the Greenworld care more about feeding their children than they do about being holy.

'He said he's going to attack us, whatever you think about it being holy. There's going to be a battle. A real one. So what are we going to do about it?' I'm suddenly so angry I can hardly contain myself, hardly keep a respectful tone, but if I start yelling I'll have lost her. I need to convince her that war is coming to us; we can't think of it as something that happens to other people thousands of miles away any more.

'I don't want a battle,' she says, peevish.

'You don't want one? No one wants to fight, Lowenna. But if they attack, we have to fight back.'

'We aren't warriors. We're peaceful. We don't have guns,' she protests.

'Melz has a shotgun.'

'Demelza is a rule unto herself.'

I sigh, for the first time wishing that there were more hard-asses like Melz in Tintagel.

'We saw it happen, Lowenna. You saw yourself in battle. I saw . . .'

I can't describe the memory of the boy with his throat torn out. I feel as though if I say it, it will come alive in front of me – the battle scene, the blood pooling under his head, the thick, sweet, coppery smell.

'A nightmare doesn't have to come true,' she says, playing with the tassels on her worn easy chair.

'We don't have any choice, Lowenna. If he says there's going to be a battle then there's going to be one, isn't there? So what are we going to do? We can't just sit back and let it happen.'

A deep voice bounces across the flagstone floor, and I look up to see Omar standing by the door, arms crossed across his barrel chest.

'We fight, boy,' Omar says.

I jump up and run across to him.

He envelops me in a bear hug and claps me on the back repeatedly. 'How're you doing, Dan?' he rumbles.

It's so good to see him. I hug him back as tight as I can. He ruffles my hair and I don't even care – it's like being a kid again in his safe aura of sweat.

He nods at Lowenna over the top of my head.

'Heard about what happened at the eclipse. Came straight here. Zia sent me,' he says by way of explanation.

How did she hear? I wonder, then I remember — bush telegraph.

'Have you heard something about a battle too?' Lowenna asks with a fearful tone. She really doesn't want to know still, I can see, and she starts pacing the room.

'Yeah. He's tried coming through the back door. Now he'll try a more direct approach,' Omar sits down, flexing his shoulders. 'I saw one of my gang contacts just before the eclipse. He said that there was a battle coming and they were stockpiling weapons. That it would happen soon.' He looks Lowenna square in the eye. 'That's why I came, to warn you. This isn't going away, Lowenna. You're going to have to fight for every scrap of this world you've created. Roach is serious, and he's organized. The gangs have been collecting weapons for a long time. They were even doing it when I was with them.'

Lowenna's cheeks flush with anger. 'No!' she shouts, and bangs her hand down on the circular table, the one the witches sit round at covenstead meetings. 'I've worked too bloody long and hard creating peace in this village, and across the villages, for him to come and take it away now. The audacity of it! When I think that I housed him under my roof, fed and watered him, taught him the mysteries! By Brighid!' She is shaking with rage.

Omar doesn't get up, just breathes out a long sigh. 'There's no point getting upset about it,' he says in his gravelly voice. 'You must have known this would happen one day.'

She is standing with her back to both of us at the window to the garden, hands clasped behind her so tight that her knuckles have whitened. There is a long pause.

'I just never thought it would come so soon,' she says quietly. She turns round and makes herself smile, but she has tears in her eyes, and something else, finally. Acceptance.

'So the only way to keep control of the portals is to fight Roach?' I ask Omar.

'We'll have to mobilize the villagers sooner than we thought – at the meeting tonight. There are hundreds in the gangs. We're going to need everyone in the village who's capable to fight,' he replies.

'Though Brighid knows what with,' Lowenna mutters. 'How are we going to fight them? With blunt vegetable knives and archaic gardening equipment? How can we possibly have an advantage over them?'

'If needs be. War has come. You didn't ask for it, but no one ever does. It's here anyway. All you can do now is defend what you have with passion. You want to protect something you love. They want to destroy something they envy. Theirs is the weaker motivation, Lowenna. That's your advantage.' All his usual cocky banter has gone; this is the Omar that fought for the gangs, against them and everywhere in between. This is a man who knows what a battle is.

'I thought that we could remain on the side of peace, but perhaps I was wrong. Perhaps it's unnatural to expect anything else of human nature,' Lowenna says sadly, looking out of the window at her garden.

'Humans are full of conflict inside themselves, and so create conflict outside themselves,' Omar says. 'Zia taught me that.'

Lowenna smiles ruefully. 'Your mother is a good witch,' she says to me, and I think about the lines in Mum's face, about the grey streaks she blacks out with indigo powder. She's a great witch, but she's tired. Weakening, maybe, and whatever Linda is doing with Roach to undermine her in the village can't help. Roach wants control of both portals. There'll be a battle for this one, but maybe he thinks he can take Scorhill from Mum slowly, painfully.

'What about guns, though? Weapons? We don't have any. Really and truly, Omar.' Lowenna looks downcast. 'How are we supposed to fight with no weapons?'

'That's what I'm here for, Wenna.' Omar grins, his cockiness returned, and puts his feet up on the table. She frowns at his muddy boots but lets him do it. 'Let's talk. Something to eat would be nice.'

She looks less than happy, but philosophical. This is happening.

She turns to me. 'Danny! Go and get some rest.

Do some reading or something if you can't sleep. You must be shattered.' And so, obediently, feeling as if I'm being got out of the way, I trudge up to my room. I hear Omar's voice rumbling and Lowenna's being raised. Bargains being made, alliances agreed.

But I know he's right. A battle is the only way now. Omar's words become my heart pumping my blood around my body – *We fight, boy. We fight.*

I'm lying on my bed reading *The Common Herbal*, when I hear Saba's voice outside my window. I get up and look out. She's in the garden with Tom. Ugh. Just what I need to see. I know I should look away, go back to my reading, but I can't; jealousy clutches me in its clammy talons and squeezes just a little tighter every time Saba laughs or he smiles. I lean as close as I can to the glass so that I can see and hear as much as possible.

I hate both of them in that moment – their perfect blondness, the way they look together: clean-cut, kissed by the winter sun. I hate Tom's hand round her waist as they sit in the hammock, swinging, talking, his voice rumbling under hers. How much longer have I got to wait? He can't love her as much as I do, and I know she wants me more, so why is she playing this game? Why are we waiting? Why am I hanging on this string, this noose, holding my breath, hands tied behind my back, waiting for a smile or a touch? All the time with the rope biting into my skin.

I start pacing around my room, feeling the fire

in my blood from talking about the battle. I'm not relishing a fight, but at least it's movement; at least a decision has been taken, and we can move forward and do something. I can't stand this other uncertainty any more, this anxiety over Saba. The beat of battle starts pounding through me.

Saba knows I'm in the house, knows it's pretty likely that I might be able to see her and Tom right now. That annoys me even more. She's playing us off against each other. Making herself feel even more desirable, even more powerful. And we've just slept together for the first time – since it happened I'd been feeling euphoric, thinking that surely now we could be together, boyfriend and girlfriend. We hadn't waited for Tom to disappear. We made love, and it was mind-blowing. Beautiful. But she still hasn't done anything, and by the looks of this little chat they're having outside, she's not using this perfect opportunity to break up with him.

I get angrier and angrier as I pace until I'm stamping so hard I'm making the books by my bed rattle. This is war. We're going to war with the gangs? Yeah, well, I'm going to war with love. With perfect Tom and his perfect-guy shit.

Books. Books. Bloody books. What can a book do to help me? I think angrily, and kick a pile of them that are by the door.

And then I remember. There's one book that might be able to.

I open my bedroom door warily and peek out into

the hall. No one around. I listen to the voices coming from downstairs – Lowenna and Omar are still talking. Good. I tiptoe along the corridor to Lowenna's room and open the door carefully. The doorknob creaks, making me cringe – I stop and listen, but the voices carry on. All right. I sneak into the room and look around me, trying to remember.

'Where are you?' I whisper into the murk. She was ranting on about the Greenworld when she showed me it. The thing that could make people do things. The grimoire. I just have to remember where she got it from.

I start carefully flicking through the pile of magazines and books against the wall, but it's not there. No. It's too precious to be in a messy pile. It's going to be in a drawer, in a cupboard. I look around. Lowenna's personal altar, with a Brighid figurine and some candles, is set on top of an ancient oriental cabinet. It has to be in there. I open the clasp slowly, hoping it doesn't break or creak. Excitedly, I look inside, holding my breath, but all that's inside are rows and rows of half-melted candles, stacked haphazardly on top of each other. I peer round them to the back of the cabinet in case the book's wedged behind the candles, but there's nothing there.

OK. Maybe the obvious place is too obvious. I look around again. A rickety wicker chest of drawers by the window. Look there. I open the top drawer only to find Lowenna's undies. Ugh. Riffle through them as lightly as possible. No book. I check the other drawers, and apart from discovering where Lowenna keeps her stretched-out band T-shirts – I mean, who were Journey? – I'm drawing a blank.

OK, so this book is something to be kept out of idle hands. But my hands aren't idle. I've got power and I can use it. And I want to use it. Conventional methods aren't working, so magical ones will have to. I lean my head out of the door, just checking again that there are still voices downstairs. OK. Still voices.

I duck back into Lowenna's room and close my eyes. I scan the room with my imagination. Show me the magic, show me the magic, I think. Something as powerful as a grimoire will have a psychic resonance that I should be able to pick up. I concentrate. There's nothing, nothing . . . and then, suddenly, I look over at a tatty apple crate that is covered with teacups. It's got a soft glow about it to my eyes. That's it. I'm sure of it. Carefully I remove the dirty teacups and a couple of sad-looking plants, heart pounding. She could walk in at any time. I lift up the crate, and there it is. The grimoire. I snatch it up, re-make the makeshift coffee table and slip back into my room, wedging a chair under the doorknob, just in case anyone feels like coming in without knocking.

I sit down on my bed and turn it over in my hands. A leather cover the colour of dried blood, but nothing else on it as far as I can see. I open it up. It's handwritten in ink, faint and spidery. *Grimoire Mandragora*. Spooky.

I turn the title page carefully. I need something good. Something that will make Saba all mine. No more cosy chats, hugs, intimate moments with Tom. He's not right for her. He's not the one she's meant to be with. I am, I know it. I know it deep, in my guts, in the unsteady sweetness that blooms in my belly when I see her.

I flick the pages. I don't understand a lot of it. Pages of symbols, shapes inside other shapes, labelled with backwards letters and numbers. Then a section of diagrams of the body. Basic biology for ancient witches, I guess. I keep looking. The thick pages have absorbed the old brown ink like flesh absorbs tattoos over time – the writing is faded, the pages fragile and delicate.

I stop suddenly at a page that catches my eye. To triumph over another for the beloved. Bingo. I light a candle and hold it up to the book to make out the writing, careful not to drip wax on the page.

I trace my finger lightly over the words.

Make a poppet of the other. Light a candle and call down the dark goddess. Request thee Her aid in your task. Sew the mouth closed, so the other cannot speak love; for the greatest effect, pierce the heart so it may not feel love. Soak thy poppet in tea of Melissa officinalis. Take thy poppet and hide it in the coldest place. Their ardour will cool as the poppet freezes, as will their appeal to thy beloved.

The dark goddess – well, I suppose, to us, that's the Morrigan. The beautiful woman whose battle cry gives courage to soldiers, but also the crone of death, taking the dead to the next world when they have fought all they can.

The tea – Melissa officinalis. Finally some of this book-learning's coming in handy. I lean over to where I dropped *The Common Herbal* and check if I'm right – yep, lemon balm. Easy enough. There's tons of it in the garden. And making a poppet – that's a cloth doll. I can do that too. Sew the mouth closed, sure. But I'm not sure about ramming a needle into its heart. I can do the rest, though.

I slip out into the hall, into Lowenna's room and hide the book back under the makeshift coffee table, hoping that I replace the mouldy teacups in the right order. Now for lemon balm. I slide down the stairs and out into the garden without going through the kitchen, straight to the herb patch. Saba and Tom are still canoodling in the hammock, but I don't say anything to them – I follow the path along the other side of the garden. It's not unusual for any of us to pop out to the herb patch. I pull some of the fragrant leaves off the big bush of it and stuff them in my pocket. Going back through the kitchen, I take some still-hot water from the kettle and pour some into a mug, and take it back up with me to my room. It's only Omar in there, and he's snoozing in a chair, his conversation with Lowenna apparently over; in a sudden moment of inspiration I open the compost bin and pull out some vegetable peelings too.

Back in the safety of my bedroom, I relight the

candles and look at the clock. Still enough time, just, before the town meeting tonight. I crumple the leaves to stew in the hot water and go to my cupboard, riffling through for an old music T-shirt of Lowenna's. Cos I left in a hurry, the Hands put together a hand-me-down wardrobe for me when I arrived. It's just as well I'm skinny, cos most of it's Beryan's or Lowenna's old work clothes; most Greenworld clothes are unisex, uniformly dull and unattractive. I pull out a holey old grey shirt with a faded pre-Greenworld band logo on it and cut a rough man shape out of it through both layers with my athame, then pull out a needle and thread from my drawer. We all learn basic sewing at school, and everyone has needles and thread. You can't get by without mending and remaking in the Greenworld. It occurs to me that I'm only supposed to use the athame for good magic, but I ignore that thought.

I kneel and call out to the Morrigan in my mind. I don't know her that well – she is Brighid's dark sister, goddess of death and rebirth; mostly she gets a mention at funerals, as we don't have battles. I remember she is Melz's goddess, and realize the appropriateness – Melz as the Morrigan. Saba is much more the Greenworld's ideal: the fiery, beautiful, earth goddess Brighid incarnate.

I feel the Morrigan's power fill me: a starkness, a single-minded focus and a war-like conviction that Saba is mine. Hoping it's OK to invoke her in my mind, cos I don't want anyone to overhear me, I think what I feel:

O Great Goddess Morrigan. Crow woman. Help me. Make me victorious. Let night fall on Tom and Saba's relationship. Let the cold of winter shrivel their love. Give me your power.

I stitch the doll together in the candlelight, thinking of it being Tom, stitching on some potato peelings for hair. He's a gardener, after all. When there's just a small gap left in the stitching, I stuff it with the ripped-up remainder of the T-shirt and close it up. Next, I draw a face on it and then stitch over the mouth with the cotton. To stop Tom telling Saba he loves her. I imagine them, out on the hammock, right now, and pull the stitches hard, criss-crossing the rough drawn-on mouth. It's not that I dislike him. I really don't. But I want Saba. I really want her. I pour the tea over the doll. It looks back up at me, dumb and soggy.

I sit there and look at it. Do I really, really want to do this? My conscience has woken up and is waving a sleepy hand in the rough direction of my libido. The grimoire flashes into my mind. Lowenna's used it – she told me. I'm a witch, same as her. Where's the harm? I've got power. A grimoire's just a spell book. Just a recipe book for people with power. I should be able to use it if I want. So why does she keep it hidden? my conscience pipes up. Why don't we all use it all the time?

I don't want to answer that. I'm different. I've got more power than them. The rules aren't the same for me. I want that all to be true. But really, I don't believe it. I know this book is powerful – and, more than that, that what I'm doing is definitely grey magic. Pretty dark grey, really. I'm obeying my own desire, and not doing something for the highest good of all concerned. I'm taking control, and it makes me feel powerful and thrilled, but sick too.

I leave the doll sitting in the cup and look back out of the window. They're still there, and as I watch, Saba leans in to Tom and they kiss. Not chastely either. Hell, hell, hell. That's all I need.

I go back to the doll, take my pen and draw a heart on its chest. I look at it, with its stupid potato-peel hair, and visualize Tom's face on it. The power charges through my chest, the heartbreak and disappointment booming down my arms and into my fingers, into the doll. The tattoo on my arm starts to throb. Curse you, Tom. She's mine. Stop loving her, I scream inside myself, and grab the needle from where I left it on the bed. Mine! Mine! Mine! I sob, and ram the needle into the heart of the doll over and over again.

Chapter Nineteen

> Then the Morrigu, daughter of Ernmass, came, and
> heartened the Tuatha De to fight the battle fiercely
> and fervently. Thereafter the battle became a rout,
> and the Fomorians were beaten back to the sea.

> From *The Second Battle of Mag Tuired (Moytura)*,
> author unknown

Later that night we all file along to the village hall for
the covensteads' meeting with the village. The Hands
walk with the other witches from across Devon and
Cornwall in a kind of ceremonial line, pacing the
cobblestones, and attracting stares and whispers from
the other people on the streets. I wonder when the last
time was that they saw so many of us all together.

I catch Bryony's blue eyes following me through the
crowd and smile thinly at her, but I'm freaking out. I've
hidden the doll behind the shed in the garden, where

it'll get nice and cold, like the book said, but it seems as if it's my heart that's getting colder and colder with every breath, every step. I shouldn't have done it, but I don't know how to take it back. I've been a witch long enough to know that magic feels good when you're using it in the natural way, the good way. It's euphoric. But this feels terrible. My arm, the one with the brand, throbs painfully with every step, and I'm avoiding Saba's eyes. I can't look at her. The guilt is too much. I'd rather do anything than stand shoulder-to-shoulder with these witches, these good souls, right now – I feel like they'll know what I've done, smell the wrongness like rotting meat on my skin. But I don't have a choice. I have to go.

It's already packed in the hall, and the village people look scared but also full of a kind of anticipation. There's an electric hum in the air. People are standing cos there's no seats left, laughing and murmuring, darting glances and raised eyebrows at each other and at us when we come in. I stand at the side of the hall, towards the front, with the many witches that have come here from other covensteads nearby – I see Tressa, Lowenna's sister from Boscastle, and some of her group, a metre or so away and nod politely to them. There are witches from Treligga and Port Isaac, even some from as far away as St Breward and Newquay. Lowenna, dressed in some kind of ultra hippy-chick purple tent dress with yellow smiley faces all over it (and a bit ripped at the seams under the arms, I notice), is standing on

301

a platform at the front of the room, flanked by Beryan and Melz. When she sees we're all in she raises her arms and calls for quiet. She gets it, but there's a lot of simmering down, shushing and scraping of chairs. She waits patiently for them all to settle.

'Fellow villagers of Tintagel: welcome. I bring to you all a very warm welcome on this cold coastal night when the taste of evil is in the air.'

The villagers shuffle their feet and exchange wary glances. This is out of the ordinary.

'Tonight, I have called you together, along with witches from many local covensteads, to address a serious problem. Many of you know the nature of this problem, and we will discuss it in due course. But first, I want to commemorate the special nature of this meeting.

'You'll know that this is the first time that a covenstead meeting of witches has joined with a local village meeting. We hope that you don't consider it an imposition, and that so many witches in one room doesn't give you cause for concern. It shouldn't, as we are all good and true women—' Here she breaks off, looks at me and smiles before she says, 'Yes, and a man too, as you can see – all good and true dedicated people, committed to your protection and health. But we are also dedicated to something else – the goodness of the Greenworld. The purity of our way of life together here. Cooperation. Wholesomeness. Non-pollution. And not polluting, friends, means more than the physical ways that we all work to make our soil, air and water pure and renewable.'

I feel worse and worse the more she talks about purity and goodness. My arm throbs hotly. It looks normal, but it feels like someone's lit a fire under my skin. I scan the crowd for Tom. Finally I see him at the side of the hall, listening and frowning. I don't know what I expected – for him to be clawing at his mouth, signing manically at us to help him cos someone's sewn it up, or clutching at his heart – but of course he's fine. I breathe a little easier. Maybe it was just all crap anyway – I mean, soaking a doll you made out of a T-shirt in tea and hiding it behind a shed – it's not that bad. And the needle through the heart – the book just said that would stop loving feelings. Nothing more. There's no need to feel so guilty.

I focus back on Lowenna.

'There is a mural on the outskirts of this village that shows Tintagel being held and protected by five outstretched hands. Those Five Hands are here tonight, as you know: your protectors.' She looks at me and smiles. 'Five, and now six. Most of you have met Daniel Prentice, our new witch.' I nod at the crowd and there's a generally positive murmur, though nothing overly enthusiastic. They're OK with me, but nothing more. 'I can't say in great detail how we protect you, but enough of you understand that we are engaged in magic. There is a . . . magical source . . . in Tintagel that we look after, something that really is as important as life and death. That source is under threat from the gangs. As is the village.'

There are a variety of responses from the crowd – clearly, some people have heard there's something up and have maybe got wind of what it might be, but there are also quite a few shocked faces. Mention of the gangs is never welcome. The gangs are a constant threat in these people's lives, and for a moment I feel sad for them. They are imprisoned in this small village, here in the relative middle of nowhere, with little communication coming in or going out. They don't have the liberty of being able to skip out here and there as we witches do, whether we're supposed to or not – they don't have the powers that we do to elude capture, to defend ourselves.

'We suspect that the gangs, led by Roach, the gang leader, will attack the village in the next few days to assume ownership of the village and the magical source I have mentioned. We are asking you, the people of the village, to stand with us. Stand with us against this threat to our liberty.'

There is a sudden babble of voices.

One of the gardeners that came to dinner at Yule, Aaron, stands up, scratching at his shaggy beard. 'Won't your magic be enough to keep them out? Why do we have to fight? Isn't that why we live in the witch villages – to be protected?' he shouts.

There is a surge of 'Yeah' and 'That's right!' from the people around him.

A woman stands up – she looks familiar, an older woman, maybe in her sixties, with grey-streaked black hair and kind creases round her eyes. She's wearing the kind of clothes most women in the villages wear – flowing, loose, colourful, a bit worn. I'm trying to place her, then I remember it's Maya, Ennor's mum.

She holds up her hands for some quiet so she can be heard. 'I'm old enough to remember the Redworld; there are many of you here who aren't,' she begins, and her voice is gentle but firm and clear. 'I can tell you that persecution and violence were quite usual in those days, especially at the transition to what we have now. We were in a lawless state and we fought hard for our liberties, for the freedom to live by new rules. Our witches serve us well and have kept our lives protected and free from chaos thus far, but human nature will out, and the time will always come when there must be a battle. In these situations, no man is an island, friends. Now is the time to band together and do what we must for the good of the Greenworld.'

She sits back down on one of the wooden benches that line the hall to a quiet respect. I look at Maya's face, which is composed and peaceful. The people around her are nodding and mumbling assent.

'Thank you, Maya,' Lowenna says, grinning her big-eyed grin. Seems that it's not just the witches that are passionate about the Greenworld philosophy. I catch a glance of Ennor's proud face as he looks at his mum, and I think, Yeah, man, you should be proud of her.

'So! A show of hands. Do we fight Roach and his gang? Those against?'

There is a fair show of hands in the hall. Scared faces. It's understandable. They are peaceful people. They just want to get on with growing their vegetables. They're frightened for their families.

Lowenna nods and counts the hands. 'All right. And now: those in favour?'

There is a sudden groundswell. Hundreds of hands are thrust in the air.

There is a shout from somewhere in front of me – I crane my head round and see Omar striding through us and into the crowd. They make way for him, and as he walks through, a chant starts. I'm not sure whether it starts from him or someone in the crowd, but it rises and swells like baking bread, here in the stuffy, hot little wooden hall. 'Fight for the Greenworld! Fight for the Greenworld! Fight!'

I join in and punch my fist in the air, following in Omar's wake, and try to forget the pain in my arm and the tortured Tom-poppet, slowly freezing in the dark.

A few nights later our gang meets at the apple orchard again. The branches on the trees are bare and black in the rain and the bonfire is belching out acrid black smoke – whatever wood's on it tonight, it's an evil mix. I've come with Melz and Saba and I'm still freaking out.

I'm seeing two of the five girls here and they don't know about each other, and absolutely no one knows about me and Saba. I've cursed Tom, though I don't know if it's had any effect cos Saba still seems to be seeing him. It's a cauldron of trouble just waiting to boil over.

It's bloody freezing tonight too – February in Cornwall, and yet here we are, too cool to be cold, shivering in the wet frigid night. I've left Gowdie at home with Lowenna in front of a roaring fire, and think of them both enviously as I tug my wool cloak round me.

Ennor and Skye are here already, tending the bonfire. Skye's wrapped her arms round his neck, standing behind him, her long blonde hair draped over his shoulder.

'Hey, witches,' Ennor calls.

Skye unwinds herself from him, picks up three beers from a pile and hands them to us.

'Hey, Boy from the Boundary,' Melz shoots back at him.

'Why do you call him that?' I ask

'That's the Cornish meaning of his name,' she says curtly.

'Is it?' asks Skye curiously. 'Makes sense.'

'What do you mean?' grunts Ennor.

'Going out with me. You're the boundary between Tintagel and the gangs.' She tickles his ribs. 'You're on the edge. You're breaking the rules. You're BAD, Ennor! You're BAD!' She squeals with pleasure as he turns from the bonfire and starts tickling her in return. They fall to the ground and roll around, play-fighting.

'Who's bad?' Tom's voice is husky in the smoke.

He walks out of the farmhouse, carrying some bottles. He sees Saba and comes over to us. Kisses her, a good kiss. When he opens his eyes there's just a flicker, but I catch it – he looks at me to make sure I'm watching. Claiming what's his, or so he thinks.

'Hi, gorgeous,' he says to her. Maybe they don't always kiss like that, but it's still bloody irritating, and I'm jealous as hell that it's not me standing in front of everyone with my arm round her, all tall and Viking-like.

He looks over at me and nods. I rub my arm through my sleeve absently – not that rubbing it makes any difference. It still hurts.

'Dan.'

'Tom.'

It's the classic absolute-minimum-politeness greeting.

'Hi, Tom,' says Melz, nudging him. Don't forget about me, her eyes say, and again I think how wrong this all is. It should be Melz and Tom, me and Saba. He grins and musses her hair, like she was a dog or a little sister. Like I do to Beebs.

'Melz! Which goddess is it you're channelling tonight, then?' He circles round her, looking her up and down – black gown, cloak, black eye make-up and the ever-present cowboy boots. 'Hmm. My goddess knowledge isn't that spot on. I can't remember which one it was that spent her time cattle-rustling?'

She just laughs. Melz never laughs, but put her in smiling distance of Tom and she turns from Priestess of Doom to Cheerleader for All Things Perky. I haven't come across anyone else who could get away with saying anything like that to her either. You don't make fun of Melz unless you want a world of trouble for breakfast. She sits down by the fire and gets out her sketchbook and a piece of charcoal, her hand making confident, quick movements across the page. I wonder who she's doing this time.

'So what does everyone think about the battle? I'm pretty freaked,' says Ennor.

Bryony and Jennie appear through the broken gate and make their way through the stark trees. Here we go, I think, and smile over at Bryony, who comes to stand by me.

'We are PETRIFIED!' exclaims Jennie, hearing Ennor and somehow making it sound as though she's actually quite excited about hand-to-hand combat with hundreds of gang members. 'I mean, what are we going to do? I don't know how to fight! It's too extreme!'

'There are classes going on, Jen,' Melz says, looking up briefly from her sketchbook. 'You need to get to one. Learn some basic self-defence. Fingers crossed, you won't need to fight. It won't get as far as where you'll be.' The plan is that the witches and the people who actually know how to handle firearms, or fight, will be at the front. Children, pregnant women and the elderly will be protected at the centre of the village and everyone else in between.

Jennie shivers. 'I don't want to, though. I don't see why we have to get involved.'

'Me neither,' Bryony adds, and takes my hand. I kiss her and snake my hand round her waist. I keep my eyes on her, as if fascinated by what she has to say, but I'm avoiding Saba's stare. She's noticed – there's no mistake.

I look over at her. Her eyes are like swords and her mouth is pressed in a line as tight as the spidery handwritten lines in Lowenna's grimoire, but she knows she can't say anything.

'I don't want to sound negative,' says Tom. 'But I think we've got a more pressing problem here, right now.'

Oh crap, I think. He's going to call me out. He knows. He knows about me and Saba. It's all going to kick off.

But instead Tom turns to Skye. 'You and Bali need to go. You can't hang out with us any more.'

I hadn't even seen Bali, but he unfurls himself from a ball on the floor. I thought he was a pile of coats. He blinks unfocusedly. 'What? What's happening, man?' he slurs. He's started on the wine already, I guess.

'You need to leave. And Skye. Both of you. Go.'

Ennor stands up. 'Wait a second, Tom. Don't be so bloody rude. Skye's not going anywhere. She hasn't done anything wrong.'

'Don't let your cock do your thinking for once, Ennor,' Tom says, and we all kind of recoil at that. Tom's usually so gentle. Everyone loves Tom. Tom the boy next door. He doesn't swear or be mean. 'We're at war with the gangs. There's going to be a battle. We've got to win. How do you know that these two aren't going home and telling their dad, or Roach, everything we say? How does it look for two of the Hands to be consorting with the gangs? It's not right—'

'Hang on, Tom. You don't have to be such a shit about it,' Saba breaks in, removing his hand from her shoulder.

He looks surprised at her words and the sudden change in mood.

'"Consorting?"' continues Saba, 'I'll decide who I consort with, thanks. And you never had a problem with it before. We've all been hanging out for ages. Skye and Bali keep it on the down-low, you know that. We can trust them.'

Now, that is her opinion, I'm sure – but Tom's picked a bad moment to say anything controversial. Only I know it, but Saba's pissed off, and she'll jump on any excuse for an argument right now. She can't say what she really wants to say, which is something along the lines of 'What are you doing with your hand on Bryony's arse, you lying cheating bastard Danny?' And,

311

as well as that, I suddenly wonder if this is the curse starting to work. Saba and Tom arguing? Trouble in paradise, finally? My stomach churns uneasily between dread and excitement – at the curse working, and at getting Saba. My arm feels as if it's going to burst into flame. I roll up my sleeve to let the cold air get to it, but that doesn't help.

Tom snorts. 'How do you know that, Saba? Know for sure, do you? Your trouble is you're too trusting.'

Whoops – shouldn't have said that I think, and I'm right. Saba gives him a stare I have never seen before, and don't want to see again – hard, flat, serrated and cold, like an ice sword.

'I'm too trusting? I think you're forgetting, Tom, that Melz and I have some pretty trustworthy methods for knowing whether people are betraying us or not. Just think about that before you go throwing your weight around.'

The thing is, I understand where Tom's coming from. It is shaky ground. Nice as Bali and Skye are, we don't really know what they're doing when they go back home, and who they're talking to; they could be Roach's spies, or not even that, just telling their friends or their dad what they've seen and heard, and that would be enough. Saba can say she knows she can trust them, but even witches are fallible.

Tom looks surprised that she's turned on him so quickly. I feel a glimmer of sympathy for him, but only a glimmer.

Saba whirls round the rest of us, challenging us one by one. 'Am I the only one that thinks this is crap? Bali and Skye are our friends.'

She catches my eye. I cough. 'I know, but . . .'

'But what? Don't defend him, Danny.'

'I wasn't going to. But you have to admit it's weird for us to be socializing with them. Witches and gangs don't mix.'

'Oh, by Brighid! They're just kids. Skye's about as dangerous as a hedgehog, and Bali's so pissed all the time he can hardly remember his own name. I'd know if they were spying on us.'

'Thanks for talking about us like we're not here,' Skye says quietly. Bali's just frowning.

'Would you, though, Saba?' I say, knowing I'm not helping myself but unable to stop talking. 'Would you really know? Cos I'm not sure you would.' But I know she knows what I mean – we've both been lying, morning, noon and night – both of us having two relationships. Keeping secrets isn't as hard as you think. We're not really talking about Bali and Skye. We're talking about ourselves.

'No. I'd know,' she says, but she doesn't sound as sure.

'I don't think you would, maybe,' I say gently. 'And when you found out, it would really hurt.'

Skye stands by Saba. 'Thanks, Sab. We appreciate you sticking up for us.' She smiles wanly and Saba pats her arm reassuringly, though she's distracted, taking in what's happening. 'It's just that we don't really have many friends.'

'I'm sorry, Skye. I know it must be hard,' Saba says, giving her a hug. 'Don't listen to Tom. He's having his period, or something. I know you're OK.'

Skye just nods.

There's a silence. Tom tries to take Saba's hand. She wrenches it away and walks off. He catches her shoulder.

She pulls away. 'Don't grab me!'

'I'm sorry. I just want us to be careful. All of us.'

'I can't deal with this right now. I'm going home,' she says, and the tears in her eyes are because of me and not Bali and Skye. I know that. She strides off through the orchard. I can see from her back she's fuming; she's so stiff and brittle it looks as though she might crack. I don't know if this is anything to do with the spell and the grimoire, but it just feels like everything's going wrong and I don't know what to do about it.

Saba stops and turns round, looking back at the group. 'Melz? You coming?' she calls, but Melz is standing beside Tom, clutching a sheaf of paper. Her drawings.

'I'm staying,' she says with a combative note in her voice. Making a stand. I see her glance at Tom, and adoration flashes in her eyes. How can anyone else not see it?

Saba gives her a long look but doesn't say anything,

just turns round and strides off. Ennor, Bali and Skye run after her.

'We're not staying here another second if that's how you all feel,' Skye says, arms wrapped round herself as if protecting herself from Tom's glare.

Ennor gives Tom the dirtiest look imaginable and spits in the dirt. 'You think you know people,' is all he says, and follows Saba, pulling Skye to his side.

Bali shambles out after them too, though it's entirely possible he has no idea what's going on.

'Wow. What was that all about?' Jennie says, taking a swig from her beer.

'I don't know. I didn't know she cared that much about Bali and Skye,' Tom says, concerned. 'I'd better go after her. Say sorry. But I really do think it's weird having them here when we're going to battle with them. Am I wrong?'

'I don't think so,' says Melz. 'Saba's too proud. She won't admit she's wrong. But she knows she is, deep down.' She looks at me meaningfully, and I get the feeling she's not just talking about Skye and Bali.

Tom looks at me. 'I'm surprised you agree with me. You and Saba are so close, after all.' There's a barb in his voice, though when he sees Bryony next to me his expression changes. He didn't expect that.

'Doesn't mean I agree with her about everything. We're not joined at the hip,' I shoot back.

He looks at me for a long beat. 'I can see that, man,' he says slowly. He throws his bottle into the corner by the wall where it shatters into the mound of broken glass we've built up there. 'Well, I'm going after her,' he says, and we both hear the rest of the sentence: if you aren't.

I turn back to the bonfire with Bryony, Jennie and Melz, and my heart's in ashes. She'll end up his warm, familiar arms. I know it. 'Do what you want, man.'

I look away and into the fire to stop the others from seeing me cry, and as I do, I notice a couple of pieces of the thick handmade paper Melz sketches on curling up in the flames. Even through the smoke, the likeness is good; my face stares back at me arrogantly just before it's consumed by the heart of the bonfire.

I look up to see Melz staring at me. 'Still not happy with your drawings?' I ask, and she smiles oddly.

'Something like that,' she says, and turns away.

Chapter Twenty

Cuchulain stirred,
Stared on the horses of the sea, and heard
The cars of battle and his own name cried;
And fought with the invulnerable tide.

From 'Cuchulain's Fight with the Sea'
by W. B. Yeats

We have several battle plans. Omar and Lowenna have been working hard to make sure everyone knows what they're supposed to do, both witch and villager alike.

A few weeks after my fight with Saba at the bonfire, Omar leads us to a huge walk-in cupboard at the back of the stuffy little village hall, which has become our battle HQ. He flings open the doors and gestures inside. Rows of guns glint back at us: rifles, pistols, lots I don't recognize. Big things, some painted in camouflage, some black. Boxes of ammunition. Grenades. Basically, a worrying amount of firepower.

'Enough for an army in there,' he says, and grins at our astounded expressions.

'Where'd you get all those?' Beryan asks, incredulous. It's a huge stash.

Omar grins. 'The gangs aren't the only ones who steal weapons,' he says. 'I've been pilfering them for years, just in case. From Roach's gang, from the Redworld. From anywhere really,' he says.

Lowenna and Merryn have tiptoed their way into the cupboard and are looking at the piles of ammunition with a kind of quiet awe. Goddess knows what was in there originally – maybe hymn books – but it's enormous, that storeroom.

'How do you get guns from the Redworld back here?' I'm curious – I mean, what does he do? Sneak them out under his coat?

'It's not that difficult. If you've got skills the security forces want, they can pay you in guns. Goods. Whatever you need. Redworld money's no good here, so I took these.'

'What skills?' Beryan asks suspiciously.

Omar laughs. 'Better if you don't know, m'dear,' he booms, making her frown.

I can guess. Ironwork, carpentry. Not everyone, even in the Redworld, would know how to repair an armoured truck. But perhaps there were other things he did too. He's a strong man – a scary man, I imagine, in the right circumstances. With years living with the gangs, Omar must have some pretty unsavoury skills for sale too.

Lowenna runs her hand along a shelf, which is straining under the weight of several semi-automatic machine guns. 'This is all ours? For us to use?' She looks like she can't quite take it all in.

He nods. 'Yeah. But we're going to have to be really careful about this, you know? I mean, putting powerful firearms into the hands of vegetable-growers. Healers. Mystics. Teachers. They've never held a weapon before, most of them. We're going to have to teach them how to use these, but we don't have much time.'

Melz is standing outside the storeroom still, looking pensive. Thoughtful. There's something bothering her.

'What's up?' I ask.

Surely goth cowgirl Melz is up for using some heavy artillery. This must be right up her street. In terms of fashion, all she's missing is a gun belt and a Stetson.

'I'm not sure about this, that's all,' she says. 'I mean, the ethics of it. No, the villagers don't know how to fire weapons, and there's a good reason for that. They're peaceful people. They chose a peaceful life. Sure, you've persuaded them that they've got to fight for their village, their lifestyle, but what will that do to their energies? To be so aggressive, so violent? I just can't see this ending well, even if we do win,' she says.

We all look at each other. Of all of us, it's Merryn

319

that speaks first, which is a surprise. She's pretty quiet most of the time, kind of blends into the background, and you can forget that she's one of the Hands and a powerful witch in her own right.

'You're right, Melz. You're right. But what can we do? We can't very well let Roach's gang just overrun the village and take what they want. We can provide psychic protection but we can't fight a whole army of them, just the seven of us. There's just no choice now, my dear,' she says, and puts her arm round Melz's bony shoulders.

Melz bites her lip. 'I know,' she says. 'I just wish it hadn't come to this.'

Lowenna looks round at us with a frown on her face. 'There's something wrong too. Can't you feel it? Something dark going on. I just started feeling it yesterday or the day before. Something out of whack. Cold, somehow. I can't put my finger on it, though. Do you know what I mean?'

I look at the floor, panicking. She has to mean the curse.

'Hmmm . . . maybe,' Merryn says, looking thoughtful. 'I mean, I think I know what you mean, but I'd just assumed it was anticipation of the fight, and probably all the negative energy around that.'

Lowenna furrows her brow, wrinkling up her face in concentration. 'Perhaps, but I've been feeling that for weeks. This is different, new. Anyone else?'

I look over at Saba but she also is looking at the

floor, and it occurs to me that she might be thinking that it's our illicit meetings her mum's picking up on – I mean, maybe it is, but I know that it must be my curse. Spells have an energy signature, and it's just as Lowenna described – dark and cold. Cold like a cloth doll soaked and freezing. I shiver, but don't say anything. How can I now?

Lowenna raises her eyebrows at the guns. 'Well, maybe it's all this that's giving me nightmares. You can't get more aggressive energies than a cupboard full of munitions, after all.' She shrugs. 'Forget it, then. But if you do feel something new and you can't get a handle on it, let me know,' she says seriously, and we all nod dutifully.

I try to catch Saba's eye again but she avoids making contact – she's been avoiding me since the bonfire, in fact. I don't know what happened after Tom went after her, and a big part of me doesn't want to. It hurts too much to think of them together, kissing under the stars, him hugging her and telling her it's all right, reassuring her – cos that's exactly what I should have done, not stood with my arms round Bryony, arguing with Saba like an idiot. I have lost her, and the fear of fighting in any battle or invasion or war will never be as bad as the sorrow I feel. It's as if the warm arms that were wrapped round my heart have turned to claws that are ripping their way out of my chest. I haven't been seeing Bryony either – it feels wrong to lead her on even further, and I can't find anything in me for her right now. I'm even avoiding her bread stall at the end of the street.

And Tom's still alive – I'm not that powerful after all, it would seem. But my arm's still hurting. Burning. My body reminding me I've done wrong. And somehow Lowenna knows. She doesn't know exactly, but she can feel something's wrong in the circle, and if it wasn't for our impending possible doom, what with the fight with the gangs, she wouldn't be letting it go that easily. It's a sobering thought, as if I needed another.

I was all for taking the fight to Roach: smoking him out, luring him out of his lair and then stamping the crap out of that lair. But Omar shakes his bear-like head. No. Our strength is in our village, he says. Here, we have defences. We have greater numbers than them. We can use the tools we have. So, here I stand, sentry at the village boundary, not far from the Witch's Gate. Every hundred metres there is someone, witch or villager, and we're on rotation day and night.

Tonight, the full moon is just starting to rise in the evening sky. It's not that late, maybe seven thirty. It's a crow moon tonight: the first full moon of March. The last moon of winter, when spring is heralded by the cawing of crows.

Bored, I pace out the hundred metres to my left, walking towards Denzil, the gardener. Since we've been on boundary patrol I've got to know him well enough to pass the time of day with. He's not that much older than me and when he's not protecting boundaries with a shakily held rifle, or gardening, we work out that we're both Redworld buffs – the music, the books, the crazy stuff. So we talk about that, and gardening. He's got a real talent for it, cos Goddess knows it's hard to produce something that isn't completely mangy without chemicals of any kind. It's an art, organic gardening. You can't just whack a handful of seeds in the ground and expect to feed hundreds of mouths.

The fruit and veg chat is terminally boring, but it's better than chatting with Melz, who is a hundred metres to my right.

As I wander over to Denzil, Gowdie trotting loyally at my heels, he smiles at me and reaches into his pocket. 'All right, Danny? Tempt you with a pasty?' he asks.

'Hell, yeah.' I'm starving. He hands me a golden, flaky pastry parcel. He takes another out of his other pocket and bites into it. I give half to the dog.

'Dig in,' he says, smiling as he chews.

I bite off one end and the savoury, peppery taste fills my mouth. The pastry is buttery and soft in my mouth, and the filling is mouth-watering – potato, carrot, squash, celery. I chew slowly, trying to make it last, but it's hard and I end up stuffing my face.

He smiles and taps the side of his head. 'Secret ingredient, see,' he says. 'Best in the village. I'd challenge anyone to make better.'

'It's pretty good,' I concede. 'Thanks. Just what I needed. I'm so bor—' I start to say, but I don't get a chance to finish cos there's a sudden bang, followed by another couple of sharp retorts.

'What was that?' asks Denzil. He's standing there, pasty in hand, rifle lowered, looking utterly bewildered, as I see maybe twenty men break through the trees off to our right and start running towards us. They're dressed in camouflage clothes, some in old jeans, old-looking Redworld clothes like the ones in Mum's photo albums. The clothes look oddly archaic, especially compared to our standard-Greenworld-issue handmade, hand-knitted browns and greens. Except Melz, in black as ever.

'Hell! Gang! Gang at two o'clock!' I yell and turn away from Denzil, adrenalin pumping through me. I run as fast as I can back to where I was supposed to be.

I turn again towards Denzil and shout over to him, cupping my hands round my mouth to make the sound carry. 'Make the signal!' I scream, and turn to my right.

I gesticulate madly at Melz who is looking the wrong way. 'Melz! Melz! We're under attack! Gang! Gang!'

Gowdie is barking like mad and running around in circles. Melz starts at the sudden commotion and looks at me, and then to her right, and sees more men rapidly approaching. She seems to panic for a moment and then calms down and nods over at me. We know what we're going to do.

As my eyes meet Melz's across the grassy edge of the village time seems to slow down. I can see the gang members – more and more of them: thirty, fifty, a hundred, more – a whole field's length away but running hard towards us, and it's all happening in slow motion. The blood behind my eyes thumps in slow motion. Melz's mouth shapes the magic words we have rehearsed in slow motion. It's all happening to someone else. Except that this is real: the earth is shaking with the reality.

Magic can only do so much with this many people in one go, so we still need to fight. Still, Melz and I start chanting our prepared protection spell, both visualizing a great wall of water rising in front of the men who are running towards us. A tidal wave, rolling towards them, gaining height and width with every second. With just two of us, the power is limited. Good, but limited: we didn't know which way the gangs would approach. If it was to the south, then Lowenna and Beryan would do the same thing; to the east it would be Saba and Merryn. Melz and I are on the west side of the village, outside the Witch's Gate, closest to the forest. It would be hard to attack from the north, as that's the ocean and the cliffs. We don't know how effective the wave will be, but it should buy the village a little time.

As we're sending out our shockwave, Denzil has signalled the person to his left, and that person has signalled to their left, and so on, all around the village. In a matter of a minute or so everyone will be on alert and know that it's started. That we are under attack. At the same time, word will go down another line to

Omar within the village walls. He's waiting with our army and will lead them to the point of attack. Melz and I have to buy him as much time as possible, and I'm praying he won't need that long to mobilize our ragtag group of heavily armed pacifists.

I try to concentrate on visualizing the wave as vividly as I can – feeling its power, speed and lashing cold edge deep within me. Pushing it ahead like a rolling net, a relentless water boulder, to trip up and imprison the coming hordes. I stretch out my arms as far as I can, and power zings from my long fingers. Almost visible, like lightning. I can feel the energy rising in me, getting hotter and bigger with every breath. It's almost overpowering, but as long as I keep focusing on spooling it out through my fingers and into the magic wall of water, I remain in charge. But I know that if I lose my focus now, that power will come back on me and blow me away. I try to ignore Gowdie, who is going mad, racing around and barking at the attackers.

The wave hits the first row of men just seconds after I stretch out my hand, although it feels like a lot longer. I have to keep my focus, not let the wave decrease, lose its volume or be distracted by the men that have already started shooting at us. But even so, I can still watch as the men lose their footing and fall backwards or into each other, faces startled and suddenly panicky. Some of them are gasping as if they've swallowed water: a salty sting at the back of the throat. They can't work out why they're tasting it here in the open air; the wave is invisible unless you are used to seeing energy like witches do. I narrow my eyes and push the wave on and on, through the coming ranks.

Men topple, falling unexpectedly in the twilight, like the wooden bottles in a skittle alley. The ones behind can't see what's tripping them up – and there's nothing to be seen anyway – but it's all happening so fast that they press on regardless, guns firing even though they're still just out of range. We can't make them stay on the ground for long, but we can stop them temporarily as the wave pushes through the crowd. I look over at Melz. A smile plays around her thin pout; she's enjoying this. Enjoying the power. I don't have time to wonder whether I am too.

The first thirty or so of the gang members that got hit by the wave are now picking themselves up and starting to come forward again when I hear a distant horn blowing three times. My rational smart-arse mind surfaces for a moment – What is this, Narnia? – but any non-essential thoughts are luxuries I can't afford right now. Omar's signal may be old-timey and kind of clichéd but it does the job. We know he's coming. All we have to do is hold the gangs off until he gets out to the boundary from the village hall, the central point of Tintagel village.

I catch my breath and look over at Melz. I know she's wondering how long Omar will take to get here, just like I am. We are only two witches, and there are more and more of them every minute.

327

'Use your gun!' I shout at Denzil, who is standing very still, mouth gaping at the men. Perhaps two hundred now. He looks at me confusedly. 'Shoot! Bloody shoot them, Denzil!' I scream, and shoulder my rifle. I fire into the crowd; they're close enough now to be hit – and for their bullets to hit us. Psychic protection won't guard against bullets. I reload and shoot again. Not the most effective weapon – slow and heavy, but I took what I could get. The recoil slams hard into my shoulder and I wince, but fire again. Melz is doing the same with a pistol. She reloads and repeats; a better shot than me. *An incredible shot* – I remember her saying that to Roach what seems like years ago, when he was at the boundary. A different part of the boundary, a different time, and yet, here we are again.

I fire until I run out of ammunition, and look over at her. She is standing with the gun in her hand, squeezing the trigger repeatedly, even though she's run out of bullets and all that comes is an empty click; it's surreal that I hear it.

She throws the gun down and shouts at me. 'Wave!' she cries, and we roll another one at them. Bigger this time, harder, but we're more desperate. I see it maybe three metres high, slamming into the front line of the approaching men that haven't been shot; again the wave rips through them. We are unaware of the return fire that screams past our ears and thuds into the grass at our feet. At the beginning of each watch, we created a protective bubble around ourselves, and tried to show the villagers how to do it too, but I don't know how effective it will be. You need time and training to do something like that. Magic doesn't work just by reading an instruction manual.

I stand and try to summon up the energy for another push and watch the men pick themselves up, spitting to try to get rid of the saltwater taste in their mouths, looking confused at what just happened, but stumbling forward anyway. I find Melz's gaze, and in my mind's eye I reach out for her hand. I feel the power flow between us, and feel Lugh and the Morrigan standing behind us, their power filling us, making us more than who we are. We push the wave out from us: huge, unstoppable, inevitable.

There is a loud crack, and the sound pulls my attention. I feel the wave leave us and surge towards the gang, and I lose the presence of the Gods.

It's Denzil.

I run over to him, calling to Melz. 'He's been shot! He's been shot!'

I cradle Denzil's head in my arms, trying not to look at his chest, where a dark stain is spreading.

'Oh no. Oh, Brighid, no,' Melz says when she sees him, and puts her hands straight over his heart. I know she's giving him healing, trying to keep him with us. 'Stay here, Denzil. It's not your time. It can't be your time,' she pleads, and I watch her dumbly.

She grabs my right hand and places it on Denzil's temple. 'Heal. NOW!' she hisses, and I try, summoning the energy, but I know it's too late. He slumps in my arms and the life goes out of him; I recognize his moment of death as definitely as I know it was the wrong moment, years too soon.

Melz starts crying and rests her head on Denzil's bloody shirt. A boy. Just a boy.

I look up and see that some of the gang men have got to their feet again and are making their way doggedly towards us, some still firing.

I get up and try to pull Melz off Denzil's body. She snatches her hand away from mine. 'Come on. Come on! Melz!'

She looks up at me. 'Go. I'm staying with him.'

'You can't. They're coming. You'll die.'

'Then I'll die. If that's my destiny. I'm one of the Hands. It's my job to protect him. To protect all of them.'

I pull her up roughly. 'This isn't about destiny. It wasn't his destiny to die here and it isn't yours. Don't be stupid, Melz. He's gone. You owe it to the rest of the village to stay alive.'

Before she can reply, the Witch's Gate swings open, and a swarm of pissed-off villagers spew out and swallow us up in the crowd. We are pulled forward by the momentum. I hear Gowdie barking madly somewhere. I look for Denzil's body but I am pulled, stumbling and tripping, forward, forward. I lose sight of Melz.

I pull a sharp kitchen knife from inside my boot. My

witch's blade is no good here. I start running forward. Once the battle starts, the Hands haven't made any plans that involve sticking together – the only plan is fight and win. By whatever means necessary.

I look briefly around me at the crowd as we surge forward. Farmers, artists, bicycle-riders, vegetarians. Their faces are frightened but resolute. I face forward again as one mass meets the other: full-frontal assault. The battle for Tintagel begins.

I've been swallowed by the crowd so it's a few minutes until I see any fighting, and then suddenly it's all around me. I can hear Omar's shouts ahead, spurring us on. The gang members have a variety of crude but effective weapons: guns and knives, but also planks of wood with nails hammered in, mallets, hammers. I pass a gang man being pummelled by two reedy-looking village guys – they can't be more than sixteen, but they've got him where they want him. I see a discarded pistol and pick it up; my mind steps out of itself for a minute and I watch myself checking it for bullets. It has four left.

I am shoved back into the present by an elbow in my ribs; there's a fight going on next to me. I look to my left and am horrified to see a familiar face being ground into the dirt. Ennor's mum Maya is lying on the floor being kicked by some half-witted-looking thug in heavy boots and a crew cut. I go to pull her up, but before I can get her up, a meaty fist grinds into my jaw like a missile.

'Boy.' The fist rings out and catches me again. 'Boy. Don't interfere with what don't concern you,' he shouts over the chaos. His hand feels like it's made of diamonds and my jaw is jelly. I push him away as hard as I can and bend to pick her up — as I try to pull her up by the arm, she screams. It's broken. I can feel the fracture in the way that the weight is all wrong in the arm. I look into her wise, attractive face and it's pained and terrified. This poor woman. Brave enough to persuade others much stronger and fitter than her to go into battle alongside her to protect what was important. And now lying broken under the boot of an animal. Rage wells up inside me like vomit. It's impossible to stop: a tide of bile that explodes from inside.

My fingers swivel the gun and squeeze the trigger twice. One, two. The cracks ring out across a plain of violent sound, and the man plunges to the ground, screaming and clutching at his legs. I look at him briefly: I have shot him in one knee and the other foot. He'll live. He lies on the grass, bleeding and crying, and I turn away and kneel beside Maya.

'Can you walk?' I ask.

She nods grimly. 'Think so,' she winces.

She's so pale I think she's going to pass out any minute.

'OK. Hang on to me with your good arm,' I say and hoist her up. It's chaos everywhere I look: people screaming, crying, groaning; people tripping over the bodies on the ground; mud everywhere. The sound of hard objects thumping into flesh. And through it all, a kind of surreal pause that stops and starts; where everyone wonders if the other person is really going to hit them again, in this sudden shift from the polite everyday rules of interaction. And I can see in many cases that people don't, or can't, fight these complete strangers. Sometimes weapons are dropped, and people stand back. Sometimes people run away.

I catch sight of Merryn in the distance. She's waving at me and I know she can see Maya. Her voice sounds in my head: *bring her to me.* She's the great healer of all of us – sweet Merryn. Plump and docile as a well-fed cat, but here she is in battle like a witchy Florence Nightingale, on the sidelines, already caring for the injured.

And there are so many. I see them as I wind my way through the crowd. The air is thick with noise and the kicked-up dirt from under our warring feet, but not thick enough to stop me seeing the carnage. Old men, young women, bloody, pale, crying, suffering. Is this really what the Greenworld is all about? Is it worth this? Is it worth one drop of blood, one broken bone? I really don't know at this moment.

Merryn runs up to me and holds out her arms for Maya. 'I'll take her, Danny,' she says. 'Well done. I saw what happened. Sickening. They're thugs, just thugs.'

Maya slumps into Merryn's ample grasp. You'd think Merryn might have trouble supporting such a dead weight but she's stronger than she looks, cos she bears Maya's weight as if she were a child. She turns to me. 'Your place is in the battle,' she says. 'I'm OK here. Bring me any others you find.' Then she turns away. No time to chat.

I don't know where Saba is. I'm worried for her. What if she gets injured, or worse? I wish I was with her, but I can't see her anywhere. I'm scanning the field to no avail when something pushes me from behind, hard, and I fall on my face in the mud. I feel a boot in my back.

'One of the witches, is it?' I'm rolled over and stare muddily up at a squat, bullish-looking guy with a beard, probably in his late forties, dressed in jeans and an old brown leather jacket. He kicks my ribs. I cry out.

'Yeah. You're the one. Look just like your picture, don't you, pretty boy?' He chuckles and waves a grubby, grainy photo at me.

How has he got that? I wonder briefly. Nobody has cameras any more. Do they? A hazy memory of the bonfire nags at me. Something I'm supposed to remember, but I can't quite get it.

I try to get up but he sits on my chest. I groan again. It feels like the air is being pressed out of my lungs by bricks.

'No, no, my bab. You stay where you are. Reward for you, in'nt there? Yeah. And I'm going to get it.' He's got that old Cornish way of talking – not someone who came here to be part of the Greenworld – he's been here all his life. 'Now then, I just need to—' But he stops talking as there's a loud crack and his head and shoulders plunge forward towards me.

I crane my head back just enough to avoid my nose being broken. 'What the—' I exclaim, and I look up to see Tom with a cricket bat in one hand, blowing his thick blond Viking hair off his forehead and smiling.

'Getting quite the sweat up what with all this fighting.' He winks at me and pulls the man off me. 'Come on, Grandpa. Leave him alone.' He pushes the guy away with some force and leans down to pull me up.

'Thanks,' is all I can get out. 'I . . . I . . .'

'Don't worry about it.'

'He had a picture of me.'

'Yeah. They want you. Goddess knows why anyone would.'

We stand there grinning at each other for a minute like a couple of idiots. Once again I'm reminded why everyone likes Tom, and in a flash, just like that, I see myself sewing the doll's mouth shut. I look down at my feet in shame. 'Thanks. I . . . Thanks, Tom.'

'All part of the service.'

I look around at the fighting throng. 'How are we doing?' I ask.

'Not bad. Holding the village.'

'Have you seen Saba?'

'She took some of the wounded back to the town hall.'

335

I'm relieved. I hold out my hand. 'I know we haven't been the best of friends, but . . . Thanks, Tom. I really appre—'

I'm stopped from saying the rest of what I want to say, which is something about making it up between us, cos Tom, instead of shaking my hand, is gripping it hard and is suddenly very, very pale.

He lets go of my hand and crumples to the floor, and a red stain starts to seep slowly through his green gardener's shirt.

The frozen cloth doll, made out of an old T-shirt and my own malice, swims up again before my eyes. It's not the cobwebs that spiders have spun over it while it's been wedged behind the shed, or the mould that's starting to climb up one of its legs that I see in my mind's eye; it's the thick darning needle poking out of the crudely drawn-on heart, which merges into the tip of a long knife sticking out of Tom's heart – his good, strong, honest heart.

I look up and Skye is standing where Tom was, with Tom's blood on her hands. Her brown eyes meet mine, and she smiles the brilliant smile Ennor must have fallen in love with.

As I stand there gaping, I feel a blow in my shoulder. It feels as though a train has run into me and left a searing hot pain worming through my collarbone. I gasp, desperate for air and stagger forward. The pain is incredibly intense and I'm in sudden and complete confusion. In slow motion again, Skye tucks her knife away in her pocket. 'Good shot,' she says to someone else. And there's a slow and blurry voice I recognize but I don't know what it's saying.

All my bearings are lost. Everything seems to slow to a dream, and I hear my own heart thumping crazily: Ba-BUM. Ba-BUM. Ba-BUM. I think of Jack and the Beanstalk. *Fee-fi-fo-fum, I smell the blood of an Englishman.* The giant has come to get me. My head's reeling. Then strong arms lift me so I'm dangling, head downward, in a fireman's lift over a broad shoulder, and I am borne away. I black out.

I wake, spluttering, as a bucket of cold water sluices my head like a demonic baptism. I gasp and try to breathe and not choke; it tastes like muddy seawater, salty and brackish. Ugh. The second sensation I have is searing red pain across the top of my body. I reach to rub my shoulder but a rope bites into my wrists and the tops of my arms. I'm tied up, and as I look up I realize I'm in a lot of trouble. Roach is standing in front of me smiling unpleasantly. He's running his thumb along the length of his athame. I recoil from it, from him.

'Awake, then, are we, Sleeping Beauty? We must stop meeting like this,' he rasps.

I look around me wildly, looking for escape, and realize where we are: the grassy, rocky top of windy Tintagel Head.

He looks at a goon: a massive man-mountain, all

bull neck and cauliflower ears. 'Bring her over,' he orders.

The goon steps away for a minute and there's a stifled cry. A female voice.

It's all happening behind me and I'm craning round to see who it is, though in my heart I already know. I just don't want to.

'Say hello to your . . . Well, what shall I call her? Girlfriend? Fellow witch? Cave dweller? Oh, I've had my eyes on you both for a while now!' Roach laughs and drags her forward by her tied wrists.

Saba's tawny eyes meet mine. I can see she's furious but scared too. Rage floods through me and I struggle to get free – all I want to do is take that knife and run it through his chest. Whatever he wants with me – well, that's one thing, but hurting Saba is another. And I'm so angry at myself for not being at her side to protect her. And angry that Roach knows about us. We thought we'd been so careful going to the cave. And I think, If we get out of this, I'll never let anything bad happen to her again.

'So! Here we are, my witchy friends,' Roach laughs.

'You're no friend of ours,' Saba spits. 'You can't win this battle. There's too many of us,' she says confidently. She's brave, but we all know that even though there might be more of us, the gang members are better fighters. We can hear the roar of the battle from here.

Roach shrugs. 'I doubt that,' he says. 'But anyway, I'm where I need to be right now. They can rage on without us for a while, don't you think?'

He leans forward and runs the blade of his knife under Saba's chin.

'What do you want with us?' I bark to distract him from Saba.

He raises his bushy eyebrows and gestures around him with a sweep of his arm. 'I want you to witness me taking what's yours. Or, what's not yours, I should say.'

'What do you mean? Whatever you think you can do, Roach, you can't. Just give up now,' Saba says, and as she speaks, she catches my eye.

It's an infinitesimal moment, but I see her eyes flick to one side. No one's looking at me right at this second, so I risk a look in the direction of her eyes. I see she's holding her hand over the pocket she usually keeps her tarot cards in – sort of to keep them warm, keep her energy in them.

I frown. OK. Tarot. What about it?

Roach has turned his back to us and starts to move his hands through the air meditatively. 'Look familiar?' he asks over his shoulder.

Saba and I exchange a worried look.

'You're opening the portal? You can't! I—' I wince as the goon slaps me in the shoulder to shut me up. The pain is incredible – a sick throbbing going right into the bone.

A gunshot, I think, not quite believing it. Somebody shot me.

'Why?' Saba asks. 'Why are you doing this? What do you think you can get from it?'

There's a pause, and Roach places the last symbol into the air. It's a demanding process. The portal bulges, pulses, suddenly alive. I feel the familiar pressure to breathe as the pounding beat thrums though my broken body.

Roach turns to us again, shaking out his elbows. 'Energy,' he pants. 'Power. That's what it's always been about. The Redworld, the Greenworld. All about energy. The Redworld wants to use it up. The Greenworld has opted out and lives without it. But it controls some of the greatest energy sources in the world. Not even witches really understand them, but I do.'

He's got a zealous look in his eye as he talks, making him look even madder than usual.

'Shut up, idiot. We understand them all right,' Saba snaps, controlling her breathing, but he just laughs.

'Course you do. Haven't you ever thought about the kind of limitless power the portal has? All that inter-dimensional energy, just flowing away, waiting to be harnessed?'

Saba and I exchange glances.

'There are people who will pay a very high price for a new energy source. Powerful people in the Redworld.

And I can give it to them. Now, how attractive do you think that makes me?' He laughs.

'You wouldn't dare do it! Brighid will have her vengeance!'

Saba is outraged, but he cuts her off. 'Oh, come on. Give it a rest. Do you really think there would be some heavenly retribution? What about all the wars, Saba? All the evil acts that humankind has ever perpetrated? Where was your goddess then? She didn't step in.' He takes a deep breath and I can see that he's not trying to align his breath with the portal. He's fighting it, and that means he's not as accomplished as he thinks he is. Sometimes the smallest things are the most important. Controlling your breath is key to working with the portal.

Roach has had a long time to practise his rhetoric in the years spent with the gangs and there is a part of me that somewhat agrees with what he's saying. His methods are vicious, but what if the energy from the portals could be harnessed to help the world? To change the remaining Redworld forever? And help the Greenworld move on too?

'So I'm not worried, thanks. Anyway, how can you presume to know the mind of Brighid? Her will? Who knows what the divine plan is, if any? Maybe it is that the portals should be harnessed for the greater good of humankind. Now what's so wrong about that?'

'Nothing at all, boss,' says a Cornish voice. I look up and see the same squat, bullish man that attacked me, walking along the top of Tintagel Head towards us.

Roach smiles at my outraged face. 'You've just met Gawen, haven't you? Not in the best of circumstances, I suppose. Gawen could tell you a thing or two about the Redworld, eh, Gaw? It's not so bad, is it?'

They both laugh.

'Not bad a' all, in my experience,' he grins, and hands Roach something. A piece of paper.

Roach glances at it. My photo. 'Did its job, then. Good lad, your son. Remind me to thank him.'

Gawen's son. I think of Skye standing over Tom's dead body, the knife in her hands, smiling. Bali took the photo; I finish the realization that started when I saw it in Gawen's hand, right before Tom knocked him over. I even remember when Bali took it. That first night at the bonfire, when I was too pissed to think about what he was doing, or why. They needed a photo of me so they would all know who I was. I think suddenly of that stupid little book Skye had about witches. How having an image of a witch was power over them. In this case, it was.

Amid my thoughts I hear Saba's voice in my head. 'The cards,' it says. 'Make them real.'

I see her hand over her pocket again. The tarot: the thing that brought me here in the first place. The night in the cave when the Empress came alive flashes into my memory, and she nods imperceptibly as I catch her eye. Now I know what she means, but can I do it?

I rack my brain to remember the way to animate the cards. Cos there are a lot of forces in that pack, and they're not all deer-herding queens of the harvest. There are knights and kings with swords and sticks and flames, warrior queens and princesses. And, if I need them, there is suffering and pain, and there is Death. Quickly, I recite the words in my head and try to concentrate as hard as I can on the tarot pack. It's doubly hard cos Roach is talking and I can't see the cards, and the combination of pain in my shoulder and the urge to heave in great lungfuls of air to counterbalance the pressure from the portal is almost unbearable, but still I concentrate as hard as I can and mentally flick through them. I need help to escape. I look back to the mainland to the battle and hear the cries of the villagers. They need us. They need all the help they can get. I hope this works.

It works.

There is the sound of heavy hoofs on rock. Wind blows across Tintagel Head, stronger than usual: there is a whinny and a bright flash of steel. Before we have time to speak, two living, breathing horses with riders emerge from the choppy waves below us and sort of fly-gallop to the top of the rock: the Knight of Swords and the Knight of Wands, bright and aflame with bravery. The Knight of Swords wears a bluish metal suit of old-fashioned armour with a guard over his face, and a huge silver sword flashes in his hand. The Knight of Wands is dressed in medieval-style red leather – all flapping tassels and knee boots. He's wielding a massive club that is on fire at the top.

Maybe this is why the trick worked at the cave; maybe water is the element malleable enough to be shaped into magical objects – it's like it's forming these tarot figures in response to my thoughts. I remember the morning at the beach, the Procession of the Maidens with Saba, when Brighid materialized over the sea. Maybe that was the same thing. But right now I don't have the headspace to theorize.

The big goon practically shits himself and Gawen holds out his hands as if to protect himself, but one of the horses rears up and hits him straight in the face with its hoofs. Boom, out cold. It's scary; I may be powering these beasts, but I don't know what they'll do next.

The Knight of Swords cuts through our ropes and hoists Saba on to the back of his horse (even in the panic, I'm tempted to think 'steed' instead of horse. It's a real Robin Hood moment). Roach has turned from the portal and is staring open-mouthed at these two huge horses champing and snorting. Before he can use magic to do anything, the Knight of Wands whacks him around the head with his club, almost setting Roach's hair on fire. He crumples on to the floor. It takes everything I've got but I pull myself on to the Knight's horse and slap its flank.

'Away!' I yell, and we stampede across Tintagel Head and across the thin, rocky bridge to the mainland. I feel the pressure in my lungs releasing as we power away from the open portal, but know I still have to keep concentrating as it's me that is driving them forward – my will, my mind. I can't think for a second that they aren't real, cos if I have the slightest doubt, they will disappear. And we need them in battle.

We ride at full speed from the coast rocks up into the village and into the warring crowd, the Knights with their weapons high. I see immediately that we are losing the battle.

I look across at Saba; her face is a blur. It is ecstatic, wild: she is clinging on to the muscular back of the horse with her thighs and her arms are clasped round the waist of the Knight. Suddenly I feel her mind meet mine and push the horses onward faster and harder. She knows what I'm doing and now that she can draw a breath she's making this a team effort; we don't want to lose these valuable forces on our side.

We ride through the fighting, swords flashing. The crowd has thinned out and there are more gang members left than villagers. There are too many wounded for Merryn to help and I can see that if we'd got here even a few minutes later it might have been too late. The village hangs in the balance; without us, now, it might be lost.

Many of the gang members are simply ridden over by the Knights. I feel a kind of dark elation as the Knight of Wands knocks one gang guy over and tramples his legs. I hear the bones crack; I feel his scream run up my spine. I should feel something more – he's a human being, like me, but I'm so concentrated on the magic that humanity fades into the background.

And then something even stranger happens. I feel power coming to me from the rest of the Hands — we're used to connecting together in this magical, telepathic way — and I start to imagine other figures from the tarot. And they appear. A knight wielding a heavy, sharp-edged pentacle. A knight bearing a magically refilling cup; whatever's in it isn't pleasant when he pours it all over a gang member, then another. And warrior queens and princesses too, armed and lethal, riding in Celtic body armour: bronze and leather, their hair plaited in complicated patterns round bronze and silver headdresses.

Because I have six lots of power at my command, I realize I can create more tarot figures from the sea. I start to visualize others: the Chariot; the Devil; the Magician.

In moments there are loads of riders on horseback slashing their way through the gangs. A rider in a horse-drawn chariot, spinning a lasso above his head; a huge horned goat-man striding forward, butting men out of the way; a magician in long robes with a wand in one hand and a sword in the other, spinning them like nunchuks.

I start to get creative with it. Even cards that don't have obviously battle-useful qualities appear on the battleground. I even imagine the holy nun-like High Priestess, and she appears, striking our enemies blind and binding their arms to their sides with a glance from her luminous eyes. And I bring the figure of Death with his scythe as a warrior on our side, although death is here for people on both sides of the battle.

The gangs are terrified, as are the villagers, but they soon get the idea that the Knights and all of these strange figures are on our side. When the leaders of the gang fighters see the goat-man and the Magician they gape, watching the crowd part in front of them like a river. When there is nothing between them and the sword-wielding Magician but dead air, one holds up his fist.

'Fall back! Back!' he shouts, and within minutes the gangs start to recede. They want to live to fight another day, and who wouldn't be massively freaked out by this kind of enemy force? I don't blame them. The ones that can still walk fall over their own feet to get to the forest.

When the last of them are stumbling to the trees, Saba and I look at each other, exhausted. We nod at each other, and together we shout, 'Stop,' and clap our hands together. I brace myself but it doesn't make any difference; we fall on to the hard Cornish ground as our mounts magically disappear.

I look around and see all the tarot figures vanish, like lights being turned off. Within a minute they've all gone. I roll on to my back and groan. I might lie here for a long time.

Chapter Twenty-one

> And hence it is that Badb (i.e. the Morrigu) also
> describes high deeds. 'Hast thou any tale?' said
> everyone to her then. And she replied:
> 'Peace up to heaven
> Heaven down to earth
> Earth under heaven
> Strength in every one.'
>
> From *The Second Battle of Mag Tuired (Moytura)*,
> author unknown

After a few seconds gasping for breath, I roll over
to Saba who has fallen close to where I am — a
muddy corner of blood-soaked battleground, which
just an hour before was a nondescript grassy field
between a nondescript forest and a scruffy village
boundary.

'You all right?' I ask.

She groans. 'Think my ankle's broken,' she whispers.

'Oh Goddess.' I roll over clumsily, sit up and pull her into a sitting position. 'Do you think you can put any weight on it?'

She nods but grimaces as we both stand up and look around us. From ground level it looks even worse. The dead and wounded are everywhere, and the air smells of sweat, discharged guns and blood.

Victory comes at a price, says a voice in my ear, and three crows settle next to us.

'The Morrigan,' Saba whispers. 'Did you feel her today? I sensed her on the battlefield. Giving us courage. I think she helped us, you know. To win.'

I look around at the bodies, at the terrible waste. 'It doesn't feel like we won,' I say.

'Well, we did. We won the battle, thanks to you,' she says.

'It wasn't me,' I say.

She smiles. 'It's always you,' she says and squeezes my hand.

I look again at the bodies. We didn't all win. I think of Tom.

Be careful what you wish for, that voice whispers in my ear.

I want to tell Saba then, confess it all, how I cursed him to die, but there's a flurry of barks and Gowdie races across the kicked-up grass to us – I don't know where she's been, but she's pretty muddy. She jumps up at me and licks my face enthusiastically.

'Good girl,' I say, and check her over for scrapes and cuts, but she seems fine.

Lowenna comes puffing up to us, her hair wild and muddy. She looks like she's gone a few rounds, fighting dirty. 'Thank Brighid you're both all right!' she exclaims and envelops both of us in a massive hug.

Saba yelps.

'Oh, oh! Sorry! Saba! You're hurt! Oh, and Danny! You're bleeding! We have to get you home, both of you. And this one!' she says, bending over and giving Gowdie a brisk stroke. 'Quite the doggy heroine! I was fighting this big bearded fella and Gowdie came to my rescue! She got hold of his arm and wouldn't let go. Brave dog!'

Gowdie actually looks proud.

Lowenna pats me on the arm, making me wince. 'What a piece of magic that was, though! I've never seen anything like it! It was amazing! I didn't know you could do that! I mean, it took incredible strength! And talent!'

I interrupt her excited babble. 'Thanks, but right now we've still got a problem. Roach may still be back at Tintagel Head, and when we left he'd just opened the portal. He got a whack on the head, but I don't think it will have slowed him down for long.'

'What did he say he was going to do?' Lowenna asks.

I shake my head. 'I'll tell you on the way, but you'd better bring your gun and as much ammo as you can find.'

She nods. 'Of course, Danny. Of course. I'll follow you,' she says. For the first time she seems a little beaten, and her reply – *I'll follow you* – fills me with a strange feeling, but I say nothing.

We all pace back to the island of rock, not talking, the crow moon now high in the sky. It occurs to me that it may not have been the best plan in the world to escape leaving Roach with the opened portal, but what else could I do? We had to act in the moment, and we did. The fact that we have repelled the gangs – and with such spectacular results – hasn't quite sunk in. And we're tired. Exhausted. I feel like I'm running on thin air, like being up a mountain. I feel light-headed. It's the effect of the magic. Not forgetting the bullet through the shoulder. As we walk, I see that she's trying to hide it but Lowenna is limping pretty badly. There's no time to ask, but I can see a dark red stain on the leg of her trousers; she's injured too, but she's not saying anything. I watch her face, and she's concentrating on controlling the pain, I can tell.

As we walk back we pass many wounded townspeople. Bloodied clothes, pain stretching their faces. Lowenna rubs my arm as we walk on. 'It's all right, Danny. They'll be cared for,' she says softly.

'But there are so many!' I can't help my reply.

'I know. I know. But Beryan and Merryn are leading the healing,' she says.

I know that as well as the energy-healing techniques employed by Beryan and Merryn – and they really are pretty impressive – the town has a good number of doctors and nurses, some trained in Redworld hospitals.

I'm reassured by them. Even though I'm a witch too, and my healing ability is coming along (though it will never be my strong point) I think there's a place for the old technical kind of nursing. Bandages and antiseptic. At this moment I can't bring myself to enquire about the dead – that's for later. Nevertheless, Tom's surprised face darts across my consciousness, the red stain spreading across his chest.

I look at Saba, wondering if she knows, if anyone knows yet. She can't know; her expression is clear and purposeful. Not the face of someone who has lost her childhood sweetheart. I consider telling her as we make our way over to the island, but it's not the right time. The words choke in my throat; the guilt sits behind my tongue like a toad. Soon will be enough time.

As we approach the island I can feel my nerves tingling. What will happen when we get up there? But as I look, I can sense he isn't there. The rock looks blank in the darkening night. We can't see any figures on it.

Saba, Lowenna and I exchange glances. That's not good.

As we reach the top of the rock, it feels all wrong. Everything is very quiet. Usually there's a psychic hum when you walk on to Tintagel Head. You might not hear it when you first visit, but once you've been a few times, and worked with the portal, and worked with magic – then you get it. You can almost hear all of the machinations and visions and mantras and spells that have ever been woven here, but now it's eerily silent. Blank. As if all of the magic has been spring-cleaned away like kitchen grease.

Gowdie runs around, sniffing at the ground, but she knows something's wrong. Roach has gone, and not just that: the natural peace of the place has gone. We all feel it.

I look quizzically at Saba.

She shakes her head. 'I don't know,' she mouths.

And then Lowenna, who has gone ahead of us, cries out. 'Oh! Oh . . . no! How could he? How could he? This is a holy place. That animal. That utter, utter animal, I . . .'

We run over and look down at the ground where Lowenna stands. Roach had a point to prove. You don't scare me, he screams back from the ground, which has been splashed with red paint and mud – maybe worse. Glass broken, strewn everywhere. Lowenna starts to sob when she sees it all.

Even though I was just here an hour ago it feels totally alien now. But what makes my breath catch in my throat is the huge muddy reversed pentagram that's been daubed on the ground. Point facing down rather than up: The wrong polarity. The wrong energy flow. And inside it there's a whole group of symbols and glyphs I don't understand and don't like the look of. Something is very, very wrong.

We exchange looks.

'What is this?' I ask.

'Never seen anything quite like this before,' Lowenna says, shaking her head.

'What is it – dark magic?' Saba asks.

'It's nothing I ever taught him. He must have found this somewhere else. I don't know what it is.'

'He's gone into the portal,' I say. 'He must have. He's been trying all this time.'

Saba frowns. 'We have to get in, then. We have to stop him before he does something to the energies. Mum, when he had us captive up here he was talking about selling off the portals to the Redworld again.'

'Well, all the more reason to find him and stop him. All right. Let's try to get in. Concentrate, kids.'

I calm my breathing and centre myself. Nothing to be gained by panicking. When I feel grounded, I nod at Lowenna and Saba and direct my power at opening the portal.

Lowenna traces the movements to start the opening procedure. It's like wading in treacle. Nothing happens. She tries again. Nope. Again. This time there's the faintest glimmer of orange, and a kind of whirr, and then nothing. Like someone deliberately blowing out a match when you're trying to light a fire. With the sweat breaking out on my top lip, I focus as hard as I can on directing my power to where the portal should be.

We finally get the portal opening on our fourth go, but it's tough. The energy is all wrong. The usual deep thrumming heartbeat is a wavering trill. It's hardly having an effect on my body at all in the normal way, but its weight on my lungs would be way better than this sick feeling of dread.

Lowenna waves at me. The effort needed to open it even this much shows in her face.

'Danny,' she pants. 'You need. To go in. Saba. Look after things this. End.'

There's no time to argue. I widen the portal as much as I can and pass through into it, concentrating on making myself fuzzy, blurring my outline, but it's really hard and I'm already so tired. I find myself in the multicoloured tunnel again and walk forward slowly. I concentrate on Roach, hoping I'll pick up his signal, or a trace of him somewhere. No old ladies catapult themselves into the tunnel this time, but the feeling of wanting to stay here starts to announce itself in the instinctive part of my brain. Like, wouldn't it be nice to sit down here, on the weird cloud-like floor, and just relax, just become one with the colours? I feel really tired. I could do with a rest. But I recognize that feeling as part of being in this in-between place, and press on. This time I have to go to the end of the tunnel. I have to find Roach, and I can only assume that's where he went.

I plod on and on, trying to keep fuzzy enough to stay here but stay as myself: keep alive, and not become some kind of weird zombie spirit. The further I go, the harder it is, and I start to feel a strong desire to turn back. I shouldn't be here. It's wrong. But I keep going, putting one foot in front of the other, and remembering that I have feet. I have a body. I will not disintegrate.

Suddenly I find myself standing on a muddy shore, looking at a wide, dark lake. There are hundreds, maybe thousands of people here, all sitting on the water. The River of Death, Beryan called it. So these people must be in the process of passing over to the next world, the place of the dead. There's a very charged feeling to the river: intensely emotional. I can feel it gagging me. Waves of joy and sorrow pass through me; I'm catching it from the souls here like hay fever on a summer's day.

I remember Beryan telling me about it. These almost-invisible people – these spirits, souls, whatever – they're reliving their lives before taking the last step. Learning from what they've done. I take a deep breath. I am trespassing here.

'I am not dead, I am not dead,' I whisper. But this is a place for the dead. I am a witch, and my skills can keep me here, and my body alive, temporarily, if I'm smart about it.

I feel strongly that I need to get over this lake to the other side, which I can dimly see in the distance. But I know instinctively that this muddy shoreline is the last permitted place for the living. If I step foot into the river I might never be able to go back, but I have to find Roach and stop him doing something terrible. I know deep in my bones that Roach is on the other side, and if he's got that far then I must be able to as well. I close my eyes, clear my mind and my heart and pray for help.

It's quiet for a few minutes as I stand there, head bowed, and then dimly I hear a plashing sound, something hitting the water softly. Out of the gloom appears a rowing boat. It's painted black but some of the paint is peeling off – it looks very, very old. The oars, when the rower lifts them from the water, are carved in an intricate knot design. They are black too, heavy wood, and the handles are bound with a frayed black fabric. My eyes travel up the oars to the bony white hands steering the boat and the thin arms circled with blue woad.

She is robed entirely in black, hooded with black feathers, but I see Her face underneath, with the symbol of the dark crescent moon in the same flaking blue paint on Her forehead. The Morrigan: Goddess of death and rebirth.

The soles of my feet ache as Her voice resonates inside my head. 'Here we are at the end of things, Daniel. Will you go further?'

'I-it's you!' I stutter, remembering Her voice in my ear, Her presence behind me on the battlefield. I can't think of anything more inspired to say.

She smiles. 'Indeed it is. And here we are together. What do you seek?'

'I need to find Roach. He's crossed over. He wants to sell the portals to the Redworld – do something with the energy – so they can use it. I've got to stop him!' I say in a rush.

'Roach has his own path,' She replies, Her eyes on the still water.

'But I've got to stop him!' I repeat.

'If you cross the river you might never be able to come back. That way is Death,' She intones.

'But there is a way back?'

'Yes. For some. But it is not advised.'

'I need to find him,' I insist. I'm doing this for Mum, for everyone in the Greenworld. It's my job to protect them, and to protect the portals.

The Morrigan looks at me for a long time, as if sizing me up, weighing my soul in Her deep eyes. Then She smiles and gestures to the seat next to Her. 'Well then, Danny. Allow me to row you across,' She says.

I step into the boat. The Morrigan leans into the oars and pulls, and we drift across the murky surface of the water. Three crows circle over the boat, cawing. The souls move to let us through as if gently parted with a giant hand.

She says nothing as She rows. Shyly I check out the blue-woad tattoos on Her arms. I see that rather than one long ongoing spiral, the lines are formed of words, circling her bony wrists, forearms and upward into the heavy, ripped folds of black. She is covered with words: spells, incantations maybe; I don't know. I only get glimpses when Her arms pull the oars.

She catches my eye. 'You have one of these now,' She says, nodding to my arm. I roll up my sleeve and look at my witch-brand.

'Yeah . . . I just don't know what it's for, or why I have it. Or why Roach has the same one. What do we have in common?'

She doesn't answer, just pulls the splintered oars through the still water, nudging aside the floating souls.

'They do not see us,' She says in response to a question I haven't asked. 'They can only see themselves. This is why they are not ready to cross over. Until they have stopped seeing themselves, stopped looking back at their own lives, they will stay here. Seeing what they could do differently for the next time.'

I look around me: the shore we came from is far away, and we are approaching a grassy island. I put my hand on Hers, on the oar, and She stops rowing.

'Really, though, why us? The ones that have it? What are the brands for?'

I think of Melz, Roach, Lowenna. Mum. What is it about us that makes us different? Why do we have these brands?

'They are magic on your skin. They are a spell, a blessing, an incantation. They are my power given to you. Lugh's power. Brighid's power. All the marks have a different energy.'

'What does that mean? Like, the brands make us more powerful?'

'It makes your trueness truer, your darkness darker, your magic stronger, your resistance higher.'

'Was that why I could make the cards come alive in battle? So many of them, all at once?'

'Yes. You have power of your own. But the words in your skin lend you His power too. Lugh. He is a magician, among other things. He brings life where there was none. Moulds the elements to his desire.'

She gently removes my hand from Hers and starts rowing again.

'Is it only men that can have his brand? Roach and me?' I keep on. It's only so often you have the opportunity for a one-to-one with a deity, after all.

'No. Any of the chosen ones may have it.'

'Why are we the chosen ones?'

'You will find that out in your own time.'

'Are we the same, Roach and me? Am I evil too?'

Her willowy arms pull the heavy oars through the black water evenly, strongly. We are almost there.

'No one is evil or good. No one is the same. Some are similar; some make one choice, some make another. It is never too late to make another choice.'

'So do we have some kind of destiny together?' I ask. 'That's what he thinks.'

'You will make your own destinies, together or apart.'

Another enigmatic non-answer. I sigh. 'I'm afraid he's trying to find a way to steal the energy from the portals,' I say. It sounds stupid even as I say it.

She just laughs, a long low jangle. 'Why would he do that?'

'He thinks he can make money out of it. To make fuel for the Redworld.'

'If there is a need for energy in your world, and if the portals can provide it, why shouldn't they?'

'Because they're sacred. They're not something you can sell.'

'What no one owns no one can sell. But they can be used in whatever way is needed,' She replies.

'How can we use portals to provide energy to others? I mean the type of energy to power machines, keep us warm, cook with?'

'This is something for what you call "magic" and "technology" to discover together,' She replies.

'So it's possible?' I ask, flabbergasted. Is Roach actually on to something?

'Anything is possible. But your task is to ensure it is done right. To maintain the portals as sacred sites even as they power the world. You can harness that power, but it has to be truthful. It has to be right.'

The Morrigan smiles, and a huge warmth enters my veins like a gulp of ritual wine. The boat has stopped. She holds Her hand out to me. 'We are at the other side,' She says, and I step on to the bank.

The boat plashes gently away. 'Where can I find him? What about me? How can I get home from here?' I call after Her.

Her voice floats across the water. 'Once you go over the top of the mountain there is only one way back.'

'What is it?'

'To be called back by someone you love. Only that can pull you away from what lies on the other side of the mountain.'

The boat disappears into the mist, and I am alone.

The mountain looms above me, full of rocks, and the ground immediately in front of me is packed with tall weeds. I put my head down and force my way through, knowing that each step takes me closer to death, to never being able to go back. Every step is riskier than the last. It's my life at stake.

Panting, I look up to the summit. Nothing. But as I drop my gaze I see a speck moving through some of the large rocks ahead. It's Roach.

I start to run forward and uphill. He's a long way in front and I sense I need to get to him before he makes it to the top. But as fast as I run and climb he still seems to be the same distance away. I'm panting and sweating like a horse. I have to stop for a minute and double over, lungs heaving.

I put my head down and will myself to climb as fast as I can. I'm so tired, but I use everything I've got and just focus on each rock immediately in front of me until I come to a kind of plateau. I stop again there, chest heaving. I swallow hard and look at the ground under my feet. Just a few more steps and I will die, I think. I'm on the boundary of life and death. I could go back. I turn round and look down at the mountain, at the river and the green land beyond it. There's still time to go back safely. But if I leave now I risk letting Roach do something terrible. I have to stop him. If it's my destiny to die trying, then I am living out my destiny.

Slowly I put one foot in front of the other, and cross over to the other side.

Chapter Twenty-two

Ad regen eumenidium et reginam eius:
Gwynn ap Nvdd
qui es ultra in silvis
pro amore concubine
tue permitte nos venire domum.

To the king of spirits, and to his queen:
Gwyn ap Nudd,
Thou who art overlord of the woodland
for the love of thy mate,
allow us to enter thy domain.

> Verse used by soothsayers,
> from a fourteenth-century
> Welsh manuscript, author unknown

I don't know what I expected, but it's not this. I'm standing in the garden where I first met Lugh and got my witch-brand – the same marble bench, the same owl hooting, the same bushes cut into animal shapes.

Only, this time Roach is sitting on the bench waiting for me.

'It's nice here, isn't it? Except for that bloody owl,' he says and taps the space on the bench next to him. 'Come on, Danny boy. Come and sit down. You must be knackered.'

Well, I'm probably dead anyway, I think, and sit down cautiously next to him. What's the harm?

He motions to the garden. 'Look familiar?'

'Umm . . . yeah,' I hedge.

'Come on. This is where you came to meet Lugh, in your vision. When you woke up with the tattoo. Don't worry – it was the same place for me. But I haven't been back since.' He takes a deep breath of the heavy, lily-scented night air. 'Funny how the smell of somewhere can take you right back. A special place, this.'

'You need to come back with me. You can't do whatever you're trying to do. I won't let you,' I say, serious, but he laughs that big laugh.

'Aren't we a bit beyond that good and evil pantomime by now? I mean, we are technically dead. Maybe you ought to start thinking of me as a friend. I could still be a helpful friend to you, Danny. The rules are different here, you know.'

'You still killed a lot of people in the battle. And you want to control the portals. That sounds like evil to me – it doesn't matter what garden you sit in.'

He gets up, stretches his neck and his shoulders and starts pacing around the bench. Around me. 'Look, Dan. Being here with you – it's weird, obviously. You hate me: that's fine. I can see why. But maybe it's fate, us being here together, just us, in the quiet. Maybe at last we can understand each other a bit more. I don't hate you. In fact, I've always wanted us to be friends. To work together. You know that.'

'But I'm not interested, Roach. That's what you seem to keep forgetting. I only followed you here to stop you doing something terrible.'

He smiles craftily and traces his finger along the granite bench. 'What was that, then?'

'I don't know – you were going to do something to the portal. For fuel.'

He grins. 'And why couldn't I do whatever I wanted on Tintagel Head? Why did I have to come this far? Why did I have to lead you here, past the living world? Tell me that if you can.'

'Lead me here?'

He paces around to stand behind me and places his hands on my shoulders.

'I never gave up on you, Danny. You got away from me three times before I had the chance to persuade you: so I knew that this was the only option I had left. Lead you in here, at the end of life itself, bring you back to this place. The place that's special to both of us.'

'So you're not here to do something to the portal?'

He waves his hand dismissively. 'No. That needs

other stuff. Machines that haven't been built yet. We need to prepare that together. No, this is about you. I knew if I could get you here then I could show you properly what your true potential is. Show you your destiny. What you were born for.'

'Why here?'

'This is a magic space. The Palace of Death. The rules of space and time are different here. Here we can travel in time – see the future, maybe even change the past.'

'How? And how can we have already been here, if this is death? If we had to go through all that palaver to get here today? Crossing the river and everything?'

'In a vision you see a facsimile of this place. A copy that you can visit while alive, while in the normal world. Like a neutral ground where Lugh could meet you, be seen by you. But this, here, is the real Palace of Death. And only the real place has these kinds of . . . possiblities.'

'What possibilities?'

He turns to look at me, excitement burning in his eyes. 'Don't you want to see your future, Danny? The greatness that you have in you? I know you feel I'm right. I know you've been curious about me all along. Let me help you, Dan. Let me help you realize your true power.'

He takes my hand in his. I try to pull it away but he grips my fingers. 'Just try it. You don't have to do anything except see.'

And the thing is, I'm curious. I can't deny it. I want to see my future, and unlike Lowenna, Roach is offering me real power. To see my real potential, not just trusting in the lame old good of the future and hard work being its own reward. He's offering me real results. At least he's nailing his colours to the mast – he's all about the magic, the power that we share. That's more than a lot of people will do – Mum, Lowenna, Omar – they hedge, they say we'll see, and all the time Rome burns.

'What do I have to do?' I whisper.

A smile plays around the edge of his mouth like a kindling flame. 'Ask to see *The Book of Daniel Prentice*.'

'What book?'

'It doesn't matter. *The* book. There's only one.'

'What do I do? Who do I ask? There's no one here.'

'There is. Just ask out loud. It's simple.'

OK. I clear my throat. 'In the name of Lugh, Brighid, the Morrigan; show me *The Book of Daniel Prentice*,' I say into the night air.

Roach is still gripping my hand, and he turns our hands over. I look down and see that where I thought our hands were touching, I am now holding a leather-bound book. Worn brown leather cover and heavy rough-cut pages.

He nods. 'Now open it to the first page.'

My hands are shaking a little. I take in a breath to keep them steady.

The opening page has my name and date of birth,

Mum's and Dad's names and Biba's. I trace my fingers over the letters. 'What is this?' I breathe, fascinated.

'It's the record of your life. Everything you've done; everything you could do. We all have one. But not everyone knows how to read theirs.'

'So everything from my life so far is in here?'

'Yeah.'

'What, even tiny things? Like how I used to throw my toast into the cupboard under the stairs cos I didn't like marmalade?'

'Even that.'

'What, everything?'

He smiles. 'Yes. Everything.'

I leaf through some of the pages, trailing my finger over the words, and as I do it, moving images leap from the pages and play out in front of me. I watch a six-year-old me playing in our garden, and a slightly older me with his face pressed against a rainy window, watching Dad walk down the garden path and out of the gate. The day he left.

'It isn't just a book?' I ask.

'It's a whole singing-and-dancing review of your life. You can use it to look over what you've done, see what lies ahead. We're special, being able to see it without being dead.'

'I thought we were more or less dead, being here?'

'More or less – maybe more, maybe less than you think. It's possible to go back from here.'

'Right. Called back by someone you love.'

'Oh, that old lie. I don't need someone weeping and wailing for me to get back. But, look, we're here now. Be in the moment, Danny.' He sees my finger hovering over that day – the last time I saw Dad. 'You can see people you haven't seen in years,' he says softly.

I snatch my hand away from the book. 'I don't want to see anything else from the past.'

'Fair enough. What about the future?'

'How do I see it if it hasn't happened yet?'

'Look ahead in the book. There are, shall we say, a number of possibilities based on your current actions. Some more likely than others.'

Nervously, I look at the thick pages. A sudden breeze flutters them in my hand.

'Look, and learn, Danny. Look, and be wise,' Roach says quietly, and puts my right hand on the pages.

Slowly, I turn them over.

The first thing I see is Saba. I smile; as always my heart lifts to see her. And I see her dressed like a medieval queen, draped in luxurious velvets and furs, and I see me too. We're in some kind of amazing, opulent bedroom. Green silk on the walls; gold everywhere. Gold furniture. Huge carved doors. A fireplace I could stand up in. We're drinking from golden cups. We both wear golden circlets in our hair.

'Where are we?' I whisper to Roach.

'The future. A possible future. Where you're rich and powerful, Danny. Richer than you can imagine.

You'd never have to be cold or hungry again – or compete for Saba's love.'

I look up quickly, but he just nods. 'Tom. Yes. I know what you did. I've been so focused on you. I've been in your dreams, in your visions. You know we have that connection. So I saw you work that curse too.'

'What?' I stand up, taking my hand away from the book. 'What do you mean?'

'I mean, I saw the stake through the heart. Crude, but effective, but the blood's on Skye's hands now, Dan. Not yours. Now you can have Saba. Forever. She never has to know what you did. No one does.'

I feel sick. 'But I didn't want him dead! He was a good guy! How can you think I wanted that?'

'I have absolutely no idea, Dan. Maybe it was the voodoo doll with the needle through its heart,' he snaps sarcastically. 'It was Skye's decision to kill him just like it was your decision to set the curse. She responded to what you put out there. Your power made it that powerful. The same curse in someone else's hands—' he blows out his cheeks – 'it probably wouldn't have been fatal. But you have to remember how strong you are. I don't think you really understand it yet.'

I look at my feet. 'I didn't mean to kill him. I just wanted her. Saba,' I say quietly.

He shrugs. 'Well, you did kill him. So you see, you're not so different from me after all. You've already made your first kill, and won the princess. Aren't you curious what else you could do – what we could do together?'

'I don't understand exactly why you need me. What the possibilities are.'

He sighs. 'All right. If you want me to spell it out. There's a way to transfer the energy that comes through the portal into fuel. I've been studying for years and I think I've worked it out, but it would need your power too.'

'And you want to sell this fuel to the Redworld?'

'Yes. But that would only be the start, Dan. Just the beginning of what we could do together. Our combined power could be huge. That's what I'm trying to show you.'

He sits down beside me and hands me the book.

'Don't think about it as a bad thing. Tom probably would have died in battle anyway, even without the curse.' He opens the book again. 'Look.'

Not really looking, I turn back a couple of the thick, rough-cut pages. I can't stop thinking about what I've done. The guilt is overpowering. I didn't want Tom dead. Did I?

'Don't think about that now, Danny. Just look at the book,' breathes Roach's voice.

I gaze hopelessly at the page, lost in a sea of emotion, and the strangest thing happens.

One minute I'm bereft – confused about Tom, full of guilt, full of a sick regret for everything I've done wrong, and then I look at this strange symbol on the page Roach has stopped at. The next thing I know is a huge surge of energy – like a sexual rush. I feel a level of power I've never felt before rip through me – not unpleasant, but incredibly intense, and I feel myself getting bigger, taller, wider, as if I had become . . .

'A god . . .' I breathe. I am standing on the ragged Cornwall coastline, arms stretched out to the horizon. Wherever I rest my eyes energy shoots out of them like lasers. The sea boils at my gaze. I push clouds away with the flick of a finger. I know, without trying, I can cleave the cliffs in two should I want to. I am all-powerful. I laugh, and the sound booms back over the waves. I have instantly forgotten everything except how good this feels. I want to stay in it forever.

'This is what your power could be, Danny. This is what I could give you. The means to become a god. We can be gods together. Harness the true power of these portals for ourselves, as well as sell them to the highest bidder. Rule the Greenworld in Lugh's name. The warrior of light. We can be rich and powerful beyond our wildest dreams, Danny. This is your future. Choose it. Choose this power. Choose the most beautiful women in the world. Anything you want, you can have. Anything, Danny. Anything. The universe is at your disposal.'

Roach's voice weaves itself like a vine, creeping along the clifftops, budding with succulent fruit, just crying out to be eaten. His promises fill the air like heavy perfume: dense, dreamy. I feel the power coursing through me and wonder why it's taken so long to find this, to realize my potential. Why didn't Mum, Lowenna, even Saba – why didn't they tell me it could be like this? My hand reaches out to pick one of the luscious fruits, to fuel the furnace of power within me. My fingers graze its velvety skin.

'That's it. Take it. It's yours,' says the voice, and I pick it and bring it to my mouth. The thick perfume in the air grows stronger.

And out of nowhere, the fruit is knocked from my hand. Someone pushes me, and I am back in the garden, feeling as if a knife has been removed from my guts. The book has snapped shut in my lap.

'Wha . . .?' I mumble. 'What's going on? I . . . hey, stop!'

Omar is standing in front of me, hands on my shoulders, where Roach's had been. Shaking me violently. 'Danny. Danny! Come back!'

'All right, bloody hell, stop shaking me!' I mutter.

He stops, and glares at Roach and me.

'Omar! What're you doing here?' I mumble groggily, wrenched from my vision of greatness.

'I could ask the same thing,' Roach says drily.

'I came to get you. Come on, Dan. Let's go. This is no place for you,' he says, and pulls me up from the bench, but I wrench free of his grip.

'How did you get here anyway? You're not a witch.'

'Well, you forget that I was once. Just not a very

373

good one. I dunno though . . . I just knew where to come to find you. Lowenna helped me get in. I knew you were in danger. I knew I had to get you.' He turns to Roach. 'Leave him alone. He's just a boy, Radley.'

'That's up to him, isn't it? He followed me here. Anyway, he's not a boy, are you, Dan? You're a man. You can make your own decisions.' Roach is looking at me keenly, his gaze like arrows. 'In fact, he was just about to make a very wise one. Claim what's his. His power. You can't take that away from him, Omar. Back off.'

'I'm not trying to take anything away from him that is rightfully his. But, Danny – whatever Roach is offering you – if it seems fantastical, then it probably is. He can't offer you anything other than a skewed reality.'

'Shut up, Omar. Take your goodwill back to the Greenworld, eh? You don't know anything about magic. You don't know the potential Danny has. You don't have the witch-brand. We do. You aren't a visionary. I was just showing Danny—'

'Oh, I can imagine. I'm not that thick, you know. Might look it, and might not have as much in the way of magic as you and Zia and the rest, but I know you, Radley. Don't forget I've known you a long, long time. You were showing him what? His bright future, rich and powerful? You're persuasive – you always have been. But persuasion isn't something you need if you've got the truth on your side.'

Omar turns to me. 'Whatever he's shown you, Dan,

it's an illusion. If you think there's some kind of fantasy land you can live in, just because you're a witch, you're wrong. Look at your mum. Does she live in some kind of palace, with servants and jewellery stashed under the bed?' He sees a flash of recognition in my eyes. 'Yeah. Thought as much. Palaces and princesses and all the gold you can eat, right? Look, Dan. He's a smart guy. He knows how much you Greenworld kids want all that crap – money, possessions – all the stuff you've never been allowed to have. He knows how appealing that must be to you. But it's not real, Dan. And even if it was, is that what you really want? They're just things. They don't make you happy. People you love, learning your craft as a witch, protecting the Greenworld. That's what's important. You know that. In your heart of hearts, you bloody know that.' He holds out his hand. 'Come on. Come back with me. You know it's the right thing to do.'

I look up at him, at his hand, and feel the rush of guilt return as I think about Tom. Poor Tom, who I killed with my desire for Saba. For wanting her and seeing her in secret. For not being strong or honest enough. I lower my eyes. I can't meet his strong gaze. I'm too weak. I'm not strong enough to do what he wants me to do.

I sit there, between them both. I look at Roach, and down at the book on the ground. 'But I saw it. In the book. This is my book,' I say, looking at them both. 'My story. I saw it,' I add to Omar.

He smiles and picks the book up, and hands it to me. 'Damn right it's your story. It's yours to write. But nothing in here is definite. There's the things that have happened, but every page after today is blank, ready for your choices.' He flicks through the pages, and I see he's right – blank pages. 'If you saw anything, it was Roach feeding off your subconscious fantasies. Making them pretty pictures for you to look at. But they weren't real, Dan. Real is muck and dirt and cold water and rain and wind, and the people you love and making the best out of what life hands you.'

I look back at the book. 'But it was so real,' I mumble. And, I want to say, it was so much better than real life.

Omar's right, and I'm angry with him for being right. Angry with him for coming in here and making me think, making my conscience tap me on the shoulder. And protecting the Greenworld, coming from someone who's never really been part of it – someone who goes from one side to another, never making a commitment either way?

'If you're so bothered about the Greenworld, why don't you live with us instead of coming in and out, appearing then disappearing for months on end?' I chip back, and see Roach smile. I ignore him. 'Mum's miserable when you're gone. She always was. She's lonely. She needed you, needs you, and you just aren't there. She needs you,' I blurt out. 'We need you.'

'Yeah, Omar. Stop pretending you're such a great

376

guy. You're just like the rest of us,' Roach sneers, but Omar squares up to him.

'Like you? No. I'm not like you. If I had a kid I wouldn't make her life hell like you did with Sadie and Linda. They're terrified of you. Afraid that you're going to steal Sadie away and make her do evil things. I'd never do that.'

'You don't know anything about it,' Roach says sulkily. 'Sadie's got the gift. I knew I could use her.'

'What were you trying to do?' I ask. 'They've been causing all this trouble for Mum. Stealing her stuff. Was that you, making them do it?'

He purses his mouth meanly. 'I didn't make them do anything; I just gave them a choice. Help me and I'd leave them alone. They helped me to block the portal in such a way that Zia will have no choice but come to me to get it working again. When she does that, we'll mine Scorhill for fuel as well as Tintagel. You and me. And when we've proved we can do it, we can do all the rest. We'll be the most powerful people in the Redworld cos we'll have what they all need.'

I look at them both. Both fathers, in a sense, but both guys that felt they couldn't do the normal dad thing of sticking around and being decent. They just don't get it. How hard it is to be a boy without a dad. A role model, someone to look up to. Mum's great, but she can't teach me about being a man, and the witches can't either. I'd like to be like Omar, but he's never around long enough. At least Roach seems interested in me. He thinks I've got something. And who knows? Maybe he's right about the portals and fuel. He can teach me, be a mentor or something. Something.

Omar puts his hand on my shoulder and looks me in the eye. 'Listen, kid. I'm sorry your dad's not around, and I'm sorry your mum and me . . . Well, I'm sorry we're not a normal couple. I see you growing up and I know you need a man around.' He sighs and looks up to the stars. 'Maybe I should have settled down, moved in. But it was never me, being that husband and father type. And your mum made it hard too, Dan. She's got her responsibilities and she puts you, Biba and the whole village before me. Goddess knows I love her, but she's got a hard shell. She wouldn't let me stay.

'Look, I'm not going to promise you the world, cos I can't give it to you. No one can. And anyone who says they can is lying. But I can be your friend. And I know I'm not your dad, but I've always thought of you as a son. And if your dad was here I can tell you he wouldn't leave without you either.'

'What do you know about my dad?' I fire back. 'He wouldn't leave without me? Is that what you think? How come he did, then? Walked off pretty happily, as I recall.'

Omar sighs. 'I know. I'm not defending him for doing that. Your dad chose the palaces and princesses over reality. Sure, it's not luxurious out there in a strange country, fighting a dirty war. But he chose action, excitement, something different, instead of

378

you. He didn't see what he had. He didn't see that he was most needed here – that you needed him. That Biba and your mum needed him. Even so, Danny, he loved you. And if he was here now he'd want you to choose the right thing. Make the choice he didn't. War and power – it's not real life. You know that.' He pauses, and holds out his massive meaty hand, dirt under the fingernails. 'So, what's it going to be?' he says softly.

I look at Roach. He holds out his hand too. 'You've seen what I can offer, Dan. Be smart. Take what's yours for once. You'll regret it if you don't.'

I look at Omar, bull-necked, broad, covered in tattoos, and mark the irony. Omar's covered with ink, but he doesn't have the one thing that sets Roach and I apart – the magical words on our skin that make us different, powerful. The witch-brand. How can he ever really understand me, understand what it's like to have this power?

I look at the heavy moon hanging in the sky, here in this strange garden. I look at the quiet ground under my feet, at the bushes shaped into animals, birds. It's peaceful here. Maybe I should just stay here on the bench. The soft breeze plays in my hair. I think of how far I've come – as a witch, as a person. How I've changed. But most of all, I realize, I think about my family, and about how much I want to see them again. I have a place there, back in Dartmoor. And though I've changed, and whatever power I might gain or lose in the future, they are the ones who understand me. And if I've done wrong, and if I've got Tom's blood on my hands — well, I'll have to find some way of making it right.

I reach out for Omar's hand. I feel so tired. Weak. It's the effect of my body being here for too long. 'Let's go home,' I say, and he squeezes my fingers tight.

We turn round to return to life and make the hard scramble back down the mountain. It was hard enough getting up it — I'm not that sure it's going to be any easier getting down.

'Are you sure we can get back?' I whisper to Omar. 'I mean, technically, this is death.'

He stares unflinchingly at the horizon as we walk up the stone steps to the top of the hill, leaving the garden below us. 'Only one way to find out,' he says grimly, and we breast the hill and look down. The mountain tails away into the distance — a long, long way down, I can see the lake, dim among the tall reeds.

He clasps my hand tight. 'Ready?' he asks, and as bearish as he is, he looks scared.

Rightly. I'm petrified — are we stuck here? Have we been away too long? And if we do get back, what will be the effect on our bodies, having been in close vicinity to death for all this time? I don't know if we'll be able to go any further — whether the atmosphere will repel us from going forward, back into life, like a pane of strengthened glass.

But we have to try.

I take the first step, and Omar follows.

Nothing happens. Gingerly, we take another step. We're definitely on the top of the mountain now, heading down. Still OK. We give each other a wary look. Slowly, we put one foot in front of the last, until we have gone several paces down the mountain.

Omar looks at me with a tentative smile. 'I think we're being allowed back,' he says.

'Let's just keep going. Slowly,' I say. This is a perilous journey, and we're not safe yet, not for a long way. We start forward again, and something makes me look behind us, to the top of the mountain. Roach is standing there, watching us. Waiting to see what would happen.

'Look,' I say, pointing.

Omar looks up and we watch as Roach takes his first step on to the downward slope of the mountain, but something's different. Something's wrong. He stops with one foot in the realm of death and one foot in the last place of the living – the summit of the mountain – and freezes. His mouth opens in a soundless O, and his eyes are a mixture of terror and surprise.

'What's happening?' Omar asks me, gazing up at Roach.

'I don't know. I don't think he's being allowed back,' I reply slowly. The Morrigan said something. What was it? 'She said when you cross the border, you can't come back unless someone you love calls you back,' I remember aloud. I look at Omar. 'Did you know that?'

He looks grim. 'No. I just came on instinct. I knew it had to be me, somehow. I didn't think about it. I just followed you.'

'You could have died.'

He looks at me, and looks at Roach. 'I could. But I didn't. I haven't. Not yet.'

And that's when it happens. Roach's eyes stretch wider, like he's seeing something he doesn't believe, and he lets out a cry. A long, wailing, desperate cry. And he bursts into flames; bright, white-hot, sudden, like an explosion. Fire streaming from his fingertips, his nose, his knees, everywhere. Not consuming him; more that he looks like he is wearing fire. Covered in it. A coat of flames. I gasp – it's exactly like my vision, only we are inside the portal, not outside it, and Roach isn't laughing.

And then he disappears.

I lose my footing with the force of the blast and start rolling down the mountain, falling, hitting my head, my arms, shoulders, legs, everything, on rocks as I go down. Dimly I'm aware of an avalanche of rock and earth all around me, and I don't know where Omar is, though I know he's fallen too. The world is sky and rock and earth and pain, and I scramble to try to find my feet but it's too hard; the fall is too fast, and I keep falling. Down.

Down.

Down.

Chapter Twenty-three

I am the Morrigan, bridge between realms; water and earth, life and death. I pace my blessed country, my dogs skirting the battlefields, and the rain washes the blood of my children from the rocks. I keen into the wind, lamenting those I have lost. The mother mourns her lost children as the wind screams over sharp cliffs and misted valleys. As the wise watch their fires, I remember the eyes of the dead. I remember their prayers and dreams. I weave my wise ones into one cloth, one many-striped wool. I call them all home.

> Suggested funeral reading from *The Book of the Morrigan*, *Greenworld Prayers and Songs*

When I open my eyes it's dark. I have no idea where I am: the real world or the portal, life or death. Gingerly, I sit up, and the wind howling around my head, and the sound of the lash of the seawater below me tells me that somehow, miraculously, we have made it back to Tintagel Head.

'It might not be a palace, but it's real,' says a croaky voice.

Dim pre-dawn light bathes Omar's meaty face and flickers around the shadows under his eyes. He sits up painfully. 'All I remember is falling down the mountain. The blast . . . Roach . . . I got hit so many times . . .' he says, groaning.

I rub my eyes. I feel terrible. Weak, bruised. 'Me too. But something must have brought us back. How did you know what he was going to do? Roach?'

'I didn't really. But Zia warned me. She had an inkling he was going to tempt you in there and then either lose you there or make you go over to his side.'

'Bloody hell. What happened to him, back there?'

'I don't know. Is he still alive, do you think?' Omar asks.

I remember the terror in Roach's eyes; the agonizing cry.

'I really don't know. He seemed to think he could get back out.'

Omar closes his eyes wearily. 'I guess he was wrong,' he says.

Suddenly there are footsteps and a voice calls out. 'They're here! They're back!'

Beryan's striding over the castle ruins, calling

behind her, and Saba and Lowenna appear, coming up the walkway.

'What time is it?' I ask Beryan, blinking up at her moleishly.

'About three a.m. Here, get up,' she says, offering me her hand.

I heave myself up, feeling about a hundred.

Omar gets up unaided, but shakily. 'Could murder a cup of tea,' he croaks.

Beryan grins. 'Expect we could manage that,' she says and pulls me towards her so I can lean on her wiry frame. 'Come on, Dan. Take it easy. Let's go home.'

We hobble slowly back to Lowenna's house.

I lose my footing, following the walkway to the mainland, and Saba takes my arm. 'Thank Brighid you're all right. I've never seen anything like it, Danny. We tried to reverse that pentagram from the outside for ages, but nothing worked. I was so worried that we'd sent you in alone, and then Omar came along and went in after you. All we could do was call you back and hope you heard us.'

Lowenna walks in front of Saba and me, talking to us over her shoulder, with her arm through Omar's. She's the only one big enough to support him.

So they all called me back. Gratefulness flows through me. For a moment Roach's flaming body flashes before my eyes, and I feel pity. Who loved him enough to bring him back? Perhaps no one ever did.

'Your shoulder!' Saba points. Gingerly, she lifts the blood-soaked shirt off my chest.

'Are you hurt?' Beryan asks, confused. 'The blood . . .'

I flex my shoulder and realize it doesn't hurt any more. Neither does my arm. I grope under the collar of my shirt, but my fingers only meet smooth skin. Somehow, I've been healed.

'I was. But I guess I'm not now.'

Finally, we get back to the house. I lower myself into a kitchen chair, and squeeze Saba's hand. Merryn's off, tending the wounded. Melz is nowhere to be seen.

'So where is Roach?' asks Beryan, anxiously running her fingers along her long plait.

'I don't know. Dead, I think.' I say, and tell my story.

'So he wanted to convert you to his side?' Saba asks.

I shrug. 'I guess so, and get me to help him with this portal-takeover thing. He needed my power to do it, apparently.'

Omar pats me on the back, and I wince. Not so much with pain but guilt. I try not to think about the terrible thing I've done to Tom. I look down at my hands. They feel to me as if they must be dripping blood.

I smile wearily. The witches smile back at me, but I can imagine they're thinking: What price your brilliance, Danny? How many lives did we pay for it? There's a silence.

'We've got to bury the dead,' Beryan says quietly.

'How many are there?'

I don't want to know the answer, but everyone has to know.

She doesn't look up from her lap. 'Forty. So far. Several more injured, some that will get infected.'

'Where are they now?'

'The ones that need care are at our house. The dead . . .' She chokes a little. 'The ones who have passed are at the town hall for now.'

'Including . . .?' I can't bring myself to say his name.

Beryan nods. 'Yes. Tom's there too.'

My heart sinks. I turn to Saba. 'I'm so sorry, Saba. He died saving me.'

'I know. It's not your fault. I . . . I can't believe he's gone. Just like that,' she says, and a tear trails slowly down her cheek.

It is my fault, I think, but I push it away. She can never know that.

'Were you . . . I mean, I know it's not the time to ask, but . . . that night after the bonfire . . .'

Still, after everything, I'm jealous. Jealous of a dead boy. I'm sick with my own callousness, but I can't help asking. Did they make up after the argument? Did Saba go with him? Sleep with him? Love him?

'No. I was angry at you. He caught up with me and walked me home. Nothing happened. He tried to kiss me; I pulled away.' Her face crumples. 'Oh, Dan, that was the last time I saw him!' She sobs as if her heart has broken.

Eventually Saba's sobs tail off into hiccups.

Lowenna brings her a glass of water and gently wipes the tears from her cheeks with a dishcloth. 'We've got to replace all that water, now, haven't we?' she soothes. 'Poor love. And poor Tom. We will all miss him so much, Saba. He'll always be a hero.'

She turns to me, folding the cloth neatly into a square. 'Seems to me that this is a good time for you to leave us, Danny. Go back home. I think they need you,' she says, looking me in the eye. I can hear what she's not saying. *I thought there might have been something going on, and now that I do know, there's no way you're staying here to corrupt my daughter.* Like I'm some dirty perv hiding in the bushes, watching Saba get undressed at night.

But the thing is, she's right. I do have to go. Mum needs me; even if Roach is dead, he still tried to take the Scorhill portal from her and I'm not happy about Sadie befriending Biba, and trying to be a witch. I've done what I had to do here, at least for now.

'I'll go with Omar,' I say. 'When are the burials?' I ask Beryan.

'Tomorrow,' she replies tiredly, her hands twisting a frayed cushion.

I'm not surprised. In the Greenworld we don't have means of preserving bodies, so we get them in the ground and back to nature as soon as possible.

'You'll stay for them?'

'Of course,' I say.

There's a silence, and Saba's face clouds over again at the mention of the burials. 'I'd better go and pack, then,' I say in the awkwardness, and leave them to it.

I don't have much to pack, but more than I arrived with: my tarot set, my books, my witch knife and wand. A few clothes bartered for in the village. An illicit half-bottle of scotch someone swapped me for a tarot reading. I smile to myself. I'm just like Mum now.

There's a knock on my door.

'It's open,' I call, and Melz slides in like a kicked cat. Her kohl-rimmed eyes are smudgy, her eyes red. Head to toe in black as usual, with cowboy boots. Goddess knows where she got them from in the first place – they're not exactly indigenous to Cornwall.

'He warned you!' she sobs.

'What?'

'At the bonfire. Tom. He warned everyone. About Skye and Bali.'

'I know. I'm sorry. I wish I could go back and do something about it. We just thought he was being stupid.'

'Well, he wasn't. Tom . . . he . . .' She breaks down into sobs.

She sits down heavily on the bed next to me – I put my arm round her tentatively.

'They set you up. They set us all up!' she cries.

I don't know what to say to her. I can't tell her the truth, that my curse is responsible for Tom's death, but even though I don't like her all that much and I know for damn sure she doesn't like me, I still don't want to be responsible for breaking her heart any more than it already is.

'I'm so sorry, Melz,' I say, and she wails into my shoulder. That's all I can say. 'I'm so sorry.'

She shakes her head, snuffling. 'Don't worry. I've already taken care of them. Roach isn't the only one that knows dark magic,' she says blackly. Her tone is dead and flat.

'What have you done?' I feel a slug of dread creep into my stomach, and the grimoire's thick, fusty pages flash into my mind. I can almost smell the sweet stench of cold lemon balm tea. *Light a candle and call down the dark goddess. Request thee Her aid in your task.*

'I've done what's right.'

I push her away from me and make her look at me. 'What have you done, Melz?'

'I worked a curse on both of them. They're going to regret messing with me. I'm a priestess of the Morrigan.'

'What kind of curse?'

'You don't need to know.'

I shake her. 'Yes I do! You know you shouldn't use black magic!'

She sniffs. 'Listen to the expert all of a sudden. I've been a witch since I was eight. Don't tell me what I should and shouldn't do.'

I tell Melz what I should have told myself, but didn't. 'Even I know that sending evil out will bring it back on you tenfold. Not just on you, Melz. Maybe on everyone. Goddess, how could you be so stupid?' I run my hand through my hair in frustration – at her, at myself.

'I don't care! I don't care. I'm not the only witch ever to have done something dark. The worst has already happened to me. Nothing can be this bad. I had to. I couldn't let them take him unavenged. I'm sick of nobody noticing me. Being in the background. He was so strong, so kind. I . . . I . . .' She sobs. 'I luh . . . luh . . . I loved him!' she cries suddenly, and slumps on to my bed. 'They're paying for taking the one I loved away from me! I've sat back and been overlooked all my life. Despite having this.'

She pulls down her black blouse, stretching the collar, and I see her witch-brand at the base of her neck. The triple spiral, the triskele. Life, death and rebirth – the endless cycle.

'D'you know what I've learned from the Morrigan, Danny? I don't have to be in the background. I am not powerless. No one messes with me and gets away with it. No one!'

'Melz, I . . .'

'It should have been you. It should have been you!' She bangs her balled-up fists on to the lumpy mattress in frustration and sorrow; her fingers are black with charcoal.

You don't know how right you are, Melz.

'I'm sorry, I couldn't help it. He saved my life.'

'No! Don't talk to me! I hate you! I hate you!' She

strides out of my room, and I hear her bedroom door bang.

I stare at the wall. I am the lowest, most despicable person that ever lived. Not only did I kill Tom, more or less; as a consequence, I'm now responsible for Melz's descent into revenge and black magic. If Tom hadn't died she wouldn't have worked this curse. Her bitterness wouldn't have taken over.

With this on my mind, it occurs to me that I should probably retrieve the poppet doll from behind the shed. It's unlikely that anyone will go there, but you never know; and it's done its job now. Done it far too well.

I tread lightly along the hall and down the stairs, and slip out into the night. No one sees me, or at least I don't think they do. I scuttle down to the bottom of the garden and to the shed; it's flimsy, the wood rotten. I reach behind it gingerly and feel around for the doll. I lean in again and reach down, and down, and finally my fingers clasp something clothy and wet. I pull it out, and my stomach lurches when I see its stitched-up mouth and the needle through the heart. I pull the needle out and throw it away. Too little, too late. And it's me that has to be close-mouthed now, as if my lips were stitched together.

I rip the doll apart in frustration until it's nothing more than a clump of damp, mouldy cotton, and throw it in the compost bin. I poke it down, far into the mulch, and re-fasten the bin lid.

I go back into the house, and as I walk back up the stairs I find myself staring at Melz's portrait of her sister, hanging on the wall. She's always drawing. Even when the gang meets. Like that time she was drawing Tom and Saba, then threw it in the fire. A perfectionist: not happy with her work unless it was exactly how she wanted it. Unless it did exactly what she wanted.

And then, suddenly, it clicks. All of it. I realize what she's been doing; I realize how she has cursed Skye and Bali.

Write the witch's name across her portrait or photograph and throw it into the fire.

She must have tried it a few times. That first time at the bonfire, when I caught her burning Tom and Saba's picture. The one where they were looking in opposite directions. No doubt on purpose – like my curse, she wanted to distract their attention from each other. But that didn't work, I'm guessing, because they stayed together. But the second time, it was my picture – the day before I got shot in battle. She knew about Saba and me, and she must have been incensed that Saba was still seeing Tom too. I think if I was Melz I could have just about coped with the idea that Tom and Saba were truly in love, but knowing that they weren't, and that she was still on the outside, must have been heartbreaking.

So maybe, instead of cursing her sister again, she chose me. She never liked me anyway. And whatever the burning-picture curse entails, she did it right that time, cos if it wasn't for my experience at the edge of death healing me, I might be one of the dead in the town hall awaiting burial right now.

And then, once she'd seen that it worked, she knew what to do for Skye and Bali, the ones who took her beloved Tom away. Only it wasn't them that killed him, really. It was me. I shiver involuntarily. I always knew you shouldn't make Melz angry.

I go up to my room and stare at the wall for a long time before falling into a restless sleep, full of nightmares.

Early the next morning, we make our way to the beach. A heavy grey mist is coming off the fields.

'It's as if the weather is mourning them too,' Saba says in a low voice as we walk. She's dressed in mourning – honey-blonde hair cascading over her shoulders, a black cardigan thrown over a long black wool dress. She doesn't say much else, and she hasn't said that much about me leaving. Either she's concentrating on her grief, or she's secretly relieved I'm going. I don't know. I don't think she knows either.

The bodies are each carried by six pallbearers, meaning that most of the villagers are either dead or carrying a dead person. The Hands lead the procession, chanting the funeral rites.

I've only heard about this before – we bury our dead on Dartmoor, but in villages close to the sea bodies are put in special rafts, crafted from willow. They have a thickly woven base and a narrow space for the body; a tall lip surrounds it and keeps it in place. Around the inner lip of the raft is a wooden reservoir for fuel and spaces for candles. The idea is that we light the candles and set the rafts adrift, and when the candles burn down low, they catch the fuel and the whole thing goes up. It's not enough fire to destroy the body – the sea does that when the raft burns – but it's more of a ceremonial thing. The body is earth; the sea is water; the flames are fire, and they're fed by the air. So in death, we are returned to the elements. But the goddess in charge is the same: the Morrigan. The death-crow. The voice in my head on the battlefield. I've felt her presence so much more here, in Tintagel, than ever at home. On the other hand, I wasn't a witch at home.

'I am the end of things. I am the hag on the battlefield. I am the sweet release of death. I will take you to the forever lands,' Lowenna intones, black crow feathers sewn on to her cloak.

When the rafts are prepared and ready, we say our last goodbyes. I walk along the series of caskets along the tideline and trace a five-pointed star on each forehead. 'Blessed Be,' I murmur every time, the words almost sucked from my mouth by the harsh winter wind that screams off the sea.

Tom's casket is towards the end of the row. As I approach, I see that Saba and Melz are standing by it. They aren't speaking, just looking down at his face. I wonder what will happen to Melz. She looks so pathetic;

she looks like I feel. Whatever happens to her will probably happen to me too.

I hang back until they move on and bless Tom's body like the rest. When I look down his eyes are closed, and he has the peace of death on him like all the others. He doesn't rise up stiffly from the casket, pointing a dead finger at me and intoning 'Murderer! Murderer!', but I almost wish he would.

'Blessed Be,' I say quietly to him. 'Go with Her.' And, when I'm sure no one can hear: 'I'm sorry. Forgive me, Tom.' I wipe away the tears that are flowing down my cheeks and walk on.

When there is nothing more to say or do, we light the candles and set the rafts adrift, watching the waves pull the crafts slowly towards the horizon, against the grey, cloudy sky and the green, foamy waves. One by one they burst into flame. We watch until they are all alight, and then turn away.

Saba walks back to the house with Melz – I don't know what they're talking about, but both of their heads are bowed. Suddenly, Melz shouts and we all look up from our trudging, muddy feet. She's standing in front of Saba, pointing at her, and she's angry.

'How can you say that?'

Saba looks shocked. 'What?'

'How can you stand there and say that when we both know you never loved him? Don't try to make out you did!' Her hand is shaking, her eyes popping.

Saba grabs Melz's arm, trying to calm her down,

but Melz pulls free. 'Get off. Don't touch me. I've never known anyone as self-obsessed as you. You vain, callous, heartless BITCH!'

'I'm not a bitch. I'm just being honest.'

Saba's trying to speak quietly, but Melz is having none of it. 'Honest. Oh, well done. Yes, you're so bloody honest, aren't you. Sneaking around behind his back, letting him adore you. Why have one boy when you can have two hanging on your every word, Saba? Yes, I can see the honesty in that.'

Melz stands with her hands on her hips, a sneer on her lips. And there's a big part of me that's right behind her on this one.

'Look. All I said was I'm glad that I didn't have to break his heart. That he died thinking I loved him. And I did, really. Just not in the way he thought.'

Melz shakes her head furiously. 'By Brighid, you're incredible. You're glad you didn't have to break his heart. Don't you think it would have been better for everyone if you did it years ago? Maybe then he wouldn't be burning on a sea raft today. Maybe he could have been with someone who really loved him. Someone who would have never left his side.'

Saba laughs then, a cruel laugh. 'Who? You? Never left his side? He wanted a woman, not a dog. He never thought of you as anything other than a little sister, to be humoured and patted on the head. Look at you. What kind of weirdo would want you? We were the same, me and Tom. Healthy. Normal. We looked right together.

If you want to find someone you look right with, go and find those tattooed thugs in the gangs. They'd love a freak with a chip on her shoulder like you.'

Melz steps back as if she's been slapped, and I can't say I blame her. I've never seen this side of Saba before. I mean, I know she's mourning Tom, but still.

'Chip on my shoulder? Are you surprised? What d'you think it's like, being me? Coming second all the time? Even though I've got the brand, and you don't!'

Saba makes a dismissive motion with her hand. 'The brand, the brand. Who cares about the bloody thing? It's only a tattoo, Melz. Not even a very good one. So what? You're not more powerful than me. You might work harder, but I'm more talented. You know it. So shut up and stop whining.'

Lowenna comes running through the crowd that's gathering around the sisters, and glares at them both. 'Demelza! Bersaba! That's enough! I can't believe the two of you. We've just honoured the dead. How dare you sully their memories with this catfight?' She gets them both by the collar and pushes them ahead of her. 'Walk. No talking. NOW!'

I look back to the column of villagers, who are all watching Saba and Melz fight, and see Bryony approaching me.

'Goddess, Bryony, are you OK?' I say, hugging her. I haven't had a chance to think about her since the battle, and now that I see her I know I've got to end things with her. It's the right thing to do.

She hugs me back. 'I'm OK. What about you? I heard you got shot!'

I wiggle my arm. 'I did. Healed, though.'

She frowns. 'But it was only a day ago! Wounds don't heal that fast.'

I smile, despite the day. 'Magic,' I say.

We step aside, out of the stream of mourners making their way back home.

She frowns, looking at my sombre face. 'What's wrong?'

I sigh and make myself say it. 'I'm really sorry, Bryony, but I can't see you any more.'

'Oh . . . Why not?' She looks deflated.

I feel like even more of a heel than before, if that's possible.

'Well, I'm going home soon. There's stuff there I've got to do, but it's more than that. See, I should have told you, but I've been seeing Saba. At the same time as I was seeing you. That's what they were just arguing about. I'm sorry.'

There's a silence as more villagers tramp past us.

Bryony stares at me. 'Oh,' she says again, more quietly.

'I'm sorry. I shouldn't have started anything with you. I just . . . you were there, and Saba was with Tom, and . . .'

'I was there? Nice. Thanks, Danny.'

'I'm sorry. That's not what I meant to say. I just meant . . .'

'I know what you meant. I was an easy distraction when your real girlfriend wasn't paying you any attention. That's pretty clear.' She starts walking off.

'Hey, Bryony! Don't walk off, I—'

She cuts me off. 'What? What else is there to say, Danny? I thought you liked me. I was wrong. Have a nice life.'

She strides off, and I think about going after her, but what else can I really say? It's not like Bryony was going to say, 'Oh, well, now you put it like that, I totally understand, Danny. I don't mind at all the fact that you used me. Congratulations on your final honesty. The deed has been done, and it's raw, but at least it's honest.'

I don't go straight back to the house with the others. I want to be on my own for a while, so I walk around the village, looking at it for the last time. It's been my home during an important time in my life: I guess a time I'll look back on in years to come and think about what I learned. But at the moment all I can think is, this is where I learned to lie. Death and lies hold the bricks together; insecurity grows up under people's windows with the roses. The cobbles are sharp as needles under my shoes.

I get back to find the house in chaos. Beryan runs out of the kitchen and into the hall as I come back in.

'What's going on?' I ask, hanging my cloak up.

'Melz. She's run away.'

Oh holy hell. I look at Beryan, aghast. 'How do you know?'

'She's taken everything. There's nothing in her room — all her clothes, her books, her drawings. Her magical tools. Tarot, athame, wand, crystals. She went off after we got back from the funerals and we just thought she was licking her wounds after the row with Saba, but Lowenna went up later and found her room cleared out. She's gone.'

I run into the kitchen and find Lowenna and Saba sitting at the gnarled table. Lowenna's got her head in her hands, and Saba looks up at me tearily as I come in.

'I didn't mean to upset her that much,' she says, and I give her a smile, but it must come across worriedly. Neither of them understands that this is even worse than they think. Melz is tainted. She's used black magic. And now she could be anywhere, doing anything. She's bitter and angry and full of grief and she's not thinking straight.

I look up at Melz's pencil portraits of the Hands, heavy with dread. I look back at Saba.

Lowenna sees the look on my face and sits up. 'What is it? Danny. Tell me.'

'It's about Melz,' I say, not knowing where to start.

'If you're keeping a secret about another of my daughters, I can tell you now I really won't appreciate it,' she says tersely.

'I know. I just don't want to get her in trouble.'

She frowns. 'Well, I can't say you won't until

401

you tell me what it is. But she's missing, Danny. Any information would be good right now.'

'The thing is, I know who shot me. And who killed Tom. We both do,' I say, looking at Saba. 'It's a couple of kids we know.'

'What do you mean? Someone from the village? That's not possible.'

'No . . . someone from outside the village.'

'Outside the village? Where?'

I explain about Bali and Skye, and our group, and the bonfire parties at the edge of the village. And I repeat what Melz told me about the curse, and how Melz was in love with Tom. But I can't confess my part in Tom's death, like I should. I'm not strong enough. I'm tainted now, dark.

Lowenna's frown gets deeper and deeper. 'So you were hanging around with gang members and you never thought to say anything? Didn't you think it was odd, those kids in your little gang? Them wanting to spend time with you? Approaching you? Bersaba! I can't believe you would be so duplicitous!' She's up and pacing round the table.

'W-we did at first, but it all seemed all right, so . . .' Saba stammers, glaring at me.

Lowenna harrumphs and stands next to the spare easy chair, absently running her fingers over its frayed fabric. 'So how much do they know about what we do?'

I shrug. 'No idea.'

She groans. 'That's not good enough, either of you!

A boy is dead because of this. Tom is dead. I've known Tom since he was a baby. Do you know what that's like, to see a young man cut down, just like that, when you can remember him being born like it was yesterday? Do you?' Her voice wavers, but she takes a deep breath to steady herself.

'What about Melz, and the curse?' Saba asks, eyes wide.

'I'll deal with Demelza,' Lowenna says darkly. 'Did you know she was in love with Tom?'

Saba looks at the floor. 'Kind of . . . yes, I suppose, yes I did.'

Lowenna shakes her head and stares at the glowing fire in the hearth. 'And yet you did nothing. Tortured her. Continued to see Tom even though you didn't care about him, if this morning's completely disrespectful performance was anything to go by.'

'But I did care, Mum, I just—'

Saba tries to explain, but Lowenna cuts her off. 'I expect better from you, Bersaba!' she shouts. 'Even you. Brighid knows you can be a selfish bitch at times, but this . . .' She bangs her fist hard on the stone fireplace.

Saba looks crushed, but says nothing.

'It's not her fault,' I say. 'Melz, I mean. She was hurt. People who are hurt do bad things sometimes.'

Poor Melz. All she did was love someone she couldn't have. Just like me.

Lowenna looks grim. 'We're all hurt, Danny. There's a lot of pain in the Greenworld today,' she snaps.

403

*

Omar and I leave at dawn the next day. All the other Hands, minus Melz, are gathered in the hallway to say goodbye. There's been no word at all. We've sent out scouts, as much as we can, and we've all been up most of the night dowsing maps of the local area with our crystals to try to find her. No luck. Nothing.

Lowenna looks older than when I first came, and haggard from being up all night crying. Still, she catches me in a bear hug so that I'm squashed up against her T-shirt. 'Give my love to your mum,' she says. 'And thanks for all you've done, Danny. You're a really talented witch.'

I smile ruefully. I can't return the warmth in her embrace; guilt and grief has woven a poisonous mesh round my heart. She doesn't know that it was me that pushed Melz to do what she did.

I turn to Saba. 'I'll miss you,' she says.

Will you? I wonder.

'We'll see each other soon,' I say, only half believing it, and only half caring.

I killed a boy for this, I realize. This lukewarm feeling, this will-we-won't-we crap of ours.

We kiss, and I turn away before she can see the turmoil in my eyes. Before she can look into my traitorous heart and see how it kills everything it loves.

'I love you, Danny,' she says, clutching for my hand at the last minute, but as I look at her beautiful face I see the desperation in her almond eyes. I don't know if she does really love me. I think she wanted me because I was different, interesting, exotic, all that crap, and now . . . Now I'm familiar, and she's ticked me off her list. And I think it's an unbearable thought for her to not be loved, not have someone adoring her, for one single second. And in a matter of days she's gone from two boys saying they love her to one boy who's not sure any more.

I squeeze her fingers, but I can't say it back, even though I do still have feelings for her. But it's not the crazy, passionate, do-anything love it was. I don't know what it is now. I don't know whether it's enough, and whether it can survive. We've both changed. Or, I know I have. Maybe she hasn't. Maybe it's just that I can see her clearly for the first time now. Maybe she isn't a goddess. Just a girl who's made mistakes.

'Come on, Omar, let's go,' I say and turn away, my heart aching for the dreams I am leaving with her, with regret for the love I thought I saw for us. That heartbreaking, crazy, big dumb love that didn't need a reason, a time or a place. I will myself not to cry.

Omar nods to the witches. 'Ladies. Stay in touch.'

We leave, and I don't look back. Can't look back, or I'll be turned to stone.

As we pass through the streets I look at Tintagel waking up one last time. I watch the grocers setting up their veg stalls, the barter shops getting ready to open, the gardeners tending blackfly and watering their tomatoes, all as if the fighting had never happened. Only it did happen, and I can't forget the dead.

I'm taking a new Danny with new power back to Gidleigh, but with a gut-wrenching secret too. As I open the energy circle around the village and we slip out, past the Witch's Gate and into the in-between land, my thoughts are, strangely, with Melz. It's as though our transgressions have brought us closer together. Only I truly understand what she's feeling. I know her secret, though she doesn't know mine. I remember how it was her voice, her shadowy presence that pulled me out of Roach's vision that first time, not Saba's.

If she can hear me, I send her a telepathic message. *Be careful, Melz. It's dark outside the Greenworld. Go home and be part of the light. It's not too late.*

Her face stays in my mind as Omar and I make our way back safely to Dartmoor and Gidleigh, past Scorhill stone circle, back to the peeling-paint walls and the faded single-hand motif at the village boundary. I know once I see it that there's trouble here. But at least it's new trouble – not connected to me. I'm home, I think tiredly. I don't feel ready. I don't know who I am any more. I don't know if I can do this.

Omar looks at me as I stand there, gazing at the boundary.

'You've come home a man,' he says gruffly.

I breathe in the Dartmoor air and feel the power in the rock under my feet, and it makes me feel stronger. This is my home. I belong here, like the heather and the standing stones.

'I've come home a witch,' I say.

Sources

The text used in the opening paragraph is an excerpt from 'The Charge of the Goddess', authored by Gerald Gardner and Doreen Valiente, a vital part of a traditional Wiccan ritual.

Skye reads excerpts from *Cornish Charms and Witchcraft*, published by Tor Mark Press in 1991.

The spell for cooling the ardour of a love rival is based on Eileen Holland's spell for cooling attraction in *Spells for the Solitary Witch*, published by Weiser Books, 2004; the sewing of the poppet's mouth and piercing the heart are my own more grisly additions and purely for fictional purposes.

The Greenworld Archive held in Boscastle refers to the wonderful Museum of Witchcraft, also in Boscastle – *www. museumofwitchcraft.com*

The quotes opening the chapters are taken from *The Mabinogion*, a collection of ancient Welsh Celtic myths and legends; other ancient Irish texts; and the poetry of W. B. Yeats. These sources refer specifically to ancient Celtic tales, which provide the framework for the Greenworld's belief system.

The other quotes are from the Greenworld's own sacred texts and provide an insight into the daily worship inside this community.

Acknowledgements

Thank you first to Jim, whose patience and support is always very, very appreciated. His passion for wilderness survival was one of the inspirations for this story.

Thank you also to Peter and Margaret, early readers and constant enthusiasts for Danny and the Greenworld. Thanks for all the belief and love.

I am deeply indebted to John McLay and Gabriella Apicella for giving so much of their time to reading and thinking about the book, helping me ask the right questions of the story and shaping it into something a publisher was interested in.

Huge thanks also to my agent, Ben Illis, a truly Arian bundle of energy, who not only found a great home for *Crow Moon* but knows his rising and moon sign.

Huge thanks and general worshipping also goes to Celtic warrior maidens Roisin Heycock and Niamh Mulvey, my editors at Quercus, who were so patient and helpful in getting the best out of the book. Big thanks too to Lauren Woosey and Jennie Roman, the other key members of Team Crow, for planning world domination (right??) and amazing attention to detail.

Big crow love goes to all the priests and priestesses of the Morrigan, especially my good friend Laura Daligan, who is always an inspiration and a wellspring of help, beauty and wisdom.

Scientific advice and chat around green energy was kindly pondered by green-energy guru Richard Hiblen of Green Square – *http://greensquare.co.uk/* – and proto-Greenworld-envirowarrior Melanie Hiblen whose passion and commitment never fails to impress me.

Thanks also to Katherine Woodfine, Claire Shanahan, Nikesh Shukla and all my Booktrust friends for your enthusiasm and excitement, and to my dear friend Katie Clapham for bookishness and taking over the world – you're an inspiration.

A damn fine coffee and maybe even a cheese pig goes to Stephanie King who gave up her valuable time to talk to me about the book and the process of being a debut YA novelist in the early stages, and an order of cherry pie to the lovely Carolyn Koussa for putting the book under her nose in the first place.

As ever, I have my grannie to thank, for being a writer herself and for being my loyal and literary penpal for many years, and, last and always, my mother, the original Greenworld single mum, for believing that magic is real. Thanks, Mum, for everything.

With Melz on the run,
and unrest in the Redworld growing,
can the witches protect their world
from the outside?

Don't miss the thrilling sequel to

CROW **MOON**

Coming March 2016